Not Quite Perfect

Not Quite Perfect

Annie Lyons

CARINA

This edition is published by arrangement with Harlequin Books S.A. CARINA is a trademark of Harlequin Enterprises Limited, used under licence.

This Edition Published in Great Britain 2016
by CARINA, an imprint of Harlequin (UK) Limited,
Eton House, 18-24 Paradise Road,
Richmond, Surrey, TW9 1SR

© 2013 Annie Peters

ISBN 978-0-263-25035-0

Annie Lyons decided, after leaving university, that she 'rather liked books' and got a job as a bookseller on Charing Cross Road, London. Two years later she left the retail world and continued rather liking books during an eleven-year career in publishing. Following redundancy in 2009 she realised that she would rather like to write books and, having undertaken a creative writing course, lots of reading and a bit of practice, she produced *Not Quite Perfect*. She now realises that she loves writing as much as coffee, not as much as her children and a bit more than gardening. She has since written another novel and is about to start work on her third. She lives in a house in south-east London with her husband and two children. The garden is somewhat overgrown. One day she hopes to own a chocolate-brown labrador named John and have tea with Mary Berry.

For Rich

CHAPTER ONE

Emma Darcy wakes to the brain-imploding sensation of another hangover and wishes she had more self-control. She opens one eye and, finding the prospect of daylight nauseating, closes it again and rolls over with a groan. She wants the duvet to comfort her, to wrap its arms around her and cure her but all it is doing is making her feel sweaty and restless. She glances at the empty space next to her and moves into it, breathing in the musty aroma of man. She can already hear said man, also known as her fiancé Martin, in the shower, cheerfully murdering a Stevie Wonder song. She pulls the pillow over her head and prays for sleep or death or both.

The volume of the singing gets louder as Martin makes his way back into the bedroom and flings open the curtains. Ignoring her protests, he prises the pillow from her face and kisses her forehead. She opens one eye and attempts a weak smile. It doesn't feel good.

'Wake up, Bungle Bonce. It's gone eleven and we've got to be at your parents' in an hour.'

'Nnnnnnnng' is the only sound Emma can make.

'Someone should have stopped after that first bottle of champagne, shouldn't they?' grins Martin, running a hand through his dark brown hair, still wet from the shower.

Emma can find no reason to disagree.

'Magical Martin's Hangover Cure coming right up!' he whispers, stroking her cheek and gently kissing the corner of her mouth. 'I hate to say it, Em, but I wonder if you might want a shower before we head over to your parents'. You smell like a barmaid's apron!' Emma aims a feeble punch in Martin's direction, which he sidesteps with ease. He laughs and jogs down the stairs, whistling happily.

Emma marvels at this man: he drinks far more than she does and yet never seems to have any side effects. She seems to have a permanent hangover of late. It's hardly surprising as ever since she and Martin announced their engagement a month ago it's been a steady round of celebratory drinks and dinners with friends and family. Last night, it was just the two of them with a Chinese takeaway and yet they still managed to polish off the champagne from Emma's godmother, Rosie, plus another bottle and possibly something more potent in a smaller glass.

They had been in celebratory mood as Emma had picked up some honeymoon brochures and they had worked their way through them narrowing it down to a beach holiday in Bali or a safari in Kenya. They had then celebrated this decision by casting the brochures to one side and indulging in passionate sex on the living-room rug. As she fell asleep that night, Emma couldn't imagine being happier. As Sunday morning dawned, she couldn't imagine feeling worse.

While waiting for the shower to warm up, she shudders at the thought of lunch at her parents' with a hangover, her sister, her brother-in-law and their three not particularly quiet children. She stands underneath the jet of water, its warmth slightly masking the feeling that her brain is trying to exit her body through her ears.

Martin is kind and presents her with a poached egg, which she nibbles, a cup of coffee, which she sips, and a glass of water with two paracetamol, which she almost inhales. She is feeling nearly human again as she staggers to the car for the short drive to her parents' house.

Her recovery is short-lived as Emma's mother opens the door and Buzz Lightyear leaps out in best Space Ranger form, fixing her with a determined eye, his stubby finger poised over his wrist-laser.

'Prepare to be eliminated, evil Emperor Zurg!' he squeaks.

'Fuck!' cries Emma in genuine surprise.

'Gra-neeeeeee. Auntie Em said fuck. Again.'

'Emma, honestly,' chides her mother.

'Sorry. He just sort of scared me.'

'Em's a bit shaky today, Diana,' says Martin, putting an arm around his fiancée. 'She's tired. She's been working far too hard and then of course there's the wedding to think about.'

Emma rests heavily against Martin's shoulder, grateful for his attempt at damage limitation.

'Auntie Em, Uncle Martin!' squeals Lily with unmitigated glee, darting down the hall towards them.

'Ah my darling Pica-Lily.' Emma scoops up her niece and tickles her delightfully chubby little ribs.

'Doppit, doppit, doppit!' shrieks Lily and then, 'Again, again, again!'

'Let them come in, you horrible lot,' interrupts Emma's dad. 'Gin and tonic, Mart? And maybe just a tonic for you eh, lovely girl?' he says, wrapping Emma in a restorative embrace. She kisses him on the cheek and puts an arm around his middle as they walk into the living room, where Rachel is flicking through the Sunday newspapers.

'I warn you, your mother's current favourite topic is weddings,' he whispers as he disappears into the kitchen to fetch the drinks.

Emma grimaces.

'Who's talking about WEDDINGS?' says Rachel in a too-loud voice, giving her sister a playful nudge as she flops down next to her on the sofa.

Emma pulls a face. 'Keep it down, Rach. I've got a hangover the size of Wales and could really do without Mum on my back today.'

'What? I only said the word "WEDDING",' smirks Rachel.

Alfie appears at Emma's side and seeing his mother's smiling face, decides to join in the game. 'WEDDING! WEDDING! WEDDING!' he cries with glee.

Emma gives her sister a look. 'Could you ask him not to do that?'

Lily appears alongside him and starts to join in. Rachel grins at her sister and shrugs her shoulders. 'I'm so sorry. I've lost control of my children,' she says innocently.

'Yes, well, not for the first time, Rachel,' declares Diana, appearing behind them. 'Emma, we need to talk menus, dresses and flowers.'

Emma and Rachel roll their eyes at one another as Edward returns with the drinks. 'At least let them have a drink first, eh darling?' he says, handing out the glasses and winking at the girls.

Diana adopts a look that suggests she is not to be trifled with. 'Well Emma is the one who's decided to get married. If she wants our help I think she needs to co-operate a bit more. Yes?'

'Yes, Mum,' says Emma with tired resignation.

'And you can stop this conspiratorial "Mummy is a villain" thing, Edward. I only want what's best for my family.'

'Yes, dear,' says Edward, suppressing a smile.

'Right, I've made quiche and salad. I don't expect the children will eat it as it's not fish fingers but I've done my best.'

Rachel opens her mouth to protest but sees Emma looking smug and decides to change tack. 'Sounds delicious. Let's eat so that we can talk weddings,' she says, looking victoriously at her sister.

Emma manages to pick her way through lunch feeling more and more miserable as her mother attacks each item on her list with the gusto of a military commander.

'So Lily will be your flower girl and Rachel your matron of honour.'

'Of course and I want Ella to be a bridesmaid too.'

'Who is this Ella? Do I know her?'

'She's my best friend at work, Mum, and no, you've never met her.'

'Yes, but don't forget that Daddy and I will be putting money towards this so we don't want people there we don't know.'

'Look, Mum, I know you're doing this with the best intentions, but we haven't even set a date yet. It is up to Martin and me.' Emma's painkillers are starting to wear off and she can feel a dull throbbing at her temples. She looks around for an ally.

Rachel is sitting with her arms folded enjoying every second of the spectacle while her husband, Steve, talks to Edward about football. Meanwhile, Martin is being coerced into the role of Captain Hook by the three children.

'I'm only trying to help. I know how stressful these things can be and I'm just trying to take some of the pain out of it. By the way, my cousin Eunice has already said she will do the flowers and I think it has to be white lilies, yes?'

'Mum, just stop it!'

'I beg your pardon?'

'I said stop it. You're not helping, you're interfering!'

Rachel is watching Emma wide-eyed and impressed.

'Well really, there's no need to be rude!'

'I'm sorry. It's just that – '

'I only wanted to help.'

'I know but – '

'I'm just trying to make it special for my little girl. I mean Rachel just eloped so I didn't get the chance then.' Her eyes are beginning to fill with tears and Emma is wishing she could dig a large hole and crawl into it.

'Mum, please!'

The tension is broken by a piercing cry as Alfie falls off the lowest branch of an apple tree having been made to walk the plank by his determined older brother, Will. Chaos ensues and everyone runs over offering advice. Steve and Rachel bundle the hysterical patient into the car with Diana following them, barking instructions about where to park when they get to A&E. Edward reassures the distraught Will, and soon has him and his sister distracted with a spot of blackberry-picking.

Martin looks sheepishly at Emma.

'I hope you'll take better care of our children,' she jokes.

Martin wraps her in his arms. 'I will always take care of my family,' he says.

Sensing an exit plan, he and Emma take the chance to leave, but she is still wound up on the journey home.

'I mean, what is she on? How many years exactly do you get for matricide?'

'You probably won't want to hear this, but I think she is just trying to help, Em.'

'Oh why do you have to be so bloody reasonable?'

'It's why you love me.'

'I know and I do feel bad because I guess she is trying to help and I'm just tired and hung over, but it's our big day and I don't want anyone hijacking it,' she says resting her hand on Martin's knee.

He smiles at her. 'It will be fine, try not to worry. We'll find a way to manage your mum. We probably just need to put her in charge of something like the cake or flowers or something.'

Emma feels a little consoled and leans over to kiss him on the cheek. 'I knew there was a reason I was marrying you.'

'What apart from my infinite charm and the fact that I'm so much better looking than Daniel Craig?'

'Yeah, that as well.' Emma's phone beeps and she flicks it to read the text: 'Hope you're not too nervous re tomorrow. Get an early night, lovely. Exx'

Emma smiles at Ella's message and is suddenly filled with nerves at the thought of what lies ahead tomorrow. She is pitching for a new book, which, given the buzz in publishing circles, is destined to become the next big thing. Her anxiety and waning hangover make her feel tired so she foregoes Sunday evening TV and a glass of wine for an early night curled up with Allen Chandler's potential new bestseller. Martin comes up to find her and picks up some of the scattered pages.

'*The Red Orchid*. Sounds a bit poncey.'

'It's not poncey: It's going to be huge and I'm going to publish it.'

'Well I hope you do, my sweet. Have I ever told you how proud I am of you?'

'Never,' says Emma with a grin.

'Would you like me to show you?' asks Martin, prising the pages of the book from her fingers, kissing her hand and along her wrist.

'I really should finish this,' sighs Emma, as Martin works his way up her arm and onto her neck.

'Well if you really have to,' he adds, continuing to kiss her chin and face and the corner of her mouth.

'Oh sod it. I'll do it on the train!' says Emma, casting the manuscript to one side, wrapping her arms and legs around him and pulling him down on top of her. There is an urgency and intensity to the movement so that minutes later they are pulling at each other's clothes and Martin is exploring Emma's body with his tongue: down the curve of her breast to one nipple where he toys a while, inciting and enjoying her reaction. Emma's body rises and she lifts her pelvis in a moment of pure pleasure and lust. And suddenly, he reaches down, moves her underwear to one side and is inside her causing Emma to gasp and pull him deeper into her. Later, after they have both come and Emma has retrieved her underwear from the nose of an indignant looking giant toy frog they won on a trip to Brighton, they lie together like spoons, both heavy and warm with sleep.

'I do love you,' says Emma, reaching an arm up to stroke his face.

''Course you do,' says Martin and she can feel the grin on his face. 'I'm bloody lovely.'

Rachel throws miscellaneous chunks of Lego and tiny dolls' shoes into whichever receptacle is nearest.

'Glass of wine?' asks Steve.

'Lovely,' she answers without looking up.

He returns smiling, placing the glasses on the coffee table and stretching out an arm to her. 'What a day, eh? At least Alfie's OK though.'

Rachel nods, accepting the embrace for a second and then pulling away. 'Just got to reclaim the living room before I sit down.'

'Sure, sweet-cheeks, you do what you gotta do,' says Steve turning on the TV and flicking to the sports news.

'Maaaarm!' yells a small voice from the top of the stairs.

'Alfie,' says Rachel in a weary voice.

'I'll go. You sit,' says Steve.

Rachel accepts with gratitude, slumping onto the sofa and sipping her wine.

'He's fine. He'd just dropped Raggy,' reports Steve on his return.

'Good. Thanks. So, do you want to watch *Grey's Anatomy* or *The Wire*? I've got them both on Sky Plus.'

'Actually Rach, I need to talk to you.'

She looks at his weary face and realises how little she actually looks at him these days. The early months of their relationship had been spent memorising every part of each other's face and body, but with time and children their faces became somewhat obscured as they were replaced by younger, smaller and more impatient versions of themselves. Looking at him now, she recognises the man she fell for, but his face is punctuated with more lines and his eyes are underlined with purple-grey shadows. She looked at her own face in the mirror recently and had been shocked when she realised that the lines were now caused by too much frowning rather than too much laughter.

'OK, sounds serious. What's up?'

'Well – ' Steve looks unsure where to begin and Rachel is starting to feel a little worried.

'You're having an affair? With Kate Winslet? Again?'

Rachel's attempt at humour makes Steve smile, but only just.

'Yeah, but apart from that. It's about work. They want to promote me.'

'Wow, that's fantastic! Congratulations! To do what?'

'To open up a new office.'

'Brilliant. Where?'

'Edinburgh.'

'What?'

'I know. It's a long way from everything but it's a huge step up and a big pay rise.'

'It's in Scotland.'

'I know, but it could be fantastic.'

'How?'

'It's an amazing city.'

'It's in Scotland.'

'I know.'

'That's north of here.'

'Yes but – '

'Where it rains.'

'OK, but – '

'A lot.'

'Look, Rachel, I knew you'd be like this but I'd at least like to discuss it rationally.'

'Oh, so I'm irrational now, am I?'

'A tad.'

'You want to drag your family a billion miles up north for the sake of your career?'

'No, of course not, but we do need to consider our future and I am the breadwinner.'

'Yeah and don't I know it!'

'What's that supposed to mean?'

'I've given up everything for this family. Everything. You just don't get it, do you?'

'Not very often, no.'

'Ha bloody ha. So that's my lack of job and sex drive at fault, is it? I mean, do you ever actually think about me or what I need?'

'That's why I'm trying to talk to you. Why do you always get like this?'

Rachel can't speak. She lets out an enraged yelp like a trapped animal and storms out. The phone interrupts her moment of fury and she snatches it to her ear.

'Hello?' she says.

'Rachel, darling?' trills her mother oblivious to her daughter's tone.

'Oh hi, Mum.'

'We just wanted to check how Alfred is.'

'He's fine thank you. He's sleeping.'

'And what about my other naughty grandchildren?'

'Naughty.'

'Excellent. Now, darling, listen, we need to take that sister of yours in hand. I thought a spot of dress shopping might be in order.'

'OK.' Rachel can't even muster any glee at the thought.

'Super. I'll call Emma and set a date.'

'OK. Mum?'

'Yes, darling?'

'Nothing.'

'All right. Kisses to the children.'

'Will do. Give our love to Dad.'

'I will if I can ever persuade him to come out from behind the Telegraph.'

Rachel replaces the receiver feeling about three years old again and wishing that there was someone to look after her. She can't remember a time when she felt anything less than exhausted. She loves her kids and Steve but can't always find the energy to tell them. She feels so far away from her previous life of skinny cappuccinos and dynamic, creative ad agency meetings. Life now is all about trying to leave the house in a non-stained top and asking everyone if they want ketchup with their fish fingers.

She is still angry with Steve but is too tired for an encore. Unlocking the back door she retrieves the secreted packet of Marlboro Lights kept in the shed for occasions like this. After padding a little further down the garden, she curls herself up on a garden chair tucked out of the sight of the house, behind a sickly rhododendron. She lights up and inhales deeply, shivering against the chilly evening air. Feeling herself relax she gazes out into the night but can see nothing but the molten orange glow of her cigarette.

'Gotcha!'

Rachel shrieks and then laughs as she sees her neighbour Tom's amused face grinning over the fence.

'You bastard.'

'Good evening to you too, Mrs Summers.'

'Good evening, Mr Davies. What are you doing, creeping round the garden like a pervert?'

'Snail patrol,' he says flashing torchlight over the fence. 'It's the only way to catch them, you see.'

Rachel looks amused.

'All right, I know. It's a sad life but I'm a single man with only my hostas for company. And I do love my hostas.'

Rachel laughs. 'And there was me thinking you were coming to rescue a damsel in distress.'

'Do you need rescuing then?' asks Tom, suddenly serious.

In the half darkness Rachel can just make out his face. At first look it could not be described as drop-dead gorgeous, in fact it is slightly pudgy at the edges, but there is a twinkle in his eye that Rachel has decided is handsome and she has always wondered why he's never been snapped up.

Steve and she had assumed he was gay until she'd been chatting with him for a bit one day and he'd said, 'I'm not gay by the way.' After that she'd worried that he'd heard them through their paper-thin walls and had felt guilty for gossiping.

'I don't really need rescuing,' Rachel says feeling disloyal. 'It's just been a bit of a day.' She recounts the saga of Alfie but doesn't mention her row with Steve.

'Ahh, you love it really.'

'Do I?' asks Rachel. 'Do I really love all this? When will it all end?' She loves the kids, that's a given, and Steve has always been her best friend: 'Sod 'em all!' they used to sing when times were tough. But now they barely have time for themselves, let alone each other.

Tom is eyeing her now, looking uncertain of what to do next.

'Well, back to your snails, saddo,' says Rachel, trying to put him at ease.

'If you ever need to chat, you know where I am,' Tom says, and Rachel is touched.

'Rach?' Steve's voice echoes across the garden. 'Are you out here?'

Rachel makes a face at Tom like a scolded teenager. 'Yeah, what?'

'Alfie wants you.'

'Great. I can't even have a sneaky fag now. See you later, neighbour.'

'Bye, Mrs S, and remember what I said.'

'Thanks.'

She stalks down the garden and into the house, ignoring Steve. When she enters Lily and Alfie's bedroom, she feels a little sheepish as her maternal role suddenly washes over her again. Their room still has that sweet scent of young children. Rachel remembers the intoxicating smell of them as newborns and although it fades over the years, she still finds breathing them in, especially after a bath when it is restored, gloriously satisfying.

Alfie is blinking at her, holding out his fat palms. 'Want Mummy.'

'Alfie, you should be asleep. Is your arm hurting?'

'No. All better,' he says. 'I am a big boy.'

'Yes you are, darling, but you need to go to sleep.'

'Want Mummy,' he insists and she cannot refuse. She lies down beside him and strokes his mop of hair.

'Poo-ee, Mummy smells.' Rachel remembers the cigarette.

'Alfie love Mummy?' she asks.

'Naaaaooo,' croons Alfie, teasing.

'Boo-hoo.' Rachel feigns weeping.

Alfie laughs. 'Mummy, cry again.'

Rachel plays along for a bit, and then says, 'Sleep now, baby boy.'

'Mummy sing,' demands Alfie and after a couple of rounds of 'Twinkle, Twinkle, Little Star' his eyelids droop and Rachel creeps out.

Steve is watching the news as she skulks back into the living room, uncertain of what to say next. He flicks off the TV and pats the space next to him, eyes imploring. 'Sit. Please?'

She does so grudgingly, not wanting to be the one to give way and hating herself for it.

'Friends?' he asks stretching out an arm like a peace offering.

Realising it would be churlish to refuse, she leans towards him. 'Look, Steve, I know we need to talk but I'm just too tired tonight.'

'I know, I know,' he says. 'Why don't we see if Emma or your mum can babysit at the weekend? We'll go and have lunch, talk properly, get drunk and say sod 'em all! Waddya reckon?'

Rachel chews her lip and looks at her husband. Dear dependable Steve, her best friend and constant; she finds it impossible to stay angry with him for too long. 'Sod 'em all!' she says, kissing him on the cheek and feeling instant relief. 'I'm going up. Are you coming?'

'Just going to watch the end of Match of the Day 2,' he says, picking up the remote and flicking on the television again.

She nods and pecks him on the cheek before climbing the stairs, exhausted by life and longing for the passion and energy of her twenties.

CHAPTER TWO

The cavernous room is filled with a murmuring hubbub as two thousand or so publishers, authors and their celebrity guests look towards the stage in anticipation. Stephen Fry stands at the podium, smiling; wise and waiting for hush.

'Esteemed guests, ladies, gentlemen and publishing scamps, it is my unbridled pleasure and bowel-clenching joy to announce that the winner of this year's Best Novel Category is the astounding, *The Red Orchid* by Richard Bennett.' Thunderous applause. The crowd are on their feet. Richard rises to greet his public pausing only to kiss his beloved editor, Emma Darcy. There are cheers from the Allen Chandler table. Richard is greeted and embraced by Stephen Fry. A sea of photographers capture the moment with a myriad of clicks and flashes. The applause is enthusiastic and heartfelt. Richard speaks to his people.

'I would like to thank the judges for this great honour. I am truly humbled, but I have to say that I could never have achieved it without the singular devotion of one woman: Emma Darcy, this one's for you, babe.'

Babe? Emma looks up confused as Richard grabs the microphone and starts to sing a heartfelt version of Dido's 'Thank You'. As she looks closely at his face, she is astonished.

'Martin! Is that you?'

She is even more surprised when Stephen Fry picks up the backing vocals and the people in the room join in too, all turning as one to smile at Emma.

'Oh. It's another bloody dream,' mumbles Emma as her brain tunes in to the song playing on her radio alarm clock. She opens her eyes feeling queasy at the thought of the day ahead. 'Today is the one day I will not, must not be late,' she says to the room.

'Drop you at the station, gorgeous girl?' asks Martin returning from the shower and pausing to kiss his fiancée.

'Brillo pads. Thanks, handsome.'

'Can I suggest, endearing as it is, that you don't use the phrase "Brillo pads" in this meeting?'

'Right-ho. Good point.'

'Or "right-ho".'

'Understood,' she says with a small salute.

On boarding the train, Emma makes a beeline for her favourite seat: second carriage from the front, facing forwards in a two-seater. She pulls out the manuscript and her notes. A few stops later a man listening to an iPod takes the empty seat next to her. They have a barely perceptible tussle over elbow territory, and she is just settling into her work when he cranks up the volume and starts to hum along.

Emma is considering making a comment when she notices that he is reading her notes. She snatches them to her chest, like a schoolgirl trying to prevent her neighbour from cribbing.

'Sorry,' he says grinning.

'It's fine but actually would you mind turning down your music please,' says Emma trying to sound as reasonable as possible.

'Sure. Sorry, again.'

Emma looks at him for the first time. He's quite good looking in a public school sort of way. His smile reveals a dimpled cheek, which reminds her of Martin.

'You must be busy, having to work on the train,' he says gesturing at her papers.

'Oh, I've got this pitch meeting today with an author. I'm an editor you see,' she says proudly.

'Oh wow. You're an editor – that must be fascinating. Who's the lucky guy?'

Emma smiles, enjoying some innocent flirting. 'He's a relatively new writer called Richard Bennett. His novel is amazing but I've heard a rumour that he's a bit of a lothario,' she says conspiratorially.

The train is making its final, slow passage into Victoria past the gasholders and dormant power station that Emma thinks makes this part of London look abandoned.

'Men, eh?' smiles the man. 'Well I hope he doesn't give you too much trouble.'

'Thanks, I'm hoping I can charm him.'

'I have no doubt you will. Well good luck – ?'

'Emma. Emma Darcy.'

'*Emma Darcy*. Like a character in a novel. I hope you get your book, Emma Darcy,' he smiles and then disappears into the crowd of commuters. Emma gathers her belongings, takes a deep breath, and steps off the train into Monday morning chaos.

'Want breakfast naaaaaow!' yells Alfie.

'Ok, Hitler-in-a-nappy. Mummy's going as fast as she can.' Rachel throws crisps, a drink and a packet of something claiming to be 100% fruit into Will's lunch bag and counts down the seconds until the microwave gives its final *ping*. She snatches open the door to find that the milk has boiled over and Alfie's porridge now resembles molten lava with a temperature to match. 'Bollocks!' she mutters as quietly as she can, emptying the rest of the carton of milk into the bowl in a desperate attempt to cool it down. It now has the consistency of slurry and Rachel knows that this will not pass the Alfie taste-test. She bins her first attempt and gives the microwave a cursory wipe before starting again.

'Naaaaaow Mummeeee!'

'Look, young man, either you wait or you work out a way of making it yourself. I'm doing my best, OK?'

''kay,' says Alfie uncertainly. 'Mummy cwoss.'

'I am not cross,' and then she catches sight of his chubby jowls and blue eyes and smiles, 'Mummy's sorting it, sausage.'

'Cuddle, cuddle,' he implores, and Rachel gives in, nibbling at his soft little neck.

'Nooo, Mummy,' he giggles.

'Right you, into your chair. Lily! Will! Breakfast time!'

'Coming!' shouts Will. 'Just got to take this penalty to win the World Cup for England.'

'I'm having a poo!' bellows Lily.

'Breakfast in paradise, darling?' asks Steve, grabbing a banana on his way through.

'Oh yeah, baby, it's like a week in Mauritius.'

'Bless you, Mummy. *Achoo!*' says Alfie mishearing.

Rachel removes the second batch of cereal from the microwave and pours a pot of something pink, gloopy and organic all over it.

'Naaaaaoooooo, Mummy, want bananaaaaa!'

'Oh for heaven's sake, Alfred!'

'Maaaarrrrm,' shouts Lily, 'I've run out of bog roll!'

'Did you teach her to call it that?' Rachel asks Steve.

'Darling, I thought you were the queen of spade-calling. Got to dash.'

'You're a bit early, aren't you?'

'Lots to do, my sweet. Got to start early so I can be home on time. Let's talk later. Properly? Over a bottle of something nice? Love you.' He plants a kiss on her cheek and on each available child's head.

'Bye, Lils!'

'Bye, Daddy. Love you.' Her voice is sweet and charming and then changes as she shouts, 'Maaarrrm!'

'OK, Lily. I'm coming!'

'Mummy, banana!' insists Alfie.

'OK, OK. Will, please can you sort out your brother while I attend to your sister.'

Lily looks disappointed at Rachel's entrance.

'I want Daddy.'

'Well, unfortunately you have Mummy.'

'Oh.'

Five minutes later, the ladies of the house come downstairs to a suspiciously peaceful kitchen.

Rachel looks pleased and then horrified. 'Will, what have you done?' she cries, seeing that Alfie's face is smeared with the remains of a packet of Giant Chocolate Buttons, which his obliging brother has tipped over his cereal.

'What? He likes them.'

Rachel is about to open her mouth when her phone beeps with a text. It's from her friend, Sue: 'Fancy Baby Bump and Grind aka Bounce and Rhyme at the library at 10?'

Rachel fires off a reply: 'In the absence of an offer from George Clooney, you're on. Got to pop home after school run. Save me a tambourine.' And then as an afterthought, 'Shall I text Christa?'

The answer pings back: 'Good idea.'

Christa, who has recently moved from Switzerland, is clearly pleased to be asked: '*Danke viels*. Roger and I would that love. *Bis bis*.'

Rachel smiles and takes a deep breath, making ready to coax, cajole and nag her family out of the house.

Emma walks into Allen Chandler's impressive, marble lobby. She smiles at Derek on reception, who gives her a wink and a thumbs-up.

'Hold that lift!' orders a voice.

Emma turns to see Joel Riches marching through the door radiating an air of self-importance. He ignores Derek, who in turn shakes his head in disgust. Emma is tempted to pretend she hasn't heard, but knows this won't work. Joel is a persistent force in her life. Every book she publishes or pitches for, he's there 'thinking outside the box' or 'campaigning above the line', ready to disassociate himself from things which don't work and take the glory for things that do. As a member of the 'say what you mean and mean what you say' club Emma loathes him.

'Hi, Emma,' he says with a condescending lilt. 'So Richard Bennett? It's either going to be a huge opportunity or a complete drain on resources and the bottom line. Thoughts?'

Emma bristles at his patronising tone but answers as calmly as she can. 'I think it's a formative work for an emerging talent in a brave new world of modern fiction destined to win awards and generate sales and profit for the company.'

'Well done, Emma. Good work,' he says, which makes Emma want to stave in his head with the manuscript she's holding. 'Personally, I prefer something a little meatier. Did I tell you I'd read *Don Quixote* last summer?'

'Several times.' They have reached the twelfth floor and the lift doors open. 'Got to dash, Joel. Got a book to buy.'

'Good luck. Don't be nervous. Mind you, I would be. Digby's relying on this one.'

'Tosser,' mutters Emma under her breath as she makes her way into the open-plan office. Ella has left a small bunch of butter-yellow freesias on her desk with a card that says, 'I know you can do it.' Emma is touched, but at the same time feels a little inadequate as she doesn't know if she would have been so thoughtful herself. Behind the lovingly placed flowers is a less lovingly placed Post-It note slapped onto her computer's blank face. It's from Miranda and it simply says, 'Emma – please pop in at 9. Digby wants a word.'

Emma feels as if she might regurgitate her breakfast. It's not that she's afraid of Digby: He's a pussy cat compared with the bottom-line obsessed powers that now run the company. But he is one of Miranda's oldest friends and was a traditional, independent, gentleman publisher, who launched a whole host of seminal works, as well as being the founding member of the day-long publishing lunch. Emma takes a deep breath and knocks on Miranda's closed door with what she hopes is an air of quiet authority. There is no answer, so Emma inclines her ear towards the door, just as it is flung open by the literary powerhouse that is Miranda Winter.

'Ah, Emma. I thought I heard something. Morning. Morning. And how is my brightest and best on this exquisite day? Come, my child, don't be shy. Digby won't eat you. He's had his breakfast.'

Miranda's office is a shrine to the great and good of publishing, books and reading. Her walls are adorned with photographs, sketches and mementos from her forty-odd years as the matriarchal founding editor of Chandler and now Allen Chandler. The world of books and publishing may have changed, but Miranda Winter is not a woman to be trifled with and the newer suits at Allen Chandler simply wouldn't dare. They're terrified of her and she makes them far too much money. The photographs of Miranda with everyone from John Gielgud to John Updike read like a history of cultural movers and shakers from the post-war years. Emma is particularly impressed by the rumours that Miranda has slept with most of the men photographed here, even the gay ones. They are like the photographic equivalent of notches on her bedpost.

As Emma enters the room, Digby is perched on the edge of Miranda's dark oak monster of a desk, a pudgy hand pawing at one of his many chins. Although publishing today is a very different world to that of fifty or even twenty years ago, when lunch neatly segued into afternoon tea, cocktails and dinner, no one seems to have told Digby and he remains the very picture of old-school corpulence. He is suited by a little man in Savile Row and his Oxford brogues are always shiny. He prefers a dicky bow to maintain the air of an eccentric publisher and today his pink shirt looks fit to burst as his belly extends over his blue pinstriped trousers.

'Ah Ella,' he begins, raising his fat hands in a sort of waving gesture.

'It's Emma.' She corrects him. 'Ella's the other one.'

Digby snorts with amusement as if having two people with vaguely similar names is the funniest thing he's ever heard.

'Sorry, so sorry. Now, Emma, I know I don't need to tell you how much our hopes are resting on you today. And I just wanted to say good luck. I know you can do it.'

Emma tries to speak but only manages a squeak of agreement.

Miranda leaps to her rescue. 'Well, Emma and I will do our darndest to bring home the bacon, eh Emma?'

Emma nods vigorously, deciding that it is probably best to remain mute for now.

'Quite so, quite so,' says Digby with customary vagueness. 'Well, the very best to you both. I look forward to hearing good news!' And away he shuffles.

'So tell me how you're really feeling,' says Miranda when he is gone.

'Honestly? I'm bloody terrified. I mean, this is the most exciting book I've read since Marquez. Do you really think we can get it?'

'The agent is touting it hither and thither after the publisher with the most money, but I know we have more to offer.'

She looks at Emma with glassy eyes. It's the look Ella and Emma call her 'mirror to the past'. Ella always jokes that Emma is her protégé and it is clear that Miranda does see something of herself in Emma. At last year's Christmas party, Miranda threw her arms around her and told her that she was like Boudicca, but they were all very drunk.

'Ten o'clock then. We pitch our ideas, gush, enthuse and generally plump up their egos like sumptuous cushions. OK?'

'OK. Do you think Richard will go for it?'

'Oh, it's not Richard we have to worry about, darling. It's the agent.'

The light is flashing on Emma's phone when she gets back to her desk. It's a text from Martin: 'Good luck Mrs Almost-Wifey. Hope you get the book. I'm proud of you. Love M.' She smiles but is starting to feel a bit sick and desperate to get on with it. She checks her watch: 9:34. Twenty-six minutes to go. She leafs through her notes again and realises that her hands are shaking. The book is beautifully written and Emma desperately wants to be the one to publish it. She gives herself an internal pep talk: 'You can do this. You are good at your job. You love this book and you want the world to love it too.'

The phone rings shattering the peace. Emma leaps up, knocking coffee all over her notes. 'Fuck!' she says involuntarily into the mouthpiece.

'Emma?' asks Miranda with no notable surprise at the outburst.

'Yes? Sorry. I'm here.'

'And so are they. Are you ready?'

Emma looks at the coffee-steeped notes and realises that she's going to have to wing it. 'I'll come straight over.'

'Fine. I'll go and welcome them, roll out the red carpet as it were. And remember, you should be bloody nervous but it's just another book. OK?'

'OK,' says Emma feeling anything but.

Miranda's office is filled with the heavy perfume of pink lilies, mingled with the welcome aroma of freshly brewed coffee. Emma realises that she needs to pee, but daren't leave the room now. The table is covered with a selection of Danish pastries. Her stomach groans appreciatively, but she decides against the risk of icing down her top and flaky crumbs on her upper lip. She can hear Miranda coming, jollying their guests along in a warm but business-like way. She decides that standing is the best option as sitting might seem somehow presumptuous or complacent or both.

The woman who enters first is known to Emma by fearsome reputation only: Joanna Uppington is ball-breaker number one of the publishing world. Emma is pretty sure she's never smiled in her life. She is immaculate and tiny in her fitted, designer trouser suit. The only aspect to her that gives her any height (and which Emma suspects is the actual source of her power) is her hair with its impressive four-inch power-bouffant held in place with enough hairspray to finish off the ozone layer.

'Joanna, this is Emma Darcy, our most talented editor.'

Joanna looks Emma up and down as if seeking to identify a new life form and thrusts out a bony hand like a poison dart. 'And this is my most talented author, Richard Bennett,' she retorts.

And there he is. Of course. As if God, Beelzebub and his wizards, and the spirit of Joel Riches were all conspiring as one against Emma. The man from the train.

CHAPTER THREE

Rachel looks at the kitchen and tries to ignore the Weetabix-encrusted carnage. She presses the button on the washing machine, waiting with impatience for it to release the laundry. She can hear Alfie and Lily shouting their usual morning chorus of 'I hate you's' and decides to let them resolve it for themselves, like the books tell you to. She unlocks the back door and picks her way across the dewy grass. She is just prising apart a mass of trousers and socks, when she hears the phone ring.

'I'll get it!' calls Lily. Rachel curses. Moments later, her daughter pads into the garden.

'My socks are wet and it's Grandpa,' she announces. Rachel accepts the phone and waves her daughter away with the international semaphore sign for 'Go and find some dry socks.'

'Hi, Dad,' she says at last.

'Morning, daughter number one. Your mother was fretting so she made me phone you,' he says with a chuckle.

Rachel laughs. 'I'm fine thanks, Dad. It was lovely to see you all yesterday, despite the apple tree incident.'

'Yes and how is the little man this morning?'

Rachel can hear her mother talking in the background, directing operations. 'He's absolutely fine. No lasting damage. What's Mum saying?'

Edward doesn't speak for a moment, as he tries to listen to two separate conversations. 'Sorry, Rachel. Your mother wants to know if you and Steve are all right?' says Edward. Rachel hears her mother exclaim at his lack of subtlety.

She laughs again. 'We're fine. Why?'

'She wants to know why,' Edward reports back to his increasingly exasperated wife.

'Oh for heaven's sake, Edward. Give me the phone will you? Honestly, if you want something done in this family. Rachel?' says Diana as she takes the phone.

'Yes, Mum?'

'Now don't you "yes, Mum" me. I know what you and Daddy are like when you get together. I simply wanted to check that everything is all right between you and Steve.'

'I've just told Dad we're fine. Why do you ask?'

'Steve has asked us to have the children on Saturday night.'

'Oh right, yes, well we just want to have a little time on our own as a married couple.'

'Yes all right, Rachel. There's no need to be coarse. So I don't need to worry then?'

Rachel contemplates this question and then immediately rejects the idea of telling her mother about Edinburgh. 'No, of course not.'

'Well good, because I've got enough to worry about with this wedding of your sister's. I'll hand you back to your father.'

'Rachel? Sorry about that. You know what your mother gets like when she's been listening to the *Today* programme. Two hours of John Humphrys and she just won't let things go,' says Edward.

'It's all right, Dad. I know.'

'You know you can always talk to your old dad, if there is anything, don't you?'

'I know, Dad. Thanks. Look, I've got to go.' Rachel replaces the phone and glances at her watch.

'Kids! We're – '

'Yeah, yeah, we know. Late again!' says Lily. 'It's OK, we've done our shoes and coats. We're a bit more organised than grown-ups, you know.'

'Well thank you, Lily,' says Rachel through gritted teeth, grabbing her bag and ushering them out of the door.

It's fortunate that Emma is not the sort of girl who blushes. She does her best to shake hands with Richard without betraying what can only be described as her almighty cock-up. Looking at him properly for the first time, she notices his dark brown eyes and the dimple that appears when the subject is amused. The subject is now extremely amused.

'Hello, Emma. So good to see you. I feel as if we've met somewhere before? Or maybe not?' He plonks himself down into the nearest chair, grabs a pastry and grins at her. Happily, no one else seems to notice this display.

'Coffee anyone?' asks Miranda.

'Tea thanks. Lapsang souchong if you have it – with lemon,' says Joanna.

'Yeah. Coffee's fine. Milk, no sugar thanks,' says Richard folding his arms behind his head in a 'so what can you offer me?' type way.

'Of course. I'll get Andrea to do the honours,' says Miranda disappearing.

Emma is panicking inwardly like a child whose mother has left the room, but she fights the urge to throw herself on the floor and beat the carpet with her fists, offering Joanna a seat instead. Joanna looks horrified and turns to inspect the chair, dusting it with a manicured hand and perching awkwardly, as if this is the first time she's sat down in her life. All the while Richard is eyeing Emma with vast amusement.

'So,' booms Miranda on her return, 'thank you for coming today. We're tremendously excited about this book and hope you decide that Allen Chandler is the best home for it. Emma has prepared some data on the current market, our comparable titles and what we can offer Richard.'

'Oh come on, Miranda, never mind that. This is a brilliant and original book. We all know that. Every other publisher is telling us that. Great. Fantastic. We're thrilled. But what are you prepared to pay?' Joanna's voice is direct, fierce and as terrifying as her reputation. Emma gulps. No one speaks to Miranda like that. Her eyes betray thunder, but her smile remains fixed.

'No, Joanna, it's OK, I think we should hear what Emma has to say.' Richard's voice is amused and almost mocking.

'Do you?' Joanna says in surprise. 'Oh all right then. Let's hear it.'

Emma's heart is in her mouth. 'Right, well I've prepared some data.'

'Yes, yes. Miranda said that. Let's see it.'

She passes round the pages.

'Ooh, PowerPoint. How modern!' says Richard, and Joanna sniggers.

'The first slide shows what we view as the benchmarks for this title and sales data to support,' says Emma ignoring them.

'*Life of Pi*? *The Book Thief*? Surely *The Red Orchid* is better than these?' says Joanna looking unimpressed.

'Well, I think so, yes. If you look at Allen Chandler's own, comparable titles from the past five years we have exceeded sales of these industry benchmarks, and I see no reason why we can't go even further with *The Red Orchid*.'

'How?'

'Well, it will obviously be picked up by the key retailers and reviewers.'

'Ha! A Waterstones' 3 for 2 and four inches in the *Guardian* does not a bestseller make.'

'Well, then there's the awards.'

'Yes, but there's no guarantee, is there?'

'Of course not, but – '

'What I want to know is, how are you going to make the UK's most talented and original author since McEwan into an out and out bestseller?'

'As I've said – '

'But you haven't said. It's all hot air and promises you can't keep, isn't it?'

Richard is grinning, enjoying the spectacle, but for Emma it is turning into another fight with her mother. She is waiting for Joanna to tell her to go and tidy her room.

'No, it's not all hot air and promises,' says Emma surprising everyone in the room including herself. Joanna looks at her sharply. 'In the past ten years the fiction market has changed beyond recognition.'

'Tell me something I don't know,' yawns Joanna.

'Publishers are under incredible pressure to deliver profit, but are being squeezed by the demands of agents and authors for ever higher advances.'

'And I suppose that's my fault, is it?' Joanna wants to spar. Emma won't bite.

'There are a whole host of publishers who will offer you more money than they can ever earn just to win your book.'

'And?'

Emma address her directly now, refusing to be cowed. 'And, those with the fattest cheque books don't necessarily have what you need to turn a book from an emerging talent to a bestseller to a classic.'

'Oh please impart your wisdom. What would that be?'

'One word: Passion.'

Joanna snorts with derision. Miranda is watching Emma with what she detects is a glimmer of pride. Emma takes courage from this and addresses Richard directly. 'Your characters, particularly Alexander and Newton, are the lifeblood of this book. They leap out and grab you by the throat, and Alexander's unrequited love for Stella is one of the greatest love stories ever told. It's a story that will stay with readers for ever.'

Richard's eyes are fixed on Emma now, calm and steady. He has lost his earlier cockiness. He opens his mouth to speak but Joanna butts in. 'Listen, I'm sure you're a great editor and it's lovely to hear that you've read and loved this book. Ya di ya big deal, but what are ya gonna pay?' She spits out the last six words with venom.

Miranda clears her throat. 'Joanna, I think it's time we drew this meeting to a close.'

'I'm sorry?'

'Yes, so am I. I think we have been upfront, honest and searingly enthusiastic for Richard's book. If it's all about the money, it's not for us. Shall I see you to the lift?' Miranda appears calm but the area of neck just below her ears has reddened.

'But I thought – ' Joanna blurts.

'Then you thought wrong. If other publishers are prepared to let you throw your weight around and patronise their editors, then more fool them. I, for one, am not.'

Joanna opens her mouth to speak but stops when she sees Miranda's face. She raises herself up on her bony twig legs and pats her immobile hair. 'Come on, Richard, let's go to another, less short-sighted publisher.' Joanna Uppington breezes out of the room on a waft of Chanel No. 5.

Richard is still staring at Emma.

'Richard!' shouts Joanna from the corridor.

Richard jumps up ready to follow, but stops at the door and turns to address Emma and Miranda. 'I'm sorry, I have to, erm, it was lovely to meet you – '

'Richard!' screeches Joanna again.

Richard holds up his hands and smiles like a defeated man. 'Bye,' he says and darts out of the door.

'Tell me his written word is better than his spoken,' says Miranda after a moment.

'It is. Unfortunately,' says Emma with a sigh. 'Why does Joanna behave like that?'

'Because, my dear, she is a bully and frankly we're better off without them both.' Her phone chirps and she glances at it, looking weary. Emma feels guilty. 'It's Digby. I better update him.'

Emma takes this as a signal to leave and tries to creep back to her desk unnoticed. She realises that the god of shit days has got it in for her as she turns the corner and Joel appears out of nowhere. Emma jumps. 'Jesus, Joel!'

'Ahh, thanks for the accolade, you can just call me Joel though. Sooo, how'd it go? Ooh. Not so good, eh?'

'I don't know. We'll just have to see.'

'Ouch. That bad, eh? You should have asked me to come along, Em. I would have been happy to help.'

Emma bristles at his familiar use of her name. Realising that homicide is probably not the best course of action, she tries to muster some dignity and shambles back to her desk. Almost immediately, Ella is by her side confirming that the Joel bush telegraph is fully operational.

'Come on,' she says, 'we need Oreo cookie cheesecake and we need it now.'

The over-enthusiastic librarian has her hand up a surprised-looking crocodile puppet as Rachel arrives hot and flustered at the library. As the highlight of pre-school entertainment in this town, the tiny space is packed with fifty or more mums and dads and their wriggly offspring. Rachel attempts to park her double buggy by the door.

'Can't park there, love,' insists a red-faced man with a bunch of keys on his belt.

'Can't I?' asks Rachel irritated.

''ealth 'n' safety innit?' he insists.

'Right. Fine.' Rachel can't be bothered to argue and steers the buggy round to 'Large Print'. She turns round to see that Alfie has escaped, while his sister is still calmly disembarking. 'Lily, where's Alfie?'

'I don't know,' says Lily with a complete lack of concern.

'Oh shit!'

A large lady in her sixties, who is dressed like a duchess, tuts loudly in Rachel's direction.

'Sorry, it's just that I've lost my – '

'Boo!' Alfie jumps out from behind a Catherine Cookson display.

The woman is unimpressed. 'This isn't a crèche, you know.'

Rachel wants to respond but Alfie is tugging at her leg.

'Let's go and see Joe, Mummy.'

'All right, darling. Silly old bag,' mutters Rachel.

Lily giggles. 'Silly old bag!'

The woman looks around and Rachel smiles trying to look innocent. 'Bye!'

After a row of 'sorry's and side-shuffles, she reaches Sue and Christa and their respective sons, Joe and Roger. 'What did I miss?' she whispers to Sue.

'Just a couple of "Bobbins" and an energetic "Sailor Went to Sea".'

The librarian, a bony woman of indeterminate age, is now handing out musical instruments. Alfie shakes his sleigh bell enthusiastically resulting in a glancing blow to Roger's bemused face.

'Alfie! Say sorry.'

'Sorreeee,' sings Alfie with a grin.

Roger looks unsure, but then joins in as Joe takes this as a cue for an impromptu sword fight.

'Boys! Stop it!' commands Lily. 'I can't hear the lady.'

The boys comply and Sue smiles, impressed. 'Got her mother's way with men, has she?'

'I wish. Wait until I tell you what Steve's got lined up for us.'

'I'm hoping it's an all expenses paid trip to a 5-star luxury beach resort with hot and cold running nannies but from your face, I'm guessing not.'

'Ok, mums, dads, boys and girls, are we ready to be jingle-jangle scarecrows?'

'Tell you over a latte,' says Rachel with a rictus, ready-to-sing grin.

Emma lets Ella take her by the arm like some doddery old dear and they make the short walk to Auntie Mabel's, the favourite haunt for any day when they're in need of a consolation doughnut or celebratory bun. Emma has always thought it a shame that there is no Auntie Mabel: The proprietors are Simon and his partner David and they happily dispense cake and wisdom as a favourite auntie would.

'Ohmygod. David? Look at that face. Bad news, is it, sweetie?' says Simon as the bell above the door signals their entrance.

Emma lets out an enormous sigh in response and nods, adopting the look of a dejected child.

'Oh my darling, bring those puppy dog eyes here. Uncle Simon will make it better.' He embraces her and guides them to a table covered with a red check cloth and tomato-shaped ketchup bottle. 'Here, have Audrey's table. I'm guessing it's two caps and two cheesecake?'

'Simon, you're as perceptive as a girl and yet such a loss to the female race!' says Ella.

'Ah but, gorgeous girl, I am seriously high maintenance and would spend much longer in the bathroom than you. Apart from that and the aversion to fannies, you'd turn me in a heartbeat.'

Ella giggles like a schoolgirl. When Emma brought her mother here for lunch, Simon had her eating out of his hand and Diana kept trying to hook her up with David: 'What a catch he'd be, Em!' Emma didn't have the heart to tell her, but luckily Martin came along and she had another prospective son-in-law to fix her hopes on.

'Are we in full-scale "don't be nice to me" mode?' enquires Ella.

Emma looks up at Audrey Hepburn gazing down at them in that 'yes, I am more beautiful than you could ever hope to be but I won't make you feel bad about it and could actually be your best friend if we met' way. 'I think we are,' Emma replies.

'Right,' says Ella feeling uncomfortable at the prospect of having to insult rather than hug her friend.

David appears with their order. 'Here we go. I've given you a dollop of homemade vanilla ice cream as well. All on the house today, girls.'

Ella sees Emma's lip begin to wobble and ploughs in. 'Who wants to publish that kind of fiction anyway?'

'I do,' says Emma. 'Can't you do any better than that?'

'OK,' says Ella unsure. 'Well it won't make us any money and will just be a pain in the arse to get off the ground.'

'Now you sound like Joel.'

Ella looks crestfallen. Emma knows she's just too lovely for this kind of thing. Then she surprises her. 'Well you're a crap editor and it will better off at another publisher.'

'Ella, steady on!'

'Sorry, you know I'm not much good at this game. How about "the author's probably a tosser"?'

'Actually, that might be true.'

Ella raises her eyebrows quizzically.

'Well there are the rumours that he's a ladies' man and he did seem to enjoy watching me squirm during the pitch meeting.'

'There you go then,' smiles Ella, pleased to have found a negative for her friend to cling to. 'That probably explains why he writes about relationships so well.'

'Yes, all right. Aren't you supposed to be telling me about how much better off I am without this man and his novel?'

'Oh yes, sorry. Well it has its flaws.'

'Like what?'

'Well the title's a bit girly.'

'Girly?'

'Yeah, I mean how many blokes want to read a book with a flower in the title?'

'OK, it's a viewpoint. What else?'

'Erm, it's too long?'

'Too long?'

'A bit.'

'Do you think Tolstoy would have created one of the masterpieces of fiction if his editor had told him *War and Peace* was a bit on the lengthy side?'

'S'pose not. Do you think you would stop feeling sorry for yourself with a gob full of cheesecake?'

'Good point.'

Despite a noble effort from Ella and two more pieces of cheesecake, Emma returns to the office with a heavy heart and even heavier stomach. Her phone shows two missed calls from Martin. She calls him back. "Lo?' she says in a flat voice.

'I take it we're not celebrating this evening.'

'Oh, Martin, it was bloody awful.'

'You poor thing. Do you want me and Charlie to go round and sort him out for you?'

'It's a kind offer but I'd rather have a hug.'

'Now that won't be difficult. Listen, I'll cook you your favourite tonight and we'll drown our sorrows. Spaghetti Bolognese is it, madam?'

'Thanks, darling. I love you.'

'Love you too.'

***

After a morning of trying children, a nagging mother and cheery singing, Rachel is ready for something far stronger than a skinny latte. However, the coffee shop does offer the next best thing with its promise of grown-up interaction and sugar-infused treats for the children to prolong this grown-up interaction. Despite its coffee chain décor of dark wood tables, fat dark-brown sofas and sepia pictures of corpulent grinning 'roasters' and couples enjoying the coffees of their lives, Rachel has a fondness for this place. She has come here since Will was a baby and knows most of the baristas by sight. Plus they welcome the mothers of the town and don't balk at mashed muffin or spilt smoothie. They have circled their buggies like wagons, bought their coffees and the children are distracted with cake. Rachel is recounting the details of last night's argument with Steve.

'Edinburgh?'

'I know!'

'Wow!'

'I know!'

'It's an amazing city, really beautiful.'

'Yeah, OK but I'm wallowing in self-pity here and you're supposed to be helping.'

'Right, sorry. It is bloody far away too.'

'Exactly.'

'And the weather's shit. Al went to uni there. He loved it but always says the weather was appalling.'

'Precisely.'

Christa laughs. 'You English and your weather. It's a national passing of time, isn't it?'

Rachel smiles. 'I just don't want to bring up my kids so far from my family. Sorry, Christa, that was a bit insensitive of me. You must miss your family terribly.'

'It is OK, Rachel. To be honest, I do not really get on with my family, not since my mother's sex change.'

Sue nearly chokes on her muffin. 'Her what?'

'*Ja*, she was name of Wilhelmina and now she is just Wilhelm.'

Rachel notices Sue ramming the rest of her muffin in her mouth to stop herself from laughing.

'*Mein* poor father did not see it coming. I think it was the shock *das* killed him.'

'God, that's awful Christa,' says Rachel unsure of what else to say.

'*Ja*, that and the prostitute he was with the night he died. His *herz* was never very strong, you see.'

Rachel doesn't dare make eye contact with Sue and pats Christa's arm, trying to look earnest.

'But I'm so sorry, Rachel, you were saying about moving away from your family. Are you very close?'

Rachel thinks for a moment. She adores her father, her mother interferes but means well, and Emma is, well, her baby sister.

'We're as close as any family and I just don't really want my kids missing out on the chance of those relationships.'

Sue has regained her composure. 'What does Steve say?'

'Well, he, erm,' Rachel says, 'actually, I don't know. I kind of shouted him down and didn't really ask him.'

'Sorry, dear friend, I'm as ready as the next militant feminist to blame men for everything from global warming to why the plughole's always full of hair, but even I think you need to talk this one through properly.'

'I know, I know. You're right. What would you do then, oh wise and rational one? Would you up sticks and go?'

'No comparison, my friend. The family is all tucked up safe and sound in the North. I'd probably jump at the chance to be honest. I mean, London's all right, but this south-east corner isn't exactly Hampstead and you don't really get the benefit of living in the big smoke with kids. I mean, when was the last time you went to the cinema or a gig?'

'2003. Duran Duran reunion gig. Bloody fantastic. Anyway, I grew up round here and it's not that bad. I bet more people get mugged in Hampstead.'

'Maybe. I just don't know if I want Joe to be a teenager around here. All those knives and gangs. I say think about it. Rationally,' says Sue with a grin.

'You're supposed to tell me to stay,' says Rachel crestfallen.

'Rach, you know I'll probably just take the kids to the pub and the bookies if you ever leave us, but all I'm saying is think about it.'

Christa is looking wistful. 'It must be nice to have a husband who is there and who values your opinion. My Rudi is never here.'

'He works for a drinks company, doesn't he?'

'*Ja*, he is Russian and spends a lot of time in Moscow. I think he has a mistress.'

'Christa, that's terrible!'

'*Ja*, but I have my boy and Rudi would never forget his responsibility to his boy.' She ruffles Roger's ginger mop of hair.

'Now, let's have another coffee and perhaps some *kuchen*? My treat.' Christa smiles broadly as if she has just given them details of a lovely holiday rather than a life in turmoil.

'That poor woman,' whispers Rachel while Christa is ordering for them.

'I know. Fancy have a mum with a willy, called Willy!'

Rachel explodes with laughter. 'Susan, you are going straight to hell!'

'Yeah, baby and you're right behind me!'

CHAPTER FOUR

Rachel stacks the plates from lunch into the dishwasher and listens, enjoying the sweet sound of silent children enjoying the chaotic capers of a talking dog and his hippy friends. Will has declared *Scooby Doo* to be a 'baby's programme', but Rachel has noticed how he grasps one of Lily's hands when the janitor dressed up as a ghost tries to spook the characters. She looks in on them now; three perfect forms with wide eyes and open mouths, rapt in a state of unbridled joy at the action playing out on screen, barely aware of her presence. Lily glances round.

'Look, Mummy, Scooby's going to have another snack!'

'Oh my goodness! Is he? I bet that's his third or fourth so far!' says Rachel.

'Fifth actually, Mum,' corrects Will, ever hot on his facts.

'Well enjoy, my darlings; Mummy is just going to do something on the computer.'

'Can Alfie look too?' asks Alfie, his eyes not leaving the screen.

'In a bit darling, you watch *Scooby* with Lils and Will.'

Rachel takes her chance and sneaks away, tragically excited about a few precious moments away from motherhood, even if it's just to pay some bills. She feels a mild thrill as the computer starts up and she connects to the internet, her mind filling with expectation at what she might find. It reaffirms that there is still a world out there, even if she often feels disconnected from it. It seems ridiculous that her house is filled with chaos and yet she feels so lonely and detached from it, like a character watching life play out before her. Rachel stares at the glowing screen, its possibilities welcoming her, inviting her in: *Do you feel lucky? Just click here, madam. Not sure what you're after? Just punch in a couple of words and we'll do the rest.*

She is methodical, however, and goes straight to her e-mails. She sends her sister a message asking about the book pitch and gets a response almost immediately: 'Cock-up of the century. Too depressed to speak. Have just eaten my own body weight in cheesecake. How's Alf?'

Rachel grins. She considers telling Emma about the possible move to Scotland but can't face it. Instead she writes, 'No lasting damage. Never mind about the book – bet it was a pile of crap anyway. Let's go and drown our sorrows soon. R x'

'OK. Speak soon. Big hugs to you all. E x'

Rachel looks around her, trying desperately to remember what she is supposed to be doing on the internet. She finds her brain increasingly unable to retain this kind of information, like some kind of leaky bottle. The other day, she had stood in front of the fridge for a good five minutes before she remembered that she was looking for the cheese.

She glances to her right and notices that Steve has left his BlackBerry at home. She looks back at the screen trying to ignore the urge that is starting to overwhelm her. She looks back at Steve's phone. Its blue flashing light seems to tempt and console her at the same time: *Go on, have a look. No one will ever know. It's not as if you're going to find anything incriminating anyway.*

Rachel shakes her head and turns back to the computer, desperately trying to remember what she was going to search for.

'Oh bollocks!' she mutters grabbing Steve's phone and clicking it into life. She's not sure why she's looking or what she's looking for, but almost without knowing it, she finds herself looking at Steve's e-mails. One is from someone called Sam and is entitled 'Coffee'.

Hmm, thinks Rachel, *never heard of Sam before*. She clicks on the message feeling a bit sordid for checking up on her husband.

'Hi Steve, are you still OK for coffee at 11 today? Need to talk about rolling out training on new IT system to your team. Thanks, Sam.'

Rachel sighs, feeling guilty for even suspecting infidelity when all Steve is doing is having coffee with some geeky bloke from IT. Suddenly, her eye is caught by an e-mail entitled 'Edinburgh' and she has clicked on it before she's had the chance to question her actions. The message, from Steve's boss, Doug details, 'our discussions regarding a possible move to start up a new office' and was sent a month ago. Rachel is outraged. She reaches for her mobile and punches buttons until she finds Steve's office number. It clicks straight through to his voicemail. Rachel flings the phone across the room with a growl of anger. Her heart is pounding and she has scared herself by flying off the handle so readily.

'Mum?' Lily appears at the door looking concerned, but not surprised by her mother's outburst

Rachel is caught off guard. 'Darling, sorry, Mummy was just – '

'When's Daddy coming home?' asks Lily interrupting her.

Rachel is irritated by the question. 'No bloody idea,' she says.

Lily looks unimpressed. 'Don't swear, Mummy. It's rude.'

Rachel watches her go, amazed that this bundle of morality is her child. Her mobile chirps into life and she sees the caller ID. She stabs the button and thrusts the handset to her ear, ready for a fight,

'Rach? Everything OK?'

Steve's calm voice seems to fuel her anger. 'No Steve, everything is not OK. Tell me, when exactly did you know about this move to Edinburgh?'

'Rach, can we talk about this later?'

'No, I want to talk about it now.'

'Rachel, I've got a meeting and I'm going to be home a bit late. Sorry.'

Rachel continues, not wanting to miss her moment. 'Over a month. Over a sodding month, Steve, and you didn't have the balls to tell me.'

'Look, Rach, I'm sorry, really I am, but is it any wonder I didn't tell you?'

'I beg your pardon?'

'Listen to yourself, Rach, any excuse for a row, any chance for a fight and you're there, aren't you?'

'Excuse me?'

'Face it, Rach, you do have the tendency to be a bit unreasonable. I was just trying to pick the right moment.'

Rachel is struck dumb for the second time that afternoon and furious that Steve is stealing her moment of thunder. 'Steve?'

'Yeah?'

'Piss off.' Rachel cuts him off before he can respond and immediately phones Sue.

'Hi, love, are you OK?'

'No, not really. Steve is being a prick.'

'Had that rational chat then?'

'Hmm.'

'Do you want some company?'

'Yes please.'

'OK. I'll be round in twenty minutes. I hope you've got a bottle chilling.'

Rachel stalks downstairs to a peaceful living room with the children slumped coma-like now watching *Tom and Jerry*. Rachel watches with them for a while. She'd always hated Tom, and found herself as a child, rooting for the cheeky chancer, Jerry. On watching again, she realises that he's actually a pretentious little tosser and Tom is the eternally tortured soul, whom no one understands.

'Unbelievable,' she mutters to herself as she heads to the kitchen. 'I'm empathising with a cartoon cat now.' She checks the fridge first for wine and then decides to be an über-mother by preparing something wholesome for the kid's tea. On further inspection of the contents of the fridge, she decides that another dose of Omega 3 via the medium of fish fingers will do them no harm.

As she scans the surprisingly tidy kitchen, her eye is caught by a picture Will did a month or so ago entitled 'My Family'. It had made them laugh because he had drawn them all as Power Rangers. Rachel looks closely, smiling to herself, but this time notices the expressions on the faces. He has drawn himself, his siblings and Steve with enormous cartoon grins but she notices that her face is not smiling but slightly turned down. She tries to dismiss it with her usual humour, questioning whether he is a new Leonardo and is seeking to recreate the *Mona Lisa*, but something about it makes her feel sad and rather lonely. She is interrupted by a polite tap at the front door.

'You took your time,' she declares flinging it open.

'I did?' says Tom smiling.

Rachel is momentarily flummoxed. 'Sorry, I thought you were someone else'

'Oh.' Tom looks slightly disappointed and then grins again.

'No, it's OK. It's nice to see you. Are you all right?'

'Fine thanks, Mrs Summers. I'm just playing Postman Pat. I took this parcel in for you this morning.'

'Oh, thanks very much.'

'Where's Postman Pat?' Alfie enquires suddenly at Rachel's legs, peering up at Tom.

'I'm here and you must be Alf Thompson. Hullo Alf!' says Tom putting on a Postman Pat Yorkshire accent.

Rachel is impressed. 'Good knowledge!'

Tom winks at her. 'My nephews and nieces have trained me well. I can do them all, Fireman Sam, Bob the Builder.'

'Where's Jess?' asks Alfie, oblivious to the mild flirting going on above his head.

'She's at home having a rest. We've had a busy morning delivering all these parcels.'

'Where's your van?' continues Alfie.

'Er, round the corner.'

'Ha!' laughs Rachel. 'You're rumbled, mate!'

Tom laughs. Alfie screws up his face with scepticism and runs back to the living room.

'Fancy a glass of wine?' Rachel asks, surprising herself.

'Erm, OK, why not? Only if I'm not in the way though.'

'Don't be silly. You can keep us entertained with your repertoire of children's characters.'

Rachel leads him down to the kitchen just as her mobile starts to ring. It's Sue: 'Listen, darl, I'm really sorry. I'm not going to make it. Joe's just thrown up everywhere. Can we speak tomorrow?'

'Of course. Don't worry. I hope he's better soon.'

'Take care, lovely, and talk to Steve. He's one of the good guys, you know.'

'I know,' says Rachel feeling suddenly exhausted.

Rachel turns to find Tom filling up two wine glasses from the bottle he's found in the fridge.

'Sorry, I took the liberty.'

Rachel accepts the glass feeling suddenly shy. She is relieved when two sets of three-year-old feet come stampeding down the corridor. Alfie and Lily appear in a state of heightened excitement.

'That's him,' says Alfie pointing at Tom.

Lily looks Tom up and down, like an old lady inspecting a joint of meat. 'Why are boys so stupid? That's not Postman Pat. It's Tom from next door.'

It's getting dark as Emma leaves the office, joining the flow of commuters in a hurry to get home because it's Monday and no one goes out on a Monday. The sky has that London light-polluted glow which means it never goes completely dark, even at night. It's chilly and a little rain has dampened the streets. Emma is feeling fed up and ready for a bath, a large glass of wine and the welcoming arms of her fiancé. She feels her phone vibrate in her bag. Fumbling through a mess of keys, lipstick and receipts, she locates it just in time, seeing Martin's caller ID on the screen.

'Hi, handsome. I've just left and I'm looking forward to my spag bol and maybe an encore of last night's performance?' says Emma with a smile.

'Hey, Em,' says Martin sounding guilty. 'Thing is I forgot I'd said I'd play five-a-side football with Charlie. Any chance we could postpone it 'til tomorrow night?'

'Oh, right.'

'Look, Em, I'm really sorry and I'll come home if you want me to. I know you've had a crap day,' says Martin in a tone that is begging to be let off the hook.

Emma sighs, knowing that she'll feel mean if she forces the issue. 'No, it's OK. You go. I'll probably just head home and have a bath and an early night. I'm a bit knackered.'

'Sure?'

'Sure.'

'Sure you're sure?'

'Yes, you loser, now bog off to your little football game,' laughs Emma.

'OK, well spag bol tomorrow night and then how about that encore?' says Martin. 'I'll do anything you want.'

'Anything?'

'Apart from the washing-up. I'll see you later, OK? Love you, Em.'

''Course you do. I'm bloody lovely!' she declares. She throws the phone into her bag and starts to trudge towards the Tube feeling like a lost soul.

'Emma! Emma!' The voice is an unwelcome interruption to her thoughts of home and at first she thinks it's Joel. She spins round, her face set in a scowl. 'Woah, woah, woah!' says the voice's owner. 'I come in peace!'

Richard Bennett stands before her, an apologetic smile on his face, his hands held up in surrender. Emma is unsure what to do or say, so he jumps in. 'Look, we didn't have the best of starts.'

'Slight understatement,' says Emma, arms folded. She's let one man off the hook this evening, Richard Bennett isn't going to have such an easy time. He looks floored for a moment and Emma would almost feel sorry for him if she weren't so fed up. 'Well, if that's all you came to say, I would really like to go home now please.'

He blocks her path. 'Look,' he begins again, 'come and have a drink with me.'

'Why?'

Richard considers the question. 'You want to know why?'

Emma detects that he doesn't get turned down that often. 'If it's not too much trouble.'

Richard's brown eyes flash with amusement. 'I'll give you three reasons actually.'

'Go on then.'

'One, I am really very sorry for what happened today. Two, I thought your pitch was wonderful. And three, your boyfriend stood you up so you may as well.'

Emma is gobsmacked. 'You were spying on me!'

'No, I just came along at the right moment. So what do you say? One drink. I get to absolve my conscience and you get to spend an hour in the company of a glittering literary talent,' he says grinning.

She considers her options. One drink can't hurt and she is intrigued by this man. Even if he has an ego the size of Big Ben, he does write a bloody brilliant book and that's always of interest to Emma. Plus it's not as if she's got any better offers and she could murder a glass of something crisp, dry and white. 'Oh all right then.'

'Brilliant,' says Richard seeming genuinely pleased.

The nearest drinking establishment is one of those central London pubs that would have been lovely if they hadn't let an eighties wine bar designer get his hands on it. The once dingy brown ceilings and walls, which always remind Emma of pubs she used to go to with her dad, have been replaced with a light airy space and pale wooden floor the size of a football pitch. The bar and surrounding tables and stools seem a little higher off the ground, giving the impression that they have wandered into a giant's kingdom.

'What can I get you?' drawls the ponytailed man behind the bar. Garen, as his name badge declares him to be, is surly but smart in his black shirt and silver tie with a Premiership footballer-type gigantic knot. The glass in which he serves Emma's Sauvignon Blanc is the size of a goldfish bowl and could easily house the whole bottle. Richard's Czech beer is the colour of gold with a price to match.

'That'll be nine eighty thanks guys,' says Garen with as much cheer as he can muster. Richard waves away Emma's purse,

'You can get the next one,' he says with a grin.

They find a seat and Emma takes a large gulp of wine feeling herself relax a little.

'So,' says Richard at last, watching her carefully.

'So,' replies Emma.

'Look, I'm really sorry how things turned out today.'

'Are you? You seemed to be thoroughly enjoying yourself. As did your cohort. '

'Oh Joanna's, you know, an agent. She's a bit fierce, but she knows what she's doing.'

'Oh and what's that? Eating editors for breakfast?'

'OK, maybe she's a bit heavy-handed, but we authors do need a bit of protection from you merciless publishers you know.'

'Publishers? Merciless? How very dare you. We act with integrity at all times.' Emma is getting into her stride now and the wine is making her feisty and flirty.

'Yeah, yeah. Whatever,' grins Richard making a sign with his fingers.

'Well I act with integrity.'

He fixes her with a piercing look. 'Do you know, Emma Darcy? I believe you do.'

It might be the wine or the dodgy lighting, but Richard is starting to remind her of some actor she used to fancy. She pats her cheeks, which are starting to feel warm and fixes him with a look. 'Then why did you give me such a hard time?'

'Well you weren't very nice about me on the train.'

'I didn't know who you were then.'

'And that makes it OK, does it? You listened to the tittle-tattle of others before you made up your own mind. That doesn't show too much integrity, does it? Shame on you, Emma Darcy,' he says with a superior smile.

'OK, I'm sorry. I'm sure it's all lies,' she says, daring him to contradict her.

'Complete lies. I am actually very choosy both when it comes to girlfriends and editors.'

'Well that's very reassuring.'

'I'm glad you think so. But enough about me, tell me about you. What's your favourite book?'

'*One Hundred Years of Solitude*,' says Emma without hesitation.

Richard looks pleased. 'Mine too.'

'You're kidding me.'

'Why would I do that? It's not as if I'm trying to get you into bed. You're attached and I respect that.'

'Again, very reassuring,' grins Emma.

Richard gives a little bow. 'Favourite film?'

'*Il Postino*. Yours?'

'*Cinema Paradiso*.'

'That's definitely in my top five.' They continue to talk and Emma is amazed at how quickly the evening passes and that she has managed to put away three glasses of wine before she notices the time. Her stomach is growling from emptiness and she is feeling decidedly woozy. 'I really should be getting home. I was only going to stay for one,' she says, fumbling for her handbag.

Richard sits back in his chair. 'I've had a great evening, Emma Darcy, and the best is yet to come. Do you want to know the real reason I asked you here tonight?'

'Surprise me.'

'Well, despite our faltering beginning, I think you understand my novel and you get what I'm trying to say. So, for that reason and the fact that you've got really nice legs, I want you to be my editor.'

Emma is blown away and slightly flattered by the leg comment. 'What about Joanna?'

'Oh she'll come round. She'll still get her fifteen per cent and she needs to keep England's most promising new novelist happy doesn't she? So, what do you say?'

Emma hesitates. Something deep inside her brain is trying to warn her off this one, but the wine and the fact that she has decided she quite likes this man makes her say, 'I'd love to.'

'That's wonderful. I'm so happy,' says Richard grinning. 'Let's have champagne to celebrate and if you insist on paying, I'll accept. That was a joke by the way.' He reaches for her hand, kissing it in a mock gentlemanly way, looking up at her as he does. Emma's mouth goes dry. 'The deal is sealed,' he says.

Rachel plods down the stairs glancing at the wonky display of what Steve calls their 'Rogues' Gallery' of family photographs. She looks at the pre-children photo of Steve and her at a friend's wedding and notices, not only that she was half a stone lighter and Steve's hair was several tones less grey, but that they look happy. It's not the happiness of stories or romantic endings but the happiness of possibilities, of what might be; that pre-marriage, pre-children happiness, when you still think you might write that novel or open your own business. It's not that she feels bitter that she hasn't achieved these things, she's just resigned to the fact that she probably never will.

Tom appears at the foot of the stairs wearing a pair of pink marigolds and clutching a tea towel. 'All sorted?'

'Yes, thanks. Have you done the washing-up? You really didn't have to.'

'It was my pleasure. Along with my sad devotion to hostas, I also take a tragic delight in cleaning baked bean encrusted pans.'

'Goodness, I married the wrong man,' declares Rachel and then wishes she hadn't.

'Well, I should let you put your feet up.'

'You don't have to go. Steve probably won't get home until midnight and if you go I'll only watch some reality floozie's TV show. If you want to be a friend to me it's your absolute duty to stay and save me from such purgatory.' Rachel fears she is sounding a bit needy.

'Very well, you can save me from another night watching eighties sitcom repeats and I will save you from ITV4,' says Tom immediately.

'Deal. I'll get the wine, you put on some music. Fancy a game of DJs?'

Tom looks bemused.

'It's a game Steve and I play. Each person selects a song of choice and the other person judges. Anything too pretentious or cheesy and you face a penalty, usually of a drinking nature.'

'OK, but I warn you, despite my cuddly bear exterior, I am a bastard when it comes to competition and I rarely play fair.'

'Hurrah, that's fighting talk!'

When Rachel returns with the drinks, Tom has selected 'Major Tom' by David Bowie and is smiling and singing along.

'Excellent choice but careful with the karaoke, sunshine, or you'll be knocking this back.'

Tom laughs. 'My dad used to sing this to me. He loved music but was completely tone deaf. It's where I inherited my talent.'

Rachel laughs and is strangely touched by this shared confidence. 'Do your parents live nearby?'

'They're both dead, I'm afraid, and in answer to your question, we grew up in Norfolk.'

'Sorry to hear that.'

'Ah Norfolk isn't so bad.'

'No, I meant – '

'Rachel? That was a joke. It's OK. It's few years back now and they were older than your average parents. Dad got cancer and died within a few months and Mum couldn't really survive without him. She had a heart attack about six months later. My older sister, Viv, and I always say she died of a broken heart.'

'Oh Tom, that's so sad.'

'Yes it is, but they had each other for nearly fifty years and surely it's better to have that kind of connection with another person?'

'Better to have lived and loved? I've always thought so.'

'Come on then, your turn. Bowie's nearly finished. Surely you need to have a tune on or penalties will have to be faced?'

'I see the man plays to win, no? Right, try this one, mate.' The opening tones of Stevie Wonder's 'Lately' fill the room.

'Nice move. Although of course, if you had chosen "I Just Called" you would have been downing that bottle.'

'True, but even geniuses have their off days.'

'Indeed we do. So how are you then, Mrs Summers?'

Tom is looking earnest now and Rachel isn't sure if she wants to take the conversation down this route. She's enjoying a bit of flirtatious banter and doesn't want to spoil it. She sighs and looks slightly vague. 'Oh, you know.'

'Ah, you don't want to talk about it.'

'No, it's not that, it's just that I really need to talk to Steve and haven't had the chance.'

'Hmm, sounds serious.'

'Well, not as serious as Third World poverty, but important in our lives.'

'Sorry, Rachel, I didn't mean to pry.' Tom looks slightly embarrassed and Rachel feels guilty.

'It's OK, really it is. Oh shit I'm making this into more than it is. Right, well Steve can't be bothered to come home and talk to me properly, so you are officially my designated male for the evening.' Rachel thinks Tom might be blushing, but she's had too much wine to stop now. 'Steve wants us to move to Edinburgh.'

'Right,' says Tom as if he's waiting for the punchline.

'That's it.'

'Right,' repeats Tom, 'and that's bad because – '

'Because it's so far away from everything we have here; from my family, my friends. I mean, surely you'd miss me!'

'Of course, of course,' says Tom nodding with enthusiasm.

'And he knew about it over a month ago and didn't tell me about it.'

'Ah.'

'So I'm frankly furious and would like to discuss it with him rationally.'

'I see.'

'Well?'

'What?'

'You need to tell me why I should go and how great it could be and how unreasonable I'm being.'

'Do you think you're being unreasonable?'

Rachel considers this question. She knows the answer. 'I just wish he could have talked to me about it earlier, discussed it properly, from the beginning. Not waited until it was a done deal.'

'Well, on behalf of Steve and men everywhere, I would like to apologise for our general crapness. We are weak and feeble beings and essentially simpletons at heart.'

Rachel laughs. 'OK, I'm sorry, I shouldn't be ranting at you.'

'It's OK. I have very broad shoulders.'

Rachel's mobile starts to ring. 'It's Steve.'

'Look, you go ahead. I've got to go on snail patrol anyway. And remember, don't be too hard on him, he's just a weak and feeble simpleton.' Tom squeezes her shoulder and Rachel feels a little jump in the pit of her stomach.

'Hell-o,' she says uncertainly into the phone.

'Rach, look I'm sorry. I should have spoken to you about the move earlier. I know. It's just that we're so exhausted and it's difficult to find the right time with the kids and everything.'

Rachel listens to his voice and watches Tom leave, giving her a little backward glance and mock salute as he leaves.

'Rach?'

'Hmm?'

'Can we start again? Please?'

''kay.'

'I've asked your mum and dad to have the kids on Saturday. We can go for lunch and talk it all through properly? OK?'

'OK,' she agrees knowing she's been unreasonable too. 'Sorry for snooping. I sort of wish I hadn't but I guess it's better to have everything out in the open.'

'I guess. OK, no more secrets and no more snooping. We're a good team and we need to stick together. Listen, I've got about another hour to do here and then I'm coming home. Don't wait up, sweetheart. I love you.'

Rachel can hear him waiting for her reply. 'I love you too,' she says and she means it.

CHAPTER FIVE

It's not until Emma has switched on her computer and made herself a coffee, that she notices the bottle of champagne on her desk. 'We got it!' shouts the note attached to its front. She races round to Miranda's office. Digby is there.

'Ah Emma.' Emma is almost touched that he's remembered her name. 'Congratulations – wonderful news. We must have lunch to celebrate. I'll get my secretary, er – '

'Fiona?'

'Ah yes, Fiona, to arrange. Quite so. Well I must – '

Lose some weight? Find a proper job? Finish my sentences properly? thinks Emma.

' – go to a meeting. Yes. Quite so. Well done – again.' He shambles off.

Miranda sweeps over and folds Emma in a mother-hen embrace. 'Well done, Emma. Passion never fails eh? At least not with authors.' She holds Emma at arm's length, studying her face as if considering a particularly tricky cryptic crossword clue. 'Richard seems to have taken a shine to you.'

Emma tries to hold her gaze, but fails and pretends to study the photograph on the wall of Miranda as a young editor with Evelyn Waugh.

'Just be careful, Emma. Creatives can be complex creatures, you know.'

'I know. I'm just his editor. Strictly professional at all times. How much did we pay in the end?' asks Emma, changing the subject.

'Enough, but not as much as Joanna wanted so at least that's some blessing. Richard is coming in to sign the contract this afternoon. I called *The Bookseller* and they're sending a photographer to mark the happy occasion.'

'Great.'

'See you later then and well done, my dear.'

Emma practically skips back to her desk and is delighted when she bumps into Jacqui, head of publicity and Joel's sidekick. Emma observes that her scarlet nails are looking particularly talon-like and her pouting lips shine with matching lipstick and gloss.

'Emma, darrrrling. I hear we got the booook – haauuuw splendid,' she rasps sounding like the snake from *The Jungle Book*.

'Thank you,' says Emma smiling. Jacqui looks perturbed that she has mistaken her comment for congratulations.

'We-ell, if yoou'll excuuse me, I'm just orff to see Jooel.'

'Oh lovely, I'll come with you,' says Emma. Jacqui frowns but says nothing.

Joel's office is the size of a broom cupboard, but he does have an impressive view over the roofs and occasional spire of central London. Pictures of every kind of motivational speaker and business guru, whose flesh Joel has pressed, hang on his walls. His favourite is the one of Alan Sugar pointing accusingly out of its frame signed with the words 'You're bloody fired, Joel mate'. As Jacqui walks in his face lights up and then falls as he sees Emma behind her.

'Jacqui. Emma.' The two names are uttered in tones relative to his feelings for each of them.

'Hi, Joel. I just wanted to check that you'd heard the good news? About Richard?' asks Emma, grinning shamelessly.

Joel's face remains fixed in a smile, but his eyes betray panic.

'Oh, didn't Digby tell you?' says Emma without mercy. 'We got it. Isn't that fantastic?'

'Congratulations, Emma. You must be delighted. I suppose Jacqui and I will have to do our best to market the unmarketable, eh?'

Emma is almost impressed by this neat left hook, but nothing can dampen her mood today. 'I'm sure you will, Joel. See you later,' she says, skipping back down the corridor like a schoolgirl who's just got one over on the mean kids.

Diana Darcy looks at herself in the mirror and is satisfied. Despite the onset of grand-motherhood and the advent of her sixties, she senses that she is still a good-looking woman. Her mother taught her that to dress well is to live well, and it is a sentiment she carries with her still. Sometimes, when she is shopping in town or out with the children in the park, she notices the fat people, the unkempt, the careless and their appearance disgusts her.

'Mum, don't be such a snob!' Rachel hisses as her mother wrinkles her nose at another overweight child in a tracksuit getting wedged at the top of a slide.

'Rachel, dear, it's just indicative of our society. I read about it in the paper. Overweight mothers breed overweight children. It's tragic really.'

Diana pats her hair, fixes a bracelet onto her wrist and dabs a little of her perfume behind each ear. She checks her appearance once more, smoothing her skirt and removing a hair from her black cashmere jumper.

'Ah, my vision, my life.' Edward appears at the door, bowing in a mock-romantic gesture.

'You old fool,' laughs Diana fondly. 'Right, I'm going to meet daughter number one and those recalcitrant children for coffee. What are your plans?'

'Oh don't worry about me. The *Telegraph* crossword beckons. Do we have any Kit Kats?'

'No. No chocolate for you, not with your cholesterol,' she scolds him like a mother with a sixty-two-year-old toddler.

'Very good, ma'am. Anything else, ma'am?'

'Yes. You can stop being cheeky and maybe put in those bulbs? It's a glorious day. Much too nice to be sitting indoors.'

'All right, my darling. Have a wonderful time. Send them all my love.'

The phone rings and Diana answers with impatience. 'Hello?'

'Diana, darling. It's Rosie. Are you well? Good, good,' she continues without waiting for Diana to answer.

'Rosie, I'm just off out to meet Rachel.'

'Of course, you run along, darling. I wanted to speak to Teddy anyway.'

Diana balks at Rosie's use of this name. It's a vestige of the past, of Edward's university days, before he knew Diana. She hands the phone to Edward. He looks nonplussed and holds the phone to his ear.

'Oh Rosie, it's you. How the devil are you?'

Diana feels suddenly invisible as Edward is lost in conversation with one of his oldest friends. She knows it's ridiculous to feel jealous after nearly forty years of marriage, two children and three grandchildren, but somehow Rosie can provoke this feeling. She has tried to bond with her, but all the time she has this nagging sense that Edward should have married her instead. Rosie has it all; the brains, the career in Fleet Street, the contacts. She's the mother the girls might have preferred; the one who can get them the jobs, the restaurant bookings and, even now, she's wooing the grandchildren with trips to the CBeebies studio and tickets to film premieres. Diana should be grateful and magnanimous, but she feels churlish and undermined.

She rallies herself now, pecking her husband on the cheek, mouthing 'Be good,' then sweeping out of the door without a backward glance.

She loves driving into town, finding a parking space and having a potter around the shops before she meets Rachel, who is always late.

'I've got three children to manage, Mother. You're just one person,' Rachel observed when her mother brought it up.

'Rachel, darling, you were never on time before you had the children.' This is true and Diana was quite pleased by her quick-witted observation, which had made Rachel laugh.

She pulls into the car park situated behind a budget supermarket branch, which Diana can't bring herself to use. Rachel laughs at her mother's superciliousness, but Diana knows she is right. She doesn't expect everywhere to be as nice as Waitrose, but she knows that they keep the lighting dim so people can't see what they're buying. Also, the entrance hall smells of urine, which to her mind can never be conducive to a happy shopping experience.

Diana finds a space by the exit. She is just placing a ticket on her windscreen when she hears two squeaky voices: 'Granny, Granny, Granny!' Diana turns at the cacophony of excited greetings to see Lily and Alfie waving frantically from their pushchair as a weary-looking Rachel plods across the car park towards her.

'Rachel, you're on time,' she says with a wry smile.

Rachel rolls her eyes. 'And good morning to you too, Mother.'

'Just my little joke,' trills Diana dismissively. She has never found small talk easy, particularly with Rachel, who often seems so quick to take offence. 'Now who wants some cake?'

'Meeeeee!' chorus Alfie and Lily with glee.

They reach the coffee shop and Diana leads the children to a table, while Rachel places their order. Alfie and Lily scramble onto the furniture and Diana sinks into an armchair blinking at the sunshine, which is filtering in through the window. She looks over at her daughter and notices how tired she is looking. Her shoulders are hunched, as if she's doing battle with life, not like the cocky teenager who used to give her so much trouble.

'Here we are.' Rachel puts down the tray with care just as Alfie kicks the table spilling milk from the too-full cups.

'Alfie!' shouts Rachel with more force than she intends. Two middle-aged women look over unimpressed.

'It's all right. There's no use crying over spilt milk, as my mother would say,' declares Diana, smiling at the women, trying to make up for Rachel's outburst.

Irritated, Rachel hacks at a chocolate muffin with her teaspoon, setting the portions in front of the children, who fall on it like hungry lion cubs.

Diana sips her coffee and wrinkles her nose. 'Too hot,' she complains.

Rachel remains silent, but can feel her annoyance increasing by the second. Most people could make comments like this, but with her mother the negativity is suffocating. Rachel can't remember the last time Diana paid a compliment. She takes a sip of her own coffee, burning the roof of her mouth, but refusing to acknowledge it.

'I tell you what you should do,' says her mother without any small talk, 'you should bring the children over one day and treat yourself to a trip to the hairdresser's.'

'Why? What's wrong with my hair?' says Rachel immediately offended.

'Nothing, darling, nothing. It just looks as if it could do with a cut. You could make a day of it. Go to Bluewater, have some lunch and get yourself some new clothes.' This body blow is dealt with a quizzical look at Rachel's baggy grey jumper.

'Look, Mum, I know you're trying to be nice, but you sound like you're criticising me.'

'Well, if you don't want to.'

'No, I'd love to, really. Thank you.' Rachel doesn't have the energy for this conversation today.

'So,' says Diana, changing the subject, 'how is my favourite son-in-law?'

Rachel's reply is curt: 'Your favourite son-in-law wants to move us to Edinburgh as it happens.'

'What?'

'That's right. He wants your grandchildren to grow up on a diet of fried Mars Bars and in a climate more akin to the North Pole.'

'Oh darling, but you can't go, surely?'

'I don't know, Mum, we need to talk about it. Are you still OK to have the children this weekend?'

'Of course. Oh, Rachel, we'd never see you.'

'I know, I know. Oh Mum, I just don't know what to do any more.' The tears spring easily into Rachel's eyes and Diana is suddenly lost.

'Oh look, darling, there, there.' She pats Rachel's hand and smiles with embarrassment at the women on the next table, who are looking over nosily. 'Come on, don't cry. I'm sure you'll sort it out.'

Lily and Alfie have noticed their mother's tears and Alfie starts to cry as well, his face a mess of chocolate muffin and snot. Lily offers her arms to her mother and scolds him. 'Stop it, Alfie, and give Mummy a cuddle.'

Rachel can't believe that her children are the ones comforting her instead of her mother. She wonders at how they must appear; her mother looking awkward and embarrassed and her, a crumpled mess with two small children covering her in sticky kisses and fierce little hugs.

Miranda's PA, Andrea, has dressed one end of the boardroom with fresh flowers and bottles of Moët. At the opposite end, a table is lined with chairs, as if Allen Chandler is about to announce a major football signing or host the ratification of an international treaty. Miranda has e-mailed the company to make sure that Richard is welcomed properly into the fold and the designers, always first at the mention of free booze and Twiglets, are already gathering, making the place look cool and a little untidy.

When Joanna and Richard enter the room, the atmosphere prickles with excitement as if a couple of celebrities have just walked in. The assembled company part to make way for them and Emma notices a lot of the females nudging each other as they clock Richard who, with his floppy schoolboy hair and grinning demeanour, is looking undeniably handsome.

Ella sidles up to her friend and whispers in her ear, 'Well, isn't he just the dish of the day?'

'Can't say I'd noticed,' smiles Emma.

'Liar.'

Miranda is a stickler for punctuality, so the clock has only just struck three o'clock when she booms out her welcome: 'Ladies and gentlemen, I am delighted to be able to gather you together today to witness a truly exciting event. As most of you will know, we have been working tirelessly to lure Richard to Allen Chandler. I am delighted to announce that he has accepted our offer. Richard, we normally get our authors to sign in blood but for you we will make an exception. Would you do the honours?'

A cheer goes up and Richard bows to the crowd, who laugh. The contract is signed and the photographer ushers Richard and Miranda into the shot. Emma is mortified when Miranda drags her into the frame and is amused to see Jacqui muscling in on the action too. Emma hears her spelling her name to the journalist.

'That's Moss, as in Kate Moss. No, no relation but thank you, people often wonder if she's my sister.'

Emma watches as Joanna whisks Richard over to meet Digby, who embraces him tightly, much to Richard's surprise. She is feeling a little light-headed due to a combination of early-afternoon champagne and last night's excesses. She wanders over to the window to take in the view. She is suddenly aware of someone standing next to her and turns to find Richard at her side.

'Hello, Emma Darcy,' he says with a smile.

'Hello, Richard Bennett. Welcome to the family. I see you've met Digby.'

Richard chuckles. 'It was like being hugged by a bear. He seems like a decent chap.'

'He is. Actually most people here are.'

'Miranda terrifies me.'

'So she should.'

'And what about you, Emma Darcy? Do I need to be scared of you?'

Emma looks him in the eye. 'Petrified.'

'That's what I thought. Well, I shall make sure I wear my thickest body armour to all our meetings. When is our first meeting by the way?'

'How are you fixed next Monday? I thought we could meet at Kew seeing as it's the backdrop for so much of the book.'

'Sounds perfect. By the way, I just wanted to say what a fantastic time I had last night. I think we're going to work really well together, don't you?'

She looks up at him. He really is very attractive, just her type in many ways and if she were single then she'd probably be having some pretty inappropriate thoughts about him. As it is, she intends to just enjoy the ride. 'Yes I do as a matter of fact.'

'Right, well I have to be somewhere. I'll see you on Monday. Looking forward to it.' He kisses her on the cheek before he leaves.

'Lucky cow,' says Ella, nudging her friend as they watch him disappear down the corridor.

'I know,' laughs Emma, putting an arm around her. 'I'm a very lucky girl indeed.'

***

Martin looks at the table and feels pleased with his efforts.

'Chicks love candles and flowers. Chuck in the champagne and you've got yourself a night to remember,' says Martin's best friend, Charlie, helping himself to another chocolate digestive.

'Yes, thank you, mate. With comments like that, I'm starting to feel sorry for Stacey. Now, isn't it time you buggered off?'

'I'll have you know, my Stacey is very well looked after, thank you,' says Charlie patting his groin.

Martin groans and rolls his eyes. 'They say romance is dead and now I see they're not wrong.'

'Oi, I'm romantic! I'm always buying Stace flowers.'

'Erm, I don't think the ones with the orange discount stickers count, mate.'

Charlie shrugs. 'They're still flowers, aren't they? Only mugs pay full price.'

'Of course they do, Charles. Now, don't you have a home to go to? Emma's going to be back soon,' says Martin, rearranging the flowers on the table like a professional.

'All right, all right, I get the message. Muff before mates. I know.'

Martin ignores him. 'See you later, Charlie,' he says, wresting the biscuit tin from his grasp.

'See you later, geeze,' says Charlie, heading for the door.

Martin looks at the table again and checks his watch. Emma should be home in around half an hour so he turns on the oven and goes upstairs to the spare room to print out the details of the weekend away he is planning. He sits back in his office chair and feels happy. Charlie may mock, but he and Stacey are practically married and soon Martin and Emma will be settled too. He gathers up the printed pages and practically skips downstairs as he hears Emma's key in the door.

'Well, if it isn't the sexiest, cleverest, most beautiful editor in the world.' Martin folds her in his arms and kisses her on the mouth.

'Mmm, I should almost fail to get a book and then succeed in getting a book more often,' she says, pulling him towards her. 'Shall we just skip the dinner and go straight onto pudding?'

'All in good time, my little sexpot. I have many surprises for you first. Come in, come in.' He leads her to the kitchen. 'Look! I bring you good things to eat and flowers and candles and – ' he pulls open the fridge, swiping out a bottle, 'champagn-a!' he says in a mock-Italian accent.

Emma's stomach does a little flip at the thought of her third dose of champagne in less than twenty-four hours but is touched by his kindness. 'Thank you darling.'

'And for my final trick – ' continues Martin, fanning out some printed pages in front of Emma like a magician. 'Ta-da!'

Emma studies them. 'What's this? Wow! The Clevedon? For this weekend? That's amazing. You spoil me!' she cries, wrapping her arms round his neck.

'Well, you deserve it,' says Martin, stroking her face and kissing her tenderly. 'I love you so much, Em. Now, sit down. Chef Love has a feast to prepare and you, my darling, have champagne to drink.'

Emma sits back in the comfy kitchen chair, propped up with mismatched cushions. She kicks off her shoes and accepts the glass of champagne Martin has poured for her.

'Here's to you, Emma Darcy, editor-extraordinaire. Congratulations.'

They knock their glasses together and Martin strides over to the work surface to check on the bubbling pot of bolognese. He lifts the lid and scoops up a spoonful, blowing it before taking a tentative taste. 'Ooh, hot, hot, but oh so good,' he grins. Emma laughs and sips her champagne, feeling cosy.

'So, who did you end up drowning your sorrows with last night?' asks Martin.

'How do you mean?'

'Well, when I last spoke to you, you were on your way home, but you sent me a text at about ten telling me not to wait up.'

The lie is out of Emma's mouth before she has a chance to stop it. 'Oh, it was just Ella. We were going to go for one and ended up staying for more. How was the match?' she asks, changing the subject.

'It was great. I scored a hat trick,' grins Martin proudly. 'I'm top goal-scorer this season. Expecting an England call-up any day.'

'I'm proud of you, darling. Hopefully that means I'll get to give up this publishing lark and hang out with Coleen Rooney,' laughs Emma as the phone rings. She picks it up and hears Martin's mother's voice.

'Emma?'

'Hello, Daphne. How are you?' Emma has an uneasy relationship with her mother-in-law to be. She's never been anything less than civil, but Emma knows she doesn't really like her. It's partly due to the fact that Martin is an only child and she's fiercely over-protective, but she also once overheard her remarking to a neighbour that Emma was a 'flibbertigibbet'. Rachel had snorted with laughter. 'I'd take that as a compliment, sis. You should hear what Steve's mum calls me.' Emma knows she's right but does want to get along with her prospective mother-in-law and she knows she tries too hard.

'Well, I can't lie Emma. I've had the most terrible bowel problems of late.'

Emma sits eyes-wide listening to Daphne's very detailed descriptions. She does her best to avoid looking at Martin, who has picked up the gist of the conversation and is doing his best to make her laugh.

'Well, that must be terrible,' says Emma, biting her hand to stop herself from giggling. 'I had no idea it could come out that colour.' Martin mimics someone sitting on the toilet and Emma sticks two fingers up at him.

'So, are you looking forward to the weekend?' says Daphne abruptly changing tack.

'Er, yes. Actually, I only just found out about it myself,' she replies slightly annoyed that she wasn't the first woman in Martin's life to know.

'Oh good, because we're so looking forward to seeing you.'

Emma is confused and then notices that Martin is looking sheepish. She glances again at the hotel booking, realising that it's just around the corner from his parents' house. Daphne is twittering on about seeing her engagement ring and how much they are looking forward to her becoming their daughter-in-law.

'Yes, we're really looking forward to seeing you too. Martin's just made me a lovely dinner, so shall I get him to call you later?' says Emma eventually. She replaces the phone, fixing Martin with a look.

'OK, Em, I'm sorry. I was going to tell you and we'll only need to pop round for half an hour or so.'

'It's OK,' says Emma pecking him on the cheek. 'It's probably a good idea. Kill two birds and all that.' She takes another sip of her champagne. 'Now, where's this dinner you've been promising me?'

CHAPTER SIX

Rachel watches Will disappear in a flurry of seven-year-olds. He looks small and even though she knows he doesn't give their partings a second thought, she still feels sick to her stomach when she thinks about him growing up. She turns away quickly, trying to avoid conversation with the other mothers, but fails.

'Rachel! Hi!' It's Verity, the toothy, overly keen year two PTA representative. Rachel has made it her life's work to avoid people with the word 'representative' in their title. Today she is particularly keen to be on her way as Steve is starting work late so that he can drop Lily and Alfie at pre-school. Rachel is eager to enjoy some quality time with this week's *Grazia* and a skinny latte.

'Rachel,' says Verity again with a sincere smile, the 'like me, like me!' vibes oozing from every pore. 'I just happened to notice that you hadn't signed up to help at our annual Nearly New Sale.'

Rachel's heart sinks. It's not that she objects to helping at school events, it's just that socialising with the school committee members is more competitive than the Olympics. Last term, she had nearly come to blows with another mother when she suggested that they buy some cheap costumes for the end of term production from the pound shop. The mother had told Rachel that she was 'creatively repressed' and 'morally corrupt' for not making Will's crab outfit herself. Rachel had then spent a miserable weekend constructing a papier-mâché crustacean that Will had refused to wear. Since that day, Rachel had vowed never to let middle-class guilt get the better of her again.

'Oh sorry, I didn't see the letter home. When is it?'

'It's on Saturday.'

'Oh, we're busy, we have a family do,' says Rachel too quickly.

'Week,' finishes Verity.

'Ahh, I think we might have something on that day too,' she says knowing she has been rumbled.

'Really?' says Verity her tone changing. 'Because it would be a shame if people didn't make the effort for their child's school, don't you think?'

'Erm, sorry, Verity, I really have to go.'

'Fine, Rachel, that's fine. Just don't expect to be voted onto the school committee. Ever.' She delivers this final utterance like a judge who has just issued the death penalty.

'Fingers crossed,' mutters Rachel and scoots out of the school gates. Her mobile rings. It's Emma.

'Tartface! What news?'

'We got the book!'

'You are kidding me? A thicky like you?'

'Whatever.'

'Seriously little sis, well done. That's very good news. When do we celebrate? I could do with a night out.'

'Are you OK?'

'I'll tell you when I see you. How about drinks tomorrow? At the Pickled Pig?'

'OK, great. You can buy me a drink and tell me how clever I am.'

'Don't push it. See you around eight.'

Emma tosses her phone into her bag and returns to the manuscript before her. She really wants to get started on *The Red Orchid*, but has promised that she'll wait until Miranda has read it through first. Saskia, the brilliant but slightly fluffy fiction designer, pokes her head over her pod.

'Hieeeeee!'

'Hello, Saskia.'

'Coming to Joely-Joel's meeting?'

'What meeting is that? The one where he patronises everyone in sight?'

'Noooooooooooo sill-ee!' trills Saskia. 'It's our monthly review of all the scrummy books coming up in the next three months,' she adds cheerfully, curling her hair around her fingers in the manner of a six-year-old. In fact, today she is dressed just like a six-year-old apart from the inappropriate T-shirt with the slogan 'Spank Me Hard'. This is teamed with a red check puffball skirt, blue and green striped legwarmers and silver ballet pumps. Her hair is pulled into two bunches like a Pekinese dog's. It probably looks very hip, but Emma shudders at the sight of her and the dawning realisation that her opinions are starting to align themselves with those of her mother.

The prospect of a meeting in the company of Poochy Poo and marketing's answer to Goebbels makes Emma want to quit her job and do something more fulfilling, like treating sewage. She takes heart at the fact that Philippa will be there and although she never gets a word in because of her fool of a boss, she's a silent, eyebrow-raising ally of sorts. When Emma reaches the meeting room, Joel is sitting at the head of the long table talking in a loud voice on his mobile.

'Yep, yep, will do, OK, of course I can sort it. Speak soon, boss. Bye!'

Emma plonks herself next to Philippa.

'On the phone to his mother again?' she whispers with a wink. Philippa grins.

Saskia bounces in, her arms full of print-outs which she always refers to as her 'children'. She takes her seat and Joel begins.

'So the purpose of today is to review the past three months, look forward to the next three, see where we are and where we want to be. OK, people?'

No one speaks so Joel continues. 'So, Emma. Talk us through the latest on these.' He fans out copies of a crime series set in Cornwall written by an eighty-year-old female author. Joel doesn't wait for her to speak. 'You see, I think we should either bin these or look to re-jacket. Book Data seems to indicate around a twenty per cent sell-through, which is very poor.'

'I don't think three months of sales is enough to say one way or the other. I think we should publish at least six before we take any kind of decision,' says Emma irritated.

'Mmm,' says Joel not listening. 'Saskia has kindly mocked up some roughs. A bit less Miss Read and a bit more "read me",' he snorts vastly amused by his own joke. Philippa winces.

Saskia's covers are horrific depictions of severed limbs, mutilated heads and general carnage.

'Joel,' says Emma, trying to remain calm, 'the author is a lovely lady called Queenie and the books are really more Miss Marple than Slasher Central. I think we should continue as we are for the time being.'

Joel is riled. 'Well, I think Digby would disagree.'

'Well, Digby isn't Queenie's editor and while I am tasked with producing books that are fit for publication, I will have the ultimate say on covers, OK?'

'Like I say, I think Digby might have something to say.'

'And so might Miranda,' retorts Emma aware that they are starting to sound like five-year-olds.

Philippa and Saskia shift uncomfortably in their seats. The rest of the meeting passes without further confrontation, but beneath it all Emma is seething.

'I mean, who does he think he is?' she complains to Ella on returning to her desk.

A beautiful array of pink and white lilies is waiting for her. She picks up the card. They're from her godmother, Rosie: 'Clever girl. Well done.' Her phone rings. She picks it up smiling. 'Hello-oo?'

'Emma? It's Mummy. You sound pleased with yourself.'

'I am, thanks, Mum. Auntie Rosie just sent me the most gorgeous flowers.'

'Oh.' Her mother sounds perplexed. 'Did I miss something?'

'Oh sorry, I forgot to tell you. We got that book I was telling you about.'

'Oh. Good. Well done. It's a shame you didn't think to tell us before your godmother. We're only your parents.'

'Sorry, Mum, and I didn't tell Rosie. She must have heard. You know what she's like.'

'Yes I do. Anyway, Emma, Rachel and I are going to take you dress-shopping. How about this Saturday?'

'Sorry, I can't do this Saturday. Martin's whisking me away for the weekend.'

'Oh. Right. Is there anything else you haven't told us? You're not emigrating like your sister are you?'

'What do you mean?'

'Oh well at least Rachel tells us things first. Your brother-in-law is planning to move them all to Scotland.'

'What?'

'Exactly. So when you've finished living your life in isolation from your family, maybe we could set a date to look for wedding dresses?'

'Don't be like that, Mum. Look, I'll take a day off. Maybe Dad can look after the kids and we can have a girly day with Rach?'

Diana doesn't want to give in, but Emma can tell she's softening. 'All right, let's say Monday week.'

'Perfect. Wow, that's big news about Rachel. I'm seeing her tomorrow and I thought there was something up.'

'Yes well, maybe you can try talking some sense into her. Goodness only knows I've tried.'

Rachel takes a sip from her Styrofoam cup of coffee and does a quick head count. Lily and Alfie are engaged in a stand-off with an older boy on the play-bus, while Will is scaling the rope climbing frame, SAS-style. She sees Christa and Roger and waves. Roger jumps out of his pushchair with great excitement and runs over to join Lily and Alfie.

'Halloo,' cries Christa kissing Rachel on both cheeks. 'Could Sue not make it?'

'Joe's still poorly. How are you?'

'Good, *danke*.'

'Coffee?' asks Rachel finishing her first and ready for another.

'*Nein danke*, your English coffee tastes like *scheisse*.'

Rachel laughs. 'It's actually Nescafé which I believe is a Swiss company?' she says with a grin.

'*Ja* perhaps, but they are not as bad as your Pot Noodles, hey?

'Touché! So, how are things with you?' asks Rachel as they find a bench.

'Fine. I think you and Sue were perhaps a little shocked by the things I told you on Monday, yes?'

'It does sound like you've got a lot on your plate.'

Christa laughs. 'I love you English and your metaphors. My life is really not so bad. Rudi is a good man really. He looks after us. We are going to have a wonderful family holiday next month.'

'Oh lovely. Where are you going?' asks Rachel thinking of Disneyland or a villa in Spain.

'We are *sehr* lucky as that lovely Cowell man is letting us use his yacht.'

Rachel is amazed. 'As in Simon Cowell?'

'*Nein!*' Christa snorts as if this is the most ridiculous thing she's ever heard. '*Nein*, silly, his brother, Nicholas. He is not nearly as rich. He only has one yacht while Simon has, I think, six or seven.'

'Well, that will be fantastic.'

'*Ja*, for sure. You should come!'

'Oh I don't think so.'

'*Ja!* It would be so much fun. There are always many famous people dropping in. Last year Paris Hilton was there and Bruce Willis. Paris was so sweet with Roger and Bruce is lovely. He told me to call him if Rudi and I ever split up.'

'Really?' says Rachel, wishing that Sue was there.

'Well, you know. Have a think about it. Talk to Dave,' she adds.

'Steve,' corrects Rachel.

'Yes, him too. Roger!'

Christa strides off to rescue her bilious-looking son from the roundabout, which Lily and Alfie have been spinning a little too fast.

'Mum! Look at me!'

Rachel looks over to see Will at the top of the climbing frame.

'Well done, Will. Clever boy.'

She catches sight of Verity talking with intensity to another mother. She lifts her hand to wave, but Verity looks away, pretending not to see her. Rachel sighs as her phone beeps with a text. It's Steve: 'Dn't b md bt gt 2 wrk l8 agn. Lkng 4wrd 2 w/e. Love u, sx'

Rachel punches a reply 'OK. Going fr drnks wth Em 2mrrw. Pls cn u b on time, r'

Steve answers: 'Wll do my bst. C u l8tr. x'

Rachel throws her phone into her bag and calls to the children. 'Right who wants pizza? Mummy's treat!'

Richard Bennett is feeling smug as he strides into the entrance hall of the Battersea riverside apartments. The lobby is tastefully decorated with modern-looking canvasses and the discreet lighting gives a warm glow that says 'you really want to live here'. Richard breathes in the aroma of a new and untouched world, a million miles away from the piss and vomit stench of his East Dulwich flat's corridor.

'Mr Bennett?'

He turns smiling, ready with effortless charm. He is delighted by the form and features of the person before him. She holds out a perfectly manicured, soft hand.

'Sophie Chancellor. Delighted to meet you. I think you'll like what I'm about to show you,' she adds with mild innuendo.

'The pleasure will be all mine,' Richard replies, knowing that this sounds corny, but also knowing that he is talking to a casual acquaintance. He has nothing to lose.

'Please follow me.'

He follows her into the lift, enjoying a shameless view of Sophie's perfectly sculpted behind, enveloped as it is in an hourglass-tight, knee-length skirt. As they travel to the ninth floor, Richard observes the curve of her neck and notices her checking him with a coy, sexy smile. They emerge from the lift and she leads him to the end of a corridor, then takes a sharp right, stopping at door number 915.

'Here we are. Home,' she says with a smile as she turns the key.

Richard pushes the door and is impressed. Every corner of the flat screams 'I'm modern, I'm hip. You want me.' From the granite breakfast bar and six-ring stove to the Bose stereo which blinks into life at the flick of a switch, it is everything Richard has longed for. All the endless research trips, the hours spent doing time at the British Library and the years writing, getting rejected, rewriting and then getting accepted as a proper writer, have been worth it. Richard turns towards the French windows that flank one side of the apartment and is breathless at the view. London in all its mish-mashed glory stretches before him looking wonderful. Richard turns to Sophie who is watching him carefully, allowing him to take in his surroundings.

Good at her job and probably a good shag too, he thinks.

'You like?' she asks in a teasing voice.

'I do, but aren't you forgetting something?' he says.

'I'm sorry?'

'You haven't shown me the bedroom.'

Sophie smiles and it's the smile of someone who loves her job, who is in control of her life and who knows how to play a man. She unbuttons her blouse, slips off her skirt and stands before him looking gorgeous in black lacy underwear and as Richard correctly suspects, stockings and suspenders. Even Richard is speechless, not quite believing how his day and his life are turning out. Sophie walks down the corridor glancing backwards and beckoning to him. Richard grins and shakes his head before following her to the bedroom.

The Pickled Pig represents the waning soul of twenty-first-century public houses the country over. It once served this corner of south-east London as a cinema until the big cinema companies invented places called multiplexes and it went out of business. It then became a pub and got swallowed up by one of the big pub companies. This caused the locals to moan until they realised that the beer was actually a lot cheaper than before.

Emma is the first to arrive and selects a pint of local beer before finding a booth, far away enough from the bar to be quiet, but close enough to the action to get a good view of the locals, many of whom have been here since opening time. She studies the black and white photographs on the wall depicting old Penge and a man named Angry Tony who made his living selling potatoes and bizarrely, coffins. The evening is grey and wet and she sees Rachel push her way through the swing doors and shake her umbrella.

'Man, it's chucking it down,' she declares as she locates Emma. 'Right, what are we drinking?'

'Hello, Rachel. Nice to see you too. It's called Stinky Pete and it's quite good. Try it.'

Rachel takes a gulp and licks her lips,

'Hmm, not bad. Want another?'

'No, I'm fine for now thanks.'

Rachel returns minutes later with her drink and a packet of dry roasted peanuts.

'Kids all tucked up?'

'Yeah, but Steve still isn't home, so – '

'You left Will in charge?'

Rachel snorts. 'Don't be daft, Lily's much more responsible! No, Tom is babysitting until Steve gets home.'

'Tom?'

'Our next-door neighbour.'

'Oh, the dishy one.'

Rachel is surprised that she and her sister obviously have similar taste. 'D'you think?'

'Oh yeah, bit pudgy, but very cute. Like Russell Crowe.'

'Steady on, he's hardly a gladiator!'

'Oh, so you have checked him out then?' Emma teases.

'So what if I have. I am a respectable married lady so it's fine to look as long as you don't touch,' says Rachel in a superior tone.

'I agree with the married bit,' laughs Emma. Rachel flicks her sister the V-sign. 'Anyway, sister dearest, when exactly were you going to tell me that you're moving to Scotland?'

'Aha, you've spoken to Mother then?'

'Yes but still, Rach, I'm your sister. You could have told me.'

'Why do you think we're having this drink? I wanted to tell you face to face. Don't be so sensitive.'

Emma is irritated by the brush-off, but is interrupted by Rachel's phone. Rachel glances at the caller ID and rolls her eyes, mouthing 'Steve' as she answers with a curt 'Hi?' Steve obviously has a lot to say and Emma watches Rachel's face as her look transforms from one of mild irritation to impatient anger. Emma waits for the backlash and isn't disappointed.

'No, Steve, you bloody listen. You said you'd be home in time and you weren't. Tom offered and I actually do think it's OK to leave our children with him. He's been more supportive than you have lately. Now if you don't mind, I'd like to hang up and moan to my sister about you.' She punches the end call button with a defiant 'Tosser!'

Emma looks at her sister. 'You're really very cross, aren't you?'

'D'you think?' says Rachel. 'First he wants to move us up north, then I find out he'd known for ages and now he's playing the alpha-male working all bloody hours while my brain is dissolving due to lack of proper use. I dunno, Em, sometimes I just want to walk out the door and never come back.'

Emma is a little shocked by the outburst. She knows Rachel can fly off the handle and she knows she's found it hard to adjust to life as a stay-at-home mum, but she's never heard her talk like this before. Giving up is not something the Darcy sisters do and she's never seen her as angry as this with Steve either. She'd always had them down as rock-solid and immune to the kind of vitriol she's seen other couples develop after so many years and so many children. She knows better than to wind up her sister any further and decides that softly, softly might be the way to go.

'Come on, Rach, you don't mean that.'

'Don't I? Oh God, Em, I don't know what I mean these days.'

'Have you tried talking to Steve?'

Rachel looks at Emma as if she's just arrived from Planet Stupid. 'Of course I've tried talking to him. All I ever bloody do these days is try to talk to my husband, but he's never bloody there!'

Emma sees the error she's made but presses on like a woman on a suicide mission. 'Well, I can babysit one night if you want to go out, you know, to talk.'

Rachel realises she's been ranting and looks at her baby sister. Emma's face is twisted with concern and Rachel sees a shadow of the four-year-old agreeing to let Rachel cut her hair, just to please her. Their mother had not been amused when she'd come upstairs to find her youngest daughter resembling a child with alopecia, especially when Rachel had tried to clarify the situation with the words 'It just fell out, honest.'

Rachel smiles at the memory and at her sister. 'Thanks, Em,' she says with as much softness as she can muster. 'I think Mum and Dad are having the kids at the weekend so we can try and sort it all out. Don't worry, little sis, I'm just knackered, OK?' Emma looks relieved. 'So what have you been up to? Tell me about this gorgeous new author of yours. I presume he is gorgeous? Congrats on getting the book by the way. Sorry, should have said that before.' She knocks her pint glass against Emma's in a feeble toast.

'He's just a nice bloke who's written a really good book.'

'Wow, Em, sounds amazing,' says Rachel, feigning a yawn. 'Let's hope they don't get you to write the marketing copy.'

'Ha, ha,' says Emma. 'Oh by the way, I think Mum's planning a dress-shopping trip. Are you up for it?'

'I'm always up for it! Now drink up, little sis, it's your round!'

By closing time, they have both drunk at least one pint more than is good for them, but Rachel doesn't want to go home.

'Let's go for a curry!'

Emma hasn't eaten since lunchtime and the thought fills her with an overpowering hunger bordering on nausea, but she agrees. They stagger out into the drizzly night and across the road to the pink neon-lit Bombay Fantasy. The waiters' smiles are patient and accommodating and they are quickly led to an enormous table adjacent to the only other diners: three sweaty city boys, their faces red from alcohol, with shirtsleeves rolled up and ties abandoned. Their ringleader, a mid-thirties chancer with a receding hairline and an air of being funnier than he is, leers towards them: 'All right, ladies?'

'All right,' Rachel replies with bravado.

'So what are two gorgeous ladies like yourselves doing out alone?'

Rachel is in her element. 'Trying to avoid cretinous men, but failing miserably,' she retorts fixing him with a disappointed look.

Chancer likes this response. 'Ha ha, get you. Are you lesbians then?' he asks, as if this could be the only explanation for Rachel's sarcasm.

Emma matches her sister's look. 'We're sisters, half-wit.'

'Even better! How about we finish up here and you can shake your booties back at my gaff?' says Chancer nudging his friends.

Emma is about to open her mouth but Rachel holds up her hand to stop her. 'We-ell,' she purrs, 'that sounds like a very tempting offer. Are you going to buy us dinner then?'

Chancer grins. 'Of course.'

'Why don't we get it to take away?' adds Rachel provocatively.

'Wahey!' Chancer and his monkeys whoop in agreement.

Emma pretends to drop her napkin and hisses, 'Rachel!'

Rachel bobs her head under the table. 'What?'

'What are you doing?'

'Getting us a free takeaway. Trust me.'

'I don't like the sound of this.'

'Just meet me by the door in five minutes.'

They place their order. Rachel makes her excuses and goes to the toilet, flashing her cleavage as she passes the city boys, who wolf-whistle in appreciation. Emma attempts a smile and Chancer's weaselly, greasy-haired friend takes this as a come-on. 'I think you're in there, Jez,' says Chancer with a nudge

Emma feels as if she might vomit and lurches to her feet. 'I just need to go and check on my sister.'

'You do that, darling.'

Rachel is talking to the waiter as Emma staggers up. 'So those lovely men over there have kindly agreed to pay for our dinner. Thanks so much. Let's go, Em.'

They make for the door.

'Oi! What do you think you're playing at?' Chancer is on his feet now.

'Run for it!'

Rachel grabs Emma's hand and they sprint onto a bus that has just pulled into its stop.

'You slags!' shouts Chancer after them.

Rachel and Emma collapse onto the back seats and Rachel waves and blows kisses at their hapless pursuer, who is being ushered back into the restaurant by two burly Indian waiters, keen to obtain payment. The bus speeds off down the road leaving the city boys far behind them.

'Ha!' declares Rachel. 'Another classic Darcy girl adventure! Em, are you OK? You look a bit green.'

'Actually, I feel a bit – ' and she promptly vomits into the takeaway bag.

'Oh, very nice,' says Rachel, 'you really can't handle your drink, can you?'

They have only travelled two stops. The bus driver comes out of his cab.

'Right, you two. Off!'

'Sorry?'

'You'll have to get off the bus.'

'But she's ill and we're two lone females.'

'Not my problem, love. She's obviously had too much to drink. You'll have to get off. You'll stink out my bus.'

'Oh charming, very gallant, chucking us out into the cold. Come on Vomiting Veronica. You can stay at mine and you owe me a takeaway.'

She leads a shivering Emma off the bus and they stagger all the way back to Rachel's house. Rachel drapes her sister over the wall while she fumbles for her keys. She sees a light come on in Tom's hallway and is half-pleased and half-mortified when he opens the door.

'Ah, Mrs Summers, how was the pub? Are you drunk?'

'As a skunk, Mr Davies, and this,' she picks up her almost comatose sister and waves a floppy hand, 'is my sister, Emma.'

'A pleasure,' Tom declares. 'Need any help getting in?'

'If you could help me get old Chunder-Cheeks into the lounge that would be great.' Rachel opens the door and between them, they manhandle Emma onto the sofa. 'Thank you. You're a gent.'

'No problemo. By the way, Rachel, I got the feeling Steve wasn't too pleased to find me here tonight. I just hope I didn't cause you any grief.'

'Oh Tom, it's not you. Steve just needs to get his priorities sorted and I need to talk to him like a grown-up, but we will, I promise. Now shoo, Doris at number thirty-two would love to see you skulking out of my house in the wee small hours, but I don't want to get a reputation.'

'Of course.'

Tom moves to pass her in the hall, turning to look at her as he does so. Rachel, slightly drunk and not wanting to appear unfriendly goes to peck him on the cheek but mistimes her attack and ends up planting the kiss on the right-side of his lip. To Rachel's mind, your next action in this kind of situation is the borderline between fidelity and adultery. She is drunk, but decides to brush it off with an embarrassed giggle. Tom smiles and the moment passes without incident, but as she shuts the door behind him, she leans against it and lets out a sigh. *What are you playing at, Rachel, you fool?* she thinks.

She tucks up Emma, leaving her a glass of water. She tiptoes upstairs to the half-lit darkness of the marital bedroom. She undresses quickly and wriggles into bed beside Steve's steady breathing form.

'Steve? Are you awake?'

There is no response, which Rachel takes as either no interest or genuine sleep. She lies awake for the next hour or so, her mind heavy with worry until alcohol and fatigue transport her to a restless sleep.

CHAPTER SEVEN

Emma blinks at her screen unable to believe that she has caused herself this world of pain again. Her left eye is twitching with the effort of being open and her temple is throbbing with a dull echo, pounding the words 'Too much beer! Too much beer!' She squints at the over-bright screen and wonders if people would notice if she slipped on her sunglasses.

'Having troubles there, missus?'

'Ella, didn't your mother ever tell you not to creep up on people like that?'

'Sorry, my mother had a Stephen King obsession so, to be honest, scaring people was a family pastime. What was it last night?'

'Beer. Too much. Don't want to talk about it. All Rachel's fault,' stammers Emma, feeling bilious at the memory. 'I think I puked on a bus.'

'Euurgh, sounds like you might need one of David and Simon's cure-all fry-ups.'

'Please, Ella. Do you want to see the contents of my stomach?'

'Hmm, not especially. Shall I leave you?'

'If you don't mind. Talking makes me nauseous. In fact, being upright makes me nauseous.'

'Mmm, well I don't think you're going to like what's coming down the corridor.'

'Miranda?'

'Worse. Joel.'

'Oh crap. Have I got time to esc – '

'Ah, Emma, have you got a minute?' says Joel, striding into their midst.

'Erm, I'm actually in the middle of something quite important.'

'But you haven't logged on yet?'

'Sorry?'

'Your screen? You haven't logged onto your computer yet.'

Emma turns to her desk. 'I know that. I'm an editor. I have manuscripts to work on,' she says fumbling for the nearest pile of papers.

Joel is unimpressed. 'Look, Emma, maybe you have time to waste but I don't. I need an urgent discussion with you about this Richard Bennett book. Can we go somewhere private?' He glances over at Ella, who is in the middle of a 'loser' gesture behind his back and has to wave her arms around as if batting a fly.

'Got it!' she grins and darts back to her desk.

Wearily Emma launches herself to her feet and follows Joel to a meeting room like a pupil about to be blasted by their headmaster. Joel is already sitting at the head of the table looking like a headmaster about to blast his pupil.

'What's this about then?' asks Emma, wishing she could just curl up in the corner of the room and go to sleep.

'It's about this *Red Albatross*.'

'Orchid.'

'I know but I'm calling it an Albatross, because that's what it will be for this company.'

Emma tells herself to stay calm. She tries to fix her eyes on a point and finds herself staring at Joel's ear hair. She shudders.

'The point is, this book isn't going to work. We've paid far too much money, which we will never earn back. We have no guarantee that anyone will even like it, let alone shortlist it for a prize. And even if it does win, who says the punters will actually buy it? I mean the Booker's all very well, but what does it actually deliver in terms of revenue and profit? You editors make it very difficult for us at the coalface, you know. So, as a precaution, Jacqui's put in a call to Richard and Judy. I'm going to need your author on best behaviour at the Ivy next month, OK?'

Joel sits back waiting for Emma to show her appreciation. Emma Darcy has never been a girl to disappoint. Before she knows what is happening, she lurches forwards, grabs a handily placed wastepaper bin and vomits, accidentally splashing Joel's shoes. They look at one another astonished before Emma wipes her mouth with a tissue and makes for the door, bin in hand without a backward glance or word. She almost collides with her godmother Rosie, who is striding down the corridor arm in arm with Miranda, two extravagantly colourful powerhouses of energy.

'Darling! I'm just having coffee with Mimms. Take you for lunch afterwards?'

'Wonderful,' says Emma with a smile. 'I'm suddenly starving!'

Rachel feels one of her eyes open and realises that her eyelid is being lifted for her by a three-year-old's finger.

'Wake up, Mummy,' sings a sweet angelic voice. When she attempts to close her eye again, its pitch and tone intensify. 'Wake up, Mummy. Now!'

Rachel tries to open both eyes simultaneously and glare at her torturer.

'Alfred, Mummy has got a headache!'

'Yeah, Dad said you had too much beer,' says Will, who has just wandered into the bedroom.

'Oh he did, did he?' mumbles Rachel, feeling an attack of 'bad mother with a hangover' syndrome coming on. 'Where's Lily?'

'Downstairs, watching *Milkshake*. I turned it on for her,' adds Will proudly.

'Clever boy,' says Rachel weakly ruffling his hair and checking her watch. 'Oh bloody hell! We've got to get Will to school in twenty minutes.'

'Oh bloody hell!' shouts Alfie with glee.

Eighteen minutes later, Rachel has bundled herself and the children into the car and armed each of them with a banana. 'A good, nutritious breakfast,' she declares.

'I wanted porridge,' says Lily, doing her best grumpy princess face.

'And I want two weeks in Barbados with George Clooney. Sometimes life is so unfair,' says Rachel.

Predictably, as they near the school, there isn't a parking space to be had, but Rachel spies a car about to leave and angles the steering wheel, indicating her intentions. As if from nowhere, a shiny black 4x4 screeches behind the departing car and bulldozes its way into the vacant space.

'Oi!' Rachel bellows causing the gathering parents to turn and stare. 'I was just about to park there!'

A sharp-faced skinny woman in a velour tracksuit, her ash blonde hair scraped back in a severe ponytail, climbs out of the tank and approaches Rachel's car. 'Are you talking to me?' she snarls with the charm of a rabid dog.

'Yes. I was going to park there. I was indicating and you pushed in.'

'Ahhh,' says the woman, 'poor you. What do you want me to do about it?'

Rachel realises that the children have gone quiet and that most of the parents are now watching the show. She spies Verity looking over, nudging a fellow alpha-mother. Oh well, in for a penny, she decides.

'I want you to move.'

'Pardon?'

'I want you to move, so that I can park there. Please'

'Oh, and why should I do that?'

'Because, it is the right thing to do and I am asking you nicely.' The woman wrinkles her face with a look that says 'whatever', so Rachel continues. 'Plus, your car is new and shiny and my car is old and battered, so you wouldn't want me to accidentally scrape it when I reverse past on this incredibly narrow road, would you?'

The woman gives Rachel a look of pure venom and Rachel wonders if she is about to be punched.

'Fucking nutter!' she mutters and flounces back into her car, roaring off in an ozone-layer-destroying fug.

'What did that lady say?' asks Will.

'Chucking butter, darling. I think she was a bit crazy,' says Rachel, pulling into the space and flashing Verity a saintly smile. Her phone chirps and she sees that it's Sue.

'Hello, love. Can I call you back in a sec?'

'Sure, but I just called to say that Joe is still poorly, so I'm not going to make Soft Play today.'

'Soft Play?'

'Don't tell me you'd forgotten?'

'Sort of.'

'Well, Christa's going, so will you go along anyway?'

'Sue, I have a hangover and was hoping to go home, bung on CBeebies for Lily and Alfie and go back to bed for an hour.'

'Ahhh, poor you. It's up to you, my love, but I think Christa is hoping you'll go.'

'That's right. Make me feel even more guilty than usual.'

'That's my job! Don't forget to text me with any more of Christa's revelations. There has to be a cross-dressing brother in that family at least!'

Rachel snorts. 'Will do. Big kisses to Joe-Joe.'

She ends the call and notices that a text has arrived. It's from Emma: 'I hate you. x'

Rachel laughs and flings open the door for Will.

'See you later, gorgeous.'

'Mum!' protests Will as she attempts to kiss him. She manages to aim one on his head before he wrestles from her grasp. He bolts into the playground, following the rest of his class into school.

'Right. Good, Soft Play then.'

'Ooh, Mummy, I love Soft Play. Can I have a chocolate croissant? Pleeeease?' squeaks Lily.

'Oh yeah, baby,' says Rachel suddenly feeling a little better at the thought of an indoor venue with coffee and baked goods to hand. Her optimism is short-lived as they pull in to the car park of Jambalaya with its ambitious strapline 'Where dreams come true'. The queue of rabid two- and three-year-olds is snaking out of the door and round the wall with its cheery Eric the Elephant sign. In fact, Eric is working the queue as they arrive. He is having a tough time as one determined three-year-old hangs on to his trunk and, given the menacing look in his eyes, is pretty set on ripping it from his face. Rachel unloads the kids and scans the line for Christa. She spots her waving from the front of the queue and gesturing for Rachel to join them. Rachel is still a little shaken by her earlier run-in with the 4x4 driver and approaches Christa with caution, perfectly ready to join the back of the queue.

'Rachel, come on and join us! You don't mind, do you?' she says to the man behind her.

'Well actually – ' he begins, before a man the size of a bison and a bear bolted together, wearing dark glasses and an enormous black suit appears and growls in a thick Eastern European voice, 'Thees laydee eez weeth us, OK?'

The objector decides against further objection. 'Erm, OK.'

The gorilla slips back into the shadows and Rachel looks at Christa for an explanation.

'Oh *ja*, sorry, Rachel, how rude of me. This is Rory. He is Roger's bodyguard.'

Rachel almost doesn't want to ask. 'His bodyguard?'

'*Ja*. It is because of Rudi and his connections.' She looks around and then whispers, 'He thinks we can't be too careful.'

'Blimey,' says Rachel wondering how long she can leave it before excusing herself to go and text Sue. 'So what do you think they would do?'

'Oh kidnapping perhaps. I think Rudi worries too much, but what can you do? Rory is a very nice man. Roger loves him.'

Rachel glances over to see Roger, Lily and Alfie practising their combat skills on Rory. He does not react until Roger karate-kicks his groin. Rory flinches and groans, but then high-fives Roger.

'He is teaching Roger self-defence. Pretty good, *nicht wahr*?'

The next two hours are wholly enjoyable for Rachel. She and Christa drink coffee after coffee, while the children run around like loons. At one point the elephant-torturer attempts to pick a fight with Alfie, until he is told by Rory to 'Play nicely' and doesn't trouble anyone again.

'Wow,' says Rachel. 'It's great having a bodyguard.'

'*Ja*, it is *sehr gut*, but you have to make sure they are very discreet. The last one we had tried to sell stories to the press about us.'

'Goodness,' says Rachel. 'What about?'

'Ah, they said we were swingers. Completely *nicht* true of course. Just because I have a rubber sex-suit in the wardrobe, doesn't mean I will share my pickle with anyone.'

Rachel almost spits her latte down her front. 'That's – '

'*Ja*, I know. Terrible. You just cannot trust these bastards,' says Christa, 'but Rory is family, so it is much better.'

'Oh it must be,' says Rachel reflecting, not for the first time, how dull her life is.

Emma sits back in her chair feeling momentarily nauseous and then, after a round burp, much better. The waiter looks disgusted but changes his sneer to a sycophantic smile as Rosie sweeps past him, returning from what she likes to refer to as the 'powder room'.

'Honestly, this place really has gone downhill. There used to be an attendant handing you warm towels and now they've got hand-driers. I mean! Hand-driers! No wonder this country is going to the dogs. So, darling, feeling better for a feed?'

'Yes thank you. That was lovely.'

'What was it last night? A book launch? Dinner with an author?'

'Oh no, just an evening in the pub with Rachel.'

'Oh.' Rosie wrinkles her nose with distaste as if Emma has just presented her with a large dog turd. 'Why?'

Emma laughs at her godmother's snobbishness, reflecting how like her own mother she can be.

'It's a really nice pub and you know how Dad always taught us to appreciate the good things, like real beer.'

'Ah yes, your father always did have strange taste,' says Rosie. 'And how is dear Teddy?'

'He's fine. He seems to be enjoying his grandchildren and making the most of retirement.'

'Yes, of course. The quiet life. Never really appealed to me. And how about your mother?' She utters this last word with poorly hidden disdain.

'She's OK. She's trying to hijack my wedding, but I guess she means well.'

'Oh darling, that's awful. Well you simply mustn't let her!'

'Easier said than done, I feel.'

'Would you like me to have a little word, you know, woman to woman?'

Emma knows this will send her mother into orbit. 'It's fine, Rosie. Thank you, but I can handle it.'

'I'm sure you can, my dear, but you must let me help in some way. Shall I ask Stella to make your dress, or see if Elton can play at the church?'

'That's really kind, but we're trying to keep it low key. To be honest, we haven't set a date yet.'

'Oh well, when you do, let me know. I'm happy to offer any assistance. Just ask.'

'Thank you. I do appreciate it. Rosie?'

'Darling girl?'

'Why did you never marry?'

'Ah, the million dollar question. Actually, I was married.'

'Really? When?'

'Many years ago when I was too young to care and thought life was so romantic.'

'What happened?'

'It was in the sixties when everything was so easy and you could fool yourself that you were in love. Alas, it was just a joke to him and he did not love me. So we got a divorce and never spoke of it again.'

'Wow! Was he your true love then?'

'No, not really.' Rosie looks suddenly old, her make-up caked face sagging with some secret sorrow. 'No, I was in love with someone else but he didn't love me so I married Ralph but it didn't work out. End of story.'

Emma feels as if she's prying. 'I'm sorry.'

Rosie snaps out of her stupor and smiles at Emma. 'Don't be, darling. I'm not. It's ancient history and some things just aren't meant to be. Anyway I am far too selfish to be a wife and I love my job too much. But enough about me. This is supposed to be about you and your gorgeous new author. I take it he is gorgeous?'

Emma feels uncertain of how to reply without incriminating herself. 'He's a very talented writer.'

'Aha! Guilty as charged m'lud. Clearly the dish of the day and intelligent to boot. Wonderful.'

'Yes, but I am practically married.'

'Tish and pish my dearest. Enjoy it while you can. Flirt away and enjoy your job. It's part of the rich tapestry of life. Speaking of dishes, how is Martin?'

'He's lovely and taking me away for the weekend to some posh hotel.'

'Feeling guilty is he?' says Rosie.

'What do you mean?'

'Excuse the bluff voice of experience, but when a man spoils his beloved, he is either expecting sex or feeling guilty or both.'

Emma remembers the flowers, champagne and home-cooked dinner coupled with the revelation of a visit to his parents. 'He just likes to spoil me.'

'Lucky girl! I hope you have a wonderful time. Don't forget to pack your raciest underwear!'

'Rosie!'

'What? I still have a pulse you know!'

'Honestly, I am packed, but I'm not telling. I better get back to work. I need to show willing after a shocking morning and I want to leave a bit early so we can avoid the traffic tonight.'

'Of course, of course.' Rosie lifts her finger and the waiter is by her side with the bill before you can say 'deliciously overpriced restaurant'.

'Maaaarm! I can't find my Cinderella dress!'

'OK, Lily, I'm just trying to help Will find his Spiderman mask.'

'Mummy. I want a cuddle!' Alfie waves his chubby arms. Of her three children, he is the clingiest and the most loving, but he does pick his moments. Rachel kneels down and accepts his pudgy embrace, but tries to multitask by flinging Will's clothes into the open rucksack.

'Doan want to go Granny's,' insists Alfie.

'Oh darling, Grandpa will be there and you love Grandpa, don't you?'

'Nooooo!' shouts Alfie.

'Yes you do!' says Rachel tickling his tummy.

'No, I don't!' insists Alfie, unwilling to be pacified.

They are interrupted by a loud *rat-a-tat* at the door.

'Daddy!' cry three jubilant voices.

'No. Guess again,' says Rachel.

Will opens the door.

'Grandpa!' cheer three happy voices.

'Grandpa!' cheers Rachel, giving him a hug.

'At your service, my lovelies,' he smiles. 'Now who wants to jump in Grandpa's Balamory bus and come for a sleepover?'

'Me!'

'Me!'

'Me!'

'Thanks, Dad,' says Rachel and means it.

'You,' he says embracing her in the warmest hug she's had for a while, 'are more than welcome. Have a lovely weekend, don't worry about a thing and promise me you'll talk to Steve?'

'I promise,' she says and she means this too.

Once the kids are dispatched, Rachel mixes herself a large gin and tonic and flops onto the sofa. The home phone rings and she answers with a sinking feeling.

'Rach?'

'Steve. If you're about to tell me what I think you're about to tell me, I will not be happy.'

'Chill your beans, missus. I'm phoning to see if you want red or white tonight? I'm on my way home and I want you in bed wearing something saucy by the time I get there.'

Rachel smiles. This could actually be a good weekend.

CHAPTER EIGHT

Emma opens her eyes and tries to remember where she is. She catches sight of the four-poster bed and expensive-looking heavy curtains, and remembers the weekend break. She also spots the empty bottle of champagne, underwear on the floor and stockings still tied around the bedposts. *Must have been a good night*, she thinks, as the form in bed next to her stirs. She moves towards him. 'Fancy an encore?' she whispers.

'Mmm, yes please. Let's seal the deal again,' answers a voice which isn't Martin's.

'Aaaaargh, Richard!' Emma jolts herself awake. Fortunately, she can hear Martin singing Elvis songs in the shower and then she sees the empty bottle, underwear and stockings.

'It's like a bloody porn version of *Groundhog Day*,' she mutters.

'Morning, sexy,' says Martin from the bathroom doorway, wearing nothing but a grin. 'That was some mighty fine lovin' you were givin' out last night. Fancy an encore?'

Emma shudders inwardly. 'All in good time,' she replies. 'A girl needs her breakfast after nothing but champagne and sex for dinner.'

'Oh, boo-hoo,' complains her fiancé, giving her bottom a stinging slap on his way past. 'Woof!'

'Thank you, Prince Charming. Whatever happened to romance?'

'It died the day they invented filthy sex.'

'I'm going to cleanse myself of my sins.'

'You're going to have to have one long shower then, Sexy Pants.'

After breakfast, Emma attempts to distract Martin's one-track mind with a walk around the grounds. It's a beautiful day. The autumn leaves still clinging to the trees are the perfect mix of orange, crimson and yellow and the sky is a pale blue with only the merest wisp of cloud. The air feels crisp and fresh but the sun is taking the edge off any chill. Emma has dug out her favourite long striped scarf and warm comfy boots and is kicking a trail through a spongy pile of leaves.

'Might be dog poo in there,' warns Martin.

Emma looks around at the stately home grandeur and shakes her head. 'I doubt it. Or at least if there is, it will be super-posh five-star poo.' She picks up a handful of leaves and flings them at Martin.

'Right, you're for it!' he declares, picking up a large armful and chasing after her.

Emma squeals and runs down the hill towards the lake. She stops just on the bank by a large willow tree. 'OK, OK, I give in,' she declares, out of breath, holding up her hands.

Martin keeps walking towards her with the pile of leaves and then throws them straight up into the air so that they shower around them like confetti. 'Der-der-deh-deh!' he sings, attempting the 'Wedding March'. He pins Emma up against the tree and kisses her on the mouth and then starts on her neck, working his hands down her body.

'Martin, not here! People can see us!' scolds Emma, although she doesn't make much effort to move.

Martin glances around them. 'What people? Anyway, everyone should indulge in a little al fresco loving, shouldn't they?' he says, working his hands under her jumper.

'They might have CCTV or something.'

'Well, they're in for a treat, aren't they? Anyway, you said yourself how beautiful it is here.'

'Mmm, it really is,' murmurs Emma, reaching for his flies.

'I'm glad you think so because I've taken the liberty of making a booking for the wedding date we talked about.'

Emma pushes him away. 'You've done what?'

Martin doesn't pick up her tone and pulls her towards him. 'I thought it would be a nice surprise.'

She gives him another shove. 'Martin, have you gone mad?'

'What's the matter?'

'You should have talked to me first!'

'It was meant to be a surprise!'

'It's certainly that,' says Emma, re-buttoning her coat and marching up the bank.

'Come on, Em, I thought you liked it here.'

'I do! It's just that I wanted to be consulted and besides, I thought we might choose somewhere close to Mum and Dad.'

'Oh so that's what this is about then.'

'What?'

'It's because it's nearer to my parents' than yours.' Martin folds his arms.

'Don't be ridiculous. It's the venue for my wedding. I think I have the right to a say!'

'What? So that your mother can take over?'

'What's that supposed to mean?'

'Oh come on, you know what she's like! She'll want cousin Margery doing the flowers and Great-Aunt Pamela making the cake.'

Emma narrows her eyes. 'Cousin Eunice actually and I don't have a Great-Aunt Pamela. Anyway, you were the one who said she was only trying to help!'

'OK, fine. If you don't want to have it here, I'll cancel it. I only paid a hundred pound deposit.'

'One hundred pounds! Are you mad?'

Martin looks hurt. 'I can't believe we're arguing about what is supposed to be the happiest day of our lives.'

'Neither can I, but then I can't believe you've booked the venue without talking to me.'

'Right, well I can see we're not going to resolve this now.'

'Clearly.'

'I'm going to give you some time to cool off,' says Martin in a way that he believes is reasonable but which winds Emma up even more.

'Fine. I'm going to the bar.'

He watches her go, shaking his head. He pulls out his phone and notices a text. It's from Charlie: 'How'd Em take the news re wedding venue?'

Martin texts back: 'Not well. Don't think she likes surprises.'

A message pings back: 'No pleasing some chicks.'

Martin pockets his phone and goes in search of the billiard room.

Emma is still bristling with anger as she orders a large gin and tonic from the bar. She wanders through the maze of swirly carpeted corridors before finding a door marked 'Library'. *Perfect. My kind of place*, she thinks, relieved to find it empty. The walls are lined floor to ceiling with shelves filled with some of the more eccentrically titled books. She notices with delight one entitled *Knitting with Dog Hair* and is about to pick it up when she spots a *Wodehouse Omnibus*;

just the thing for a weekend pretending to have more money than you do. Two large bay windows overlook the garden and it is towards these and a tall, elegant chair that Emma steers herself. She inhales the delightfully musty aroma of the room and is about to settle into its sanctuary-like calm with gin and Wodehouse for company when her phone vibrates with a text. It's from Rachel: 'How's your w/e playing lady of the manor? Am in scary clothes shop trying to find sthing 2 enhance my muffin-top. lol. Rx'

Emma laughs and types back: 'Had row with M. Off to drown sorrows in gin. Hope u and S having fun.'

'Have one 4 me and hope u sort it. Rx'

She sips her drink and tries to settle into her book but her brain is whirring after the argument. She knows he was just trying to surprise her but she also feels cross that he can't see her side of it. She looks out of the window at the view. It would be a perfect setting for the wedding. The house itself is gorgeous and dripping with history. The grounds are stunning and there's a croquet lawn, which would be ideal for the reception. She quite fancies playing lady of the manor in a big white dress. It's just that she'd always thought she would get married somewhere close to her parents and start the journey to her wedding from her family home. Is it wrong to feel like that? Plus she's worried what her mother will say if she agrees to have the wedding here. Although Martin has a point: her mother does have a tendency to take over and Emma usually lets her. Rachel had the right idea by eloping but then Rachel never did things by the book. Emma envies this. No, she must do what's right for her and Martin and if that involves being upfront with her mother, then that's what she'll have to do. She shudders at the thought.

Her phone buzzes with another text. It's from Martin: 'I miss you.'

Emma doesn't want to give in but she doesn't want to ruin the rest of her weekend because of an argument. Her more mature side wins and she replies: 'Where are you?'

'In the billiard room. Fancy a game? I'll let you win.'

'In your dreams, mate. Sorry 'bout earlier. Bit of a shock.'

''S OK. Should have checked first. Look forward to making up.'

Emma smiles and finishes her drink. She looks down at the book in her lap and runs a finger along its spine as she replaces it on the shelf. 'You'd know what to do with a tricky mother like mine, wouldn't you, Plum?' she says to the ghost of P.G. Wodehouse before heading off in search of her fiancé.

The clothes boutique window is beautifully decorated with the most desirable 'of the moment' tops, dresses, bags and shoes, plus a gorgeous selection of the dinkiest outfits for only the hippest children. Rachel has always felt rather out of place here, mainly because she usually has at least two snot-ridden children clinging to her legs whenever she passes.

Shopping with the children has never been a relaxing experience. She remembers an ill-advised trip to IKEA on her own with all three of them. She thought it would be nice; they could bounce on the beds and potter around while she could browse the soft furnishings. Then she'd treat her darlings to a delicious meatball lunch. Alas, reality bit. Alfie flatly refused to get out of the car. 'Who can blame him?' said Steve later. 'It's the Scandinavian version of hell.' Lily pulled a whole raft of towels on her head and Will scarpered, but did manage to find the only person working in the store, when he realised he was lost. Rachel was so panicked by the experience, that instead of looking for a sofa bed, she bought two mismatched cushions, which fell apart three weeks after purchase, a raffia storage box and a shaving mirror, which to this day remains in its bag in the cupboard under the stairs. By the time they made it to the café, Rachel only had the strength to feed her children packet food, so their lunch was Daim bars and Fruit Shoots. The children were still bouncing off the walls by the time Steve got home.

Today, however, she is unfettered and has brushed her hair and even applied make-up in preparation for a pub lunch with her husband. She is therefore feeling brave enough to attempt a casual mooch in this most intimidating of establishments.

'C'help yoo?' the nineteen-year-old shop assistant enquires in her best south-east London drawl.

'I'm fine thanks, just browsing,' says Rachel, immediately feeling uncomfortable.

The girl looks disappointed, her eyes dark with too much eyeliner and her mouth turned down in the permanent pout of the teenager. She eyes Rachel with suspicion as if she's never seen a person over thirty years of age before and isn't quite sure how to deal with this species. Rachel flicks through the rails in what she hopes is a casual way, trying to give off a vibe of 'yummy mummy'. She can feel the girl watching her. Then comes the body blow.

'We have those in bigger sizes.'

'I'm sorry?' says Rachel and means it.

'Bigg-er sizes,' stresses the girl, as if talking to a deaf person. 'I can go out the back and find them if you like?'

'No, it's fine thanks. This is actually my size,' she says triumphantly holding up a black top peppered with pink sequins, which spell out the words 'Sexy Mutha'.

The girl looks surprised and then admiring. 'You should definitely get that,' she says nodding. 'My mum bought it last week – she's about the same age as you,' she adds sagely.

Horrified, Rachel replaces the top and grabs the nearest thing to her, which is a string of pretty, shell-pink pearl beads.

'I'll take these,' she says panicking, 'for my daughter.'

The girl looks pleased. 'Great choice. I'm sure she'll love them. That will be twenty pounds.'

Rachel looks at her as a mother looks at a disobedient child. 'What's the magic word?'

The girl scowls, but grunts, 'Please.' Rachel hands over the cash and skips happily from the shop.

The air is cold and sharp, but the sun is trying to fight through to warm the day. Rachel loves days like these: blue skies, chilly air and welcome bursts of sunshine. It makes her feel as if something exciting is on the way. She remembers this feeling as a child, when summer gave way to autumn: the first conkers, the pavements matted with spongy wet leaves and Fireworks night, which started the really exciting build-up to the ultimate joy – Christmas.

Despite her apparent toughness, Rachel is ridiculously sentimental. Steve often laughs and calls her 'the onion' as they watch Saturday night TV and she cries along to *The X-Factor*, even before they've revealed that the seventeen-year-old boy has lost his mother to cancer. She also loves her little traditions, particularly at Christmas. Last year, Will had been indignant with a 'Not again, Mum!' when she insisted that they all sit down together on Christmas Eve to watch and weep at *The Snowman*. Rachel smiles at the memory and strolls down the high street towards the pub where she is meeting Steve. She hears a loud wolf-whistle behind her. She turns, ready to scowl, and then laughs when she sees Steve walking towards her with a rose between his teeth and a vast bundle of Saturday newspapers under his arm.

'Hello, gorgeous,' he says, kissing her passionately and presenting her with the rose. 'How was the shopping?'

'Eventful. I'll tell you over lunch. Buy me a drink?'

'My pleasure.'

He takes her hand as they dodge the traffic and dart into the pub. Rachel blinks, adjusting her eyes to the dark interior, and immediately decides that they should sit by the fire. Steve fetches their drinks and they browse the menu in silence apart from the occasional 'mmm, that sounds nice' and Steve's comment that this pub does the best onion gravy in London. They order and Steve starts to read the sports pages until he notices Rachel's frown. He laughs.

'Oh, you want me to talk to you, do you? Right then, Mrs Summers, how about I start by making a little speech? Ahem!'

'Steve, we do need to talk.'

'I know, I know, but I need to say this first.' He reaches out and takes her hand. 'I know that it hasn't been easy for you what with us trying for ages to have kids and then all of a sudden we have three.'

Rachel opens her mouth to speak but Steve holds his hand up to stop her.

'And I know that it's been hard for you to park your brain for a while and do the mum thing. But I just want to say that I think you're the best mother in the world, and I really appreciate everything you do for us. And this – ' He reaches into his pocket and pulls out a small, shiny black box with the flourish of a magician. '– is for you.' He slides it over to her. Rachel stares at it and then at him.

'Well, go on, don't you want to know what's inside?'

Rachel opens it and gasps. 'Wow!'

'It's just to say thank you, and to remind you that I love you. The diamonds represent each of the kids. I hope you like it.'

'I do, I really do. Thanks, Steve. It's wonderful.' She slides the ring onto her finger alongside her engagement and wedding bands and leans over the table to kiss him.

'Sausage and mash twice?' barks the pug-faced waitress, beautifully unaware of the intimate moment she is interrupting.

They eat their lunch in good spirits. Rachel pauses to admire the ring from time to time and they talk about everything except the move, as if they're worried they'll ruin the moment. By the time they've finished, they have sunk a bottle of acceptable red wine and Rachel is feeling pretty tipsy. She moves closer to Steve and starts to whisper filthy suggestions in his ear.

'Get a room!' mutters the waitress and they giggle conspiratorially. Steve jumps up and grabs Rachel's hand, pulling her to him and whispering, 'I want you now.'

They tumble laughing out of the pub and practically sprint home, pausing to kiss and tease each other with their afternoon plans. Rachel spots Verity drive past in her roomy Volvo and waves just as Steve pinches her bum. Verity looks away appalled and Rachel guffaws.

'Stuck-up cow. I bet she never gets any.'

'Ha! We hardly ever get any.'

'Well, we're making up for it now, aren't we?' laughs Rachel, feeling happy, free and drunk.

It is with a certain air of disappointment that they round the corner and spot a forlorn looking Tom sitting on his doorstep.

'Hi-ee,' says Rachel trying not to sound peeved or drunk.

'Oh, hi,' says Tom. 'You'll never guess what I've done.'

'Got yourself a girlfriend?' quips Steve. Rachel hits him.

'Ahaha. I wish,' chortles Tom amused. 'No. I've locked myself out.'

'Oh dear,' says Rachel and looks at Steve, crestfallen. As Rachel has often said, Steve is much nicer than her. He claps Tom on the back.

'Never mind, mate. You'd better come in. What do you want to do? Call a locksmith?'

'Actually, my brother has a spare key, which I suppose I should really give you too, shouldn't I?'

'Yes you should but never mind. Come in and give him a call. Where does he live?' asks Rachel, keeping her fingers crossed that her afternoon of dirty sex won't be completely ruined.

'Only half an hour away. Are you sure this is OK?'

'Of course!' chorus Steve and Rachel with false enthusiasm.

Two hours later, Rachel and Tom are sitting at the kitchen table tucking into their second packet of digestives. Steve has gone to check the football scores and Rachel has resigned herself to being neighbourly.

'So, are you close to your brother?' asks Rachel.

'I'd like to say yes, but we're very different people,' says Tom. 'What about you and Emma, isn't it?'

'Oh you know, we get on pretty well. She's the baby and knows it, which can be annoying but then I'm the big sister and I did give her a bit of a hard time when we were growing up.'

'Oh yes, this is a side of Rachel I don't know. What did you do to your poor sister then?'

Rachel laughs and shakes her head. 'You don't want to know. I was a bitch.'

'Mrs Summers, you shock me! But don't tell me, motherhood has softened you. You're a reformed character, eh?'

'Something like that.'

'Speaking of which, where are the munchkins today?'

Rachel is amused by his use of the word 'munchkins'. 'They're staying with my mum and dad.'

'Oh lovely,' nods Tom and then a look of horror crosses his face. 'Shit! You're supposed to be having a weekend alone, aren't you?'

'Well, sort of.'

'And I'm ruining it by being here, aren't I? You and Steve should be talking and, and, doing other grown-up things too!' Tom looks mortified.

'Honestly, Tom, it's fine. Don't worry about it.'

'Rachel, I'm so sorry. I'm going to make it up to you and babysit anytime you want.'

Rachel laughs and repeats, 'It's fine.' There is a loud *rat-a-tat* at the door.

Tom leaps up. 'About bloody time!'

He dashes down the hall with Rachel following, amused and curious. An exact replica of Tom, smaller, darker and about three years younger is standing in the doorway smiling at Rachel.

'Oh hi! I'm Mark. You must be – '

'Rachel.'

'Very nice to meet you, very nice. Lucky you, Tom, having such a gorgeous next-door neighbour. Not that you'd be her type. Well out of your league, mate.'

Tom looks embarrassed and Rachel hates Mark on sight.

'Well, I better go. Thanks again, Rachel, and please say sorry to Steve. Don't forget what I said. About babysitting.'

Rachel gives him a final wave before closing the door and making her way back to the kitchen. Steve is peering at his phone. Rachel creeps up on him. 'Who are you texting?' she cries, grabbing him from behind.

He lifts the phone out of her reach. 'Nosey cow!'

She tickles him under the arm so that he buckles. 'Let me see that,' she cries, snatching the phone. Steve looks sheepish. It's from Sam, whose name Rachel remembers from when she snooped at Steve's e-mails earlier in the week. 'Your team are such a bunch of losers,' it declares.

Rachel yawns. 'Oh boring football stuff. You men are so sad,' she says, holding the phone out for him.

'Aren't we?' says Steve grabbing it back from her quickly and switching it off. He pulls his wife towards him. 'And now that Mr Nice-but-dim has gone –' he begins.

'Don't be so mean,' says Rachel hitting him on the arm.

'What? Are you scared he'll hear?'

'Yes and it's not true. He's a very nice man!'

'"A very nice man",' parrots Steve laughing. 'He fancies you.'

Rachel laughs too quickly. 'He does not!'

Steve raises his eyebrows. 'Well, who cares? He's got very good taste and anyway, you're all mine,' he declares, cupping her face in his hands and starting to kiss her neck. Rachel shivers with delight. 'I think,' he says in between kisses, 'we might be able to bring back that lovin' feeling after all.'

Rachel smiles, but gives him a gentle shove. 'All in good time, Mr Luvva Luvva. I think we should try and have that chat.'

Steve frowns. 'OK. I suppose you're right,' he agrees with reluctance. 'But I have two, no actually, three conditions.'

'Oh yes?'

'Yes. One, we do this over a bottle of wine, two, we try not to shout, and three, we still get to do that filthy thing you promised in the pub.'

'Deal.'

Rachel fetches the wine and they stretch out on the sofa.

'Right,' says Rachel, 'where do we start?'

'Well, shall I tell you about the job?'

'OK.'

Steve takes a deep breath. 'It's a real step up with a lot more money, of course. I would get my own office and staff, and it's in a really lovely old part of Edinburgh.'

Rachel nods. 'It does sound amazing. Amazing but far away.'

'I know, I know, but it's a real opportunity for us. Will's only just started school, so he wouldn't be too unsettled if we move him now. Plus the schools up there are really good and the city is beautiful.'

'It sounds as if you've got it all mapped out.'

'Well, I have thought about it a lot.'

'But it sounds as if you've already decided. Without talking to me.'

'We're talking now.'

'Yes, but after the event. Steve, you used to talk to me about everything. I mean you barely got dressed in the mornings without checking which colour shirt you should wear. And this is one of the biggest decisions of our lives. How do you think it makes me feel that you've been cooking this up for ages without talking to me?'

'I know, Rach. I am sorry, really I am. It's just that we're always so busy and knackered. I kind of thought that if I got on with it, then we could take the final decision together.'

'But Steve, you don't seem to understand. I used to have a job, a good one and I loved it and I was good at it. Then I had the kids and they're lovely and I love them more than I can explain, but there is something missing for me. Suddenly I don't have to use my brain any more and the most challenging thing I'm asked to do is open a yoghurt. It's just not very fulfilling sometimes and I feel bad saying it because you're supposed to just love being a mother and I do.' Rachel is crying now. 'It's just that I feel as if we've changed so much and we're cutting each other out somehow and I don't want to live like that.'

'Hey, hey, come on, Rach, it's OK.'

'But it's not. You can't ever really understand how I feel because you're the man and you haven't had to give up your career to look after the kids. Nothing really changes for you, but it does for me. I feel as if I'm becoming a useless blob of jelly with no personality.'

Steve laughs and Rachel giggles through her tears.

'Well, I think you're a very gorgeous blob of jelly and I wouldn't have you any other way. Listen, Rach, no one said you couldn't go back to work and to be honest with this new job, we could probably afford the childcare if you wanted to try it. I just want us to be happy and if you're not, there's no point in you being a martyr to the kids. Better a happy working mum, than a miserable stay-at-home one. Better for the kids and better for you.'

'I guess. I just feel as if I should be there for them.'

'Well you can be. You could find something part-time.'

'Even in Edinburgh?'

'Oh yes, they have jobs up there for clever, gorgeous types like you.' He kisses the top of her head. 'Listen, this could be really great for us. Will you at least come up to Edinburgh with the kids next month so we can check it all out?'

'OK,' says Rachel slowly, 'and then make the decision?'

'And then make the decision.'

'All right then.'

'That's great. That's really great.' Steve looks relieved and picks up his glass. 'To Team Summers?' he says.

Rachel taps her glass against his and takes a drink. 'To Team Summers,' she says, replacing it on the table.

Steve takes a large sip and then puts down his glass before turning to his wife, a lecherous smile on his face. 'Now what about that thing you promised?' he says, jumping on Rachel, who squeals with delight.

CHAPTER NINE

Emma is woken by a shaft of buttery sunlight inching through the tapestry curtains. She lies for a minute or two feeling drowsy and content, enjoying the peace of the early morning. She glances over at Martin who is lying on his back with his arms above his head, breathing softly. His frame is broad and muscular and his face looks soft and handsome as he slumbers. She is about to lean over and kiss him when her phone vibrates across the bedside table. She reaches over and reads the text message. It's from Rachel: 'All right cow-bag? R u coming 2 M&D's 2day?'

She punches a reply: 'Fine thx tart. Got coffee with future in-laws but might c u l8r.'

'Good luck flibbertigibbet! btw talked 2 steve - all good.'

Emma is pleased. She doesn't like the thought of her sister being unhappy, and she likes their family dynamic: largely chaotic with moments of calm and a dash of insanity.

Martin rolls over and puts his arms around her. 'Morning, beautiful. You're up early.'

'Hello, handsome. Well, we did go to bed rather early last night.'

'Yeah, but not to sleep,' he quips with a filthy grin. 'And seeing as you seem so full of beans this morning.' He pulls back the cover to reveal an impressive morning glory. 'We better not let this one go to waste!' Emma giggles and allows herself to be overpowered.

Afterwards, she runs a bath and is just settling into some Molton Brown luxury when Martin appears in the doorway and stands, smiling at her.

'What?'

'I'm just admiring my beautiful future wife.'

'Oh stop.'

'Seriously, Em, I'm the happiest, luckiest man in the world. We've set a date for the wedding, we're having a lot of sex and you are the best thing that's ever happened to me. Even if Cameron Diaz walked in here right now and begged me to marry her, I just wouldn't.'

'Well, that's a great comfort.'

'I mean it! People make life so complicated. Does he love me? Do I love him? But it's simple. All you have to do is meet someone, fall in love and *bish bash bosh.*'

'*Bish bash bosh*?'

'That's it,' says Martin, grinning like a man who has cracked the secret of life. 'I'm going for a quick stroll before breakfast. Enjoy your soak.' He disappears whistling cheerfully.

Emma sinks into her bath and closes her eyes. She thinks about Martin and his carefree view of life. She envies the way men can just accept things without analysing everything. She wishes she could be more like this. She's never been one to rest on her laurels or accept things as they are just for the sake of it. 'A restless soul,' her dad calls her sometimes, 'always searching for something new or different.' In her professional life this has often been to her advantage; fuelling her ambition and driving her career. But as she approaches marriage, it strikes her that a different tack might be necessary. Surely finding the one you want to spend the rest of your life with brings contentment and less of a need to keep searching for something. Emma hopes this will be true. She loves Martin very much. He's kind, reliable, good looking and loves her unconditionally, as well as being a bit of a tiger in the bedroom. She knows this should be enough for her and in lots of ways it is. However, she also knows that Martin is keen to get their babies out into the world as soon as possible and she shudders slightly at the thought.

She thinks about Rosie and her carefree, no strings, lots of money, 'big is beautiful' life. She seems happy. She has it all. Emma sinks under the water and rises blowing a spout of water from her mouth. And then there's Rachel with her three gorgeous, albeit slightly exhausting, children. She seems happy. Sometimes. Emma sighs.

There are times when she wishes she could stop her brain questioning everything and accept her life for what it is. But now there's a wedding to organise as well and given the start she and Martin have had sorting the venue, Emma is experiencing an encroaching sense of dread. It's supposed to be the best day of her life and she's sure it will be if she can prevent it being hijacked by her mother, godmother and, even, fiancé. She gets out of the bath and wraps herself in a fluffy white robe just as Martin returns. After breakfast, they check out and make the short drive to Martin's parents.

'Nervous?'

'Why should I be?'

'Oh no reason.'

'Martin, this is just coffee with your parents isn't it?'

'I think so.'

'What's that supposed to mean?'

'I think Mum might have invited a couple of other bods.'

'How many?'

'Oh, I dunno, four or maybe six. Don't worry about it. They'll love you.'

He switches on the radio just as Steve Wright announces, 'And this one is for Emma from her fiancé Martin.' The opening strains of 'I Won't Last A Day Without You' by The Carpenters leak through the speakers.

Emma is irritated at the prospect of fifty of Martin's relatives, but is touched by the gesture with the song. 'Thanks, darling,' she says weakly.

They reach his parents' house just as Karen Carpenter finishes singing. Martin turns and smiles at her. 'I love you, Emma Darcy. Now let's go and face the music, shall we?'

Emma nods but suddenly her attention is distracted by the dozen or so cars parked on the road and drive, and the crowd of people she can see through the window. She feels slightly sick as Martin's mother, Daphne, flings open the door with a 'They're here!' and twenty excited people spill out to greet them. Martin takes her hand and mouths 'Sorry,' as they enter the fray.

'Darlings, how wonderful to see you. Come in, come in,' trills Daphne.

They troop into the house, which is a testament to an era of chintz and frills circa 1978. Emma is horrified to enter the lounge and find a table piled high with all manner of cold meats, cheeses and bread.

'Oh Daphne, you didn't have to go to all this trouble. Coffee would have been fine,' she says looking meaningfully at Martin, who has a fixed grin on his face.

'Nonsense, nonsense! It's a celebration and I thought we'd have one of those, what do you call it, Sara? Munch?'

'Brunch, honey.'

'Brunch, of course. Sara is –' she grasps Emma's hand and whispers confidentially '– an American!' as if she's just introduced her to a new species of exotic bird. 'She's taught me so much and apparently brunch is very popular in New York, isn't that right, darling?'

'Sure is, Daph. Hey, good to meet you, kids. Congratulations and all that. Can't say marriage worked out for me. It was the old three strikes and I was out but good for you!'

'Thanks,' says Emma uncertainly.

'Well, you must come and meet everyone,' says Daphne ushering them in. 'We're all dying to see the ring. And grab some food. I decided to go all Scandinavian and do a smorgasbord or whatever they're called. Elke from the village gave me the idea. She's Swedish, you know. The pickled herring is very good.'

Emma's stomach flips at the thought of cold fish at 10.30 in the morning. She glances over to see Martin give her a little wave before making himself a cheese and pickle sandwich, and marvels at a man's ability to eat constantly, like grazing cattle. Daphne leads her through to the living room, smiling triumphantly as if she is about to present a member of minor royalty.

'Now you must come and meet – '

'Hullo, Emma!' Martin's father, Rob, shambles up and gives her an awkward hug.

'Hi, Rob, nice to see you. How are you?'

'Oh fine, fine. Keeping busy, you know, pottering around the garden. How are your mum and dad?'

'Robert!' barks Daphne.

'Yes, my tulip?'

'I thought I told you to put out all the wine glasses and did you remember the pickle forks?'

'Pickle forks. Wine glasses. Right, sorry, Emma. Duty calls.' He shuffles off, a mass of Damart trousers and old-man cardigans.

'Sorry, Emma, where were we? Ah yes. Let me introduce you. You've met Sara and this is Elke of the pickled herring fame.' Daphne laughs at her own joke. 'And this is David and Vanessa, David's our doctor you know, and Roger and Doreen, Harriet and Philip . . . ' Daphne continues to reel off name after name until Emma just wants to plonk herself down in the nearest Ercol chair and have a plate of Mortadella and pickled cucumber. Eventually the introductions are done, the ring is cooed over and Emma has talked about everything from lighting bonfires to why John Lewis is the only place to shop. She decides that she has done her duty and goes on a hunt for Martin. She finds him hiding in the kitchen with his dad.

'Hello, darling. Having fun?'

Emma makes a face and pulls him to one side. 'Let's just say that I'm not planning to invite many of your mother's friends to our wedding. Can we go soon please?'

'Can I come with you?' asks Rob with a wry smile.

'Poor Dad. Has Mum been bossing you around again?'

'I think if you removed the word "again" you'd have it about right. Look, you two get off and enjoy the rest of your weekend. I'll deal with your mother.'

'Thanks. I'm going to take Emma home the scenic way.'

'Great. Do you think we could pop in to see Mum and Dad? I want to hear the latest about Rach and Steve's move,' says Emma.

'Sure thing.'

'Oh Emma, I must give your dad a call. I want his advice on transplanting a camellia.'

'Oh all right, I'll mention it to him.' She gives Rob a hug, feeling genuine affection for him.

'Going so soon? But I've just put a strudel in the oven!' says Daphne.

'Yes, sorry, Mum, got to get back, shirts to iron, stuff to sort for work.'

'Ahh you young types, so dedicated to their work. Well, once you're married, you'll have the children to think about, and Emma will have to give up that working life, eh?'

Rob raises his eyes heavenwards and Martin looks at the floor. Emma curses the weakness of men. She pecks Daphne on the cheek.

'Right, well thanks for a lovely, er – '

'Brunch,' chimes Daphne.

'Yes, brunch. We'll see you soon.'

Emma flops into her car seat, her cheeks aching from smiling too hard for too long. Martin kisses her on the forehead.

'Well done, my darling. You survived. Now, let's play a game of Shoot, Marry, Shag, with my mother's friends!'

'Come on, Rach, we're going to be late!' calls Steve.

'Coming!' Rachel appears at the top of the stairs wearing a dark grey empire-line Karen Millen dress she picked up in a charity shop last week and gorgeously comfortable but, destined to fall apart at any second, boots from Primark.

'Wow! Who is this vision I see before me?'

'Oh stop,' chides Rachel, never able to take a compliment. 'I just thought I'd make a bit of an effort.'

'Well, I like,' says Steve, wrapping her in his arms, 'very much. All set?'

'Yes. Actually I'm looking forward to seeing the kids. I've sort of missed them.'

'I know what you mean. It's been a bit too quiet. Lovely, but a bit too quiet.'

They drive over to Edward and Diana's with Rachel flicking through the radio channels. 'I've got to find Lionel! You can't have a Sunday without Lionel! Aha!' she cheers hitting on the right commercial station and whistling along to 'Easy Like Sunday Morning'. They pull up outside the house and Rachel notices the silver Mercedes blocking her parents' drive.

'Oh bugger. I think that's Rosie's car.'

'Is that a problem?'

'It's just that, you know what she can be like. It's been such a lovely weekend; I don't fancy listening to the loaded comments and criticisms just because I'm not Emma.'

'Oh sod her. Just ignore it.'

'Steve, you know that's simply not in my make-up.'

'Yes, well I did wonder as soon as I said it.'

'Never mind, give us a kiss and let's face the music.'

As they get out of the car, two small forms come charging out of the door.

'Mummy! Daddy!' they chorus. A third, small female form follows behind shouting 'Daddy! Daddy!'

Rachel scoops up Will and Alfie breathing them in and remembering something she read recently which described boys as smelling of angels and tigers. How well that writer knows boys, she'd thought. Her father appears at the door smiling.

'Welcome, welcome and thank goodness you're here. The children and I were about to go on a moon mission and we didn't want you to miss it. They've even made moon cakes with Granny.' And then as an aside to Rachel, 'And Grandpa forgot to tell Granny that Great-Auntie Rosie was coming, so he'll probably be fired off in a rocket later.'

'Poor old Grandpa,' laughs Rachel, putting an arm around her father and planting a kiss on his forehead. 'And are the old ladies playing nicely?'

'Not especially,' he replies, kissing her on the cheek. 'And how's my favourite daughter with children? Nice weekend?'

'Lovely, thank you. Really lovely.'

'I'm glad, darling. You know how fond we are of Steve and I know he makes you happy.'

'He does.' She watches as Steve chases Lily and Alfie, who are screaming like lunatics, into the kitchen.

'And what's all this noise?' asks Diana with mock-crossness.

'It's Daddy! He's a monster!' squeals Lily.

'Ah well, no cakes for Daddy then,' says Diana. 'Darling, come in, would you like a coffee or maybe a gin and tonic. I'm going to have one.'

'Hi, Mum. Tea would be great actually thanks. Tough morning?'

'Only when your dad's little surprises turn up.'

'Rachel! Steve! How wonderful to see you!' Rosie sweeps in, wearing a vast pink cashmere wrap. 'Diana was just telling me about your move. What a shame. She'll never get to see you. Still, be good to be away from the monster-in-law, eh Steve?' she says nudging him.

'Erm – ' Steve begins.

'Diana was about to have a gin and tonic, Rosie. Would you like one?' says Edward.

'Ah, isn't it a bit early, Diana dear? Well, why not? We can all be alcoholics together!'

Rachel notices her mother disappear and goes to follow her.

'So, Rachel,' Rosie begins, 'those children of yours must keep you busy. What a delightful handful they are. Will is such a mischievous little boy. I caught him trying to pour golden syrup into my Chloe bag. Such a pickle!'

Rachel sees her mother kiss Will on the head and set about measuring a large gin.

'Ah well, it's their age you see. They like to push the boundaries,' says Rachel, feeling defensive.

'Hmm,' agrees Rosie uncertainly. 'And how are you, my dear? How are you finding it all? It must be tough and perhaps not the most stimulating. I mean, it's not like they ever want to go and see a film at the BFI or take in the latest exhibition at the V&A, is it?'

'Actually, I did take them to the V&A once,' says Rachel irritated.

'Did you, darling?' says Rosie not listening, fitting some tiny pink stilettos onto the Barbie doll that Lily has left, limbs askew on the table.

'I did, yes.' Rachel remembers a miserable day trailing the kids around London with Will declaring everything to be boring and whining because the Natural History Museum had been shut and he couldn't visit his beloved dinosaurs. Lily and Alfie screamed the place down because they both had streaming colds and it was raining. 'But you know it's very difficult – with the pushchair.'

'Quite, quite,' agrees Rosie still not listening, preening Barbie's hair. 'Well, I admire you stay-at-home mums. I could never have done it. I like my own space and the thought of childbirth, my goodness! However do you manage it?'

Rachel laughs. 'I think it's called an epidural.'

'Ah yes and of course the gas and air must make it all worthwhile, but it's a bit too barbaric for me,' says Rosie shivering and pulling her wrap tightly around her shoulders. Lily swaggers in and stands very close to Rachel as if waiting to be invited into the conversation.

'How's my little Picca-lily then?' coos Rachel tickling her under the chin and smoothing her hair.

'Mu-um! Stop it,' orders Lily, swatting her hand away like an impatient cat flicking away a fly.

'Sorry, darling, it's just that I've missed you. Did you miss me?'

Lily screws up her face as if trying to work out a tricky algebra equation. 'Sort of. Mum?'

'Yes, darling?'

Lily eyes Rosie who is smiling brightly in full-on auntie mode. Lily grimaces at her and turns back to her mother, leaning in and whispering in a mock-quiet voice. 'Why does Auntie Rosie smell like that?'

'Pardon, darling?' asks Rachel trying not to betray her panic.

'She smells. I asked Granny what the smell was and she said "a tart's boudoir". What does that mean?'

'Here we are,' says Edward bringing in a tray of drinks.

Rachel breathes a sigh of relief. 'Thanks, Dad. Lily, why don't you show me these wonderful cakes?' she says.

'But, Mum?'

'Kitchen, Lily. Now!'

Lily harrumphs from the room and Rachel fires a quick embarrassed smile at Rosie who ignores her and starts talking to Edward.

Diana is interrogating Steve in the kitchen. 'But it's such a long way, Steve.'

'I know, Diana, but they do have things called trains and planes and to be honest, we'll be able to afford a bigger place with room for you to stay as long as you like.' Rachel gives him a look. 'Within reason of course.'

But Diana is not going to be pacified. 'But I'll never see my little monkeys.'

'Mum, it's not decided yet,' says Rachel. 'We're going to go up and have a look next month. You should come!'

'What?' chorus Steve and Diana.

'Yes, why not? We could make a weekend of it. Get Emma and Martin along too.'

Steve looks concerned.

'Well, why not?'

'Because we need to go and decide for ourselves.'

'Oh-ho, you think I'm going to interfere, don't you?' says Diana offended.

'Not at all,' fibs Steve. 'It's just that it's got to be our decision.'

'Yes, but we're your family. We want to be involved.'

Steve looks defeated and Rachel feels bad for suggesting it. 'Maybe Steve's right. Maybe we should just go on our own and then you could all come to help us look at houses if we do go.'

'But then it would be too late!'

'Too late for what?' asks Edward coming in at just the wrong moment.

'Oh Edward, can you try to talk some sense into these two. They want to move to the ends of the earth and they won't listen to a word I say!'

'Oh let them make up their own minds, Diana. Stop trying to interfere,' says Rosie interfering.

Diana looks at Rosie with murderous intent. 'And who asked you?'

'I'm just saying, darling, that you do have a tendency to interfere, isn't that right, Teddy? Rachel?'

Edward and Rachel look at the floor.

'I don't hear anyone disagreeing,' says Rosie with malicious glee.

Diana does not speak, and Rachel notices that her neck is almost puce, indicating that she is apoplectic with rage.

'Maybe it's time to eat?' says Edward quickly.

'And maybe Rosie would like to play mother on this occasion. I'm not hungry,' says Diana in a quiet voice. She walks out of the room, puts on her shoes and leaves through the front door, slamming it on her way out.

'Well,' says Rosie after a pause. 'Someone's a bit tense today. Shall we eat?'

Rachel looks at her father. 'Shouldn't one of us go after Mum?'

Edward looks a little unsure. 'No, it's fine. Let her cool down a bit.'

They sit themselves at the table and lunch passes in the usual distracted chaos of trying to eat a meal with small children present. Rachel is grateful for the distraction of having to cut up Alfie's broccoli when Rosie launches into another soliloquy about how wonderful Emma is.

'I suppose you regret giving up work, do you? I mean your brain must feel like a bit of a mush now, Rachel?' she says.

Steve looks at Rachel fearful of a response as sharp and poisonous as a scorpion's attack.

'Well, it's true, it's not as dynamic or grown-up a world as working at the agency, but I decided it's what I should do and they aren't so bad.' She ruffles Alfie's hair. 'To be honest, I have bad days with this job just as I had bad days with the other one, but it's the right job for me at the moment. Anyway, Will's going to give me a promotion soon, aren't you, darling?'

'What's a promo-shon?' asks Will, failing to see any humour.

'Well, I think you're an absolute saint. I'm far too selfish to give up my lifestyle for a life of domestic thrall. I think it's marvellous.'

Rachel ignores the patronising tone and smiles at Steve, who gives her a small thumbs-up. Rosie spends the rest of the meal talking to Edward, laughing and teasing and patting his hand. They hear the front door open and the children, like Pavlov's dogs, register this as a cue to leave the table and run into the hall.

'Granny! Granny! Granny!' they shout.

'Ah, the wanderer returns,' says Rosie with no note of warmth. Rachel gets to her feet.

'You stay here. I'll go,' says Edward.

Rachel follows him out and herds the children back into the dining room. Lily and Alfie are smothering their grandmother with kisses and follow Rachel reluctantly. On her way out of the lounge, Rachel turns to see her father wrap her mother in his arms as she starts to sob. They finish the meal and retire to the conservatory. Rosie immediately slumps into a comfortable chair and falls asleep, her mouth wide open, snuffling and snoring like a piglet. Lily and Alfie watch and giggle with delight, and Rachel doesn't scold them.

Edward returns and announces, 'Granny's just going to have a little rest upstairs. You've worn her out, you rotters. Now, who wants to try these cakes?'

The small people chorus their approval and rush to the kitchen followed by Rachel, Steve and Edward. Steve dishes up thick squares of biscuit and raisin goo, and Rachel's father opens the back door.

'Just going to check on the greenhouse.'

'I'll come with you,' says Rachel.

Any warmth from the day is fading fast as the sun starts to melt into a pale yellow colour. Rachel wraps her cardigan tightly around her and follows her father up the path under the old apple tree, feeling worm casts and tiny hard apples under her feet. She has to stoop low to avoid scraping her scalp on the branches. She remembers summers with Emma under this tree: endless tea parties with bears and dolls, fairy banquets and balls with pretend coaches made from the bigger apples and acorn cup wine goblets from next door's oak tree.

'Clocks will be going back soon,' says her father looking at the sky. Rachel murmurs in agreement. He taps the greenhouse thermometer. 'Hmm, not too bad but I reckon there'll be frost next week.' Rachel wonders at her father's ability to know this. He has the skill to sniff the air and tell which weather front is coming in next. Since the BBC introduced the red button, he is forever checking the hourly and five-day forecast. It drives her mother potty, but Rachel sees how your world can shrink when you're retired and this is his way of keeping busy. Her father uncovers some seed trays and prods them.

'Better give these a bit of water. So, all square with Steve?' he asks without further introduction.

'I think so. We're going to all go up to Edinburgh in a month or so, get the lay of the land, you know?'

'Sounds very sensible.'

'Dad?'

'Sweet pea?'

'Will Mum be OK?'

'She'll be fine.'

'And what about you?'

Her father looks up from his precious seedlings, almost surprised at the question. 'Rachel, when you married Steve, you made a promise to stick by him through everything, didn't you?'

'Ye-es.'

'So, this is one of those times. He's your husband and you have three wonderful children and you must decide on your own what you should do.'

'Yes, but – '

'And, you mustn't worry about Mum and me. We just want you to be happy. We're fit and well and can come and visit you any time. OK?'

'OK.'

'Good.' He puts an arm around Rachel. 'I'm very proud of you. You know that, don't you?' Rachel nods. 'So is your mum. I know she finds it hard to say it, but she had a tough time growing up. Don't be too hard on her, will you?'

'I think you should tell Rosie that too.'

'Yes, you're probably right, but I'd rather spend my time looking after my three girls than worrying about Rosie and her sarcasm. She's got her own issues, you know.'

'Hmm, I can see that.'

Right on cue, the back door flies open and a voice rings out. 'Teddy, look who's here! It's Emma and Marvin!'

Rachel snorts. 'Marvin?' She links arms with her father and they make their way back down the garden path into the house.

Emma is trying to wrestle her way out of her coat while Lily and Alfie cling onto a leg each shouting 'Auntie Em! Auntie Em!'

Rachel laughs. 'Hello, Em. And Marvin!'

'Ha ha,' says Emma. 'Can you call off your monkeys please?'

'Children!' says Rachel with mock-fierceness. 'Put your Auntie Emma down – you don't know where she's been!'

'Goodness, what's all this noise?' says Diana, plodding down the stairs, her eyes red and her hair ruffled from sleep.

'Dear me, Diana, don't you own a hairbrush?' enquires Rosie.

Diana ignores her and kisses Emma and Martin. 'Steve, would you be a darling and pop the kettle on, please? Come on, let's go and sit in the lounge. Emma and Martin can tell us about their weekend. How are your parents, Martin?'

They all shuffle in. Rosie plonks herself down in Diana's usual spot. Diana perches next to Emma and Martin on the sofa.

'It was an amazing hotel, really lovely. Four poster beds, lovely grounds, great food.'

'Ahh, is this the Clevedon?' interjects Rosie.

'That's the one. Do you know it?'

'Of course, darling. It's my favourite weekend getaway, if you know what I mean.' She smiles lasciviously.

Emma is mortified and says quickly, 'Right, well actually, we're thinking about it for the wedding.'

It's Diana's turn to look mortified. 'The wedding?'

'Yes, it's really lovely, Mum, and we could all stay and have a wonderful weekend,' she adds, her voice squeaking as she desperately tries to sound convincing.

'But what about the golf club? Daddy was going to ask Philip.'

'Oh for goodness sake, Diana. This is the Clevedon. It's the height of sophistication. Emma is on the cusp of a glittering publishing career. She doesn't want to have her wedding reception at some tired old suburban golf club full of red-faced fifty-year-olds and their sweaty wives. No offence, Teddy.'

Emma and Rachel look at their mother. She has gone very pale, and is looking at a painting on the wall; a watercolour of a Cornish beach with children paddling on the shore. They both know that this is the eye of the storm and definitely do not want to get caught in the tornado.

Rachel seizes the moment. 'So, when are we going to go and buy this dress?'

'Erm,' Emma blurts uncertainly.

'How about the week after next. You'll have the kids, won't you, Dad?'

'Absolutely. Anything to help.'

'Oh, how wonderful! A girl's day out. I'd love to!' trills Rosie.

Rachel and Emma exchange glances.

'I'll get onto Stella first thing tomorrow. She owes me a favour, so she'll be only too happy to help. Wonderful, that's settled then. Right, I must dash,' she says checking her watch, 'I'm having supper with Nigella tonight. She's promised to give me the recipe for her Tiramisu. So divine. Not that I'll be cooking it, but I shall ask little Maria to run it up for me.' She air-kisses everyone in turn and as a parting shot says to Diana, 'I hope you're feeling better soon, my darling. You really look awful today.'

'That bloody woman!' roars Diana, when she is gone. 'The cheek of it! And now she's trying to hijack the dress shopping and my daughter's big day, and – '

'It's all right, Mum, we'll sort it,' says Rachel.

'And we haven't even talked about Rachel's move or your wedding venue. Oh, it's all too much.'

'Maaarm!' Will's voice is like a foghorn at the door.

'Yes, William?' replies Rachel.

'Lily's done a poo!'

'Oh great.'

'It's OK,' says Lily coming into the room lifting up her skirt to reveal her bare bottom. 'I've taken off my pants.'

'OK,' says Rachel, 'and where are the poo and the pants?'

Lily looks sheepish.

'Lily!'

'OK, OK, I put them in Auntie Rosie's bag. I think she made Granny sad and she smells funny. Am I in trouble?'

Diana scoops Lily into her arms and kisses her. 'No, my darling, you're not in trouble. In fact I think Granny might have some sweeties for you somewhere,' she adds with a smile.

CHAPTER TEN

The sky is heavy and grey with rippling waves of white as the wind pushes the clouds across its surface. It's as if the day couldn't really be bothered to get started and its dullness very much reflects the fact that it's Monday in London. Everyone hates Monday in London. Emma buttons her mac as she emerges from the Tube and rummages for an umbrella, sending pens and lipstick spilling onto the floor. People rush past her, tutting as she gets in their way and she feels herself panic slightly at temporarily losing her cool. Moments later she emerges onto the damp pavement and casts around looking for directions to Kew Gardens.

She buys a ticket and walks through Victoria Gate, taking in the view. The wide-open spaces of London never cease to amaze her. It's almost as if they shouldn't really be there, but for Emma, it's what makes London the best city in the world. She dodges the puddles, edging her way to the Princess of Wales Conservatory, where she is due to meet Richard. She has arrived early so that she can have a look around and acquaint herself with some of the inspiration for the novel. She also senses the need to be professional and in control with Richard Bennett. She's not sure why but there's something about this author that unnerves her. She tells herself she's being ridiculous.

The Conservatory is vast. Emma breathes in the warm, sweet earthy smells, not unlike those of her dad's greenhouse. Apart from a couple of green-booted gardeners at work, she has the place to herself. She heads straight for the orchids and marvels at their perfect forms. She loves Kew for the way it reflects a human need to be interested in the world, to understand and nurture. She wishes she had an in-depth knowledge or passion for an obscure subject. Martin once bought her an orchid – pale purple and cream, flecked with pink dots, as delicate and beautiful as a duck egg – but in her duty of care, she over-watered it and it was dead within weeks. She was mortified and Martin had laughed: 'It was only a tenner from M&S.'

Here, the orchids are exceptional. No supermarket hybrids to be seen, just pure beauty and exotic perfection.

'Remarkable, aren't they?' says a voice. Emma jumps. She turns to see Richard's smiling face. He looks handsome in a scholarly way today, his face framed by flattering black-edged glasses.

'Yes, yes they are. Wonderful. Really lovely. Stunning. How are you?' Emma realises that she's jabbering and tells herself to calm down.

'All the better for seeing you, esteemed editor.' He leans forwards and kisses her on the cheek.

Emma takes in the scent of expensive aftershave and feels her stomach dip a little. *Get a grip, Darcy*, she thinks. 'Shall we go and grab a coffee and discuss this brilliant book then?' she asks in full-on professional editor mode.

'After you,' says Richard with a gallant bow.

'No, Lily, you cannot wear your swimming costume to the music group. It's six degrees outside!' Rachel lifts the lid on the stove-top coffee pot, willing it to be ready, desperate for a hit of caffeine.

'I hate you!' Lily shouts.

Rachel shrugs her shoulders. 'Well I love you, darling,' she says with as much calm in her voice as she can muster.

'Well, I flippin' well hate you!' screams Lily, her voice reaching a pitch that only dolphins can hear, followed by a dramatic thumping of small feet and an explosive slamming of her bedroom door. Rachel considers momentarily if perhaps her child has become a teenager overnight. She pours herself a coffee and slumps into her favourite kitchen chair as Alfie waddles in.

'Is Lily cross?' he asks with pure innocence.

'No, darling, she's just got issues,' says Rachel cheerily. 'Now where's Mummy's cuddle?' Alfie squeaks with delight as Rachel grabs him and tickles him mercilessly.

'That's enough, Mummy!'

Rachel relinquishes her grasp and enjoys a leisurely sip of her coffee. 'Ahh, the nectar of life,' she sighs. She can hear Lily throwing toys, books and what sounds like small items of furniture around her room, but Ken Bruce is playing a James Taylor song and Rachel is determined to savour the moment. As the song ends, she glances at the clock.

'Holy cow! We're going to be late! Alfie, find your shoes, I'll get your sister!'

'Holy cow!' giggles Alfie with unbridled joy.

Rachel stampedes up the stairs and throws open Lily's door.

'Come on, Lils, it's nearly time for "Hello Sally" and you don't want to miss that, do you?' urges Rachel, trying not to show panic in her voice.

'Oh and I suppose we're late again, are we?' says Lily with frightening insight. Rachel realises, as she has realised many times before, that these are not the battles she will win easily. Her mother has often said how eerily similar Rachel and Lily are and Rachel has a grudging admiration for her four-year-old's intelligence.

'OK, Lilsy, I'll do you a deal. You let me get you dressed and into the car without any fuss and there's a babycino in it for you.'

'Hmm,' contemplates Lily. 'Deal or no deal? Let me think.' Rachel tries to suppress the dark thoughts she is now having about her torturer. 'OK, Mother. Throw in a chocolate chip panettone and you have a deal.'

Rachel is flabbergasted and impressed in equal measure. 'Fine, fine. Now, let's get you dressed and don't call me Mother.'

'All right. Don't call me Lilsy then. I'm not a baby. And I'm already dressed.' She peels off her dressing-gown to reveal an outfit incorporating pink corduroy trousers, a red glittery sequined top, which Rosie bought for her and which Rachel hates, and a green Tinkerbell dress. Rachel doesn't know whether to laugh, cry or take a picture. She remembers what the books tell you about praising positive behaviours and not undermining your child.

'That is a really remarkable outfit, Lily. Well done.'

''S not finished yet.' She fishes out a pair of gold glitter wings, a red and yellow Peruvian hat and a pastel pink polka dot bag.

'There,' she says checking herself in the mirror. 'Perfect.'

'You look like a Christmas tree,' says Alfie unwisely as he wanders in. Rachel waits for the backlash. It doesn't come.

'I know,' says Lily delighted. 'I love Christmas! Now, Mum, please can we go? It's sooo embarrassing when we're late.'

Rachel is speechless.

'So let's talk about Stella and what she really wants. Is she genuinely drawn to the brothers or is it all just a game to her? Does she behave the way she does due to the death of her mother?'

'Absolutely, absolutely. So Emma, are you married?'

'Well, Richard, I'm not sure it's entirely relevant to this conversation, but for your information, I am engaged.'

'Ahh, who's the lucky chap?' smiles Richard, toying with the froth on his cappuccino.

'His name is Martin and he's the love of my life. Now look, we're supposed to be discussing your plotline.'

'Oh come on, Emma, we've been talking plotlines for two hours and I think it's important that we get to know each other a bit better as editor and author.'

Emma folds her arms and surveys him. 'OK, what do you want to know?'

'How did you meet this Marlon?'

'Martin.'

'Yes of course, sorry. Martin.'

'He used to work in our IT department.'

'How romantic.'

'Are you mocking me?'

'Only mildly. No, I'm just in awe of two people who are prepared to commit to one another in this day and age.'

'I take it you're a commitment-phobe,' teases Emma.

Richard smirks. 'I just haven't met the right available woman yet,' he says with emphasis on the word 'available'.

'I'm sure you will,' she replies dismissively.

Richard nods his head looking earnest. 'I hope so. I didn't have the best role models to be honest. My father left my mother for her sister, so not a great example.'

'That's terrible. Your poor mum.'

'Mmm. It was tough on her. She ended up in a mental asylum after she tried to kill herself.'

Emma puts a hand to her mouth. 'I'm so sorry. That must have been hard on you too.'

'It was.' Richard looks into the distance for a moment as if lost in a memory. He takes a deep breath and smiles at her.

'Thank you, Emma. You see? I told you it was good to share. I feel better already.' He reaches out and touches her hand. Emma feels a little jolt like an electric shock. Richard moves his hand away. 'Anyway, tell me more about Martin. When are you getting married?'

Emma frowns. 'Next June. Although to be honest I'm not enjoying the planning so far.'

Richard eyes her. 'Interfering mothers, perchance? Occupational hazard I should imagine.'

'Actually it's Martin. He booked the venue without talking to me,' says Emma feeling immediately disloyal for mentioning it.

'Hmm, far be it from me to criticise another man but that sounds a bit unreasonable.'

'Thank you,' says Emma with genuine relief. 'It's nice to talk to someone who doesn't try to excuse him all the time. Sometimes I think I'm a bit of a pushover.'

'I can't imagine that for one moment,' says Richard. 'You strike me as a very strong, in-control woman. If you were my fiancée, frankly I'd let you walk all over me.'

Emma's not sure how but somehow Richard manages to make this sound romantic and sexy all at the same time. She gives a little cough and realises she needs to take control of the situation. 'Right, well I think that's enough social chat. Shall we get back to Stella?'

Richard gives her a devilish grin and a small salute. 'Whatever you say, Emma Darcy. You're the boss.'

Rachel is amazed to find that they are on time for the music group. The crowd of pre-schoolers is only just gathering in the church hall, with its regulation orange plastic chairs and vomit-green curtains. Sue waves wearily as they enter and Rachel has soon dumped their coats and joined her cross-legged on the floor,

'Hello, Susan,' she singsongs in the manner of the music teacher, Sally.

An immaculately dressed mother with a black bob as neat as a topiary hedge looks up, 'Ray-chel! You made it on time! What happened?' Then she sees Lily's outfit and lets out an involuntary, 'Aieee!'

'Yes, "aieee" indeed, Polly. Lily's experimenting with clothes, but at least she's wearing something today,' says Rachel recalling with a shiver the day Lily decided to strip off mid-lesson and the rest of the children copied her. Some of the mothers haven't spoken to her since.

'All right, chick?' she says, nudging Sue.

'Fine, my sweet. Just a bit tired. Joe's been a bit up and down.'

'Goodness me, you do look tired, Susan,' says Polly unhelpfully. 'You should try this ylang-ylang tea I picked up at Fortnum's. My personal trainer swears by it.'

'Ignore her,' whispers Rachel as Sally claps her hands to start the class. 'She's a Stepford wife.'

'Now then, mummies, no talking! It's time for our Hello Sallys!' trills the teacher with a high-pitched edge bordering on hysteria. The class passes with only three major incidents and Rachel is overwhelmed with schadenfreude as they all involve Polly's little boy, Jasper. Following one particularly vicious attack with a rhythm stick on doll-faced Evie and Polly's inability to quash this behaviour with her imploring, 'Come on, my little ray of sunshine, come and sit with Mummee,' Sally has had enough.

'Stop it now, Jasper!' bellows Sally, her usually smiling face now dissolved into that of a baying dog. 'You are being a very naughty boy. Go to Mummy or you will have to sit on Sally's naughty chair!'

Jasper and the other children freeze. The parents look at each other, in awe and moderate terror. Polly looks mortified and opens and shuts her mouth in the manner of a fish out of water. Jasper's lip begins to wobble and soon the rest of his face follows suit. He makes a small squeaking sound, which escalates into a medium-sized cry, then a gigantic wail, at which point he throws himself at his mother and buries his sobbing head in her lap. Some of the smaller children follow his example nestling against their mothers' bosoms.

Alfie snuggles into Rachel's lap while Lily sits defiantly on her own.

'Weaklings!' she mutters, patently disappointed by her peers' lack of character.

'Right,' says Sally, her face as pink as a beetroot. 'Shall we finish with Sleepy Bunnies?'

'I love Sally,' says Lily as they leave the hall and head out into the street. 'That Jasper's a pain in the bum.'

'Thank you, darling,' says Rachel looking over her shoulder and hoping that Polly hasn't heard. 'Fancy a coffee, Suze?'

'I better not. Joe's a bit knackered, so we should probably get home. Just tell me quickly, how was the weekend with Steve?'

Rachel smiles. 'Pretty good, actually. I managed to talk and listen and enjoy some spectacular sex. We're going to go up to Edinburgh in a week or two so we can make a considered decision together.'

Sue laughs. 'Good girl. I'm very glad and seriously jealous. I managed to go two hours without Joe vomiting all over me. But I guess you have to count your blessings and at least he's OK now,' she says, stroking Joe's hair.

'Sorry, Suze,' says Rachel putting an arm round her friend. 'Do you want me to have him for a couple of hours while you go home and have a kip? I'm sure he'll be fine. We can make a bed for him on the sofa if he gets tired.'

'Thanks, darl, but I think I'll take him home, give him some lunch and bung on a DVD.'

'OK but if you change your mind, you know where I am.' She gives Sue a big squeezing hug.

'I'll miss you if you go, Rach,' says Sue, and Rachel suddenly feels a pang. 'But then we'll be up to stay every holiday so you'll soon be sick of the sight of us,' she adds seeing her friend's worried face.

'Well, that's the last time we do Singalong Sally, I think.' Polly breezes through in her purple cape and matching cap. 'Come on, Jasper darling, Mummy take you to the toyshop, buy you that Lego fire station you wanted and then how about Pizza Express for lunch? Susan. Rachel. See you later.'

'Bye Jasper!' calls Alfie sweetly.

Jasper turns around and sticks out his tongue.

'Bugger off you rude, rude boy!' says Lily with venom. 'And don't you ever stick your tongue out at my brother again!'

'Lily!' says Rachel shocked. 'You can't say that to people. It's a bit rude.'

'You say it to Daddy,' declares Lily. 'And anyway, he deserves it.' Rachel can't disagree and leads the children home feeling rather proud of her daughter and a bit sad at the possibility of losing her best friend.

CHAPTER ELEVEN

Emma returns to her desk to find a hillock of post and her answerphone flashing red. 'Talk to me now!' it seems to be saying. She dumps her bag on the floor and spies the manuscript for *The Red Orchid*, its pages curled from being read again and again. She enjoyed her morning with Richard, although she wouldn't say she'd managed to keep control of the situation at all times. Richard was a shameless flirt but he was good company and she told herself that it was important to build good relations with your authors. He had bid her farewell at the Tube station with a kiss on the cheek.

'I enjoyed our first date,' he'd said, smiling mischievously. 'When can we do it again?' Emma had tried to steer him back to business. 'Why don't you crack on with the revisions we discussed and we'll take it from there. You can call me if you need me.'

He had clicked his heels together and saluted. 'I'll be in touch very soon then,' he said with a wolfish grin before disappearing through the ticket barrier.

'How was the dreamboat author?' asks Ella, popping her head over the partition that separated their working areas.

'Ella, you scared me!'

'Sorry. Daydreaming about literature's great new hope, were you?' teases Ella.

'Oh stop it, Ells. I'm practically a married woman.'

'Of course, of course, but you're still allowed at little low-level flirting.'

Emma smiles. 'Well, maybe a little.'

'Ha! I knew it.'

'What? I was an angel and Richard's not that easy to deal with, you know. You're lucky to have straightforward Clive and his historical fiction.'

'Yeah right. Clive stares at my breasts while I'm trying to give him sound editorial advice and, to be honest, I'd rather endure that from a good-looking man than someone who reminds me of my uncle, Dennis.'

'Poor Ella,' says Emma with a little pout.

'I appreciate your sympathy. By the way, Joel popped round. I think he left you a love note.'

Emma snatches up the sticky note attached to her computer screen before scrunching it into a ball and throwing it in the bin. 'Patronising moron. Who does he think he is?'

'Alastair Campbell?'

'With a splash of Genghis Khan. Right, I better go and see him, I guess. Wish me luck.'

'*Bon chance.* I'll come and rescue you if you're not back by home time.'

'Thanks.'

Emma strides along the corridor ready to do battle. Joel's door is slightly ajar and she can hear voices.

'I just can't stand another day sucking up to that buffoon,' she hears Jacqui purr.

'Patience, Jacqueline. It's only a matter of time before the Americans see what a drain on resources he is. I've already been exchanging e-mails with Phil. He's coming over in a few weeks. As soon as he sees Digby for the fool he is, they're bound to be looking around for some strong leaders and they won't have to look far, will they?'

'What about Miranda?'

'Oh, she's an old bag, but she's a useful old bag. I'm sure there'll be room for her in the new regime.'

Jacqui laughs like a pantomime villain. Emma freezes. She can hear movement in the room and in a fight or flight moment, chooses flight. She rounds the corner straight into the not insubstantial bosom of Miranda.

'Ahh Emma, I was just looking for you. Ella said you were on your way to see our little Marketing spin-doctor but you appear to be going the wrong way. Is everything all right?'

Emma is caught off guard. She would like to talk about what she's just heard, but doesn't want to seem as if she's telling tales.

'Er yes fine. Joel was just sort of busy.'

'Yes, he's a busy boy, that one. I need to tell you about some bloody awful course I've got to send you on. Can you spare a moment?'

'Absolutely.'

Once back in her office, Miranda rummages through the myriad of paper that covers her desk.

'Ah yes, here it is: "Communicating with Authors". Hmm. Arse-gravy of the worst kind. In my day we just slept with the good-looking ones and got the ugly ones drunk, but these days it's all about psyches and egos and analysing each other until we disappear up our own backsides trying to find whatever it was we'd forgotten we had. Ho-hum. However, it will be a good opportunity to network as they like to call it and find out what the enemy is up to. It's at a swanky little hotel just off Sloane Street, so you can go and lust after some shoes at lunchtime. OK?'

'I will suspend judgement and look forward to the shoe-shopping.'

'Good woman. So is everything all right with you and Mr Riches?'

'Fine, fine, why?' says Emma with a little too much enthusiasm.

'Look, Emma, I know he's a bit cocksure but to be honest, we're under a bit of pressure. The Americans are on our backs a little, so we need to make sure we all pull together, OK?'

'Of course, but we're doing all right, aren't we?'

'Yes, yes, but you know how things are changing in this industry. Blink and you've missed another retailer going down the Swannee. We need to make sure we're all on top form. We have to rise above it sometimes, don't we?'

Emma isn't sure if she's being advised or scolded. She nods and takes her leave. Joel is waiting at her desk.

'Ah, Emma. We need to talk. Have you got five minutes?'

'Yes, Joel, what is it?'

'It's about this new campaign for Tim Deakin. I think we should drop the above the line stuff and go with a viral approach. Thoughts?'

'Fine. You're probably right.'

'Sorry?' Joel looks stunned and slightly disappointed.

'I said, I think you're right. It's your budget and you're in charge of Marketing so I will go with your call and thanks for checking with me.'

'Oh, right, OK. Is that it?'

'That's it. Sorry, lots to do. Was there anything else?'

'Er, no. Thanks, Emma.' Joel strides off.

Ella appears by Emma's side. 'Did that just happen?'

'What?'

'Did you just agree with Joel Riches?'

'I did. Do you think it's the beginning of the end?'

'Well, I am a little concerned, but let's just dismiss it as a one-off, shall we?'

Emma laughs it off but feels strangely unsettled. She spends the afternoon editing, grateful for a distraction from real life, and trying to dismiss thoughts of Richard Bennett from her mind.

Rachel looks at her watch: 4:28. Still two hours until Steve is due home and at least an hour until she can legitimately open a bottle of wine without feeling guilty. Will is having tea at a friend's house, and Lily and Alfie have coerced their mother into a long and intricate game of Doctors and Nurses.

'You are very sick,' announces Lily. 'We will have to operate. Nurse Alfred!'

Alfie appears looking pleased to be included.

'Prepare the gas mask for the patient!'

Alfie finds a fireman's helmet and passes it to Lily who applies it to her mother's face with some force.

'Now count to ten, patient.'

Rachel does as she's told, relishing the chance to close her eyes as her torturers empty out their doctor's kit and set about cutting her open and removing the foreign object.

'Aha!' announces Lily. 'You have been eating Lego again, you naughty lady. You will have to go to prison.'

'For swallowing Lego?' asks Rachel.

'Yes. It is against the rules.'

'Sounds a bit harsh.'

'And you have to stop talking. PC Alfred, fetch the handcuffs!'

Alfie obeys and soon Rachel is shackled by her ankles because, according to Lily 'your wrists are too fat'.

'Right, Mummy's had enough of this game and needs a cup of tea. Can you bring me the keys please?'

Lily looks disappointed, but knows better than to cross her mother when she needs a hot drink. 'Aww, OK. Alf, where are the keys?'

Alfie, in true foppish sidekick fashion looks blank. 'I thought you had them, Lils?'

'No, you did!'

'You did!'

'OK, both of you stop! Now let's just stay calm and think. Where did you last have them?' says Rachel realising how ridiculous this phrase sounds and trying to mask her growing panic.

Lily looks worried. 'I don't know.'

'Oh for goodness sake!'

Alfie, always thrown by conflict, starts to cry.

'Oh for goodness sake, Alfred!' chastise Rachel and Lily together, just as the doorbell rings.

There are times in Rachel's existence when she can't quite believe what has happened. Ten years ago she was sashaying her way through life with a brilliant job, nights out, dinners at Nobu, lots of sex and the overarching feeling that she was a strong, confident woman in control and at the top of her game. Now, she is never very far away from chaos and frustration and the compelling urge to shout 'Oh for fuck's sake!' This is one of those moments.

'Who is it?' she asks pogo-ing towards the living room door, buying herself some time, and hoping it's the postman so she can open the door without revealing her shackles.

'It's Tom! Sorry, is this a bad time?'

Rachel stops and considers. She's not sure if she really wants Tom to see her like this but on the other hand, she is a take as you find sort of girl so, in for a penny. She opens the door with the words 'Please don't ask but please come in,' and hops back down the hall.

'Oh,' is all Tom wisely opts to say as he follows her into the kitchen. 'Shall I make us some tea? I've brought you some biscuits by way of a thank you for rescuing me the other day.'

'You are very kind, and in answer to the tea, yes please.'

'Do you want me to see if I've got a hacksaw?'

'Again, that would be lovely, but let's have a cup of tea first, shall we? Anyway, how come you're home so early? In fact, I don't think you've ever told me what you do.'

'Ahh well I'm actually a trained assassin so I only work at night.'

'Oh really. I don't think snails count as targets,' jokes Rachel. 'But seriously, what do you do?'

'I'm a business analyst mainly covering Asia, so I get to start very early but knock off at 3.30. It's lovely really because I never miss *The One Show*.'

'Gosh Tom, your life sounds almost as exciting as mine!'

Tom laughs and Rachel wonders at how at ease she feels with this man. He reminds her of Steve in the early days with his easy banter and ability to make each other laugh with just a remark. She is just contemplating opening a bottle of wine when the doorbell rings again.

'Oh drat!'

'Never fear, shackled maiden. I'll get it.'

'Thank you.'

He returns moments later flanked by Rory the bodyguard, Christa and Roger.

'Rachel, so sorry to drop in without the announcement, but we were just driving past and Roger was very keen to see Alfie and Lily. I hope you don't mind.'

Rachel does mind a little but is far too British to admit it, and soon they are all sitting around the kitchen table. Rachel and Christa are drinking wine, Tom is on coffee and Rory has opted for green tea. Rachel smiles to herself as Tom nervously tries to interact with the burly Russian minder.

'*Zo*,' says Christa, 'you were not telling me that you had such a handsome man living in the next door.' Tom blushes and Rachel feels oddly irritated by her flirting.

'No, well, we've had him locked in the cellar for six months. We only bring him out for special occasions,' jokes Rachel.

Christa looks perplexed and then sees Rachel's face. 'Ah yes, I see, this is one of your jokes, isn't it, Rachel? Ha, ha, *sehr gut*. Rachel is teaching me how to be funny, Tomas. You see even though I am Swiss, I am still German so I do not have the sense of humour. In fact, do you know, we don't really have a word for it. Funny eh?'

'More wine, Christa?' ask Rachel.

'*Ja*, why *nicht*? I have my driver here and we Muttis deserve a little treat, *nicht wahr*?'

Rachel has forgotten about her compromised ankles and her attempt to move is followed by her falling flat on her face. 'Shit! These bloody handcuffs!'

'Ah, *mein Gott*, what has happened to you? Oh I'm so sorry, were we interrupting you and Tom?'

'Oh Christa, don't be ridiculous! It was the children,' laughs Rachel feeling bizarrely pleased by the insinuation.

'*Natürlich, natürlich*. Sorry, Rachel. I must stop thinking that just because Rudi is having an affair, that everyone is. I might be able to help.'

'With what?'

'With those handcuffs. I have many sets of keys.' She reaches into her bag and pulls out a key ring adorned with about twenty of what can only be handcuff keys. She crouches down and looks at the handcuffs, sorts through her selection methodically and within minutes, has released Rachel.

'Thank you.'

'You are *sehr* welcome. I always carry these. Rudi and I are always getting into situations like this so it is *gut* to have them to hand, you know?'

'Erm, I'm sure,' agrees Rachel. She notices that Tom is watching Christa open-mouthed.

'Well, we better go. Roger! *Heim jetzt, mein Schatz!* Thanks for the wine and so *schön* to meet you, Tomas.'

When they are gone, Rachel and Tom burst into helpless laughter.

'Is she for real?' asks Tom.

'I know, she's brilliant, isn't she? But actually, I do feel a bit sorry for her with her husband and being in a strange country. It must be hard.'

'Hmm. Anyway, I'm sure you've got to sort the kids. I better be off too.'

'Oh, OK, of course,' says Rachel feeling a little disappointed.

'Thanks for the tea and remember to let me know if you ever need a babysitter.'

'You might regret that but thank you.'

When Tom is gone, Rachel pours another glass of wine. She looks at the handcuffs on the table and laughs to herself. Her phone rings and she sees that it's Steve.

'Hi love,' she says, making her way over to the fridge ready to select something imaginative for tea.

'Rach, hi. Listen, I'm really sorry but I'm going to be a bit late home tonight.'

'Again?'

'Yeah, sorry, love. There's lots going on with the plans for the new office. I shouldn't be too late but I won't be back in time to help with the kids. Sorry.'

Rachel sighs but doesn't want a fight tonight. 'OK, well I guess I'll see you later,' says Rachel, reaching into the freezer for the fish fingers and chips.

'OK, thanks, Rach. Give the kids a kiss from me.' Steve presses the end call button and throws his phone onto the desk. He starts to gather up his papers and carries his dirty mug to the kitchen. A woman with short hair and pretty elfin features is already there doing some washing-up.

'Hey, Sam, are you nearly ready to leave?' he asks.

'Yep, just give me two minutes to log off. Where do you want to go?'

'Fox and Hound?'

'Perfect. I'll get my stuff,' she says with a smile.

Emma opens her front door, her mind fixed solely on a hot bath and a large gin and tonic. The flat is still in darkness, which strikes her as odd, and it feels cold, which strikes her as irritating. She switches on the lights and stalks into the kitchen and is mortified to find no welcoming orange glow on the boiler controls and no flicker of life as she randomly presses all the buttons and taps at its dials.

'Bollocks! What's wrong with this bloody thing?'

She stomps around the kitchen swearing, her mind racing at the thought of no bath and the cost of a plumber. She is cross because Martin isn't home and surely men are supposed to be the ones to discover and solve these things. Then she feels stupid for being helpless. She rummages through the miscellaneous items drawer containing takeaway menus, keys, a gigantic ball of red elastic bands which Martin inexplicably decided to construct one day from all those that the postman had dropped outside their front door, and instruction manuals for everything she has acquired since 1997. Eventually she pulls out a discoloured, dusty booklet that promises to hold all the secrets of their boiler. After seven minutes of scanning pages detailing installation, commissioning and routine maintenance, Emma finds the fault-finding flow chart and a further four minutes' examination leads her to the conclusion that she needs either a degree in engineering or a plumber.

'He-llo? Shit, it's cold in here!' calls Martin from the hall.

'In here and the bloody boiler's not working!'

'Oh no! Hang on, I'll come and have a look.'

Another quarter of an hour's tinkering by Martin and he's on the phone to Charlie for the number of a 'bloke he knows'. Emma has hauled the old heater down from the spare bedroom and made hot water bottles for them both. Martin comes in bearing a gin and tonic for Emma and a beer for him.

'Oh you lovely man,' she says kissing him. They climb under the duvet and nestle alongside each other.

'This is cosy,' says Martin, putting an arm round her. 'How was your day?'

'Oh the usual, you know.' She's not quite sure why but she decides against mentioning Richard. It's just work and, after all, Martin doesn't tell her about the details of his IT world, thank God. 'Although there's something fishy going on with Joel.' Martin looks blank. 'You know, Joel, the tosser, who's always trying to undermine me.' Martin nods vaguely. 'Well, I think he's plotting to overthrow Digby.'

Martin snorts. 'Plotting to overthrow him? You make it sound like something from one of your books.'

'Shut up!' says Emma hitting him. She doesn't like the way he says 'one of your books' as if it's not important. 'It's serious.'

'Sorry,' says Martin stifling a laugh.

Emma is irritated and decides to change the subject. 'By the way, have you had a look at those photography brochures?' Again Martin looks blank. 'Martin! I left them out for you.' She rummages on the coffee table. 'Here,' she says handing him a sheaf of leaflets. Martin looks sheepish and Emma is angry now. 'Oh come on, Martin, you promised and we need to get on and book these things,' she cries.

'All right, all right, don't get grumpy. I'll do it now.' He sifts through the leaflets. 'Hmm, I'm not sure. What do you think?' he asks looking helpless.

'Right, fine, I'll do it, shall I? I mean it's not enough that I have to work, clean the house and sort the wedding. Is there any chance you could pull your weight?'

Martin looks cross now. 'That's not fair. I booked the venue.'

'Without asking me.'

'Oh not that again. I thought that was all sorted.'

'Oh you did, did you?'

'Yes I did. I mean you agreed with me in the end, didn't you? And to be honest, having been given such a hard time over the venue, I'm terrified to make any other decisions without consulting you, your mother, Rachel and Lily.'

'Now you're being ridiculous.'

'Oh I'm being ridiculous?'

Emma leaps to her feet, grabbing the duvet from him and struggling towards the door. 'Well, I am going to bed!' she declares. 'Goodnight!' She leaves him sitting on the sofa without a backward glance. Once in bed she pulls the duvet over her head in an attempt to get warm. She is still fuming and can hear her heart beating in her ears. She listens to the muffled rise and fall of voices on the television and is cross that Martin's not coming to try and resolve the argument. 'Never let the sun set on your anger,' her father would say. She finds this impossible. She and Martin are far too stubborn to apologise when they're angry. Besides, it was Martin who didn't do what he was asked and it isn't fair to expect her to do everything. She wonders at what married life must be like if the wedding preparations are this stressful. She rolls over in bed. She is hot and uncomfortable but doesn't want to move. She hears the television go off and the sound of Martin climbing the stairs. He opens the bedroom door and she can tell he is peering over at her but she pretends to be asleep.

'Em? Are you awake?' he whispers. She snuffles in a fake snore and she hears him undress and get into bed beside her. She lies awake, still angry and it is long after Martin starts to breathe in a steady sleeping rhythm that she falls into an uneasy and restless sleep.

Rachel wakes as she hears Steve's key in the door and looks over at the television, where a weatherman is forecasting rain for the morning. She glances at the empty wine glass and almost empty bottle next to it. Her head feels fuzzy and she dearly wishes she'd gone to bed an hour ago.

'Hey gorgeous,' says Steve, sticking his head round the living room door. 'Sorry I'm late.'

He embraces her and she feels his cold, bristly face against hers and smells mint on his breath. She wants them to stay like this for a while in the quiet warm of their home.

'Hey you. You're a bit later than I thought. Have you eaten?'

Steve nods, plonking himself down on the sofa and putting an arm round Rachel. 'We ordered in pizza.'

Rachel looks at her husband's weary face. She hasn't got the energy for a discussion about the move now and she can see he's tired too. She rests against his shoulder. 'Tough day?'

'Oh you know, the usual. But I do have some news. How would you like a trip to Scotland this weekend?'

'Really? So soon?' says Rachel panicking inwardly. She'd thought she'd have a bit more time to get used to the idea and maybe even get Steve to see what they'd be leaving behind. She'd been feeling flat ever since seeing Sue and realising how much she'll miss her friend if they go.

'Well, there's no time like the present. So I've booked flights and a swanky hotel near to the Royal Mile. Oh and I've also booked us in with a couple of estate agents just to get the feel for the place.'

'Oh. Right.'

'Rach? You don't sound that happy. I thought you'd be pleased?'

'I am, of course, it sounds great,' lies Rachel.

'Great,' smiles Steve. He leans over to kiss her and behind the taste of mint, Rachel can detect something alcoholic.

'Have you been drinking?' she asks.

'Oh we just had a beer with the pizzas at the office,' says Steve. 'Why? Don't you trust me?'

I always thought I did, thinks Rachel. 'Of course. I'm going to bed,' she says, pecking him on the cheek.

'OK, love. Just going to check the football scores and then I'll be up. Love you, Rach.'

'Love you too,' says Rachel. She plods up the stairs feeling exhausted and unable to shake off a growing sense of unease.

CHAPTER TWELVE

Emma wakes from a disturbing dream involving Miranda and Digby dressed as chickens and trapped in a cage with Joel and Jacqui as their captors. She opens her eyes wide, feeling the reality of her bedroom return to her.

'Go to sleep, bloody brain!' she mutters.

Her mobile starts to ring. She flicks the button. Rosie doesn't even wait for a greeting.

'Emma darling. Guess what Auntie Rosie's got planned for you today?'

'Good morning, Rosie. I've no idea.'

'A fitting with Stella. At eleven. I know!'

'Today? But I've got to go to work.'

'Not today, my dear. It's all squared with Mimms. I'll pick you up in the car at ten. Wear something glamorous but understated, OK?'

'But – '

'No need to thank me, darling. It is my pleasure. See you later!'

Emma shakes her head and throws her phone to one side. Martin appears at the door looking nervous. 'Morning. Friends?' he asks sheepishly.

Emma looks at his pleading face and doesn't have the energy to be cross any more. 'Look Mart, I'm sorry for storming off last night, but can you promise me something?'

'Anything.'

'We sort the wedding out together as a couple. If we're falling out before we're even married, it doesn't exactly bode well, does it?'

Martin wraps her in his arms. 'Agreed and I've left the brochure for the photographer I like downstairs on the table. Sorry for being a bit crap – I hate it when we argue. Look, I've got to dash. Aren't you going to be late?'

'No, Rosie is in charge today.' Martin looks blank. 'Don't worry, I'll call you later. Have a good day,' she says kissing him.

When he's gone, she flicks through the contacts on her mobile and finds her sister's number.

'Morning, Auntie Emma,' says Rachel.

'Hello, big sister. Listen I was just wondering if – '

'I'd had the morning call from Rosie? Oh yes and I've also had the explosive "that bloody woman" call from Mum too. Deep joy. We're going to meet you there. I've got to drop Lily and Alfie off with Dad first.'

'Okey dokey. That's good. I just wanted to check you were going to be there.'

'Never fear. Rosie's got some gall, but I don't think even she would leave Mum and me out. Anyway, baby sister, I wouldn't miss the sight of you in your pants next to a woman with some very sharp pins for the world.'

'Yeah well, don't forget you're the matron of honour so the pin lady's coming for you too.'

***

Emma looks around the room and feels her skin prickle with anxiety. She wishes Rachel was here to let rip with a few expletives just to pollute the very pure cool air. She also wishes that her mother was here just because your mother is supposed to be with you for these sorts of things, rather than your overbearing godmother. She looks at her watch, which tells her that her female relatives are over an hour late. She has already met Stella, who was friendly, but clearly very busy. Despite Rosie's embarrassing protestations, she was polite as she handed them over to Dietrich, 'my right-hand man who will create you something wonderful'. Dietrich had then gently cajoled Emma into admitting that she hates frills, but loves beads and dashed off a couple of designs which would make most women weep with joy. She and Rosie are now waiting for him to return with copies for her to take away. Rosie is glued to her iPhone, while Emma is trying to look elegant in her best Zara and H&M combo.

'Lovely to meet you,' says Stella on her way past. 'Gorgeous blouse by the way.'

'Oh, thanks,' stammers Emma, 'it's – '

'Gucci, isn't it, darling?' booms Rosie. 'Thanks again, Stella. Give my love to your dad. *Ciao*, *ciao*!'

Stella is on her way out of the door as Rachel and Diana bustle in. They both stop and stare, as is often the way when you come across a famous person, and for some reason, Diana bobs into a curtsey. Stella smiles graciously. 'Good luck with the wedding, Emma,' she says with a smile.

'Mum! Rachel! Where have you been, and, Mother, did you really just curtsey to Stella McCartney?'

Emma's mother blushes. 'Don't be silly, dear! I was just letting her through. Sorry we're late. Alfie didn't want Rachel to go so we missed the first train and the second one was cancelled. Are we too late?'

'Much too late,' says Rosie with a thin smile. 'You can't keep people like Stella waiting, but don't worry, Diana, I've got everything under control.'

Diana strains with civility. 'Well it's very kind of you, Rosie.'

'Not at all. What are fairy godmothers for? And to be honest, if we'd left it to you, Diana, it would have been some ghastly off the peg from Berketex Brides, eh?'

Diana looks murderous and Rosie nudges her. 'That was a joke, Diana. Oh come on, lighten up. Let's go for lunch somewhere hideously expensive. My treat!'

She looks unsure until Rachel whispers, 'Come on, Mum. Might as well fleece the old trout.'

Diana squeezes her eldest daughter's hand. 'Thank you, Rosie. That would be lovely.'

'Excellent! Emma darling, bring those copy designs, will you? Rachel, you're going to love what Dietrich is planning for the matron of honour and he's going to do a darling little version for Lily. This is going to be the wedding of the year!'

Richard stares at the screen of his laptop, inwardly cursing rewrites.

'But I've already bloody done it!' he whinged to Emma at their Kew meeting. 'And I liked it that way, otherwise I wouldn't have written it.'

Emma had been unsympathetic and almost schoolmarmish in her response. Richard had found her forthright, gently bossy nature rather alluring. In fact, she was part of the reason he couldn't buckle down today. There was something about this woman, something he couldn't shake from his brain. In the past, he'd slept his way through whole editorial departments without even having to buy them a drink, but this one was different. He hated that phrase and hated admitting it, but she was. It wasn't that he wanted to sleep with her, although of course that would be nice. This one was tricky.

He smacks his forehead and stretches back his shoulders, glancing at the now cold mug of tea, grateful for a legitimate distraction. Filling the kettle, he looks at the concrete view from his kitchen window. He shivers and flicks on the boiler, finding the biscuit tin. He tries a custard cream and spits it out, disappointed at its staleness. All the time, his brain is musing about Emma Darcy. Maybe that's it – maybe she would become his muse. She certainly understood his writing and there weren't many people he trusted with that.

Richard carries his tea back to the desk, his heart heavy with the burden of work. He glances at his phone and is delighted to see that someone has left him a message. Playing it back, he screws his face against the cheery, trying-too-hard tone.

'Hey Richard, it's just Sophie. I was wondering what you thought about that flat I showed you and also wondering if you would like me to show you any more, if you know what I mean? Ha ha ha. Well, give me a call. Anytime!'

Richard casts the phone aside disappointed. He doesn't want anything else to do with this woman, but he did like the flat. He starts to reread his last paragraph and realises that he's used the word 'passionate' five times in twenty-five lines. He sits back, despondent, and takes a sip of tea. His mind racing, he grabs his phone and finds Emma's number. Her voice sounds distant and there is the noise of restaurant chatter in the background.

'Hello?'

'Emma? It's Richard.'

'Oh Richard, hi. How are you?'

'Fine, fine. Well actually, I'm bloody awful. It's this sodding rewrite.'

'Yep, OK, understood. Listen, the only problem is I'm not working today.'

'Oh. Oh, OK. Well, not to worry.'

'No listen, we can meet tomorrow. Why don't you come to the offices around ten?'

Richard smiles. 'That would be fantastic. What would I do without you, Emma Darcy?'

He ends the call feeling like a man with what his mother calls 'a pencil full of lead'. He scrolls through his missed calls and dials again. The voice that answers is breathy and intense.

'Oh Richard, hi! I thought you were avoiding me!'

'Now Sophie, why would I do that?' purrs Richard. 'I've just been stupidly busy, but it turns out that I have a free afternoon to play with and I was very keen to take you up on your offer.'

Sophie laughs flirtatiously. 'Well, that sounds fine. I have some very beautiful Mayfair apartments I could show you. Very desirable with many outstanding features.'

'Sounds wonderful, I can't wait to see the bedrooms and then maybe the bathroom, kitchen and living room, if you have the stamina. You certainly did last time.'

'I'll do my best, Mr Bennett.'

'That's wonderful. And Sophie?'

'Yes, Mr Bennett?'

'I hope you're wearing those stockings again.'

Emma returns to the table to find her mother in tight-lipped silence and Rosie regaling them with another showbiz story. Rachel is looking desperate and hisses, 'Where have you been? It's like Rumble in the bleedin' Jungle with these two!'

'Sorry, sorry. I just had to take a call from that new author, you know.'

'Oh, you mean the one you fancy?'

'What do you mean? I do not!' snaps Emma adopting the tone of her teenage self.

Rachel laughs. 'Methinks my little sister doth protest too much!'

'Oh bog off.'

'All right small-fry, lighten up. You are allowed to flirt with other men, you know.'

Emma is keen to change the subject, but unfortunately Rosie has now picked up the thread.

'Ah! Are we discussing this scrumptious new author of yours, Emma?'

Rachel raises her eyebrows at Emma.

'So we are. Well, there's no harm in having fun before you have to start wearing the old ball and chain, eh?' says Rosie, waggling her ring finger at them all.

'Well frankly, I don't think that's appropriate,' says Diana, the colour rising around her throat.

Rosie feigns a yawn.

'Am I boring you, Rosie?' says Diana.

'Only moderately. Oh come on, Diana, you've never exactly been one to live a little, have you? I bet Teddy was the first man you slept with,' says Rosie, her voice loud enough for a few diners to look their way.

Diana looks uncomfortable. 'That is none of your bloody business!'

Rosie is merciless. 'Ha! So it is true. Well, I've got to hand it to you. If you've got to pick a man to give your cherry to, there are few better than darling Teddy.'

Emma and Rachel are mortified, as if they've actually walked in on their parents having sex. Rachel spots the maître d' talking to some diners on an adjacent table. It is moments before he appears and suggests to Rosie that perhaps it would be a good time to adjourn for coffee. Rosie staggers to her feet.

'No one,' she snarls, 'ever tells me what to do! We are leaving.' She totters towards the door but loses her footing after three paces. Waiters rush forward to help her and she turns on them. 'Don't you touch me!' she roars. 'I know AA Gill! This place is finished!'

Rachel, Emma and her mother watch as she stalks onto the street and hails a cab. The maître d' appears and Diana composes herself.

'I think we'll take our coffee now. Thank you.' He gives a little bow and ushers them into the lounge, which is filled with stiff leather armchairs and old men dozing over tumblers of brandy. They sip their coffee and Rachel suddenly looks alarmed.

'Oh shit. She's flounced off without paying!'

Diana looks a little smug and pats her daughter's arm. 'I think she gave them her card when she came in.'

Rachel looks relieved and then a wicked smile spreads over her face.

'Oh no Rachel – don't,' warns Emma.

Rachel ignores her and catches the waiter's eye. 'Excuse me, do you have any Dom Pérignon, please? 1974 or earlier would be wonderful.'

The waiter nods. Emma is still staring at Rachel, who slumps back into her armchair and grins at her sister.

'What? You're getting married. It's a celebration! Let the witch pay.'

Edward's relief is palpable as the doorbell rings. He adores his grandchildren but he does sometimes feel that he's lacking a vital negotiation skills qualification in order to deal with their needs.

When Will was dropped off after school by one of Rachel's friends, he informed Edward that he always had biscuits and crisps for a snack: 'Sometimes two packets.' Lily had backed him up. 'Mummy always gives Alfie and me the same too. Otherwise it isn't fair, Grandpa.' Edward had looked to Alfie for help but a sharp elbow from his sister and he took the cowardly route. He had looked at his grandfather with his big, cow-eyes and nodded in fearful agreement. Edward had decided that he was allowed to indulge them, indeed it was probably his job. Snack-time had gone well but adhering Rachel's rule of 'no TV before 5 p.m.' was proving trickier. Edward had decided to organise a spot of Lego building, but Lily had declared this to be 'boring boys' stuff' and skipped off to find Chairman, Diana and Edward's bad-tempered ginger tom with Alfie trailing after her. Will and Edward had spent a happy half hour building a storm trooper fort, but Will did ask a lot of questions and many of them Edward simply did not have answers to.

'Grandpa?'

'Yes, Will?'

'Why do people wear pants during the day but not at night?'

'Erm.'

'Jon-Joe Minto says it's because you don't poo at night.'

'Well, I'm not sure.'

'I don't think that sounds quite right.'

'No, perhaps not.'

'Because it's not as if you use your pants to catch the poo, is it?'

'Er, no.'

'Grandpa?'

'Yes, Will?'

'You know Father Christmas?'

'I do.'

'How does he see you all the time? I mean ALL the time?'

'Well, he has a whole army of elves and they go out into the world and keep an eye on all the children.'

'Elves?'

'That's right.'

'Where are they?'

'Everywhere. They look like normal people but actually they are Santa's elves.' Edward is getting into his stride now.

'So they stand around, watching the children?'

'They do.'

'Like paedophiles?'

'Pardon?'

'Paedophiles. They stand around and watch children, don't they? Jon-Joe Minto's dad says that paedophiles should be strung up.'

Edward is defeated.

'Grandpa, what does "strung up" mean?'

'I think I'll just go and see how Lily and Alfie are getting on and then maybe we can talk about football when I come back, eh?'

'OK, can you explain the offside rule again, please Grandpa?'

Edward feels safe again. 'With pleasure.'

He opens the front door full of hope and is not disappointed to find Martin standing there grinning.

'Hello, Edward. Emma said that you were home alone with the small people so I knocked off a bit early and thought I would offer some moral support. Beer?'

'With that kind of offer, you are destined to become my favourite son-in-law. We better tell Steve to up his game.'

Martin follows Edward into the kitchen.

'Hey, Willster, how's it going?'

Before Will can answer, Chairman the cat races from the direction of the stairs on huge thumping paws and darts through the cat flap.

'Come back, silly cat. You have to wear your special hat!' shouts Lily as she and Alfie pound down the stairs after him. They spot the visitor and immediately forget the cat.

'Uncle Fartin!' shrieks Lily.

'Uncle Fartin? How dare you!' says Martin, pretending to be cross. 'Now you must be Lily with a willy and Alfie smelly-pants. And is this your brother Will Wee-Brain?'

Impressed by his anarchic humour, the children shriek with glee. Edward pats Martin on the back. 'I'll get you a beer.'

Rachel teeters along a narrow wall singing the theme from *Fame* before doing an impressive star-jump. This is met by a curtain-twitch from the wall's owner, a guffaw from her sister and a loud tut from her mother.

'Honestly, Rachel, I do have to live round here, you know.'

'Sorry, Mummy,' says Rachel wrapping an arm around her mother.

As they reach Edward and Diana's house a voice says, 'Good evening, ladies.' They turn to see Steve's smiling face. 'Did you have a good day?'

Emma plants a smacker on his cheek. 'We certainly did, favourite brother-in-law.'

'Emma, you are clearly very drunk. I am your only brother-in-law.'

'Ah yes, but you're still my favourite.'

'Well then, it sounds as if we're having a party. Let's get this open,' he says holding up a bottle of champagne.

'Oooh, lovely,' says Emma grabbing the bottle and almost falling over.

'Honestly, how on earth have I managed to produce two girls so prodigiously unable to hold their drink?' says Diana, opening the front door and falling over the mat.

'You were saying, Mother?' says Rachel helping her up.

'I was tripped. I'm always telling your father about that silly doormat.'

The door to the lounge is closed. Rachel opens it and they are immediately blasted by the sound of two grown men and three small people shouting.

'Goaaaaaaaaaaaaaaaaaaaaaaaaaaaaaaaaaaaaaaaaaaaaaal!'

Lily then begins her victory dance jabbing her finger at the TV. 'You're not singing, you're not singing, you're not singing any more!'

Rachel closes the door again. 'I need a drink. Let's open that champagne.'

As she follows Emma and Diana to the kitchen, Steve catches hold of her hand.

'Rach?'

She turns to face him. He pulls her towards him and kisses her. His lips are warm and she leans into him feeling happy in her drunken bubble.

'What was that for?' she says with a smile.

'Do I need a reason to kiss my wife? I just love you, Rach, and I know everything's going to be OK.'

Rachel hugs him, hoping with all her heart that he's right.

'Oi, you two. Get a room!' says Emma, handing them glasses of champagne on her way to the lounge.

Rachel takes her glass and follows her. Will and Martin are arguing with the television over a penalty decision and Edward is nestled on the sofa, his arms round Lily and Alfie. Rachel looks at them and wishes you could freeze moments like this when no one is fighting and everyone is happy.

She picks up a sleepy Alfie and settles down next to Edward, replacing his arm around her shoulder and snuggling into him as she used to when she was a little girl.

'She's just like you, you know,' says Edward, gesturing at Lily.

'I know.'

They sit like this for a while, and suddenly Rachel can feel tears dripping onto her jumper and realises that she is crying. Her father says nothing but pulls her in a little closer.

'He really needs to substitute number seven, don't you think, Rach?' he says.

CHAPTER THIRTEEN

'Good morning, Ella,' says Emma sweeping into the office.

'Someone's bright and breezy this morning.'

'Oh you know, engaged to be married, very promising career, morning meeting with a dishy author. I love my job!'

'Another meeting?'

'Yes, another meeting. I like to give my authors the very best care.'

'Hmm, sounds like it. Got time for lunch? It would be good to catch up.'

'Sorry, I don't think I'll be finished in time.'

'Oh, OK.'

Emma looks at her friend. There's something different about her but she's not sure what. 'Is everything OK, Ells?'

'Yeah, fine, it's just – '

'Ah Emma, you are here. Could we have a quick catch-up?' Joel appears alongside Emma's desk.

Emma jumps. 'Joel, can you stop creeping up on me like that? As for a catch-up, I've got a meeting with Richard Bennett in half an hour, so it will have to wait,' she says firmly.

'Ah, Mr Unmarketable.' Joel chuckles to himself. 'That is a shame. We'll just have to make the key decisions without you.'

'Sorry?'

'The decisions? About our ongoing publishing strategy? Didn't you see Digby's e-mail? Oh dear. Maybe you weren't copied in. How awkward. I probably shouldn't have mentioned it. I expect Miranda will fill you in on the details once it's all decided.' The corners of his mouth turn up into an almost-smile and he strides off.

'Did you hear that?' declares Emma angrily, turning to find that Ella has gone and Richard Bennett is standing alongside Lauren the receptionist.

'Oh Richard, hi!' she says trying to regain her cool.

Richard smiles and then turns to Lauren. 'Thank you so much, Lauren. It was lovely to meet you. I have no doubt we'll see each other again.' Lauren giggles and gives Emma an envious look before disappearing back to her desk.

'Goodness, you certainly worked a charm offensive there,' says Emma. 'She usually just barks at anyone who dares to visit or phone.'

'Oh you know me, Emma, I'm just good at putting people at ease. I can't help the fact that they all fall hopelessly in love with me on sight. It's a gift I suppose.'

Emma laughs. 'Well the female race is eternally grateful. I just need to grab a few bits and then we can go and find a meeting room. Would you like a drink?'

'Actually, I took the liberty,' he says holding up a paper bag. 'I guessed skinny latte and banana and bran muffin?'

Emma is impressed. 'That's very thoughtful and also very perceptive.'

'Like I say, it's a gift. So,' says Richard looking around Emma's excuse of an office. 'This is where the magic happens eh?'

'You make it sound like Disneyland!'

'Ha, well I mean it in nicest possible way. Ah and this must be the lucky man,' says Richard plucking a holiday snap of Emma and Martin from the wall.

'Thank you,' says Emma grabbing it back. 'Right, ready and able. Follow me.'

They walk down the corridor to the vast conference room furnished with a long black table and impressive views of London.

'Right, you sit at one end and I'll sit at the other,' jokes Richard.

Emma smiles and takes a seat. Richard peels off his jacket and sits next to her. He puts on his glasses and pulls a notebook from his bag before taking a sip of his coffee. He sits up and looks at her with eyebrows raised. He knows how good-looking he is and is clearly taking every opportunity to show her. She takes a deep breath and clears her throat.

'Right, down to business. How are you getting on?'

'Honestly?'

'It's the only way.'

'Bloody awful.'

'OK, well, how do you usually deal with this sort of thing?'

'Drink. Heavily.'

'Hmm, well, it worked for Hemingway.'

'Please. I have a rule. Do not mention that man's name in my presence.'

'Sorry. Aren't you a fan?'

'Fan? It was that man who made me become a writer, but I cannot bring myself to read him again.'

'Why?'

Richard looks around him as if the walls have ears and whispers, 'Because I'll never be that good.'

'OK, well let's not worry too much about alcoholic geniuses. Let's talk about that scene with Stella and Alexander. I presume that's the one that's bugging you?'

'Telepathic and beautiful. What a combination,' says Richard taking a bite of muffin.

Emma ignores the comment, but there's a feeling in the pit of her stomach similar to how she felt when forced to have swimming lessons as a child. 'Just jump in, for goodness sake, Emma!' her mother had said, exasperated. Emma had jumped and then for a while everything had seemed dreamlike, before a couple of strong arms had arrived to rescue her.

'OK, so Stella. How do you think she is feeling?'

Richard screws up his face and shakes his head. 'You realise you're asking me the impossible question, don't you?'

Emma smiles. 'Of course. The Pandora's box for male authors and men everywhere. What women think.'

'Precisely. Which is why you have to help me, Emma. How do you think she's feeling? I mean, she's in a bit of a quandary, isn't she? She's betrothed to Newton but then Alexander has a bit more about him. Quite an interesting choice, wouldn't you say?'

Richard has pulled his chair up close to Emma's and she can feel his breath against her cheek. She doesn't want to look him in the face. The whole room is starting to swim. She gives herself a mental slap around the cheek, shifts in her seat and takes a drink of her coffee.

'Right. Stella is in love with Newton, or so she would have us believe. Alexander is his brother and best friend and has fallen in love with Stella. Both men are going to South America to search for the world's rarest orchid and both are driven by feelings for Stella. Alexander comes to see Stella before they go to tell her how he really feels and how does she react? This is a key moment in the narrative but I think you give too much away. We need to keep up the mystery and keep the reader guessing.' Emma emphasises her words here and steals a look at Richard. He is smiling at her with a look of interest but Emma sees something else. It's as if he's enjoying being entertained, playing the game.

Emma turns to face him. 'I think she turns him down.'

Richard looks surprised, the wind knocked out of his sails. 'Really?'

'Really. She wants to keep up the pretence of loving Newton so pretends to be horrified and sends him away with a flea in his ear.'

'But what if she can't resist him?'

'Oh please. This isn't a bodice-ripper. She's got her own agenda. She doesn't need Alexander.'

'True, but Newton is a bit safe with his high religious ideals, isn't he? She might be tempted by something a little more exciting.'

Emma fixes her eyes forwards again, staring at the framed book covers on the wall. She knows she should move away but she doesn't. *This man flirts with everyone*, scolds her rational self. *Martin is the one. He is reliable. He loves you, you love him. Bish bash bosh.*

Richard leans towards her and Emma feels herself turn her head.

'Emma? Is everything all right?' She and Richard turn to see Miranda standing at the door, eyebrows raised.

Emma sits upright in her chair and reorders her papers like a newsreader. 'Absolutely. Richard and I were just discussing the Stella and Alexander storyline,' she says avoiding eye contact with Miranda.

'I see. Well I just popped by to say hello. Richard, I trust you are well?' she says, smiling and holding out a hand to him.

'Very well, thank you, Miranda. Emma is putting me through my paces, but I think that's just what I need,' he says shaking her hand.

'Indeed. Well, do let me know if you need me. Emma, let's catch up later, shall we?' she says with meaning.

Emma nods sheepishly as she's been summoned to the headmistress's office.

'Saved by the boss,' says Richard when she's gone.

Emma looks embarrassed.

'Emma, I'm joking. Lighten up. It was only a bit of harmless role play in an attempt to solve my editorial dilemma. Now are you going to eat that muffin or what?'

***

Rachel has never been to Christa's house before but knows it's located in an exclusive area of town that she and Steve could never afford. She drives along the tree-lined street straining to see the numbers. Each house is the equivalent width of three of their own Victorian terrace.

'It's that one!' shrieks Lily in her ear.

'How do you know?' asks Rachel with a frown.

'Because I saw Roger's face at the window, duh,' retorts her daughter like a pint-sized teenager.

Rachel pulls in at the next available parking space and gets out of the car, releasing Lily and Alfie who are jumping up and down like excited spaniels. Christa's house is a mock-Tudor affair with a large sloping drive and enough parking for three cars. A shiny silver BMW sits on the drive. The gate has an intercom system, which immediately makes Rachel feel like an intruder.

'Ooh, can I press the button?' says Lily, elbowing her mother out of the way. Rachel sighs and lifts her up.

'I wanted to do that,' cries Alfie, his bottom lip starting to wobble.

'You can do it next time,' snaps Lily in a tone that she has heard her mother use. Rachel shakes her head feeling very much surplus to requirements.

'Hallo?' squeaks a small voice. Rachel can hear Christa in the background. 'Roger, *Schatz, bitte nicht!*' she declares. 'Hello Rachel? I will buzz you in, just push the gate.'

Rachel does as she is told and moments later Christa is at the door waving them in with a shy-looking Roger hiding behind her legs.

'*Willkommen*, come in, come in!' she says. 'Roger, stop clinging on to my leg. What is the matter with you? You were so excited that Lily, Alfie and Joe were coming.' She looks at Rachel. 'He is just grumpy because I told him off but he is always buzzing people in. Last week he let in a homeless man without me knowing. I had no idea until I found him watching television with Roger. He had even made himself a cheese and pickle sandwich.' Christa chuckles at the memory. 'But he was a very nice man and turns out he's an out of work gardener so I am getting him to come and trim my bushes next week,' she adds without a hint of irony.

Rachel swallows a giggle. 'Is Sue here yet?'

'Yes, she is in the kitchen and Joe is upstairs playing in Roger's Lego room.'

'Excuse me?' squeaks Alfie, tugging at Christa's jeans. 'Did you say Lego room?'

'*Ja, Schatz*, why don't you go with Roger and find him.'

'Lego? Bor-ing,' declares Lily.

'Lily!' chides Rachel embarrassed. She smiles at Christa. 'My daughter the diplomat.'

'No, that's OK.' Christa kneels down to speak to Lily. 'I understand, Lily, really I do. You are not wanting to build with the Lego because you can't make something as good as the boys. I understand.'

'That's not true!' cries Lily.

Christa shrugs her shoulders. 'Well, I think you should go and show them who is the boss, Lily, and I will award a jam doughnut to whichever Lego model is *das beste*.'

'Cool!' shouts Lily scooting off up the stairs after the others.

'Those poor boys,' sighs Rachel, watching her go.

'*Ach ja*, but it is good for them to learn about the strength of women from an early age, *nicht wahr*? And now, can I make you a latte?'

Rachel follows her into the kitchen, which is a beautifully decorated modern affair with a slate-slab breakfast bar in the centre of the room, gigantic fridge and vast, welcoming, range-style oven. Sue is sitting on a long-legged stool at the breakfast bar happily nursing a coffee.

'Hello, lovely,' she says, hugging her friend.

'Hey, Sue, how are you doing? Is Joe all better now?'

'He's fine but Al's come down with it now and you know what men get like once they contract the dreaded man flu. It was quite a relief to get out of the house just to escape the neediness.'

'*Ach* but, Susan, you must nurse your poor husband,' says Christa, handing Rachel her coffee.

'You are joking?' says Sue, raising an eyebrow at Rachel. 'I don't know if you know, Christa, but I'm from the North and up there you just get on with it.'

'Not like us sissy southerners,' grins Rachel.

Christa laughs. 'You English are so funny with your north–south issues. No, I mean you must pay attention to your husband so that his eye does not do the looking elsewhere.'

Sue shrugs. 'I think Al's too fond of his testicles to ever be unfaithful.'

Christa nods. 'Yes, I had a friend who cut off her husband's testicles once.'

Rachel flashes a glance at Sue. 'What happened?'

'He was sleeping with her sister and so she chopped them off and fed them to him.'

'Oh my God, that's barbaric!' cries Sue.

'No, it was OK. She was a nurse and she gave him an anaesthetic first so he had no idea when he woke up and there they were pan-fried on a plate with potato mash and pickled cabbage.'

'Fancy,' says Rachel.

Christa looks vague for a moment. 'Actually I might be mixing that up with a film I saw once.'

'Well, I'll bear it in mind,' says Sue with a grin.

'I love your house, Christa,' says Rachel, taking her coffee over to the large patio doors that open onto the garden. 'You've got so much space. I'm very jealous.'

'*Danke viels*. We are only renting as we never know how long we will be staying anywhere,' says Christa standing alongside Rachel and staring out at the day, which is cloudy and grey.

'How is Rudi then? Will we ever get to meet him?' asks Sue.

'I don't know, *Schatz*. He's away so much with work.'

'Do you still think he's having an affair?' asks Rachel.

'Almost certainly,' nods Christa.

'How did you know?'

'*Ach*, you know the little things. He bought me big presents. He's a very generous man but these were big presents – a car, a Rolex – that sort of thing, and he lies about what he's doing or where he's going to be. Last week he said he was in New York but I know he was in Moscow.'

Rachel thinks about Steve's ostentatious gift and the alcohol on his breath the other night. 'That's terrible, Christa.'

'*Ja*, I know but what can you do? That's why I say make sure you are as attentive as you can be; don't give them a reason to get bored of you. I don't think Rudi ever saw me in the same way after we had Roger. Still, Roger is *das beste* thing I've ever done so who gives a *scheisse*?'

Rachel puts an arm round Christa, who smiles at her. At that moment Lily appears in the kitchen holding up an impressive scale model of Big Ben. 'Do I win?' she asks.

'Wow, Lily, *das ist fantastisch*!' says Christa, embracing her. 'I am guessing you have come to claim your prize?' she adds handing her a doughnut. 'Now, I shall just go upstairs to take one each to the boys also.'

Lily grins and skips after Christa declaring, 'I like the way you talk! Can you teach me some German?'

Rachel smiles as they disappear and takes a seat next to Sue, who is eyeing her carefully. 'What was that all about?'

'What?' says Rachel.

'The way you grilled Christa about Rudi's affair.'

'Did I?'

'Yes.'

'I was just being a concerned friend,' says Rachel, draining the rest of her coffee.

'Are you sure you weren't having irrational thoughts about Steve?'

Rachel looks at her very perceptive friend. 'Am I that transparent?'

'A little.'

'Oh Suze, I dunno. First he gives me this eternity ring and then he came home late the other night and I could smell booze on his breath but he said he'd been working. My brain just started working overtime.'

'Rach, I hate to say it, lovey, but I think you might be getting a bit paranoid. I don't think there's a man less likely to have an affair than your Steve. He adores you.'

'I know, I know.'

'So talk to him, honey. Don't jump to conclusions all the time.'

'OK. I promise. And we're going to Scotland this weekend with the kids.'

'Well then, a perfect time to get away and take stock of everything.'

'Yeah,' smiles Rachel patting her friend on the knee. 'Can I ask you a favour?'

'Shoot.'

'Can you be really horrible to me for the next few months. It'll make it a whole lot easier if we do decide to go.'

'No problems, you fat cow,' grins Sue. 'Now hand me your mug and I'll make us another latte. I'm dying to have a go on Christa's swanky coffee machine.'

Emma sits back in her chair and sighs. She has been editing the same sentence for about half an hour now. She looks at the three mugs on her desk and decides to break the habit of a lifetime and wash them up on the day of usage. The offices are starting to empty and only the strays and workaholics remain. Emma goes into the communal kitchen, littered with its usual end-of-day detritus and peculiar cheesy smells and flicks the button on the kettle.

'Ah Emma, just the person. Have you got five minutes for that catch-up?' booms Miranda from the door.

Emma jumps. 'Of course,' she stammers following Miranda back to her office.

Miranda plonks herself behind her desk. 'Sit down, Emma, and stop looking so scared.' Emma does as she is told. 'I've never told you about James Wilson, have I?'

Emma looks uncertain. 'No, I don't think so.'

Miranda takes a deep breath. 'James Wilson was a promising new author I discovered when I was about your age. He was hugely gifted, charming and very handsome.' Emma doesn't say anything, touched by Miranda's shared confidence. 'He was also married.' She looks at Emma. 'I am not proud of what happened and cannot justify our affair by saying that I was young and foolish. I was both those things, but I should not have allowed the closeness of our working relationship to spill into real life. You see, Emma, working with an author is one of the most intimate experiences in life. They bare their very soul to you and it is easy to mistake shared passions for something more.' Emma goes to speak, but Miranda holds up her hand. 'All I am saying is that I don't judge you for what I witnessed today, but you have to be careful. Mr Bennett is a charming man, but if the rumours are true, he's something of a heartbreaker too.'

Emma nods. 'I understand. Miranda?'

'Yes, my dear?'

'What happened in the end with James?'

Miranda's face falls and Emma can see tears brimming in her eyes. 'His wife killed herself.' Emma gasps. 'It was ghastly. James moved abroad and I nearly left publishing for good. Happily though, that was around the time I met Digby and he helped me through it all. So you see, Emma, a moment's madness can be a very dangerous thing.'

'I'm so sorry, Miranda.'

'Thank you, my dear, but to be honest, it's James' poor wife you should feel sorry for. Anyway, on to other matters. How are things with Joel?'

'All right, I think. Actually, he mentioned something about strategic planning today. Is that something I need to be involved in?'

'You will. At some stage. So will Joel. I presume he was just stirring?'

'A little.'

'Well, keep your chin up and ignore it, Emma. Office politics is for those who lack confidence in their abilities or have small penises or both. I don't think that includes us, do you?'

Emma smiles. 'Certainly not.'

'Good girl. Now, don't work too late. I'm off to see some ghastly modern opera in Covent Garden. Wish me luck.'

'Good luck,' says Emma taking her leave. She returns to her desk, relishing the quiet of an almost-empty office. Half an hour later she has finished her edit and is feeling happier with the world. Just at that moment she hears a noise, like the sound of a heavy book falling to the floor. She jumps up in surprise and then hears the sound of more books falling. It's coming from the library. Emma creeps towards the noise and can see that the door is shut and the lights are off. She is just about to turn the door handle when she hears a low-pitched moaning. She freezes. The voice, obviously female, moans again and this time is joined by a male voice urging. There's a rhythm to the noise that Emma immediately recognises as the most intimate act between two people. Torn between an urge to find out the identity of the saucy pair and embarrassment at the scene, Emma runs back to her desk as quietly as she can. She giggles and contemplates phoning her sister with a 'guess what just happened at work?' tale. A few moments later, she hears the door to the library swing open and peers around the corner. She is extremely surprised to see Ella hurrying towards the exit. She ducks back to her desk feeling a little hurt at her friend's secret. She is even more horrified, seconds later, when a voice calls, 'Goodnight, Emma,' and Joel strides past her desk. Emma can hardly speak but manages to squeak 'Night!'

She plonks herself in her chair, her brain racing. How could Ella be sleeping with this man? Surely she can see what an idiot he is? Emma is starting to feel let down when her phone rings. It's Martin. Something triggers Emma's memory and she has switched off her computer and grabbed her bag before she's even answered the phone.

'Mart? Yes, sorry, darling. I got caught at the office and the Tube is a nightmare. Which pub are you in? Yep, I'll be there in twenty minutes,' she says, knowing that she's at least half an hour away.

CHAPTER FOURTEEN

A few days later, Emma climbs the steep steps into the hotel lobby, taking care not to spill her takeaway latte. The lobby has a veneer of luxury – bulging leather sofas, oil paintings of made-up dignitaries, winking chandeliers and dripping gold. She approaches the concierge desk where a bored-looking man, whose badge declares him to be 'Anthony – Happy to help you'. is checking a clipboard. He notices her and doesn't look any less bored, but does manage a thin smile, using only the lower muscles of his face.

'Yes, madam?'

'Could you direct me to the Editor's course please?'

'Three flights down follow the corridor round to your right tea and coffee on the left.'

'Pardon?'

He repeats it as if addressing an idiot and Emma, still unsure of where to go, heads for the stairwell. She has just reached the bottom of the stairs, when she hears voices.

'And I said to her, I don't give a damn if he's won the Booker, you can't write a novel without using the letter "e". I mean, Jesus!'

The woman she is speaking to nods and then spots Emma. 'Emma? Hi, how are you?'

'Oh Vanessa. Thank God. A friendly face. Good to see you.'

'You too. Do you know Stella? Stella, this is Emma Darcy.'

Stella studies Emma for a moment, unsmiling, and then continues with her story. They find their room and moments later, Emma is devouring a custard-filled almond croissant.

'Oh gosh,' gushes Stella. 'I do admire people who can eat at this time. I wish I could but unfortunately my metabolism simply won't allow it. It probably accounts for why I'm so thin.'

There is a moment's silence and then Vanessa asks, 'So, where are you working now, Emma?'

'I'm still at Allen Chandler, working for Miranda.'

'Oh, she's fantastic. Best in the business. Lucky you. So that means you've just acquired the new Richard Bennett novel. I read the manuscript and thought it was amazing.'

'Richard? Richard Bennett?' says Stella, suddenly interested in Emma.

'Yes, do you know him?'

'Let's just say, we've had our dealings,' says Stella looking smug.

'That's one way of describing it,' laughs Vanessa.

Stella adopts a saintly expression. 'You may say that, but I couldn't possibly comment.'

Emma wants to find out more, but a sincere-looking, curly-haired woman wearing an ill-fitting trouser suit and too much make-up interrupts their chat.

'Ladies!' She spots a young male editor, looking terrified at the back of the room. 'And gentleman – don't be shy! Let's get started, shall we? Bring your coffees and come and sit in a circle.'

During the course of the morning the tutor, whose name is Ros, talks about communication without looking any of them in the eye and then uses her fingers as quotation marks when she announces that they are going to do some 'role play'.

Emma is paired with the timid male editor and manages to bring him out of his shell by making him laugh.

At lunchtime, they are herded into the cavernous dining room and Emma finds a seat next to Vanessa.

'So, are you still in the same job?' she asks.

'Well actually, I've just been promoted to Editorial Director,' says Vanessa.

'Congratulations. That's fantastic.'

Vanessa looks a little unsure. 'Well, it is but actually, I don't get to do much editing these days and that's what I really enjoyed, you know, creating something really special, even if it was a car-crash when you first read it. In fact, especially if it was a car-crash when you first read it.'

'I know what you mean. I'm just going through rewrites with my new golden boy.' Emma looks over at Stella, who is on the phone. 'So, is there a history between Stella and Richard?'

'And then some. They were the Richard Burton and Elizabeth Taylor of Waterstones'.'

'Really?'

Vanessa nods. 'They were floor managers at Piccadilly. Apparently the rows were explosive and they were once caught at it in the Natural History section. She dumped him when she got the publishing job and then he got his publishing deal, had a bit of success and they haven't spoken since. Apparently, his heroines have more than a little of Stella in them, and not the nice bits. Of course, she's too narcissistic to see the true meaning but he's clearly carrying round a truck-load of baggage.'

Emma slaps her forehead as she has an epiphany. 'Of course – Stella! She's the character in the new book. It's her.'

'Very likely, but listen, Emma, just a word of warning, Richard Bennett does have a reputation as something of a lothario.'

'Hmm, yes. I think I'd clocked that.'

'Just be careful. I found him very tricky when I had to deal with him. Lucky for me I'm a lesbian,' says Vanessa with a smile.

Stella returns to her seat having finished her call, runs her hand through her dark bobbed hair and fixes them with cat-like emerald eyes. 'Can you believe it? I've just got off the phone to my builder and it's going to be another six weeks until they finish. I mean, six bloody weeks.'

Ros claps her hands, calling them to attention. 'OK, everyone, grab yourself a tea or coffee and we'll reconvene in five.'

Emma hears her phone ringing and sees that it's Martin. 'Hi, darling, how are you doing? Fancy a curry tonight while we chat about the guest list?' she says, moving out of the dining room and into the hotel lobby.

'Hey, Em, listen, I know we said we would talk about that tonight but can we do it at the weekend? It's just that – '

'Charlie wants you to play football again.'

'He's entered us into this tournament. It's an important game.'

'Not as important as our wedding.'

'No, that's true but I promise, I'll sort whatever you want me to at the weekend. Don't be cross, Em. I love you, OK?'

Emma doesn't want to give in but she hates bad feeling. 'OK, but you're buying me a curry tomorrow night in lieu of being a crap boyfriend.'

'Deal. And I'll chuck in some filthy sex too.'

'How romantic.'

'I can do romance if you'd prefer?'

'We'll see.'

'See you later, gorgeous.'

Emma throws her phone into her bag and heads downstairs to find the others feeling fed-up. She spends the afternoon keeping a close eye on Stella and wondering what it was like to be the woman who stole Richard Bennett's heart.

'Grandaaaaaad!'

'Alfieeeeeee!'

Edward spins round and catches his excited grandson as he throws himself into his grandfather's arms. Rachel and Lily are out of breath when they catch up with him.

'Alfie! You mustn't run off like that.'

'Sorry, Mummy.'

'I should think so,' scolds Lily.

Edward and Alfie exchange glances. 'That's us told, eh Alf?' says Edward and they both giggle.

It's Rachel and Lily's turn to shake their heads at one another. 'Honestly. Boys!'

'Well, anyway. Who's for a swing?' says Edward.

'Meee!' chorus the children and they hurtle off towards the playground.

'How's my favourite daughter over thirty?' asks Edward, giving Rachel a squeeze.

'Fine thanks, Dad.'

'Are you sure?'

'All right, you've got me. I just hate all this uncertainty about the move. I'm not very good with change, you know.'

Edward nods. 'Is there anything I can do?'

'No more than you do already.' She kisses him on the cheek.

'Gran-dad!' Lily is stamping her foot.

'On my way, Miss Lily!'

Edward pushes the children on the swings while Rachel fetches the coffees. When she returns they watch the children for a while revelling in their whooping glee. Rachel enjoys time with her father. They don't even need to speak to each other. She looks up at the sky and pulls her coat tighter against the autumn chill.

'Getting a bit colder,' she remarks.

'Yes, I had to close up the greenhouse last night. I'll probably put the heater on later this week.'

'Have you notified *The Times*?' she teases.

Edward laughs. 'Sometimes the quietest lives are the happiest lives, you know.'

'I know. I long for a quiet life!' says Rachel.

Edward looks at his daughter. 'Don't wish your life away, Rach. I remember how it was with you and Emma as little girls. It's over so quickly even if it is hard work sometimes.'

Rachel nods. 'It is and I wish I could find a way to enjoy it more sometimes.'

Edward puts his arm around her. 'Stop giving yourself such a hard time. You're a wonderful mother and you have three very lucky children. Don't forget that. And it is hard having small children. Your mother didn't always find it easy being at home with you two.'

'I'm sure. I know we were challenging sometimes.' Edward looks at Rachel, amused. 'OK, I know I was challenging sometimes, but Mum seemed to cope.'

'Not always,' says Edward. Rachel looks at him in surprise. 'Don't tell your mother I told you, but it all got too much for her at one stage.'

'And?' says Rachel.

'And she left us for a while. Not for long, just a month or so.' Rachel is stunned. 'So you see, everyone struggles and you can't judge them or yourself.'

'But what about Mum. What happened?'

'It was a long time ago. I probably shouldn't have mentioned it.'

'It's all right, I won't say anything.'

'All I'm saying, Rachel, is that you are caught in a moment and you must see it as that. Things will change. Life won't always be this exhausting or intense. You can't see around corners and so you have to trust your instinct.'

'So, go to Scotland then?'

'If that's what your instinct tells you. Who knows what new adventures it might bring?'

Rachel hugs her dad. 'It sounds as if you fancy it yourself.'

'If I were twenty years younger, I would, but alas I cannot leave my roses and anyway, it will make the times when we do see you all the more special, won't it?'

'Graaaandaaaaad!'

'Coming, Alfie! Duty calls.'

Edward ambles after his young grandson and Rachel watches them delighting in each other's company. Lily comes bouncing over, her cheeks red and her eyes bright with life.

'Mum!'

'Yes, Lils?'

'I love you,' she says, plonking herself on her mother's lap. Rachel is surprised, but deeply touched by this out-of-character affection. She wraps her arms around her daughter.

'I love you too, Lils,' she says breathing in the warmth of childhood.

'Well, that just about concludes things for today. Thank you, ladies and gentlemen. I think we did some excellent work. If you have any further questions, feel free to e-mail me.'

Emma gathers up her belongings and Vanessa catches her at the door.

'We're going for a quick drink,' she says, gesturing at Stella. 'Fancy joining us, Emma?'

Emma checks her watch. It's just gone five and she has nothing to rush home for. 'Why not?' The young male editor looks over and smiles. 'Do you want to come too, Josh?' she asks.

'That would be great. Thanks.'

They find a pub just down the road from the hotel. Vanessa orders a round of drinks while Emma, Stella and

Josh find a table. Stella starts to hold court and Emma is amazed by her ability to talk about herself without listening to anyone else or indeed asking anyone anything about themselves. The first drink goes down well, so Emma orders a bottle for her and Vanessa to share, a beer for Josh and a soda water for Stella – 'I never drink on a day with a "T" in it'.

Stella looks around the room and notices the Rothko print on the wall above their heads. 'God, not another bloody Rothko. He's everywhere, isn't he? So pedestrian. I bet he's rubbing his hands with glee.'

'Actually he's dead.' They all look round at quiet, mousy Josh, clearly emboldened by the influence of expensive, Belgian beer.

Stella looks at him, clearly irritated. 'Is he? Really?' she says uninterested.

'Yes he is. Committed suicide actually.'

Vanessa raises her eyes at Emma and nods towards Josh, amused. Emma feels like patting Josh on the back, but is interrupted by her phone. She feels her heart start to pound when she sees Richard's number flash on her screen. She flicks the answer button.

'Hello? Richard?'

Stella looks up sharply.

'Emma? I've done it!'

'Sorry, Richard. It's difficult to hear you. What have you done?' she asks, moving away from the table and mouthing 'sorry' to the group.

'The bloody rewrite. I've done it!'

'That's fantastic. Well done.'

'Well, it's down to you, Miss Emma Darcy. I couldn't have managed it without my favourite editor. Where are you, by the way?'

'In a bar.'

'Oh terrific, I'll come and meet you. We can celebrate.'

'No, Richard, I can't – ' begins Emma before her phone is grabbed by Stella.

'Richard! Sweetie! Guess who?' Emma watches in horror and can only imagine Richard's responses. 'Ahhhh, have you missed me? I hear you've named your latest heroine after me. How sweet. Oh come on, Richie, calm down. Yes, I'll hand her back.' She gives the phone to Emma.

'Richard? Are you there? Sorry about that.'

'Is this some kind of joke, Emma?'

'What? No, no, of course not.'

'How come you're with Stella?'

'I met her on a course. Everyone has come for a drink. That's all. She grabbed the phone.'

Richard is silent for a moment.

'Richard? Are you still there?'

'Yes, I'm here. Sorry. It's just a bit of a shock to talk to her after all this time.'

'I'm sure. It was quite a shock to meet her today too. She's very – '

'Needy? Possessive? Selfish?' says Richard, his voice filled with bitterness.

'Possibly,' says Emma with a nervous laugh.

'Look, don't worry. I'm sorry for jumping to conclusions. She's just very manipulative, Emma. It took me a while to get over her.'

'I understand. Are you sure you're OK?'

'I'm fine. Go back to your editor friends. I'll speak to you soon.'

She hears the note in his voice that tells her he isn't fine and wants to end the conversation.

'OK, bye.'

She clicks off her phone and returns to the table muttering under her breath. Stella looks amused.

'So how is the publishing industry's great new talent?'

'Fine. No thanks to you.' Emma is feeling drunk and feisty.

'Ooh, touchy. What? Is he still pining for me?'

'No, I think he's moved on actually.'

'Ahhh, so you're sleeping with him, are you?'

Emma fixes her with a Darcy stare. 'Not everything revolves around sex, flirting and you, OK? You may think that people are hanging on your every word and opinion, but they're not. You should try listening to yourself sometimes. It's actually quite dull. Oh, and have you read Richard's new book? If I were you, I wouldn't be too proud to be called Stella at the moment.'

Without waiting for a reply, Emma gathers up her belongings, kisses Vanessa and Josh goodbye and heads for the Tube, her head spinning. As she walks down the road, the cars and taxis seem a little bit louder than usual, the lights a little brighter. She is surprised at the strength of her anger towards Stella and how sorry she feels for Richard. He may flirt for England but he has a heart and it clearly has been broken. She flicks open her phone and dials his number. It goes straight to voicemail. She takes a deep breath.

'Hi, Richard. It's Emma. Again. I'm really sorry about that. It was unprofessional and you're clearly upset. So please take this as an unreserved apology and if you need to talk, you know where I am. If it's any consolation, I gave Stella a piece of my mind. It probably won't do any good, but I tried. I'm going down into the Tube. Speak soon.'

Emma jogs down the moving escalator and jumps onto a waiting Tube just as the doors slide shut. It's still hours before closing time and well past rush hour, and she is grateful to find an almost-empty carriage. Plonking herself down, she considers reading but feels too weary. She feels her phone buzz in her pocket and retrieves it. There is a text message from Richard: 'Thanks Emma Darcy, Guardian Angel.'

Rachel hears Steve's key in the door and waits patiently as he is greeted by all three of his children. He rough and tumbles his way down to the kitchen with Lily still clinging onto his leg.

'I missed you today, Daddy,' she implores.

'I missed you too, Lils,' he smiles. 'And now I have to go and hug Mummy.'

'Aww,' says Lily, but she lets go and runs back to the living room to join her brothers in front of the television.

'You're on time,' says Rachel glancing up from the chopping board.

'I'm on time,' repeats Steve, wrapping his arms around his wife and stealing a slice of red pepper. She slaps his hand playfully. 'It's good to be home,' he adds, walking over to the fridge and helping himself to a beer. 'Want one?'

'Oh go on then. Thursday is the new Friday and all that. How was your day?'

'Bor-ing,' he says parroting Lily. 'How was yours?

'Fine. We met up with Dad. He told me some interesting things about Mum actually.'

'Go on.'

'She left us for a bit when things got a bit much for her.'

'Doesn't sound like your mother.'

'I know, but I guess life gets to us all sometimes.'

'You're not thinking of going anywhere are you, my sweet?' asks Steve, his voice edged with concern.

'No, are you?' She turns to face him.

'Hey, Rach, where has all this come from?' He approaches her and holds her by the shoulders, studying her face.

'Oh, I dunno. My brain just goes into overdrive sometimes. I worry what with you working late all the time that maybe you're getting bored of me. I think I'm going mad sometimes. Maybe it's because I spend all day with Barbie and Jeremy Vine.'

'A match made in heaven,' laughs Steve. 'Listen, Rach. Life is hard sometimes and busy and, yes, I have been working late but you are the most wonderful woman I've ever known and nothing will ever change that. I love you so much. Don't ever question that.'

Rachel gives him a small smile, feeling consoled. She knows she's ridiculous to doubt Steve. Sue is right, her dad is right and it's time to start behaving like a grown-up. She takes a sip of her beer and feels a bubble of excitement in the pit of her stomach. Scotland could be just the tonic she needs.

CHAPTER FIFTEEN

'So, Ells. How are things?' asks Emma, watching her friend switch on, her computer, desperate for her to share her secret.

Ella looks up, a vague smile on her lips. 'Fine, thanks. How about you? How are the wedding plans?'

'Oh great. Really great. But enough about me, what about you? It feels like ages since we've talked. What's been going on?'

Ella goes to open her mouth and then snaps it shut, as if she's thought better of it. Emma is starting to feel cross. 'Oh come on, Ella, there must be something!'

Just at that moment, Emma's phone rings and Ella, seeing an escape route, disappears to the kitchen. Emma snatches up the phone. 'Hello?' she barks.

'Someone forgot to take their happy pills this morning!'

'Richard. Sorry, I was just a bit – never mind. How are you?'

'Tip-top thank you. Any chance you're free for lunch today?'

Emma bites her lip. 'Erm, let me just check my diary,' she says, buying time.

'Look if you're busy,' says Richard, sounding a little hurt.

'No, no! I don't have a meeting. That will be fine.'

'Excellent. Shall I come to the offices around one?'

'Perfect. See you later.'

Emma sighs as the call ends. She wonders if she's spending too much time with Richard but reassures herself that it's just part of the job. After all, she does have an editorial duty to him. She can't help it that they get on so well. At least he seems to value her. She feels let down by Ella and the situation with Martin isn't great at the moment. Head spinning, she decides to call Rachel for a reality check.

'Hello?' squeaks a small voice on the other end of the phone.

'Lily? Is that you?' asks Emma.

'Naow, silly, it's Alfie. Is that Granny?'

'No, silly, it's Auntie Em,' says Emma, horrified that she has started to sound like her mother. She hears another small, cross voice in the background.

'Give me the phone, you silly boy. Auntie Em?'

'Hello Pica-lily. Are you OK?'

'I'm bored. What are you doing? Do you want to come round and play hairdressers?'

'I would love to, Lils, but I've got to work. Is your mum there?'

'MAAAARM!' shrieks Lily into the mouthpiece. Emma clutches her ear, taking the full force of her niece's cry.

'Tart-face,' says Rachel, reclaiming the phone. 'You OK?'

'I'm fine. How are you?'

'Yeah, OK. Bit manic, we're off to Scotland tomorrow. LILY! STOP HITTING YOUR BROTHER AND PUT THAT BAG OF ONIONS BACK IN THE CUPBOARD! Sorry, Em. You were saying?'

'Oh nothing. I just wanted to check you were OK. You sound busy. I'll let you go.'

'Yeah, sorry, things are a bit crazy. Steve thought it was a good idea to drop this trip on me at the last minute and guess who has to pick up the pieces? The house is a tip and the kids are driving me – ALFIE! GET DOWN AT ONCE! YOU CAN NOT CLIMB UP ON THE BOOKSHELVES – YOU'LL F – '

Emma hears the sound of a small boy falling off some bookshelves, a four-second delay and then a cry that echoes like an air-raid siren.

'Sorry, Em, got to go. Text you over the weekend.'

'Bye,' says Emma feeling lost and unsure of what to do next.

Rachel looks at the kitchen and wants to weep. Last night's dinner things are strewn across the work surfaces, this morning's breakfast things are still on the table, the dishwasher needs to be emptied, the washing machine needs to be filled and she can hear Lily telling Alfie to 'SHUT UUUUUUP!' which will result in doors slamming and wailing within less than a minute. It's the domestic equivalent of Armageddon. Rachel makes her way towards the sink and steps heavily on a chunk of Lego.

'Shit! Ow! Shit!' yells Rachel fighting the urge to kick something but not the urge to swear.

'Mummy! That is a very bad word. I'm going to tell Granny!' says Lily, her face set in a determined scowl.

'Well if you children didn't leave your stupid toys on the floor, maybe Mummy wouldn't be in need of a new foot!'

Lily fixes her mother with a look which can only be described as withering. 'You shouldn't say "stupid", Mummy. It is very rude.'

Rachel is tempted to say something a lot worse but manages to keep it together. 'Where is your brother, Lily?'

'I shut him in the wardrobe.'

'Lily! He won't be able to get out of there.'

'He was being naughty. He has to learn.'

Rachel leapfrogs the toys obstructing her path and takes the stairs two at time, arriving at the top step breathless. She can hear Alfie now and the sound reminds her of a cornered animal from a wildlife documentary.

'Coming, Alfie!'

She wrenches open the wardrobe door to find him huddled in a corner, struggling to get his breath and shaking with fear. She pulls him to her.

'Lily! Come here now!'

After many sobs, apologies and angry words, a fragile peace is restored and Rachel returns downstairs to tackle all the jobs she has to do before she can even start packing. She hears arguing upstairs and is about to join in when there's a tentative rap at the door. Her face is set in a furious expression as she flings open the door and is confronted with Tom's kindly face. He laughs and puts up his hands.

'Easy there, neighbour. I come in peace!'

Rachel smiles. 'Sorry. No work today?'

'No, I'm on holiday today. Are you having a bad morning?'

'Did you hear us?'

'Let's just say the walls are rather thin.'

'I'm so sorry. Listen, come in for a coffee but you'll have to watch me wash up.'

'I believe there are men who pay a lot for that kind of spectacle at some of the more exclusive Soho establishments.'

Rachel laughs.

'Who is it?' demands Lily from upstairs.

'It's Tom from next door.'

'Oh I like him.'

Rachel winks at Tom. 'You lucky fella. Praise indeed.'

Tom grins.

Lily appears in the doorway in her princess heels and minces over to Tom, fluttering her eyelashes. 'Hi, Tom!'

'Hi, Lily, how are you? You look very pretty today.'

'I know,' says Lily without a hint of irony. Rachel and Tom grin at one another. Alfie comes trailing in after his sister.

'Hi, Alfie. Are you OK?' asks Tom ruffling his hair.

'Lily did be shutting me in the wardrobe.'

'Oh did she? Oh dear.'

'Alfie was being annoying!' protests Lily.

'Yes but that's no reason to shut him in a cupboard. Goodness only knows I've wanted to do that to your father a few times,' says Rachel.

'It wasn't a cupboard. It was a wardrobe,' corrects Lily, and then turns her attentions to Tom. 'Tom?'

'Yes, Lily?'

'Do you have a wife?'

'No, Lily, I don't.'

'I think that's sad.'

'Do you know what, Lily? So do I,' agrees Tom.

'You should marry Mummy!' Rachel looks at Tom and can see the trace of a blush in his cheeks.

'Lily, stop tormenting poor Tom.'

'Just for today. You could get divorced before Daddy gets home.'

Rachel laughs. 'Well, romantic as that all sounds, I think we should maybe let Tom choose his own wife, don't you?'

'OK,' agrees Lily earnestly. 'Tom? Do you want to marry my mum?'

Tom looks like a frightened rabbit. 'Erm, well, I don't know.'

'Because my mum is actually quite pretty when she brushes her hair and puts on make-up. What does Daddy say? Oh yes: "She scrubs up quite well".'

Rachel feels sorry for Tom but the wicked side of her wants to see how he will react.

'Well, your Mum is – '

'Yes?'

'Obviously very beautiful.' Tom looks at the floor, avoiding Rachel's gaze.

'Correct!' shouts Lily delighted. 'Mum? Can we go to the park now? I'm bored.'

Rachel is momentarily caught off guard by Tom's comment. It's as if she's just uncovered a secret truth. 'Erm the park? No, sorry, darling. Mummy's got too many jobs to do and I've got to pack.'

'Oh, are you off somewhere?' asks Tom.

'Yes. Scotland. You know, casing the joint.'

'Oh, so you are moving then?' He sounds disappointed.

'Not necessarily. We just need to go and check it all out. Why, will you miss us?'

Tom looks at her now and smiles. 'Of course. Who will tease me mercilessly about my snail patrol if you're not around? So, kids! Do you fancy coming to the park with your Uncle Tom?'

'Yeeeeees!' shout Lily and Alfie together.

'That's all right. isn't it? I can take them for an hour or so. Get them out of your hair?'

'Are you sure? It's not much of a way to spend your day's holiday.'

'Call it payback for when I gatecrashed your weekend with Steve.' Tom gets up and helps Alfie with his shoes.

Rachel follows them to the door. 'Well, thank you. It's very kind of you.' She touches Tom on the arm and he turns to face her. There is a second when neither of them knows what to say and then Lily grabs his hand.

'OK, you two, say bye bye to Mummy!'

'Have fun and thanks, Tom.' She watches them disappear up the road and then returns to her chores feeling a little bit happier with the world.

Emma doesn't see Ella again until lunchtime and is getting the distinct feeling that her friend is avoiding her. She is just leaving the loos when Ella comes in. She sees a flicker of panic pass over her friend's face.

'It's all right. I'm just leaving,' says Emma with teenage petulance.

'Oh, are you OK?'

'What do you think, Ella? I mean my best friend keeps avoiding me, and I know there's something up, but she doesn't seem to want to tell me, so no, I wouldn't say I was OK!'

Ella looks crestfallen. 'OK, OK. I'm sorry. It's just that it's a bit complicated.'

'Oh is it?' says Emma, assuming she's referring to Joel. 'How so?'

'I don't think I'm ready to talk about it yet.'

'I see.'

At that moment, the door swings open and Miranda sweeps in. 'Ah, my favourite editors! I'm not intruding, am I?' Emma mutters shaking her head and Ella smiles weakly. 'My, my, do I detect a spat? Can't have that. No fighting in the ranks, eh?'

'It's nothing, Miranda. Really,' says Ella quickly.

'Splendid, that's the spirit. See you both later then.'

Emma heads for the door without a backward glance. When she reaches the lifts, she senses Ella at her side.

'What's this all about, Emma?'

'You tell me, Ella.'

'I don't know why you're so cross with me. I've just got some stuff going on that I need to sort out, but I can't tell you what it is, OK?'

The lift doors open. Emma stomps through the door and turns on her friend.

'That's fine, Ella, just fine. Send me a postcard when you remember who your real friends are, eh?' The lift doors close and Emma glimpses Ella's hurt face before she turns away.

'So I've decided to kill off Stella in the first chapter.'

'Mhhmm,' says Emma.

'And take my book to another publisher.'

'Great, great. Sorry – what?'

'Emma, are you OK?'

'OK? Of course I'm OK.' She looks at Richard's face. 'Sorry, I haven't been listening, have I?'

'Not so far. Bad day?'

'There's just a lot going on. Sorry.' She draws her thumb and forefinger down in front of her face as if she's pulling on a mask. 'There, professional face now fully engaged.'

'Oh, don't be silly. I think it's good that we're like this.'

'Oh yes and how are we?'

'Well, Miss Darcy, I like your honest, straightforward ways. You're very easy to be around and you understand me, I think. Very few people do.'

Emma smiles. Richard reaches over and touches her arm. 'You know you're very good for me, Emma.'

'Oh yes?'

'Yes. I think you bring out the best in me.'

Emma discreetly pulls away her arm and pats his hand. 'Well, I am very glad and now shall we talk about this rewrite?'

'Oh, plenty of time for that. How are the wedding plans?'

'Don't ask. My godmother and mother are being control freaks and my fiancé seems to have lost interest.'

'Well more fool him. He needs to realise how lucky he is.'

Emma is suddenly aware of someone standing by her side. She turns expecting it to be David, the café owner, who has been extremely attentive today and made gestures of approval behind Richard's head. So she is mortified to see Martin with his arms folded, looking slightly cross.

'Martin! What are you doing sneaking up on people like that and how did you know I was here?'

'I was hoping to take my fiancée to lunch actually. Your receptionist told me where you were.' Emma curses Lauren's helpfulness. 'Why are you discussing me with a stranger?'

Richard stands up to address Martin. 'I'm so sorry. I don't think we've been introduced. I'm Richard Bennett,' he says holding out his hand.

Martin surveys him with narrowed eyes but doesn't take his hand. He turns back to Emma. 'I was trying to make amends for last night but I'm wondering why I bothered.'

'Martin, I'm working.'

'Why are you discussing our wedding then? And for your information, pal,' says Martin jabbing a finger back towards Richard, 'I do know how lucky I am, thanks.'

Richard reaches for his jacket. 'Look, I feel as if I'm intruding and I'm sorry if I offended you, Martin. Far be it from me to interfere in domestic spats. I'll give you a call after the weekend, Emma, OK?'

'Richard, you don't have to go. Martin, apologise!'

Martin sits down in Richard's vacated chair and folds his arms. 'I've got nothing to apologise for.'

Richard holds up his hands in a conciliatory gesture. 'Emma, it's fine. I'll speak to you soon,' he says, disappearing out of the door.

Emma contemplates running after him but realises how this will look. Instead she glares at her fiancé. 'What was all that about?'

'You tell me.'

'OK, I'm sorry, I was talking out of turn. I'm just frustrated that you're never around to discuss stuff.'

'Oh fine, well that's great, isn't it? The first sign of trouble and you go running off to your new author.'

'And what about you? Charging in like some stag about to fight for his mate.'

'At least it shows I care.'

'Yes, in a bloody alpha-male "hands off my woman" kind of way.'

'Well, sorry for giving a damn.'

They sit in a sulky silence for a while before David approaches the table nervously. 'Everything all right here, Emma?' He gives Martin a sly glance.

'Fine thanks, David. This is Martin by the way; my fiancé.'

'Oh delighted to meet you,' gushes David. 'Is the other chap coming back?'

'No, he is not,' says Martin firmly.

'OK. Can I get you anything to eat then?'

'I'll have a tuna baguette and a lime and soda thanks, David,' says Emma. 'Martin?'

'A cheeseburger and chips please. And a Coke.'

'Very good,' says David.

Emma fiddles with her knife and fork and steals glances at Martin, who is sitting with his arms folded looking cross. 'Oh come on, Mart, don't give me the silent treatment!' she says at last.

'What do you want me to say? That I'm sorry?'

'Well, you did scare my author away.'

'Well, he should mind his own bloody business.'

Emma snaps her mouth shut. She knows there's no point in arguing with Martin when he's like this. She excuses herself and goes to the bathroom. She splashes cold water on her face and eyes herself critically in the mirror. *What are you doing, Emma Darcy?* she says to her reflection. She wishes she knew the answer.

She returns just as David delivers their food. Martin flips open his burger and wrinkles his nose in disgust as he spies a gherkin. He looks over at Emma and gives her a small smile before offering her the offending object as he has done many times before. 'Peace offering?' he asks.

She doesn't want to give in but she doesn't know what else to do. 'I'll take it,' she says with a small sigh.

'Friends again?' he asks. Typical Martin: comes in all guns blazing and then just wants everything to be back to normal.

'Friends,' she says, wishing she could remember what normal was.

Diana scrapes the remains of the fish into the bin and stacks the plates into the dishwasher. Edward walks into the kitchen, phone in hand.

'All right. darling. Have a lovely trip. Mum's here. Do you want a quick word?' He passes the phone to his wife.

'Rachel? Are you all set? Now remember, don't make any rash decisions, will you? Yes, I know you're not a child. I'm just trying to help. OK, OK. Well, have a good trip and give the children a kiss from me. All right. Bye.'

Edward watches his wife as she replaces the phone and turns back to the kitchen.

'It will be all right, you know?' he says.

'Oh and how can you be so sure? You know how impetuous Rachel can be. She'll probably have them moved up there by next week!'

Suddenly, Diana is crying and Edward is at her side, putting his arms around her.

'Come on, love. You know they've got to do what's best.'

'I know! I just – it's just that –'

'What is it, my light, my love?'

'I'll just miss those children so much.' She hides her face in his chest and sobs.

'I know, but listen, they haven't said they're going yet. There's still a long way to go and even if they do, we can always visit or have the kids to stay.'

'Oh Edward, you know it's not the same,' says Diana through her tears.

'Well, we could always move up there?'

'What? Don't be so ridiculous!'

'Why not?'

'Because, this is my home and I'm too old and it's in Scotland.'

'Yes, Edinburgh tends to be in Scotland and you're not too old, you're barely in your sixties and everyone knows that home is where the heart is.'

'Oh really, Edward, stop talking in clichés. You've got to be realistic. What about if they don't like it and move back? What will we do then?'

'Move back?'

'You know that's silly, don't you? We can't just keep moving up and down the country and anyway, I don't want to live in Scotland.'

'What's wrong with Scotland?'

Diana gives him a withering look that indicates the end of this line of questioning.

'Anyway, what about Emma? We can't abandon Emma and Martin.'

'True. Let's just see how things go, eh? Let's not be too hasty. Nothing has been decided, all right?'

Diana kisses her husband on the cheek. 'All right. I knew there was a reason why I married you.'

'And there was me thinking it was something to do with my wit, charm and film-star good looks.'

The phone rings and Edward answers it. 'Oh hello, Rosie, how are you?' Diana's heart sinks. 'Look, Rosie, can I give you a call some other time? I'm just a bit busy now.' He smiles at his wife as he replaces the phone. 'Now, how about we settle down and finish this wine in front of *Gardeners' World*? I know how you like to ogle Joe Swift.'

Diana smiles and follows her husband into the living room.

CHAPTER SIXTEEN

'Is that man a terrorist?'

'No.'

'What about that man?'

'No!'

'He has a beard.'

'That doesn't mean anything. Now please can you stop pointing at people, Lily?'

'Actually, Abraham says that Muslims cut their beards off before they blow themselves up,' says Will.

'Does he? Does he?' asks Rachel wondering how long it can take one man to buy lattes, juice and a muffin. She takes out her phone and starts to text Emma: 'At airport tryng 2 stop kids talking abt terrorists. U OK?'

A reply comes back straightaway: 'Good luck! Off to lk at flowers wth Martin.'

'Good luck 2 u 2!' replies Rachel.

'Do bits of you fly everywhere when you blow yourself up?' asks Lily. A sweet white-haired old lady, who had been smiling at the children, moves to a different table.

'OK, can we stop with the suicide-bomber chat now please? Ah, here's Daddy with the drinks.'

'Sorry, sorry. Awful queue and a Japanese tourist in front of me who had to do a lot of pointing. Right, who's for a smoothie?'

'Meee!' shout Lily and Alfie.

'Euuurgh. Smoothies are for babies!' declares Will.

'THEY ARE NOT!' shouts Lily.

'OK, OK!' says Rachel desperate to avoid a scene. 'Now, who would like some muffin?'

Children appeased, they are just relaxing into the café experience, albeit the Gatwick café experience with coffee-ring stained tables and sticky floors, when an announcement comes over the tannoy.

'This is a final call for the Summers party. Would Mr and Mrs Summers and their children please make their way to gate 36 as we are about to close the gate.'

Rachel looks at Steve and then longingly at her latte. 'I thought we had at least half an hour!'

'Right you lot, who wants to have a race?' says Steve.

Happily the children are very much in favour of a race. Unhappily, gate 36 is the furthest one from the terminal building. They arrive breathless and wound-up, having had to apologise to the fifty or so people and their injured ankles. The stewardess on the door is Scottish, pasted with thick orange make-up and bright blue eye shadow, and is extremely unsympathetic.

'It clearly says at check-in that you need to leave enough time to reach the gate. We were about to unload your bags,' she drawls.

'Yes, sorry. We thought we had more time,' wheezes Steve.

The woman frowns at him and then at Rachel and finally at the three children. She processes their tickets with taloned false-nail fingers and no further communication.

'They're heeer Boab,' she calls to her colleague, a ferrety man wearing an orange tabard.

'Aye, OK.'

'Thanks very much. Sorry again,' says Steve.

'Why was that lady so cross?' asks Lily too loudly.

'Because we were a bit late for the plane,' says Rachel.

'Is that why she was a funny orange colour too?'

Rachel ushers Lily down the boarding tunnel not daring a backward glance.

'What about these?' says Emma.

'Ahh, the Calla Lily, a very popular choice for the bride to be,' says the florist with an admiring smile.

'What do you think, Martin?'

'What? Oh yeah. Lovely. Really lovely.'

Rachel looks at the man she is destined to marry and sighs. 'Martin? Can we have a little word?' she says, and then to the florist, 'Excuse us.' The woman gives her an ingratiating smile. Emma pulls Martin to the front of the cavernous, heavily scented shop. 'Earth to Martin! Do you read me?'

'What?'

'We're supposed to be looking at flowers, getting some ideas?'

'I know. I am looking.'

'OK, so what are these?' Emma points to some delicate delphiniums.

'Erm, lovely purple flowers?'

'Martin!'

'Look, I didn't realise that looking at flowers would require me to bring along my *I Spy Guide to Floristry*. Can't we just go with the ones that look the nicest? What about these? These are nice.'

'They are flaming tulips! Not necessarily ideal for a July wedding or indeed any event where you need the flowers to last longer than twenty minutes!'

'OK, OK. I didn't know that. I'm sorry. Come on, Emma, this isn't really my thing. You have to be honest. Flowers are more of a girl thing.' Emma looks at her fiancé with murderous intent and notices the florist scurrying into the safety of the back room.

'A girl thing, are they?' begins Emma with a dangerous edge to her voice. 'I suppose I should stick to dresses and flowers and wrapping flipping sugar almonds in tulle, should I?'

'Em, I didn't say that. Come on, don't be so sensitive.'

'Oh, sensitive now, am I? I tell you what, why don't I just go the whole hog with the girly thing and agree to "obey" you?'

'I thought we were going to include that in the vows. I've already told the vicar.' Emma's look tells Martin that his lame attempt at humour is a mistake.

'Is that supposed to be funny?' she growls.

'OK, all right. I'm sorry. We're obviously not on the same wavelength today. Are you still pissed off with me about yesterday? Because I thought we'd sorted that.'

'No, I'm pissed off with you because you'd promised we'd get on with sorting stuff for the wedding today but you don't seem that bothered!' Emma is actually still cross about yesterday but she's not about to tell Martin.

'I thought we were going to do guest lists and gift lists. Don't be grumpy. I'm just a bit out of my depth here. I don't really know what I'm looking at.' He prods a beautiful purple orchid and its petals melt to the ground. 'Oops.'

'OK, OK. We can do it another time. Let's go.' Emma grabs him by the arm calling back over her shoulder. 'Thanks for your time. I've got your card and we'll give you a call.'

Back on the street, they walk side by side and Emma folds her arms as Martin tries to catch her hand.

'Actually, we could go for lunch,' suggests Martin.

'Oh right, where?'

'Well, Charlie and Stacey – '

'Oh great, so not just the two of us then?'

'Well, Charlie just sent me a text. He and Stacey are in the pub watching the football so it would be kind of rude not to.'

'Martin! We're supposed to be spending the day together, sorting out wedding stuff, not sitting in the pub while you and your mate watch football.'

'Oh come on, Em. It's only round the corner and we do need to eat.' Martin sticks out his bottom lip like a small child. 'Please? For me?'

Emma assesses her options and takes his arm. 'All right, but you're bloody paying.'

Rachel takes a deep breath as the taxi drops them outside one of Edinburgh's swankiest hotels.

'Now, don't touch anything,' she says to everyone including Steve. A top-hatted man with a red face, red uniform and bulbous nose holds the door open for them and smiles. Lily grins and swaggers past.

'Oh thank you so much,' she says in a breathy little voice.

'Aye, you've got a heartbreaker there, sir,' says the man to Steve who nods politely.

'That man looked like a tomato,' declares Lily as they enter the glimmering luxury of the foyer.

Rachel shushes her daughter and looks round. 'Where's Will?'

They all turn to see a small figure spinning round in the revolving doors like a sock in a washing machine, while a queue of impatient looking people wait outside.

'Daaaad! Help!' squeals Will, his voice increasing and decreasing in volume as he spins past them.

'Will! Get out at once!' cries Rachel.

'Is there a problem, madam?' Rachel turns round to find a thin man with a melancholy face at her side.

'Erm, I'm afraid he's got stuck in your revolving door. His dad is just going to get him out.' Rachel looks over and is mortified to see both Will and Steve spinning in the revolving doors. The doorman is trying to help from the outside and Steve is trying to calm Will, who is now racing around, unable to stop, like some kind of maniac hamster. Alfie starts to cry, fearful that he will never see his big brother or dad again. Rachel and Lily exchange glances and stride towards the door.

'Release the big money balls!' commands Lily, which causes Will to laugh and shoot from the door like an Exocet missile closely followed by his father.

'Right! Is it possible that we can make it to our room without further incident?' asks Rachel.

Will looks sheepish. 'Sorry, Mum.'

'Really!' comments a superior looking woman on her way past. 'It's like being at the zoo!'

Rachel and Lily both round on the woman but Lily gets in first. 'This is not a zoo, it is a hotel, and that is my brother and he only got stuck in the doors which wasn't actually his fault so don't be so mean!' The woman looks at Rachel who shrugs her shoulders and puts a protective arm around Will.

'Well I never!' says the woman and heads for the lift closely followed by her amiable mole of a husband who turns and winks at them. 'All looked rather fun to me!' he says with a smile.

'Goooooooooooal!'

Emma looks at the two men in front of her, who are now in the middle of some kind of primal celebration dance.

'Men, eh?' laughs Stacey placing her immaculately French manicured fingernails around her straw and taking a long slurp from her drink.

'Three sausage and mash and a chicken Caesar salad!' yells the landlord.

'Lovely grubbly!' shouts Charlie.

'Oooh, what's that?' asks Stacey peering at Emma's lunch.

'Well, it's supposed to be chicken Caesar salad,' says Emma, poking her fork at a depressed collection of limp lettuce, stale croutons and yellowing chicken in salad cream.

'I told you to go for the sausage,' says Martin.

'Oi, oi, none of that!' says Charlie, laughing like Sid James on speed. Martin giggles.

'Honestly. What are they like?' asks Stacey with an indulgent smile. Emma doesn't reply. 'So, Em!' she squeaks, flicking a hair extension and patting Emma on the knee. 'Tell me about the wedding plans!'

Emma smiles at Stacey. She is a lovely girl, always very friendly and kind. Emma finds her taste in boyfriends questionable but tells herself that it doesn't make her a bad person. She and Stacey are just different people. 'Well, I think I've found my dress,' she confides.

'Wicked! What's it like?' Emma looks over to check Martin isn't listening but he and Charlie are engrossed in their food and the football.

'Well,' says Emma, with an indulgent smile. 'It's very simple, very classic.'

'Lovely. Where are you getting it from?'

Emma feels a little embarrassed. 'Erm, just someone my godmother knows. She's making it for me.'

'Ahh, that's lovely and should save a bit of money, eh?' Emma nods uncertainly. 'And what flowers are you going to have? Oh, I know what I was going to say, do you want me to ask my mum to make the cake?' Emma opens her mouth to speak and then thinks better of it. 'Because she makes these really lovely ones. They look dead professional. Want me to ask her?'

'That's really kind of you, Stacey, but we haven't really decided what we're going to have yet. Can I let you know?'

''Course, no probs. The offer's there if you want it.'

'Thank you. Very much,' says Emma relieved.

'Don't you like your salad?' asks Martin, pointing at her untouched plate.

Emma shakes her head. 'Think I might get some chips, actually.'

'That's the spirit!' says Charlie. 'Don't want you wasting away, eh girl?'

Emma smiles and watches as Charlie puts his arm around Stacey, feeling envious of their easy companionship.

'All right, gel?' he grins.

'All right, fella?' she smiles.

'Drinks?' asks Martin. He takes their orders and disappears to the bar leaving Emma wondering what to say next.

'So, what's new with you two?' she asks.

Stacey and Charlie exchange glances and Charlie nods encouragement at his girlfriend as Martin returns with the drinks.

'Actually, we've got something to tell you,' says Stacey, looking uncharacteristically shy. She looks at Charlie again who winks at her. 'I'm pregnant!' she cries. Several people look round from their lunchtime pints and cheer at them. Stacey laughs and the next few minutes are taken up with hugs and kisses and 'well done mates' among the four people.

'That's brilliant news. Really brilliant!' says Martin.

'Well, it's nice to know that the old man's doing his job,' says Charlie patting his groin.

'Charlie!' scolds Stacey laughing.

Charlie looks at Martin and Emma. 'And it means that there'll be a little fella lined up when you two finally get your act together.'

'Cheeky! It might be a little girl,' says Stacey.

Charlie raises his eyes at Martin. 'The next thing you'll be telling me is that girls can play football.' He eyes Emma waiting for the reaction. He isn't disappointed.

'Well, can't they?' she says, narrowing her eyes at him.

'Not properly,' he replies and then does a 'winding up' mime.

'Well, let's hope if it is a boy, it doesn't inherit its father's misogyny,' says Emma.

'*Ding ding*! And that's the end of round one!' cries Martin trying to inject some humour back into proceedings. Emma shuts her mouth and folds her arms. 'Right, well, it's brilliant news. Congratulations. Both of you,' he says, looking embarrassed at Emma's silence. 'I don't think it will be too long before we're joining you in the parenting game.'

Stacey pats Emma's arm. 'It'll be brill, Em. We can go to the park with the kids, share the school run. How many do you want? I want at least three,' she says without waiting for Emma to reply. She launches into a gushing commentary on babies and children without pausing for breath. Emma wishes she shared Stacey's maternal urges but she's not sure if she's ready for all that yet. She looks at Martin. Is she really ready for weekends with Charlie and Stacey in the park with their children? She shudders at the thought. Martin finishes his beer and issues forth a loud belch.

'Pardon me.' Stacey giggles but Emma frowns. Martin always gets like this when he's with Charlie. It's like he's a different person somehow and it's annoying her today.

'Are you ready to go, Martin?' she asks.

'Absolutely, darl. Right, Charlie, I'll see you tomorrow. Stacey, congratulations again, darling.'

'What's tomorrow?' asks Emma confused.

'I told you. Charlie and I are going to look at a venue for the stag do.'

'You didn't tell me.'

'Uh-oh, trouble in paradise,' mutters Charlie.

Emma ignores him. 'I can't believe you're going to look for somewhere for the stag do when we've got all the other stuff for the wedding to sort out!'

Martin looks sheepish. 'Well, it is part of the wedding and it does need to be done.'

'Right, fine. Fine,' says Emma not wanting to continue the argument in front of Charlie, who is relishing the spectacle. 'Goodbye, Charlie; goodbye, Stacey. Congratulations again,' she says walking out of the pub without a backward glance.

'Last one to the top of Arthur's Seat buys the ice creams!'

The kids bound ahead like excited puppies. Steve offers his wife a hand.

'Why thank you, kind sir.' They walk hand in hand for a while not speaking, concentrating on breathing and admiring the immense view that is unravelling in front of them as if someone is lifting a blind on the world. The sky is filled with billowing grey and white clouds, but the wind is spiralling them across the sky at such a rate that if you stood still and looked up, you would think that you were moving.

'Don't go too far, kids!' bellows Rachel.

Steve is ahead of her now. 'It's OK. I can see them.'

'When did I get so unfit?' she puffs as she catches up with him.

'That would be when you had children.'

'I thought they were supposed to make you fitter. Phew! I don't remember it being this difficult when we last did this. When was that?'

'1990 and our ascent was fuelled by a night of filthy sex, a gigantic fry-up including haggis and two pints of Heavy.' Rachel giggles at the memory.

'Ah yes, happy days and didn't we, erm, seal the deal again at the summit?'

'I think we did. Gave those Japanese tourists quite a fright, didn't we?'

'Ha, ha, Mummy and Daddy are losers!' shouts Lily as she reaches the top. Reunited, the five of them sit and share some chocolate.

'Why is it called Arthur's Seat?' asks Lily.

'Something to do with a famous king called Arthur, I think. Actually, this used to be a volcano,' says Steve.

'Cool!' shout Lily and Will.

'A volcano?' says Alfie looking around nervously as if he is about to be engulfed by molten lava.

Lily tuts. 'You're such a baby, Alfie!'

'Am not!' cries Alfie, his face turning red.

'Are!'

'Not!' A couple of tourists look round.

'OK! OK!' says Rachel. 'Time Out! Why don't you go and see what you can spot over there?' Rachel and Steve watch the kids run off, jostling and carefree.

'That's what they need, isn't it?' says Steve eventually.

'What? A walk up a hill followed by a Kit Kat?'

'You know what I mean, Rach.'

'Yeah well, we have hills in south-east London.'

'Oh yeah, where?'

'Crystal Palace is very hilly.'

Rachel looks out at the view and breathes in. 'When did life become so complicated?'

Steve falls silent for a moment. 'I think,' he says, his voice filled with sincerity. 'I think it was around the time they changed Marathon bars to Snickers.'

'Ha bloody ha.'

'Oh come on, Rach. Why does everything have to be so serious all the time? Why can't we just live a little, laugh a little?'

'Isn't that a supermarket tagline?'

'See? You can't take this any more seriously than I can. Look, the bottom line is that this is a real chance for us; something different and new and exciting! So – '

'So? Move to Scotland?'

'Why not? Look, Rach, it doesn't have to be for ever. We could just rent a house for as long as I'm doing this job. See if we like it. Move back if we don't.'

'But what about Mum and Dad?'

'Rach. They can visit. Anytime.'

'All right, steady. Don't give Mum ideas!'

Steve laughs. 'I just think we should give it a go.'

Rachel looks at the children running in the distance and takes a deep breath. 'All right then.'

'What?'

'I mean, I'm not saying yes, I'm not saying no, but I think we should go and look at some houses tomorrow.'

'Really?'

'Yes. Now let's go and have a pint. I'm gasping!'

She grabs Steve's hand and they scoop up the children on their way down the hill, whooping and laughing all the way.

Emma looks around the flat and feels her heckles rise. She is tired and dehydrated after one lunchtime glass of wine too many and is bristling from Martin's revelation about spending tomorrow with Charlie. She is starting to feel as if she is the only one doing anything towards their wedding and is also feeling a bit guilty about letting Martin chase Richard away yesterday. She did send him a text to apologise and he had sent her a short and somewhat abrupt message: 'Nothing to apologise for. Have a good weekend.' She had considered calling him but wasn't sure what the right course of action might be. He is just her author after all, nothing more.

She wants to follow Martin's example and lie on the sofa, snoozing with the papers. However, as a woman she knows this option is simply not open to her. The kitchen needs to be tidied, the bathroom needs to be cleaned, the clothes which have been hanging on the airer all week are demanding to be put away and she can not rest until she has at least attempted some of these jobs. She moves towards the kitchen surfaces and lets out a loud 'Oh for God's sake' at the open pot of jam with a sticky knife protruding from the top, the discarded foil from a newly opened tub of butter and the teabag nestled on a teaspoon in a pool of tea. Emma hates housework, but knows that she will feel a lot better once it is done. It's just that it will take a lot of swearing and cupboard slamming before she gets to that stage.

'All right, sweet pea?' asks Martin, wandering into the kitchen and, unwittingly, a domestic war zone.

'No, not really!'

'What's up?'

'Are you blind?'

'Sorry?'

'Look at the state of this kitchen!'

'Oh yeah, sorry. We left in a bit of a hurry. I meant to do that.'

'It's disgusting.'

'All right, Em, calm down. I'll do it in a bit.'

'Calm down? Calm down? Martin, does it ever occur to you to just clean up without being asked? I mean, I do work just as hard as you and yet it's always me cleaning up after us, making sure it gets done. Would it kill you to clean the bathroom without being asked once in a while?'

'No, but I just don't think of doing it. I'll do it if you remind me.'

'But I don't want to remind you, I don't want to be the nagger and the whinger!'

Martin looks at his nagging, whingeing fiancée. 'OK, so don't then,' he says with the innocence of a child.

'Aaaaaargh! You're so annoying!' shouts Emma. 'You just don't get it, do you?'

'Well, I don't think I'm going to tonight, no,' quips Martin unwisely.

Emma fixes him with a glare and points a finger at him. 'You are pathetic.'

'Emma, calm down! I said I would clear up and I will.'

'But when? When? Today? Tomorrow? The day of the next lunar eclipse?'

'Today! In a minute. Why does it matter? Why are you being like this?'

Emma shakes her head and starts to cry. 'I don't know! I don't know!' she sobs. 'I just feel so – ' She covers her face with her hands, realising that the word that is pounding in her ears but which she can't bring herself to say is 'trapped'.

Martin tries to prise her hands from her face. 'What is it? Tell me, Em, what's the matter?'

'I don't know! I told you, I don't know! Just leave me alone, will you?' She pushes him away, rushes from the room and flings open the front door just as her father is about to knock.

'Hello, youngest daughter. I was just passing and – ' he begins and then seeing his daughter's face, opens his arms to her. 'Hey, hey, what's all this?'

Martin appears behind Emma at the door. 'Oh hi, Edward, sorry, just a minor spat about domestic chores. Would you like a cup of tea?'

'Well, I don't want to intrude.'

'No, it's fine, you go and have a seat with Em.'

Edward leads his daughter into the living room and they sit down on the sofa. He reaches into his pocket and retrieves a large monogrammed handkerchief and offers it to his daughter. She sniffs and accepts it gratefully, smiling at him from behind red puffy eyes.

'Are you all right?'

'Yes. Thanks. Sorry, Dad.'

'Oh you don't need to apologise to me. I just don't like seeing you upset. It reminds me of when you were a nipper and your sister used to terrorise you. Mind you, when you were a bit bigger, you gave as good as you got.' He laughs at the memory. 'So, do you want to talk about it?'

'I don't know that there's anything to talk about. Probably just work stress or the wedding or both.'

'You know, you don't have to be a superwoman all the time, Em. It's OK to give yourself a day off every now and then.'

'I know.'

'And Martin is a good man, you know.'

'I know.'

'Men are just poor, weak souls and it's up to you women to show us the way and goodness only knows the Darcy women are better at that than most.'

Emma laughs through the tears.

'Is there anything else?'

She contemplates telling her father about Richard, but knows she can't. It's a Pandora's box that she's too confused to open.

'No. I feel better for a chat and a hug, thanks.'

'Just like when you were five.'

Martin comes into the room with the tea. 'Feeling better?' he asks.

'Much,' she lies.

'Good stuff. Well, I'll just go and sort the kitchen and bathroom. You stay and chat to your dad.'

Emma looks at her father and smiles. 'I am lucky, I know,' she says.

'Just as long as you're happy, Em. That's the main thing.'

'I am,' she lies again, wishing that she could shake off the nagging sensation that she is losing control of her life and everything in it.

CHAPTER SEVENTEEN

'This is a wonderful area for schools and as you can see, it's already a family home so you could move in straightaway,' says the matronly estate agent in a Miss Jean Brodie voice, peering at them from behind her half-moon spectacles.

'I don't like it!' declares Lily.

The estate agent behaves as if no one has spoken and looks expectantly at Rachel and Steve.

'It's very nice,' says Rachel feebly.

'I love it!' shouts Will, sliding down the wooden-floored hall on his knees.

'Let's go and have a look upstairs, shall we?' says Steve, keen to keep them on the move.

The estate agent ushers them up in front of her.

Alfie stays by her side. 'Excuse me?'

'Yes?' replies the woman, horrified to be addressed by a small child with snot streaming from his nose.

'Why do you talk like that?'

'Sorry! Sorry!' says Rachel wondering if she will have to spend the rest of her life apologising for her family. 'He's at that very direct age!' she explains.

'I see,' says the estate agent.

'Mum! The toilet works!' calls Lily from upstairs.

Rachel smiles at the woman and hurtles upstairs after her daughter.

'I thought she was lovely,' says Lily without irony as they watch the estate agent drive away.

'Excellent, great. OK, one more to go then,' says Steve with his trademark optimism.

The other members of his family groan.

'This is boring,' says Will. 'When can we have something to eat?'

'Oh come on, guys! This is our only chance to have a good look round. Alfie!' says Steve, scooping up the most compliant member of the group. 'You want to go and look round another house with Daddy, don't you? This one's got a big garden!'

Alfie looks uncertain. ''kay,' he says, burying his head in his father's shoulder.

'Weakling!' mutters Lily.

'Come on, Steve, this is the third one we've seen,' echoes Rachel.

'Rach, I promise you. You're going to love this one.'

'That's what you said about the last one.'

'Trust me.'

Rachel looks at her husband and then at the children. 'Come on, kids! Last house and then Dad's going to buy us the biggest lunch ever!'

Emma pours herself another cup of coffee and picks up the newspaper, listening to Martin singing cheerfully in the shower. They had managed to broker a fragile peace yesterday with Martin overcompensating for his failings by not only cleaning the house but also changing the bed linen and cooking dinner. They had cuddled up on the sofa but Emma had felt restless. She had excused herself and gone to bed early, pretending to be asleep when Martin came up some time later. That morning he had treated her to breakfast in bed but instead of feeling touched, she was irritated and she wasn't sure why. Her phone buzzes with a text from Rachel: 'Ednbrgh grey and S gt us on our 4th hse. L pooed in the last 1. Hope yr hvng a gd w/e and M was helpfl wth the flwrs - lol. Rx'

Emma smiles and sends back a non-committal reply. She would actually quite like to see her sister now. She's probably the only one who could help her cut through the crap and see her situation for what it is.

Martin appears in the bedroom doorway wearing a towel and a cautious smile. 'How was your breakfast?'

'Lovely, thank you,' says Emma stretching.

'Look, I'm sorry we got our wires crossed about today but I shouldn't be late. Shall I cook us a roast when I get back?'

Emma shrugs. He's trying too hard again. 'I might go out, see if Ella's around, maybe go to the cinema.'

'Em, are you still cross with me?'

She shrugs again. Martin perches on the end of the bed. 'Look, Em, I'm trying my hardest, OK. I've said sorry, cleaned the house, made you breakfast, what more do you want?'

It's a reasonable question but Emma isn't feeling reasonable today. 'I want you to think before you act and not afterwards.'

He looks at the ceiling and sighs. 'OK, OK. Just give me a break sometimes will you? I'm doing my best.'

'Well, it's obviously not good enough.'

'Obviously not,' he says getting dressed. She can tell he's angry now. He takes his wallet and keys and kisses her on the cheek. She doesn't respond. 'I'll see you later,' he says disappearing down the stairs.

She waits for him to slam the door but he doesn't and that irritates her too. Typical Martin; so bloody reasonable all the time, he even exits an argument in a rational, considered way. She picks up the newspaper and flicks to the book pages and there, staring out at her with his intense gaze, is Richard Bennett. She skims the article, which is by a female journalist who obviously fell for Richard on sight. She reports how well he writes about women and asks about his inspiration. In his answer Richard confesses to being a terrible flirt and much happier in the company of women. He says that he has known many strong and impressive women and is lucky that his latest editor is such a person and that he has drawn great strength and inspiration from knowing her. Emma almost drops the paper in shock and feels herself redden at the compliment. She tells herself that it doesn't mean anything. A lot of authors are inspired by the editors they work with – it's part of the creative process. And yet she feels as if Richard is sending her a message somehow. She picks up her phone and scrolls down until she finds his number. She looks around the room as if searching for the answer as to what she should do. She tells herself that she's merely calling to congratulate him on the article and presses dial.

He answers after one ring. 'Emma Darcy.' His voice is warm and welcoming like an embrace.

'I just wanted to say that I thought the article was great.'

'Thank you.' His voice is expectant.

'And to apologise again for Martin. I felt bad that our lunch ended that way.'

'Well, I admire your fiancé for staking his claim.' Emma detects a note of irony.

'Yes well, he has been severely scolded.'

'Lucky man. And where is he at the moment? I'm guessing he doesn't know you're making this call or is he about to come onto the phone and give me what for.'

There is a playfulness to his voice, which Emma knows should be sounding alarm bells in her brain. He is clearly enjoying the illicit nature of their conversation.

'Actually, he's out for the day.' As soon as the words are out of her mouth she knows she's in trouble. With one sentence she has made herself sound available and suggestive all at once.

'I see.' He is toying with her, she knows this but her heart is beating fast and there's another emotion. Is it longing or excitement? She is on the brink of ending their chat when he says, 'Well, I've got this lunchtime thing to go to at a pub in north London if you fancy it? A friend of mine is doing a poetry reading and I've promised to go. To be honest, I'm dreading it but it would be altogether more palatable if you were to join me.'

And there it is. The beginning of the end or is it the beginning of the beginning? Emma isn't sure. This isn't an author meeting, it isn't a discussion about plots or publication plans. There are no excuses this time. Richard Bennett is asking her out on a date.

She pauses for a moment, her mind racing. She is about to decline the offer when she remembers Martin and his trip with Charlie. It is a combination of still-simmering anger with her fiancé and a longing for a small adventure that leads her to say, 'I'd love to.' After they have finished the call, Emma runs herself a shower and lays out some clothes, trying to ignore the fact that she is taking more time than usual over her outfit.

The flat seems too quiet somehow so she switches on the radio and tunes in to *Desert Island Discs*. By the time she is ready to leave she has convinced herself that this isn't a date at all – it's just two friends, work colleagues really, meeting in a public place for lunch. Yes, that's it – just friends and nothing more. She leaves the house quickly, shutting the door firmly behind her and marching down the road to the station before she can change her mind.

'Mummy, what happens if the pilot gets sick?' demands Lily so loudly that people ten rows in front turn, some of them looking with interest at Rachel, waiting for the answer. Rachel looks behind her at Steve, who is sitting with the boys. Alfie is asleep and Will is playing his Nintendo. Steve looks up from his newspaper and gives her a thumbs-up. She sticks out her tongue in reply.

'Mummy?'

'Yes, darling?'

'What about the pilot?'

'Oh yes, the pilot. Don't worry, if the pilot gets sick, there's a co-pilot to take over.'

'Right. But what about if he gets sick?'

'Well, that never happens.'

'How can you be so sure?'

'Because it has never happened, so it never will happen.'

'But you can't say that. They said that Maisy's grandad wouldn't die, but he did. Why do adults lie all the time?'

'It's not lying, Lily. People don't always know what's going to happen.'

'See? There you go. You don't know what's going to happen so you can't say that. The pilots might both get ill and then there would be no one to fly the plane and then we would crash.' Lily delivers this final word with a loud clap of her hands. Rachel can see several people looking more than a little worried now. One of them alerts a stewardess and starts to point in Rachel's direction. The stewardess stalks towards them, and Rachel is horrified to see that it's the same woman they met at the departure gate on the way out.

'Madam?' says the woman, baring her teeth in a thin white smile.

'Yes?' says Rachel trying to maintain an air of innocence.

'Madam, we've had a complaint from another passenger about the content and volume of your daughter's conversation.'

'Oh right,' says Rachel starting to feel her primal maternal urges kick in. 'What seems to be the problem?'

'Well, some passengers are rather nervous of flying and therefore, using words like "crash" might cause them to panic.'

'You mean to say that people are being intimidated by the fanciful talk of a four-year-old?' says Rachel.

'I didn't mean to cause offence, madam,' says the woman with emphasis on the word, 'madam'. 'We just need to cater to the needs of all our customers.'

'I see, well I'm sorry for the over-sensitivity of another passenger. I will tell my daughter that she needs to be seen and not heard in future.' Rachel realises that this is the point in an argument when she would usually storm off but that being in a large metal tube prevents her from doing this. Luckily, the stewardess is called to the front for the safety announcement but not before she gives Rachel a final, disapproving look.

As she walks away, Lily remarks, 'Is that the orange lady we saw on the way out? Why is she so cross?'

'I have no idea, darling,' says Rachel kissing her daughter on the head.

'Excuse me,' says a jovial looking Scottish lady from the row in front. 'Just wanted to say good for you, lassie. These air hostesses are so up their own ends these days! Hope you don't mind me asking but would your little girl like one of these?' She holds up a box of shortbread. 'I've been staying with my daughter and she sent me home with some. Much better than that shop-bought crap! Oops, pardon my French!' Lily giggles at the woman and accepts a biscuit.

'Thank you,' says Rachel, grateful for the support.

'So have you been staying in Edinburgh then?'

'Yes, yes, actually we're thinking of moving up here.'

'Oh yes? Good for you. Best city in the world, Edinburgh. I've been visiting my daughter. I used to live here but moved to London for my husband's job. Biggest mistake I ever made. Now I have to spend my whole time going back to visit my family. I'm going to try to move back myself soon. Do you want to move?'

Rachel looks at Lily who is now bossing her Barbie collection into some order and considers the question. She takes a deep breath.

Emma has had a wholly enjoyable day. She met Richard at the pub as planned and was initially thrown off guard when it turned out that he was meeting some of his own friends there. However, they were a friendly and lively bunch; intelligent and funny and they took Emma to their companionable bosoms straightaway. One of the girls, Daisy, took an instant liking to Emma, sharing her bottle of wine and quizzing her about her publishing life.

'It's so lovely to meet you. Richard has told me a lot about you. It's a shame you're getting married as I reckon you'd be perfect for each other. You're much nicer than that bitch, Stella,' she declared, knocking glasses with Emma and taking a huge gulp of her wine.

Richard's poet friend had actually been quite good and gave an enthusiastic reading, buoyed by Daisy's wolf whistles and his other friend's rowdy cheering. Emma liked them and found herself thinking how different this pub meeting was to the one with Stacey and Charlie the day before. Was it so wrong to prefer the company of people with similar minds and intelligence? Of course, that made her sound like a snob and she didn't mean it. She just felt more at home here somehow. She didn't talk to Richard much during the lunch but she did catch him looking over at her every now and then. At one stage he raised his glass to her and she smiled in response. When Daisy disappeared to the toilet, he plonked himself in her vacated seat and smiled.

'Having a good time?'

'Lovely. I like your friends.'

'They're a good bunch. Daisy's very excitable but she looks out for me.'

'She's great.'

After lunch, they had gone for a stroll in a nearby park. Everyone was a little drunk and they laughed their way round, kicking up the fallen leaves and pushing each other like schoolchildren. Emma had glanced at her watch and seeing the time said, 'I better go.'

Richard nodded. 'I'll walk you to the Tube.'

Daisy had given her a squeezing embrace goodbye and told her to, 'Marry Richard if it all falls through with the other bloke.' Emma had looked at Richard as she said this but he was saying goodbye to someone else.

It was starting to get dark and chilly as they reached the Tube entrance and as they stopped to say goodbye, Richard had reached out to pull Emma's coat more snugly around her.

'There,' he said satisfied, his eyes shining with friendly amusement.

Emma looked up at him. 'I had a wonderful time. Thank you for inviting me.' She could feel his breath on her cheek and thought she knew what was coming. She was ready now. She tilted her head upwards and could see Richard studying her face. The kiss brushed lightly past her lips and landed on her cheek.

'I'll see you soon,' he said, turning to leave. He glanced back at her. 'I'm really glad you came.'

Emma felt as if she was in a trance as she made her way through the ticket barrier and down the escalators. She was trying to decipher her emotions as she made her way onto the platform. As the train pulled into the station, she realised that what she was feeling was a lurching disappointment that she wasn't still standing outside the Tube station kissing Richard Bennett.

'Well, good luck, dearie. It was lovely to meet you and really super to meet you too, Lily – don't forget to keep telling people the truth, will you? They need that!'

'I know, I won't. Thanks, Edie!' grins Lily and gives the old lady a kiss. Rachel enjoys a rare moment of unadulterated pride.

'Right, got the bags. Let's go!' says Steve.

Once in the car, the three children are quiet and one by one they nod off. Rachel yawns and stretches out her legs. She reaches over and strokes the back of Steve's head.

'All right, gorgeous?' he smiles.

'Yes thanks, handsome.'

'It was a good trip in the end, wasn't it?'

'Yes it was.'

'And I was right about that house, wasn't I?'

'You were. It is gorgeous and I could really see us there.'

'So?'

'So – '

'You still don't want to, do you?'

'I didn't say that, Steve.'

'But I can sense it. You've made up your mind, haven't you?'

'Yes, I've made up my mind.'

'I knew it! I knew it! You'd made up your mind before we went. You were never going to change it!'

'Now hang on a minute, matey, you haven't asked me properly.'

'What do you mean?'

'You haven't actually asked me what I've decided.'

'Do I need to?'

'Well, I do have a problem actually.'

'Oh yes?'

'Yeah, I'm not sure how I'm going to tell Mum and Emma we're going.'

'What?'

'You heard me, cowboy.'

'Are you serious?'

'I had my doubts but I was coming round and then I talked to that lady on the plane and she just made me realise what I had and what we need.'

Steve is beaming at her now. 'That's brilliant, Rach, really brilliant! God I love you.'

'And I love you too, Mr Summers.'

Steve smiles over at Rachel. Her phone beeps with a text. She looks at it. It's from Emma: 'R u movng 2 Edinburgh or not?'

She switches off her phone and puts her arm around Steve.

CHAPTER EIGHTEEN

Emma steps into the lift and checks her reflection, willing away the dark shadows under her eyes. She hadn't slept well last night. Coming home to Martin had brought her back down to earth with a guilty bump. He had been kind and attentive, too attentive in fact. As they had sex that night, she had tried but failed to stop herself from imagining it was Richard making love to her.

'Morning, Emma!' says Ella, sneaking in before the doors close.

'Hi,' says Emma, her voice flat.

'Look, I – ' begins Ella.

'Hold that lift!'

It's the unmistakeable bark of Joel. Ella presses the buttons, panicked. Emma sees this as proof that something is going on between them and looks at the ceiling, shaking her head.

Joel darts into the lift without a word of thanks. 'Ladies,' he says by way of a greeting. Emma ignores him and presses the button for the fifteenth floor.

Joel coughs. 'Actually I'm off to the twenty-first floor. The Yanks are in town and Phil Allen has asked to see me.'

'He probably wants to deliver your P45 in person,' says Emma.

Joel's laugh is accompanied by a wrinkle-faced sneer and a shake of the head. 'I don't think so. He's probably heard about some of my more cutting-edge marketing techniques and wants to sound me out.'

They have reached the fifteenth floor and Joel steps aside for them with a little bow.

'Emma?'

'What?'

'If he asks me if I know an editor with a penchant for profit-leaking books, I'll be sure to give him your name.' The doors close and Emma and Ella are left side by side.

'That man!'

'I know.'

'I just want to – '

'I know.'

Emma looks at her friend and sees desperation in her eyes.

Ella takes a deep breath. 'I'm sorry I've been a bit distant lately. I've just had a lot going on. Can we go for a coffee later? I'll explain everything.'

Emma sees how much her friend needs her and realises that she could do with a friend too. 'Of course.'

Ella smiles gratefully.

They walk into the offices and are greeted by the bustling, coffee-laden form of Joy, the formidable office manager, who is the fount of all knowledge at Allen Chandler. 'Morning, girls!'

'Hi, Joy. How are things?' says Emma.

'Oh you know, bearing up under the strain. I suppose you've heard the news?'

'What news?'

'There's a big powwow going on upstairs. Company meeting at ten.'

'Really? What's that about?'

Joy approaches them, looking around her, as if checking for spies. 'I reckon it's a bit of a management shake-up,' she whispers.

'Oh shit!' says Emma.

'What?' asks Ella.

'Bloody Joel's on his way up there. Why can't they see what a slippery customer he is?'

'Because he's good at covering his tracks?'

'Everyone knows that Philippa's been doing his job for years. It's a travesty!'

'Don't you worry, Emma,' says Joy, taking on the tone of a wise oracle. 'If there's one thing I've learned in this place, it's that every dog will have his day.'

'Well, he's bloody overdue his day,' says Emma.

'Don't let the buggers get you down,' says Joy with a wink.

Ella and Emma reach their desks and Emma switches on her computer, firing up her e-mails, not expecting anything major on a Monday. The first thing she sees is an e-mail from Richard. Her heart quickens and she notices that it was sent either very late last night or very early this morning depending on how you view your day. The subject is blank but as Emma clicks to the message she can see that this is no one sentence message. She scans the words, hungry for information and her eyes come to rest on the last sentence: 'You are the most incredible woman I have ever met.'

'Good morning, Emma; Ella,' says Miranda.

Emma jumps and clicks shut the e-mail as if she's been stung. 'Good morning,' she says, turning to face her and immediately noticing how weary she is looking. 'Is everything all right?'

Miranda inhales deeply. 'There are some days, my dear girl, when you know you are going to need a large gin and tonic by 11 a.m. and this is one of those days.'

Emma looks nonplussed but Miranda offers no further explanation. 'I take it you know about the company meeting at ten?'

Emma and Ella nod.

'Good. I'm glad to see the Joy-telegraph is still working its magic. See you anon.' She sweeps off in a blur of purple silk.

'Curiouser and curiouser,' says Ella.

'Hmm,' says Emma turning back to her e-mail.

'Coffee?' asks Ella heading for the kitchen.

'Please,' says Emma, grateful to be left alone to read Richard's e-mail in peace.

Rachel reaches the coffee shop early for once. She is meeting an old friend from the ad agency who has recently had a baby. Her mother, fearful that her grandchildren are about to be whipped away to the North at any second, was only too happy to entertain Lily and Alfie for the morning. So, having dropped Will at school, Rachel is looking forward to a visit to the coffee shop without having to wipe sticky fingers or buy an endless supply of muffins.

She orders a large skinny latte and takes a seat by the window. She checks her watch. She is still early and so unused is Rachel to this sensation, that she doesn't know what to do with herself. She stirs her coffee and sits back in the chair but feels as if she should be doing something. Realising she is experiencing restless mother syndrome, she plucks her mobile from her bag and finds Emma's number.

'Hey, Rach,' answers Emma sounding flat.

'Ooh lordy, what's up with you, tart-face?' asks Rachel unsympathetic as ever.

'Nothing,' lies Emma. 'How was Edinburgh?'

'Brilliant actually. How would you feel about having a sister who lives north of Watford?'

'You're not serious?'

'I think I am but don't tell Mum. I'm going to have to ease her into the idea.'

'Good luck with that one. Wow, Rach, that's incredible. It must have been one hell of a visit.'

'It was. I could really see us there and sometimes you've just got to seize the moment, haven't you?'

'I guess,' says Emma, thinking about her own moment-seizing.

'What's up, Em? Are you going to miss me?'

'I will, actually,' says Emma.

'Are you sure you're OK? What happened at the weekend?'

'Oh, nothing really. Just a bit annoyed with Martin because I seem to be doing everything for the wedding. Anyway, I'm sorry I've got to go as I am tremendously busy and important,' says Emma, trying to inject a note of humour to reassure Rachel.

'All right but come for tea soon, yeah? The kids love their Auntie Em. And I always like having someone around to take the piss out of.'

'OK,' laughs Emma weakly. 'Bye.'

Rachel feels a little uneasy as she puts her phone back in her bag and wonders if she should call Martin, then chides herself for reacting as her mother would.

There's a subdued air in the boardroom as Emma and Ella join their colleagues. Only Jacqui and Joel are the exception, chatting in excited voices, smiling at anyone who will look their way, perched like eager schoolchildren in the front row. Emma notices Miranda, also sitting at the front and is concerned to see her shoulders hunched and her head bowed as if in prayer. They find some seats in the middle row next to Philippa, who gives a small wave.

'Any idea what this is about?' whispers Emma.

'Not a clue, but I don't think it's good news.'

Their conversation is interrupted as Philip Allen, CEO of Allen Chandler, strides into the room flanked by a tall, well-built man and a short, compact woman. They take their places at the front. Philip turns to face the room, which is full to bursting, with latecomers being forced to stand.

'Good morning!' he begins.

The crowd murmurs in reply and Philip looks a little perturbed by this typically British response. Emma fears he's going to try it again, like some kind of corporate children's entertainer but happily, he thinks better of it.

'OK, guys, I guess you're probably wondering what's going on and I just want to say from the outset that none of you need to worry. Your jobs are all safe for the time being.'

'Blimey,' whispers Emma, 'if I wasn't worried before, I am now!'

'I wanted to bring you all together to update you on the strategic review which we initiated last year and which is now complete.'

Emma, who has an aversion to people who use words like 'strategic' forces her brain to carry on listening.

'As a result of this review we have decided to undertake a restructure at the top level and it is my duty to inform you that Digby Chandler will be taking a well-earned retirement and relinquishing his responsibilities as MD. I would like to take this opportunity to thank him for all his hard work.'

He continues to speak but Emma is no longer listening as she is watching Miranda, who is motionless. Eventually Philip stops speaking and then the well-built man, who is something to do with finance, starts enthusing about bottom lines and five-year profit projections.

Shut up, shut up, thinks Emma. *Can't you see that people are in shock?*

After a lot of arm flapping, he stops talking too and then the small woman, who announces herself to be the Head of Human Resources, tells them to come and see her if they have any questions. Her voice is as soothing as honey and Emma distrusts her on sight. They are dismissed but no one really moves and the room is silent apart from the odd murmured word between colleagues. The Americans, obviously fearing a mutiny, are quick to leave, closely followed by Joel, who can be heard calling 'Phil? Phil? Can I have a quick word please?'

'Judas,' mutters Emma, 'he's probably going to put himself forward.' As soon as the words are out of her mouth, Emma realises the horror of the situation. 'Oh my God, he's probably going to go for the job and then he'll be my boss and I'll have to kill myself!'

'Emma,' says Ella quietly and then again as her friend continues to rant, 'Emma!'

'Yes? Sorry! What?'

Ella nods over to where Miranda sits. People are starting to leave now, but Miranda continues to sit and stare into the distance. One or two stop to see if she is all right, but she waves them away and stays where she is.

Emma approaches her. 'Miranda?'

Miranda looks up and Emma sees tears in her eyes. Emma sits down beside her and takes her hand. 'Oh Miranda, I'm so sorry.'

Miranda pats her hand. 'Thank you, dear girl.'

'How is Digby?'

'Oh, he'll be fine, silly old fool. He'll just go to his club every day and write his memoirs. It's just another nail in the coffin of imaginative publishing. Another step towards letting the bindweed of pappy fiction take over the world, rather than allowing some interesting new seedling to flourish alongside.'

'That's a great metaphor,' says Emma. 'Have you ever thought of going into publishing?' Miranda gives a weak smile. 'So, what do you think will happen? Do you think the Americans will stop us publishing literary titles?' she asks, suddenly concerned about Richard.

'I really don't know, but I tell you one thing, Emma, if they start telling me how to publish fiction, I'll be off to the nearest competitor before they can tell me to "Have a nice day".'

Emma laughs. 'I'm very glad to hear it.'

'Right, well I'm off for lunch with my literary husband. Can I count on you to keep the home fire burning?'

'Always. Give Digby our love, won't you?'

Miranda stands and puts her arms around Emma.

'You are a good woman, Emma Darcy.'

Emma smiles and watches Miranda leave the room, feeling as if her world is slowly and quietly imploding.

Rachel is enjoying her morning, although she leaves the coffee shop feeling oddly unsettled. It had been lovely to catch up with her friend, Olivia. Her baby had been cute and thankfully asleep so they were able to have a grown-up conversation without distractions. Olivia was planning to go back to work once her baby reached six months and Rachel had felt a pang of envy at her confident decision.

'I just can't stay at home all the time,' she had declared. 'It would drive me potty!'

Rachel knows what she means.

'And what about you? How do you cope with it all?'

Rachel had considered the question and brushed it off with her usual self-deprecating humour. 'Oh you know, there's always a bottle of wine in the fridge but I try not to touch it until at least eleven!'

They had laughed and gone on to discuss work and the latest gossip from the ad agency. Whenever she met old work-colleagues, Rachel always longed to be told that it was all falling apart without her. Of course that never happened.

'So, Amanda, you know, who took over your job has just been promoted. She's such a lovely person and so good at her job,' Olivia said.

Rachel had nodded and smiled. *Curse the woman*. 'And how's Daniel?'

'Oh you know Daniel, married to the job but fine, I think. I think he misses you.' Rachel clung onto the sentiment like a life raft. 'So what about you and Steve? How are things?'

Rachel had confided the Scotland news and watched as Olivia's eyes grew wide with horror. 'Oh God and do you really want to go?'

Rachel considered the question. 'I think so.'

'Well, good for you,' chimed Olivia. 'I don't think I'd be up for Scotland. I'd miss London and my parents too much,' she added, giving voice to Rachel's deepest worries.

Rachel had kissed Olivia goodbye and promised to meet her for a drink soon. She could feel a knot of uncertainty growing in her stomach. She thought she'd made a decision but now the doubts were flying round her head again like a swarm of persistent flies. She had phoned her parents to see how they were getting on and thankfully her father had answered. He had insisted that Lily and Alfie stay for lunch and Rachel had gratefully accepted. So now she is working her way along the shops on the high street, relishing not having to negotiate doorways with a heavy pushchair or endlessly apologise for her children being children. She makes her way to her favourite haven; their local, independent bookshop. Once inside she scans the shelves, admiring the covers, enjoying the luxury of time. She breathes in the heady smell of new books and runs her fingers along their spines, picking out titles at random and reading the blurb on the back. She is just considering the new Anne Tyler when she hears a voice next to her.

'I can strongly recommend – ' She looks up into the handsome, round face of Tom.

'Hello!'

'Good day, Mrs Summers. Are you going to buy it then?'

'You're a fan of Anne Tyler?'

'I am.'

'Isn't it a bit girly for boys?' teases Rachel.

Tom looks at his watch. 'That's a new record.'

'Sorry?'

'Less than thirty seconds and you're already taking the mickey out of me.'

Rachel laughs.

'Anyway, haven't you forgotten something?' says Tom gesturing around him. 'Where are the small people?'

'With their wonderful grandparents.'

'Good for you. Actually, I'm just going for a quick sandwich. Fancy joining me?'

'Don't you ever go to work?'

'Not if I can help it. No, I'm using up the holiday that sad losers such as myself seem to have in abundance at this time of year. So, do you want to have lunch with me or not?'

Rachel smiles feeling more excited than she probably should. 'I'd love to,' she says.

'Of all the cafés in all the world, you have to walk into ours!'

'Hi, David. Hi, Simon,' says Emma, her voice flat.

'Oh dear. Someone's having a crapper of a day. Oreo cheesecake for two is it?'

'No, just a cappuccino, thanks.'

'Hairy Jesus, things must be bad. Simon, any of those doughnuts left?'

'Just the one.'

'Put that sweet baby on a plate for Miss Emma, and Miss Ella, how about you?'

'Just a peppermint tea thanks, David.'

'A peppermint tea? Are you pregnant Sugar-Cheeks?'

Emma suddenly catches the thread of the conversation and looks at her friend who is blushing and looking at her shoes.

'Are you?!'

'Emma, I've been wanting to tell you but actually, yes I am.'

'Oh my God! Oh my God!'

The next five minutes is spent in a frenzy of hugging and dancing as Emma, David and Simon fire questions at Ella. Suddenly, David grabs her arm.

'Do you know who the father is?' he asks looking worried.

'I think I do,' says Emma.

'Who?' says Ella in surprise.

'It's Joel, isn't it?'

Ella looks at her friend, with a confused frown. 'Are you ill?'

'Ella, I saw you.'

Detecting danger ahead, David and Simon retreat to fetch drinks.

'When?'

'The other week. I heard you having sex.' She is trying to keep her voice down but she can see David and Simon nudging each other.

Now it's Ella's turn to be cross. 'Well congratulations, Poirot, but did you honestly think I would do that to you and for God's sake, Emma, with Joel? Do you think I have no taste?'

Emma can sense she's made a huge mistake. 'Oh, I see. I'm sorry. Well, if it wasn't Joel, who was it?'

Simon and David are practically falling over the counter trying to hear.

'It's Jamie.'

'Jamie?'

'Yes, Jamie.'

'Our twelve year old post-boy?'

'He's twenty-four actually and would probably prefer it if you didn't call him a post-boy.'

'Right, sorry. Wow! That's incredible. You dark horse. But jeepers, Ella, you're pregnant! You're going to be a mum.'

'I know,' says Ella in a quiet voice.

Suddenly Emma sees that she is crying and realises how selfish she's been. She rushes to her friend's side. 'Oh God, Ella, I'm so sorry. Please don't cry. It's all going to be OK. Have you decided what you're going to do?' David and Simon appear with the drinks, offering red paper napkins to help Ella dry her tears.

'Thanks, everyone,' sniffs Ella blowing her nose.

They sit for a while and Emma takes her hand. 'Whatever you decide to do, I'll help you.'

'Thanks, Emma.'

'What does Jamie say?'

'He says he'll do whatever I want, but I don't want to get married or even be with him really. It was only meant to be a bit of fun.'

'I know,' says Emma. 'And what fun! You filthy cow!'

They laugh.

'Hey, I've just had a thought!' says Emma.

'What?'

'I could be your birthing partner!'

'Emma, you hate blood.'

'I know, but I could stay at the head end.'

They giggle and Emma pushes a strand of hair out of her friend's face. 'It will all be OK,' she says, unsure of what else to say.

Ella forces a smile. 'Just popping to the loo.'

While she is away David brings over the drinks. 'Is she OK?'

'I think so. How much do I owe you?'

'On the house, gorgeous girl.'

Emma's phone beeps with a text and she casts a glance. It's from Richard: 'Did you get my e-mail? I meant every word. R x'

Ella returns, her eyes red and puffy. 'Do I look like shit?'

Emma takes her friend's hands again. 'No, you look blooming.'

'Yeah right.'

Emma's phone starts to ring and she looks at the caller ID: Martin. She switches it off.

'Shouldn't you get that? Who was it?'

'It was no one. Now then, Ells-Bells, when's your next scan? Do you want me to come with you?'

Ella's face crumples with gratitude.

'Now, now, none of that. I can see I'm going to have to employ the "don't be nice to me tactics". Right, well you're going to get fat and your boobs will never be the same again.'

Ella snorts with laughter through a veil of tears. 'Thanks, Em. I'm glad we're friends again. I missed you.'

'Me too,' says Emma. She wishes she could talk to Ella about Martin and Richard but she realises that at this moment in time, she doesn't know what to say.

'And now I'm just feeling utterly confused about the whole thing.' Rachel pops a slice of tomato into her mouth and looks at Tom.

'Hmm, that's not easy and I don't really feel like the best person to advise you.'

'How so?'

'Well, it won't really be in my interests for you to go and live in Scotland.'

'Why, will you miss me?' asks Rachel, realising that she's fishing for compliments.

'I'll miss all of you,' says Tom blushing slightly, 'but you are my chief counsellor so yes, I suppose I will miss you most of all. Another coffee?' he adds hastily.

Rachel checks her watch and is pleased to see that she still has time. 'Cappuccino please.' She smiles.

She watches Tom make his way to the counter and scolds herself for checking out his bottom. *Get a grip, Rachel, he's your neighbour and you're married.* She tells herself it's nothing more than a little harmless flirting and it is nice to reconnect with the old Rachel, the pre-children Rachel, who was attractive to men and was more than just someone's mother.

'What are you grinning at?' asks Tom as he returns with their drinks.

'I was just thinking what a lovely day I'm having.'

'Careful, Mrs S, you're dangerously close to paying me a compliment.'

'Oh stop it. No seriously, I'm really glad I bumped into you. I enjoy our chats.'

'Me too,' says Tom, his neck flushing slightly.

They sit for a moment and Rachel, hating silence, says the first thing that pops into her head. 'So what about your love life?'

'My love life? Are we teenagers?'

'No, I was just wondering why a handsome fellow like you is still single.'

'Rachel, I wonder that myself sometimes. Usually when I'm drunk.'

'Seriously, we should try to set you up with someone,' she says not really meaning it.

'Actually there is someone,' says Tom looking a little furtive.

'Oh yes?' says Rachel hoping and fearing at what is coming next.

'Isn't your friend Christa separated from her husband?'

'Christa?'

'Yes, she seems very nice. Very straightforward.'

'Well, I think she's, erm, you know, strictly speaking, still with Rudi,' says Rachel, trying to hide her disappointment. Then she glances over at Tom and sees the enormous Cheshire cat grin on his face. 'Ha ha, very funny,' she says, relieved.

'Got you! Honestly, Rachel, I think you're losing your touch. Do I look like the kind of man who would dabble with the Russian mafia?'

'No, but then I'm not sure what that man would look like, unless he had the word "stupid" tattooed on his forehead. So no romantic leads for me to follow with my Cupid's bow?'

'Well, actually, you could offer me a bit of advice?'

'Oh yes,' says Rachel, her heart sinking.

'There is a girl at work, bit out of my league probably but very nice, very funny and single.'

Rachel masks her disappointment with humour. 'Well, ask her out then, loser! What does she look like? One or two heads?'

'Just the one. She's very, er, nice looking.'

'Nice? Gosh, make sure you tell her, won't you?'

'OK, OK, I'm not very good at this. Help me please!'

'All right, why don't you invite her over for dinner and I'll give you all the lines to help you seduce her.'

'Do you think that will work?'

'Trust me.'

'I do.'

Rachel glances at her watch. 'Right, Mr Davies, I need to fetch the kids. Lunch was lovely. Thank you.'

Tom gives a little bow and Rachel heads back to her car wondering at how quickly her thoughts and feelings have changed in just one day.

CHAPTER NINETEEN

'All set for tonight?'

Emma looks up from her computer to see Miranda standing before her. She looks tired.

'I think so,' says Emma. 'How are you? How's Digby bearing up? I did wonder if we might postpone in the circumstances.'

Miranda sighs. 'Yes, well, if it were my decision, we would have. But the Americans are in town so it was all planned to tie in with their visit. Anyway, the Author Party has been part of Chandler's calendar since the early days so we couldn't really let everyone down. Right well, onwards and upwards.'

Emma watches Miranda go, noting how she seems a little less gutsy and a little more burdened. Ella returns from her fifth toilet trip of the morning and flops into her chair

'I won't miss this about being pregnant,' she sighs.

'Poor, Ells. Do you want a cup of tea or coffee? I'm just going to make one,' says Emma.

Ella looks pale. 'No thanks. I definitely don't need any more liquids. But thank you.'

'OK,' says Emma, 'Or I've got a banana?'

Ella is now white. 'No, it's fine. I just need to – ' and she is gone, fleeing back to the toilet on a wave of nausea.

'Oops,' says Emma. Her phone rings and she picks it up with an 'Emma Darcy?'

'Emma Darcy. My literary heroine.'

'Richard. How are you?'

'I was going to ask you the same thing. Did you get my e-mail?'

Emma is silent for a moment, feeling her stomach flip. 'Yes, sorry I've been a bit busy,' she says after a moment.

'I understand. Well hopefully we can find five minutes for a chat in a dark corner at the party?' says Richard with a chuckle.

'Yes, all right. See you later,' says Emma trying to play it cool.

'Great. I can't wait to see you,' he adds hanging up.

Emma replaces the phone and stares up at the photo of her and Martin on holiday in Greece. She looks into his eyes, searching for an answer, trying to picture them on their wedding day or out on a daytrip with their children. But she can't.

On the other side of town, Rachel is folding laundry. She picks up one of Will's pairs of school trousers and wonders at how big he's getting. Her father is right, of course, blink and your children are no longer children. She fishes out multiple socks and starts to pair them, a job she finds strangely satisfying. She wishes ordering her own life could be so simple. Alfie ambles into the kitchen looking sad.

'What's up, honey?' asks Rachel concerned.

'Lily did be saying we're moving house,' he says, his little face screwed-up with worry.

Rachel sets the laundry basket to one side and holds her arms out to him. He accepts readily. He is the only one of her children that she can always rely on for a hug. He lies across her arms like a baby and she nuzzles his cheek. 'Well listen, it's not all decided yet so don't worry. Anyway, it would be OK if we move. And you liked Scotland, didn't you?' She knows it's ridiculous to expect a four-year-old to make a decision for her but she's starting to feel desperate.

Alfie vehemently shakes his head. 'No, no, no, no, no!' he cries, tears forming in his eyes.

Rachel hugs him to her. 'Oh, baby, don't cry. It will be OK,' she says, hoping this isn't a lie.

'It won't be OK. I don't want to leave my house or my toys or my telly. And what about Grandpa?'

Rachel looks at her son and wants to cry herself. She takes a deep breath. 'It's all right, Alf. We can take all your toys and Grandpa can come and visit.'

'But what about the telly?' wails Alfie, his sorrow reaching its peak.

Rachel laughs. 'We can take the telly, don't worry, sweetheart.'

Alfie seems a little consoled by this but his face is still wrinkled with concern. 'But won't you miss Grandpa and Granny and Auntie Em?'

It's like a shot to Rachel's heart. 'Yes Alfie, I shall. Very much.'

'Can I have a biscuit?' asks Alfie, sensing an opportunity. Rachel laughs and packs him off with three biscuits and strict instructions to share them with his siblings. Her mobile rings and she sees that it's Steve.

'Watcha,' she says.

'Hey, gorgeous. Would it be OK if I went out for a drink with the guys from work this evening?'

'Is this the first of many leaving drinks?' asks Rachel.

'Something like that,' says Steve. 'I won't be too late but don't wait up.'

Rachel rings off, sighs and goes back to pairing socks and pretending that everything is fine.

Emma arrives at the gallery on time to find the usual suspects already knocking back glasses of champagne. She sees Ella in one corner with 'historical fiction' Clive, who is talking to her breasts. Ella looks over and mouths 'Help!' Emma grins and is making her way over to her friend when she is accosted.

'Emma Darcy.'

'Richard! You're very prompt,' she says, kissing him on both cheeks.

On the second kiss, he leans over and whispers, 'I couldn't wait to see you.'

'Ah, Richard, darling! How are you?' His agent, Joanna has joined their cosy twosome and immediately puts a protective arm around her charge. 'Come with me. I have people I want you to meet,' she adds ignoring Emma. Richard allows himself to be led away. Emma sees him look back at her forlornly and feels her heart race.

She spots her Cornish crime writer and goes over to give her a warm embrace. She spends most of the evening catching up with her authors. Occasionally she sees Miranda surrounded by guests and marvels at how professionally she conducts herself.

After about an hour, someone taps on a glass with a knife and everyone turns to see Philip Allen with a microphone smiling and waiting for hush. He begins his welcome and Emma takes this as a cue to duck out for some air. As she turns through the door, she feels someone catch her arm. She doesn't need to turn around. She knows who it is.

'Richard, where have you been?'

'Joanna keeps introducing me to people, but I'm here now,' he says expectantly, studying her face. 'I need to talk to you, Emma.'

'Look, Richard – '

'Richard? Is this the famous Richard Bennett then?'

Emma jumps at the sound of Joel's voice but regains her composure. 'Joel, this is Richard Bennett. Richard, this is Joel. He works in marketing.'

Joel's face flickers with irritation. He holds out his hand. 'Joel Riches, Head of Marketing. Good to meet you at last.'

Richard accepts his hand and turns back to Emma. Never a man to take a hint, Joel lingers, ready to join the conversation. 'So, Richard, have you read *Don Quixote*?'

Richard forces a smile. 'Actually, I tried to once, but didn't get further than the first thirty pages.'

Joel looks smug and pats Richard on the back. 'Yes well, it is a very difficult read. It's not for everyone.'

Richard smiles. 'Very true. I can see you're a very clever chap, Joel, and I shall do my best to keep up with you,' he says.

Joel puffs out his chest and smirks. 'Well, it was good to meet you, Richard. Now if you'll excuse me, I need to go and catch up with Phil. We need to talk strategy.'

Richard gives a little bow. 'Of course. It was very good of you to spare the time.'

Joel smiles, nods at Emma and slips away. She nudges Richard with her elbow. 'God you're good! You were on to him straightaway.'

Richard grins. 'I'm a very good reader of character, Emma Darcy. Anyway,' he says taking her arm, 'when are we going to have our little chat?'

Emma looks back into the gallery. People are starting to disperse. 'Well, I suppose we could go and have a drink now?' she says feeling light-headed at her own boldness.

'I've got a better idea,' says Richard putting an arm round her. 'We're not that far from my place. Why don't we jump in a cab, have a drink there and then you're half-way home.'

Emma realises how natural it feels with Richard's arm around her. She checks her watch. It's still early and Martin is playing football. Again. She can be home by midnight without the need for any excuse. She knows that going to Richard's place is a dangerous step but it's as if she's standing at the top of a waterslide on a hot day and longing to take the plunge. She looks up at Richard. '*Carpe diem*,' she says.

'What does that mean?' he asks.

'It means I hope you've got a lot of booze at your flat,' she replies.

Richard grins and leads her towards the street.

***

'Mum! Dad! How are you? What a lovely surprise!' says Rachel, trying to mask her irritation at having her evening of Pinot Grigio and brain-mush TV interrupted.

'Oh, we were just passing on the way back from bridge, darling!' says Diana, breezing past her daughter and running a dust-testing finger along the hall shelf.

'I thought bridge was in the other direction,' whispers Rachel to her father through gritted teeth.

'It is and I did try to put her off, but you know your mother,' whispers her father in reply.

'What are you two whispering about?' says Diana frowning.

'Nothing, Mum. Glass of wine?' says Rachel, steering them towards the kitchen.

'Lovely. And are the little cherubs all safely tucked up?'

'Grandpa! Granny!' squeaks Alfie's falsetto voice from the top of the stairs.

'Oh great,' sighs Rachel, her evening dissolving before her eyes.

'It's OK. I'll go,' says Edward giving his daughter a peck on the forehead. 'You talk to your mum.'

'Thanks, Dad,' says Rachel, squeezing his hand. She follows Diana into the kitchen, where she is already helping herself to a large glass of wine.

'So. Edinburgh. How was it?'

'I'm fine thanks, Mum. How are you?'

Diana is irritated. 'Don't be sarcastic, Rachel. Can't a mother ask her daughter a simple question?'

Rachel wants to argue but doesn't have the energy. 'I don't know, Mum. There's still a lot to sort out.'

'So you're not going?' Diana looks hopeful.

'I don't know. Maybe. I need to talk to Steve again.'

Diana looks stern. 'Rachel, you have a family to think about. This is not a time for dilly-dallying. You need to make a decision.'

'All sorted. He'd lost Bear,' says Edward returning to the fray.

'Edward, you have to try and talk some sense into this girl. She won't listen to me.'

'Diana, I think we need to let Rachel and Steve sort this out for themselves,' says Edward reasonably.

'Well, they don't seem to be doing a very good job on their own!' declares Diana with customary diplomacy.

'Thank you, Mother,' says Rachel.

'Darling, I really think we should be getting home and leave Rachel to her evening,' says Edward firmly.

Diana frowns but sees her husband looking at her with eyebrows raised and gives in. 'Very well but please let me know when you've made a decision, won't you? I need to be forewarned about the prospect of having to visit Scotland.' She pronounces the place name as if it's a contagious disease. 'I'm just going to powder my nose.'

When she's gone, Edward puts an arm round his daughter. 'In case you were wondering, that's your mother's way of saying she doesn't want you to go.'

Rachel nods and starts to cry. Her father folds her into his arms and kisses the top of her head. 'It will all be fine, Rach,' he says. 'Promise.'

Rachel wipes her eyes and smiles up at him wishing she had his wisdom and foresight. After her parents have gone she pours herself a large glass of wine and flops onto the sofa. She decides to call Steve for reassurance. His phone rings three or four times before someone picks up.

'Hello?' says a female voice.

'Oh hi, who is this? I just wanted to speak to Steve,' says Rachel wondering if she's accidentally dialled the wrong number.

'Oh no, this is Sam. Steve's just popped to the loo. Shall I get him to call you?'

Rachel isn't sure why she answers as she does but she knows that she wants to end the call as quickly as possible. 'No, it's fine. I'll call him tomorrow,' she says. She puts the phone down, her mind racing. Snippets of conversation from the past few weeks flood through her mind. Sam, Sam, Sam. Sam, the IT manager who had coffee with Steve. Sam, who texted him one weekend. She thinks about the ring and the late working which Steve dismissed so casually and tonight which was meant to be 'a drink with the guys'. Rachel is adding two and two together and coming up with five and suddenly she is seeing her rock-steady husband in a different light altogether.

'But you're close to your sister?' asks Richard, his voice slurring slightly under the strain of so many glasses of wine.

'We have the usual sibling rivalries but yeah, she's a peach. How about you?' says Emma, trying to sound coherent.

'I don't know your sister,' says Richard.

'No, silly!' snorts Emma. 'I mean I know about your mum and dad but is there anyone else?'

'No, just me but that's the way I like it.'

Richard launches himself onto his feet and lurches towards the globe-adorned table by the window. Emma giggles.

'What?' says Richard half-laughing, as he lifts the globe back to reveal a well stocked drinks trolley.

'Oh my God, you have got to be kidding!' says Emma leaping to her feet. 'I've always wanted one of those!'

Richard looks pleased. 'I went out and bought it the day I sold my first book.'

Emma nods with smiling approval. 'Classy.'

'I know!' says Richard with unbridled glee. 'Now, what shall we have?'

'Oh, I think we've had enough, don't you?'

'Oh come on, Emma, surely it's time for something in a smaller glass. Anyway, I want to propose a toast.'

'Richard, we've already toasted all our family, friends, the England cricket team individually, the greatest living writers of all time – '

' – and the dead ones'

'And the dead ones. Plus John Noakes, Stephen Fry and Moira Stuart.'

'I love Moira Stuart.'

'I know, but I think it might be time to call it a day,' says Emma, starting to make her way across the room.

Richard reaches forward and grabs her arm. 'No, look, I've got one more toast to make and it's the most important one. Pleeease?' He leads her back to the drinks cabinet and pulls out two shot glasses, filling them with a cloudy white liquid.

'What is this?'

'Ouzo. I have a penchant for collecting liqueurs. This one is early nineties. A very good year.'

Emma takes a tentative sip and pulls a face. 'That is disgusting.'

'I know, but let me make the toast and then we'll down it in one, OK?'

'OK.'

Richard takes a deep breath. 'I want to propose a toast to you, Emma Darcy. You have no idea what a difference you are making to my life. You are quite the most wonderful, intelligent, funny woman I have ever met and I think – ' Emma is looking at him in surprise. He sees the look and knocks back his drink. 'Dutch courage. You see, the truth is,' he says, putting down their drinks and taking her hands in his, 'I think, in fact I know, I'm in love with you.'

The room seems to swirl around Emma, taking on a life of its own and all she can feel is her body moving towards Richard anticipating the kiss that has been coming since the moment they met. As it arrives, she feels as if she has no control over the situation whatsoever, as if she couldn't stop this happening even if she wanted to. It is as if she is watching the film of her life playing out in front of her.

CHAPTER TWENTY

Emma Darcy is confused. Someone has glued her eyelids shut and her mouth feels as if it's full of fur. She forces one eye open and is disturbed to discover that she is wearing a T-shirt that doesn't smell of Martin and is waking up in a bed that isn't her own. Suddenly, last night's events come flooding back to her like a wave of raw sewage and that's when the heart-stopping thump of this morning's hangover takes hold.

'Good morning, beloved editor,' says Richard from the doorway. *Right, time to wake up now*, thinks Emma. 'Oh dear, someone's in need of my never-fail hangover cure,' he adds, grinning at her.

Emma tries to speak, 'But did I – ?'

'Yes, you stayed here last night.'

'Oh no, no, no, no, no!' cries Emma panicking. She leaps out of bed, thankful that she is at least wearing underwear.

'Emma, it's fine.'

'No, Richard, it's really not fine. I'm supposed to be engaged. This is distinctly not fine!'

'Emma, calm down. You're overreacting.'

Emma looks at Richard as if he's just fallen out of the Stupid Tree. 'Overreacting? Look at me! I'm wearing your T-shirt, staying in your bed and I can't even remember if we had sex or not! And I'm supposed to be your editor. This is highly unprofessional and extremely immoral!'

'Emma, stop it, you're starting to sound like Ann Widdecombe and to be honest, it's a bit of a turn-on.'

'Arrrrrrrgh, Richard!' yells Emma, reaching for the nearest pillow and throwing it firmly in his direction. 'This isn't funny!' He catches the pillow in a deft movement and peers out at her, trying not to smile.

'God I love you when you're angry.'

'Grrrrrrrrrr!' is all she can say as she throws another pillow.

'Hey! Stop lobbing my pillows, they're stuffed with very expensive Siberian goose feathers, you know.'

'I'll give you bloody Siberian goose feathers,' she says lunging at him.

He grabs her wrists and pulls her in close. She tries to resist but without much conviction. He holds her face and looks into her eyes. 'Do you want to know what happened then, Emma Darcy? Do you want to know what the next strand in the plot is?'

'Stop mucking about, Richard and just tell me.'

Richard leans in and as soon as she feels his lips on hers, she responds. Richard pulls away. 'That was it.'

'Really?'

'Yes, really. I know I like the ladies, but I would never take advantage, particularly of someone I feel so strongly about.'

'Oh, right.'

'Look. Emma, I meant what I said last night. I have real feelings for you, but I know that you are technically taken so it's up to you how the story pans out. Marry whatshisface or think about what I said and reconsider your options.'

Emma's mind is racing. Isn't this what she wanted? Last night was exciting and fun. Everything is more fun after champagne and ouzo but life has a habit of dumping you on your backside when you're sober. It all seems so unreal now. She glances at her watch.

'Oh shit! I'm supposed to be at work. Miranda is going to kill me! And what about Martin?'

Richard takes her hands in his. 'Look, Emma, you have to calm down. This is your life. You can do what you want. You don't have to tell anyone anything. You can walk out of this flat now, pretend this never happened and we can carry on like before.'

'How can we? Seriously, Richard, how could we just carry on like before?' She is rushing round the room frantically retrieving her clothes.

'Because we're grown-ups and we'd have to. I wouldn't like it but if it's what you wanted, I'd respect it.'

Emma is sitting on the bed trying to put on her tights. She looks at Richard. He is staring at her with an admiration she doesn't think she deserves. She feels utterly confused and covers her face with her hands. 'This is a nightmare! What am I going to do?'

Richard sits next to her and puts an arm around her. 'It will all be all right, I promise. Go to work, see how the day goes and we'll speak later, OK?'

'OK,' says Emma sounding unsure.

'Hey, hey,' says Richard, lifting her chin and kissing her again. 'I love you, don't forget that, will you?'

Emma looks into his steady clear brown eyes and thinks she can glimpse the future. 'I won't,' she says with a shy smile.

Rachel opens one eye as the clock radio drones out the day's news. She glances over at Steve's side of the bed and notices that it's empty and on further inspection that it hasn't been slept in. She feels sick and reaches into her bedside drawer for her mobile. It's flashing with a text: 'Missed last train home so stayed at friend's – sorry. Didn't call as didn't want to wake you. See you later, S x.'

She feels reassured that he's all right and now even sicker at the thought of who he was with. Before last night, she would have put Steve down as the last person to ever be unfaithful but she feels unsure about so many things these days. She is about to phone him when the bedroom door is flung open and Alfie announces that, 'Lily did be hitting me.' In the same way that small children prevent you completing many important tasks in a day, they also serve as a welcome distraction and Rachel is almost delighted to have to referee the twins. She becomes model mum, making them breakfast and Will's packed lunch in record time. They are ready to go so early that she even puts the television on for them.

'You're the best mummy in the world,' murmurs Alfie as he settles down for a little early morning *Peppa Pig*. Will moaned when he saw what was on but giggles happily along with his brother and sister. Rachel feels a lump catch in her throat as she catches sight of the three of them laughing together. She sends Sue a text: 'Any chance you could have Lily and Alfie for me for a couple of hours this morning pls? Don't ask why – just need a bit of time to myself.'

The answers pings back immediately: 'Sure no probs – take all the time u need. Joe v excited.'

Rachel smiles at her friend's kindness, brushing away a tear and telling herself that 8:40 in the morning is not the time to fall apart. She wonders at the fact that all she had to worry about last week was moving to Scotland and now it feels as if her whole world is collapsing in on itself.

'OK, kids, time to go,' she says in a croaky voice, helping them with their coats and ushering them out of the door.

Emma teeters into the entrance lobby of Allen Chandler and uses all the strength her body can muster to press the lift button.

'Someone looks a little fragile today,' says a voice. Philippa's bright and cheery face peers at Emma. 'Big night, was it?'

'You could say that,' says Emma in a hoarse whisper. 'How are things with you?'

'Very good, thanks. Very good indeed.' Philippa grins.

'Well, I'm glad someone's happy. See you later.' Emma reaches her desk, wishing that a giant sledgehammer would appear from nowhere and finish her off.

'Ooooh, you look – ' begins Ella.

'Yes, I know. Bloody awful. Don't say it and don't ask me what happened. I can barely come to terms with it myself.'

'Fair enough. So I take it you haven't heard the news?'

'What news?'

'Ahhh, you need to read your e-mails.'

'Oh God, what's happened now? Please tell me they haven't made Joel MD? I will literally have to top myself with this,' says Emma brandishing a copy of the *Oxford English Dictionary*. Ella adopts a secretive and slightly superior look.

'I'm saying nothing. Read your e-mails.'

Emma switches on her computer and waits for her e-mails to open. Sifting through the usual trade news of the day, Emma sees an e-mail marked urgent and entitled 'Changes To Personnel'. She clicks to open it, her mouth feeling dry. It's from Philip Allen and is addressed to the whole company.

Dear Colleagues,

Thank you for your attendance at yesterday's meeting and I know many of you have questions about the future of the company and how Digby's departure will affect things. I am pleased to say that following discussions with the relevant members of staff, I can announce the following changes:

With immediate effect, Miranda Winter will assume the role of MD. This is testimony to her hard work as Fiction Publisher and her tireless commitment to this company. Furthermore, we will be enhancing the role of our Marketing Department and I am delighted to announce that Philippa Jones is promoted to Head of Marketing alongside Joel Riches. The attached document details how they will manage the marketing department between them. They will both report to Miranda.

We believe that these changes will help us to continue with our commercial focus to deliver growth as well as maintaining our strengths as a publisher of quality and integrity.

If you have any further questions, please speak to Miranda, Nancy or me.

Kind Regards,
Philip Allen
CEO
Allen Chandler

'Ha!' says Emma with unmitigated glee. 'Bloody brilliant!'

'I know,' says Ella, returning with two steaming mugs. 'I thought you could do with one of these.'

'You are a gem but do you know what, suddenly I feel a lot better. Has anyone seen Joel?'

'He's surprisingly quiet this morning.'

'Brilliant. Brill-eee-ant!' Emma's phone starts to ring and she glances at the caller ID and sees that it's Martin. She suddenly feels sick. She had chickened out of speaking to him by sending a text. She is fearful that he'll hear the guilt in her voice. She tells herself to get a grip. She hasn't even done anything. Yet.

'Hi, Martin,' she says trying to sound upbeat.

'Hey, gorgeous. I missed you last night.'

'Oh, did you?'

'Of course. How was Ella's sofa?'

'Oh fine, bit lumpy, but fine. Listen, I've got to go, Mart. I'll see you later, OK?'

'Can't wait. I love you.'

'OK, bye,' says Emma ringing off and feeling as if her whole life is turning into one big fat lie.

Rachel leans heavily against the front door as she pushes it shut behind her. She holds her breath against the silence. She pulls out her phone and dials Steve's number. She has already tried it twice on the way back from Sue's but it went straight to voicemail. This time it rings three times before Steve picks up.

'Rach?'

'Hi,' she replies, unsure of what to say next.

'Did you get my text?'

'Yes.'

'I'm sorry, darl. So stupid to miss the last train. I lost track of time. Luckily Sam lives on the Tube line so I stayed on the sofa.' Rachel feels her throat tighten. She can't do this over the phone. 'Rach? Are you still there? I've got a meeting to go to but I'll make sure I'm home on time and I'll put the kids to bed, OK?'

'OK,' she manages. He rings off and Rachel slumps onto the stairs. He's actually admitted to going back to Sam's. Surely he wouldn't do that if there was something going on? Or maybe he would. She sighs and puts her head in her hands. She doesn't know what to think any more. She can't seem to order her thoughts into something that makes sense. A loud *rat-a-tat* at the door interrupts her train of thought and makes her jump. When she opens the door, she is overjoyed to be looking up into Tom's smiling face. Suddenly, he seems like the only person she needs. She puts a hand to her mouth to try to stop the tears but she can't. She is shaking and Tom looks worried and steps into the house offering her his arms. She accepts gratefully, feeling immediately safe. He closes the door behind him and holds her tightly, letting her cry.

'Hey, Rachel, what's all this? Are the kids OK? And Steve?'

Rachel nods but can't speak for a moment. She feels a surge of energy shoot through her body at Tom's touch. He strokes her hair back from her face and looks down at her. As soon as their eyes meet, Rachel knows what is going to happen. She takes his face in her hands and pulls him towards her. He doesn't resist and now they are kissing, her back against the wall. They move towards the living room, still locked in the kiss. Rachel starts to pull at his shirt and unbutton his flies, feeling his hands all over her. They reach the sofa and she lies back, landing on one of the kid's squeaky toys. She casts it aside ready to pull Tom down towards her, but Tom is still looking at the toy.

'Rachel, we can't do this.'

'Shhh, we can, come here,' she says drawing him towards her and kissing him on his cheek and neck. This time he resists.

'No, we can't, Rachel,' he says pulling away and doing up his belt.

'Why? Don't you find me attractive?' she asks, feeling embarrassed by the way this sounds.

Tom kneels in front of her and takes her hands in his. 'Rachel, there is nothing I'd like more than to make love to you, but you are very married to a man I really like.'

'You can have him if you want!' says Rachel, sounding petulant.

'You have three beautiful kids,' continues Tom ignoring the comment, 'and I know how much you love Steve really. In a different life at a different time, I would be all over you in a heartbeat but we just can't. I know you can see that too. Listen, I'm going to let myself out and we'll catch up later over the garden fence while I'm being a saddo with my snails? As friends?'

Rachel nods weakly, feeling ashamed and sad that something she was enjoying so much is coming to an end. Tom kisses her hand.

'I hope you realise what a wonderful woman you are,' he says.

As she hears the door close, Rachel slumps back onto the sofa and sobs.

CHAPTER TWENTY ONE

Emma drags herself up the road, grateful for the end of the day and hoping that Martin won't be home yet. All she wants is a hot bath, her bed and to avoid any incriminating conversations with her fiancé. She needs time to think properly and Martin's cheery, reasonable presence won't help her with this. She had contemplated going round to see Rachel but she didn't feel ready to confess her sins yet. After all, there was nothing really to confess and she knew Rachel had a tendency to get a bit high and mighty sometimes. Plus her sister was fond of Martin. Emma feared that she might force her to confess all to him before she had worked it out properly in her own mind.

She rounds the corner and feels her heart sink as she sees the light filtering out from the hall. There's a car she doesn't recognise parked outside. She turns her key in the door and calls, 'Hello?'

'In here,' says Martin, his voice sounding gruff and angry.

As she enters the kitchen, she is horrified to find Richard sitting at her kitchen table and Martin standing by the sink, his face set in a disgusted scowl.

'Richard, what are you doing here?' asks Emma.

'I'm sorry, Emma, I had to come. I felt it was for the best,' he says rising to kiss her. She pushes him away.

'What was for the best?'

'I've told him about us,' he says.

'What do you mean "us"? There is no "us"!' says Emma.

'How can you say that? You know I have feelings for you. I thought you felt the same. What about last night?'

'Yes, Emma, what about last night?' asks Martin angrily.

'Nothing happened last night! It was just a kiss!'

'Just a kiss?' chorus the men, Richard sounding hurt and Martin mocking.

Emma sinks into a chair and longs for a fairy godmother to magic these two men away. She is too tired to sort this out now. 'I'm sorry,' she says quietly. 'I don't know what to say. But, Richard, you said you would give me time to think about everything. Why have you come here?'

'I'm sorry,' says Richard, taking Emma's hands. 'I just couldn't wait. I know how I feel about you and I sense that you feel the same. I thought it would be better for everyone if we told Martin as soon as possible.'

'Very decent of you,' says Martin bitterly.

Emma looks at Martin and realises she owes him an explanation. 'Richard, I think you should go,' she says quietly.

'But, darling – '

'Please. I need to talk to Martin.'

'All right,' says Richard with a sigh. 'But promise you'll call me.'

'OK.'

Emma follows him down the hall. On the doorstep, he stoops to kisses her on the mouth. 'I mean everything I've said, Emma.' He gives her a final wave before he drives off. She turns to see Martin staring at her, before he thumps up the stairs.

'Martin! Wait! We need to talk,' says Emma following after him. Once in the bedroom, he grabs a rucksack from

the cupboard and starts to fling clothes into its gaping mouth.
'What are you doing?'

'What does it look like I'm doing, Emma?'

'Please stop.'

'Why should I? So you can tell me more lies about where
you've been over the past few months? I mean how long has
it all been going on?'

'Martin, please. You have to listen. I haven't slept with
him!'

Martin stops ramming clothes into the bag and looks at
her. 'But you did kiss him?'

'Yes, but – '

'What? If you're going to tell me it meant nothing, then
don't. I think I'm worth a bit more than that, don't you?'

'Of course, of course you are and I can understand why
you're angry but please, Martin, can we at least talk about
this?'

'What is there to talk about, Emma? Is there really any
point? At least that tosser was upfront about it, but you've
been lying all along, haven't you? All the time we were
making plans and you were giving me such a hard time
about the wedding. Everything's been a lie and God knows
how long it would have carried on if he hadn't decided to
pay me a visit.'

'I'm sorry. I just felt so – ' says Emma, struggling for
the right word. She is suddenly hit by the enormity of what
is happening and the uncontrollable feeling that she can't
stop it. Her legs give way and she sinks onto the edge of the
bed.

'Well, Emma, how did you feel?' demands Martin with
rising impatience. 'Too loved? Too worshipped? Too adored?
Because all I've ever done is love you and if that's not good
enough, what hope do we have?' Martin crouches in front
of her, holding her by the shoulders. 'We could have been

so, so happy, Emma. Maybe I haven't got the flash words or wit of Richard bloody Bennett and I like football and I could buy you flowers more, but I love you more than any man ever does or will and that's the truth.' He goes back to his packing.

'Then don't go, please,' says Emma, the tears welling in her eyes. 'Just give me a bit of time to sort myself out,' she pleads.

She can see tears forming in his eyes too as he zips up his bag. 'I don't think so, Emma. I've got to protect myself too, you know?' He darts down the stairs and Emma hears the front door slam behind him. She runs to the window and watches him drive off. She stands there for a while looking at the pool of streetlight where his car was. Then she crumples to the floor and cries heavy, silent sobs.

'We're going on a – '
  'BEAR HUNT!'
  'We're going to catch a – '
  'BIG ONE!'
  'What a – '
  'DADDY!' shout the three children using their small-person, radar-ears as Steve turns his key in the door.

'Hello-o!' says Steve, galloping up the stairs two at a time, before he is leapt on by the children. He manages to stagger to his feet 'What a lovely welcome! How are you lot?'

The children all talk at once, telling Steve snippets of their day. Rachel notices that Steve hasn't kissed her yet, but tells herself he's just pleased to see the children.

'Now, who wants Daddy to finish the story?'
'Meeeeeee!'
'Yes please, Dad. Mum is rubbish at reading this one,' says Lily plainly. She leans in to whisper to him. 'She doesn't know how to do the bear bit properly.'

'Oh I see,' whispers Steve, not looking at his wife. Rachel busies herself by putting away the twins' clothes. 'Well, I do a very good bear so you better watch out!' he adds, tickling them. They squeal in shared delight.

Rachel kisses each child goodnight and heads for the door.

'I'll see you downstairs,' she says. Steve looks at her for the first time since he arrived home and she feels unnerved by his gaze. He looks almost disappointed that she's there. She feels sick as she plods back down the stairs. Is he about to tell her the thing she dreads most in the world? Is he going to leave her for this Sam woman? She heads straight for the fridge and picks out a bottle of Sauvignon Blanc and is already on her second glass when he appears half an hour later. He pauses in the doorway to look at her but she doesn't return his gaze.

'So,' he says, his voice sounding cold. 'What's been going on?'

'You tell me,' says Rachel, immediately on the offensive.

'Meaning?'

'Meaning where exactly were you last night?'

'I told you. I missed the train and stayed at Sam's'

'Ha! This will be the Sam who you go for coffee with and the Sam who sends you texts at the weekend and the Sam who answered your phone last night.'

Steve looks confused. 'Yes. That Sam. Why?'

'Why didn't you tell me that Sam was a woman?'

Steve laughs mockingly. 'Why should I?'

Rachel is furious now, lost in her anger. 'You let me think that Sam was a man.'

Steve laughs again. 'Don't be ridiculous.'

'You did! I remember. When you got that text from her about the football, I made a comment about men being saddos and you didn't contradict me.'

'Oh for God's sake, Rachel.'

'And you lied about working late. I know you did.'

'OK, OK, but only because I knew you'd overreact. As you are doing now.'

'So you did lie.'

It's Steve's turn to be angry now. 'No, I didn't tell you Sam was a woman because I didn't want to give you another reason to go off at the deep end. I also didn't think you needed to know because I thought you trusted me. I have been for a few beers with Sam because she's easy company and to be honest, I've missed having someone rational to talk to.'

'How dare you!' cries Rachel. 'So as soon as things get tricky with your wife, you go rushing into the arms of another woman!'

Steve shakes his head disbelieving. 'I haven't rushed into her arms. You are being ridiculous!'

'Are you having an affair?

Steve turns away. 'I can't do this.'

'Can't do what?'

'Listen to your paranoid ramblings again but to answer your question, I am not having an affair with Sam, who, by the way, is gay. What about you? Are you having an affair?'

Rachel feels as if the ground is moving away from her somehow. 'What do you mean?' Steve walks to the counter and picks up his phone. He presses some buttons and then holds it up for her to hear.

'Rachel, we can't do this.'

Rachel suddenly feels sick as she hears Tom's voice coming through slightly muffled on the speakerphone. Steve is watching her, his face furrowed with anger.

'Shhh, we can, come here.'

'No, we can't Rachel.'

'Why? Don't you find me attractive?'

'Rachel, there is nothing I'd like more than to make love to you.'

Rachel can't listen any more. She can't look at Steve and she doesn't know what to say to him. Everything is a blur as she runs from the kitchen, grabs her bag and dashes out of the door. She sits in the car for a moment, sobbing and secretly hoping that Steve will appear at the door. When it remains stubbornly shut, she starts up the engine and drives off with a loud rev, causing an elderly dog-walker to stop and shake his head in her wake.

'If you're selling something, we don't want it,' says Diana flinging open the door and then looking perplexed and a little irritated to find her youngest daughter standing in the porch wailing like a banshee. Terrified of public displays of affection, she calls for her husband.

'Edward! It's Emma. She's rather upset.'

Edward comes bustling out of the living room, an open *Telegraph* still in his hand. As soon as he sees Emma, he throws the newspaper to one side and hurries along the hall, his arms outstretched.

'Darling girl! Whatever is the matter?'

Emma is inconsolable and tries to speak but starts to cry every time she gets a word out. Edward takes her hands. 'Is it Martin? Is everything all right?' Emma nods to reassure him. 'Come in, sit down and we'll get you a drink.'

'I'll do it. Gin and tonic, Emma?' says Diana. Emma nods again, incapable of any verbal communication. She allows herself to be led into the living room, which is filled with the squashy sofas and pouffes Emma loved as a child. The walls are adorned with generations of photographs, and are testament to parental pride as all the certificates the girls have ever won are also displayed. Emma sits down and accepts the very strong gin and tonic with gratitude. She sips it and pulls a face and then takes a large gulp as if the gin will force her to get her story out.

'So, what's happened, my love?' asks her father.

Emma sniffs and takes a deep breath. 'I think Martin has left me,' she says with a loud sob.

'I knew it! I knew it! Didn't I say? I said there was something wrong. Oh goodness, we'll have to cancel the wedding!' says Diana.

Emma almost laughs. 'Thanks for the support, Mum!'

'Well sorry, but it has to be said.'

'All right, Diana, let's let Emma get her story out shall we?'

Diana harrumphs loudly but even she can see that her husband is right. She sits back in her chair and folds her arms.

Emma addresses her story to her father trying to avoid catching her mother's disapproving eye. 'Well, there's this author at work.'

'Oh my goodness – another man. Emma! How could you?' cries Diana.

'Mum, will you please let me finish?'

'Sorry, but really!' Just at that moment, the doorbell rings again. Edward and Emma look at Diana who looks around her and then throws up her hands in despair. 'Right, I'll go, shall I? Edward was never very good with axe murderers, so I suppose I better face them!' says Diana.

'I don't think axe murderers ring the bell first but your mother does like a bit of drama,' whispers Edward. Emma laughs through her tears and they both listen for voices.

Diana is back in a moment followed by a red-eyed Rachel. 'Well, I like the way you two plan your crises for the same evening,' comments Diana. 'I suppose you'd like a gin and tonic too, would you, Rachel?'

'Yes please, Mum,' says Rachel, sniffing loudly.

'And don't sniff, Rachel. There are some tissues on the coffee table if you need one.'

'Yes, Mum. Sorry, Mum,' says Rachel, like a five-year-old.

'Oh dear, what's happened? Are you all right, Rachel?' asks Edward. 'Come and sit here with your sister and me. I haven't had to do this for a while!'

Rachel takes her place next to her father on the sofa and grabs a tissue. 'Hello, Em. Are you OK?'

'Not really. You?'

'The same.'

Diana returns with a drink for Rachel and stands awkwardly not really sure whether to stay or go.

'Diana?'

'Yes, darling?'

'You can sit down if you like.'

'Oh, all right. It's just that you all look so cosy. I wasn't sure if you needed me.'

'Of course we do, don't we girls?,' Emma and Rachel mutter an unconvincing agreement.

Diana perches on the side of the chair. 'So, Martin has left Emma and what's happened to you, Rachel?' asks Diana with the subtlety of a rampant wasp.

'You're kidding,' says Rachel turning to face her sister and suddenly forgetting her own woes.

'He hasn't left me. We've just had words,' says Emma with a defensive tone to her voice.

'There's another man involved,' says Diana in hushed tones as if Emma is no longer in the room.

'There isn't, I mean there is but we're not involved. We just kissed,' says Emma.

Diana tuts. 'Well, no wonder he's left you.'

'Mum, is there any way you could be a little bit more understanding?'

'What do you mean?'

Emma sighs and wishes she hadn't come here. She should have gone to Ella's or Rosie's. It was always this way with her mother. Tea and sympathy in a battle zone. Emma takes another sip of her gin and sees a get-out. 'What about you then, Rach?'

Rachel's eyes narrow as she realises her sister's game. 'Oh, Steve and I just had a bit of a row.'

Diana's bloodhound radar leaps into action. 'What about?'

'Oh just about stuff that's going on.'

'You mean the move?'

'Well partly,' lies Rachel.

'Rachel, do you mean the move?'

'Well yes, among other things,' she says, thinking it best to keep her mother off the scent for as long as possible.

'I knew it! Edward, didn't I say? That girl is not happy, she doesn't really want to go, she's just going along with it. I said that, didn't I?' She looks at her husband who realises that a response is required.

'You did say that, darling.'

'Well, you'll just have to tell him you don't want to go. He'll have to say no to the job and either keep doing what he's doing or find something else. Or maybe you could get a part-time job and we could help with the childcare? Edward, why didn't you suggest that? Do I have to think of everything?' And on Diana goes, her voice delivering each word in a rapid machine-gun fire staccato. Edward and the girls exchange subtle glances of amusement and let her talk. They are almost content sitting close to their father, while their mother pontificates to her heart's content. It's a picture of familial bliss. After a while, Edward stretches his arms and turns to his wife.

'Diana darling, I was thinking about some supper. Would you like something?' Diana leaps up as if a ten-ton truck has just careered into the living room.

'I'll go. You'll only make a hideous mess. Girls, would you like a sandwich or something?' Both girls nod gratefully.

'Right, I haven't got much in but I can sort something out and I expect you'll be wanting another gin and tonic,' she says scooping up their empty glasses. 'Will you be staying tonight? Both spare beds are made up if you want to.' She bustles off into the kitchen.

Rachel looks at her father. 'You did that on purpose, didn't you?' she says with a weak smile.

'Let's just say I have my ways and means,' says Edward smiling. 'And now then you two, what's going on? How are we going to help you out?' Rachel and Emma look at one another. They are remembering how their father used to do this when they were upset as children. He would manage to somehow create a task or crisis to distract Diana while he sorted out their worries.

Edward turns to Emma. 'Do you love this author chap?'

'No, I don't think so, oh I don't know. He's just – '

'Different,' says Rachel finishing her sentence for her.

'Yes. Thank you.'

'You're welcome. God, I should be the editor,' says Rachel.

'So, he's different but what about Martin?' continues Edward.

'Well Martin is wonderful but sometimes, I just feel so – '

'Trapped,' says Rachel.

'Yes! That's it! It's as if I'm old and married and my life is over.'

'Thanks very much,' says Rachel. 'You should actually try being married.'

'Sorry, sis, I didn't mean it. Anyway, you're not trapped, you've got everything and you're about to fly away and have new adventures. I'm stuck in London, about to get married.'

'Sorry, did you say I'm not trapped? What about the small matter of three children and the prospect of following my husband to Scotland like the obedient wife?'

'Don't take this the wrong way, Rach, but "obedient" isn't exactly a word I would use for you.'

'Bloody cheek. Anyway, you've got your career and life ahead of you. You can do anything you want. So you're not sure about marrying Martin? So don't.'

'Simple as that?'

'Well, why not?'

'OK, don't go to Scotland then.'

'That's different.'

'How is it different? Just because you're older than me and have three kids, it doesn't make your life any more complicated.'

'Oh come on, Emma, of course it does.'

'You patronising cow.'

'Oh, grow up.'

'Girls!' Edward uses his ex-headmaster's voice to gain their immediate attention. They sit up and look towards him. 'I think you've both got a lot to think about. Emma, you need to decide if Martin really is the one for you and if he isn't, you need to tell him. He's a lovely chap and he deserves that much.' Emma nods, suddenly ashamed. 'And as for this other fellow, well I don't know, Emma, you'll have to decide but if he isn't a good man, don't throw everything away. And, Rachel, you need to really consider what you want from life. You and Steve have so much. You're at a bit of a crossroads so tread carefully.' Rachel knows her father is right. 'Girls, I really think you need to take a deep breath and take stock of what you have. You're both wonderful, clever women with long lives ahead of you. Don't spend all your time waiting for life to begin – take charge and enjoy it for what it is. Now come here and give your old dad a hug before your mum gets back and starts laying down the law again.'

When Diana comes back, the three of them are cuddled up on the sofa laughing at some seventies sitcom they've found on the television. Diana watches them for a while, envying Edward and longing to join them.

CHAPTER TWENTY TWO

Emma is hiding in her flat. She phoned in sick today doing her best flu voice and has been spent most of the day sleeping and crying. She feels so weary, as if she could sleep for a year and still be tired. It had been weird staying at her parents' house last night but she had found comfort in her dad's counselling and even her mother's bossy declarations that she'd ruined her life. There was something reassuring in the constancy of your family. Even Rachel had been consoling and Emma sensed that there was more going on in her sister's life than she was letting on. It wasn't like Rachel to run to her parents' readily; her father maybe, but to expose herself to her mother's critical scrutiny was virtually unheard of.

It's getting dark now. Emma hears the heating click into life and feels comforted by the normality of life. She doesn't think she's going to be able to go back to sleep so she gets up and runs a bath. She reaches into the back of cupboards to retrieve enough candles to light a cathedral. She dots them around the bathroom and goes to find her cosiest pyjamas and fluffiest towels. This brings on a fresh round of tears as they are the pyjamas that Martin bought her last Christmas. She is feeling weak and feeble and hates herself for this. She sets about lighting the candles and is just about to get into the bath when there is a loud knock at the door.

'Oh bugger off,' she curses under her breath, retying her robe and blowing out all the candles before hurrying downstairs to answer it.

Richard stands on the doorstep grinning coyly. 'Surprise?' he says, leaning forward to kiss her.

'Oh hi. What are you doing here?'

'I just wanted to see if you were OK,' he says looking concerned.

'I'm fine,' says Emma starting to cry again, showing that she clearly isn't fine.

'Oh darling, darling. Hey, hey, come here,' says Richard, taking the opportunity to hop over the threshold. He takes Emma in his arms, kisses her face and wipes at her tears.

'Richard, please don't,' she says, backing into the living room.

'Sorry, Emma, it's just, God, you know I can't resist you. Come on, come and sit down. Let's talk.' He leads her to the sofa and notices the empty wine glass. 'You sit down. I'll get us both a drink.'

'Oh, right, OK,' says Emma, a little peeved by his presumption. He returns with two large glasses of wine and plonks himself on the sofa next to her.

'I have to say, I feel rather responsible for all this and I am sorry,' he says offering her the wine.

'Thanks,' she says unsure of what else to say.

'But if I'm honest I didn't really think Martin was making you happy. I thought I was doing the right thing, but I do regret the trouble I've caused you.'

'Well, I appreciate you coming round to see how I am,' says Emma sipping her wine.

'I was desperate to see you. I've thought of nothing else since last night.' Richard takes her wine glass from her and sets it down on the table. He cups her face in his hands.

'You see the thing is,' he says kissing the corner of her lips. 'I have fallen.' Another kiss. 'Quite hopelessly.'

And another. 'In love with you.' The next kiss is long and lingering and Emma feels herself move towards him. 'Emma, I think we should go upstairs,' he breathes. He stands and picks up the wine glasses. Emma is completely stuck in the moment. Martin is gone, she tells herself. It's time to move on. She stands to follow him just as her home phone rings.

'I'll leave it,' she says.

She follows Richard upstairs and by the time they reach the bedroom she can hear her mother's voice on the answering machine, but can't pick out any words. I'll call her tomorrow, she thinks, have a proper chat, maybe invite her for lunch. Richard sets down the wine glasses and walks to where Emma is hesitating in the doorway. He kisses her again on the mouth and then starts to kiss her neck and work his way down. He is just undoing her robe when Emma's mobile starts to ring. She looks towards where it lies on the dresser.

'Leave it,' says Richard, but Emma glances over and sees the caller ID.

'It's my mother,' she says.

'So?'

'She never phones my mobile,' she says reaching for the phone. Richard pulls away and sinks onto the bed, sulking like a five-year-old.

'Mum? Are you OK?'

'Emma? Emma, is that you?' Her mother sounds very far away, her voice uncharacteristically small and distant.

'Yes, Mum, what is it?'

'It's your father, Emma. There's – there's – ' she stutters over her words and then breaks off.

'Mum!' calls Emma feeling the panic rising in her voice. 'What is it? What's wrong?'

'Emma?' It's Rachel's voice. 'Are you there?'

'Yes, Rach, tell me what's happened to Dad!'

'He's had a heart attack. We're at St. Mary's. I think you better get down here.'

'Do you want anything from the machine, Mum?'

Diana, her eyes red from crying, looks at her daughter as if she has just spoken to her in Lithuanian.

'Sorry, Rachel, did you say something?' Rachel sits down next to her mother and takes her hand. Diana immediately stiffens at the physical contact and draws her hand away but pats Rachel's leg to show that she is grateful. 'I'm fine. Thank you.' They are sitting on plastic chairs, which have probably won awards for 'world's most uncomfortable seat'. Rachel looks around her. A low coffee table to her right is covered in tatty women's weeklies and the odd *Saga* magazine. On the opposite wall, there is a print of one of Van Gogh's sunflower paintings. How depressing, thinks Rachel – a painting by a mentally unstable genius who committed suicide – perfect for encouraging people to get better.

'I'm going to go and get a drink. Do you want one?' she tries again.

'What? No thank you, Rachel,' says her mother and she continues staring off into the middle distance. Rachel walks down the corridor feeling slightly nauseous at the smell of chemical cleanliness and fearful of the beeps and groans she can hear coming from the wards. She finds a drinks machine and empties her change into its slot. She is rewarded with a drink the consistency of mud and sand which purports to be a cappuccino

'Excuse me, dear,' says a thin voice at her elbow. Rachel looks round to find a small, skeletal woman, carrying two heavily stuffed plastic bags, her hair a wispy halo around her head.

'Are you all right?' asks Rachel, immediately concerned.

'Oh yes, dear, I'm fine,' says the woman displaying a mouth devoid of teeth, 'I just need to know where I go for the number fifty-two bus?'

'Well, I'm not sure,' says Rachel looking around her, desperate for a nurse to appear. Just at that moment the woman lets forth a gush of urine onto the floor, some of which splashes onto Rachel's shoe.

'Ahhh, that's better,' says the woman with a grateful smile.

'Mrs Hill! Mrs Hill! There you are,' calls a genial looking West Indian nurse. She jogs up to the old lady and takes her by the arm. 'Oh, you had a little accident. Well, I'll sort that out. Let's get you back to bed, shall we?' The nurse turns to Rachel and whispers, 'Poor lady. She keeps trying to pack her bags and go back home to her husband, but he died seven years ago. It's very sad.' She leads the old lady away and Rachel hears her ask, 'When will I see my Ernie again, Grace?' Rachel feels tears welling in her eyes and is aware of someone standing next to her. She turns and is so grateful to be looking up at Steve. He wraps her in his arms and she sobs.

Richard screeches into the hospital car park and pulls up outside the modern, pillared entrance.

'Are you going to wait?' asks Emma. She looks at him and sees the panic pass over his face before he masks it with a kindly smile.

'Oh, Emma, I would but to be honest I'm not very good with family things, you know,' he says, as if she has invited him to her cousin's wedding. 'I don't think they'd want me there.'

'No, but I could do with some support.'

'Of course, of course,' he says, 'and if you need me, you just have to call me, OK?' He takes her hands and kisses her. 'I really hope your dad's OK, Emma.'

Emma doesn't answer. She opens the door of the car feeling numb and walks into the hospital without looking back.

Richard watches her disappear and retrieves his mobile. He flicks to missed calls. The voice that answers is purring but with a hard edge.

'Hey, loser, good to hear from you.'

Richard grins and stretches back in his seat. 'What are you up to?'

'Well, I'm currently lying in bed wearing nothing but a smile. It would be lovely to see you, if you're not too busy with your editor,' purrs the female voice.

Richard laughs. 'That's a very tempting offer. I'm obviously very busy but I think I might be able to fit you in, in say half an hour?'

'I look forward to it.'

'He's had quite a sizeable heart attack and, at this stage, it's a little like a volcano. We can't really say what will happen next. But for the moment, he's stable. The next twenty-four hours will be critical,' says the consultant.

Rachel is staring at the mole on the doctor's lip all the while she is talking. Diana sits looking almost serene as if this woman is delivering tomorrow's weather forecast. Emma is crying noisily in the corner. Steve is the only one paying full attention to the doctor and when she has finished he thanks her. She smiles the smile of a woman who experiences these scenes every day of her life and sweeps out of the room. The four of them sit together in silence for a while. Rachel looks at the tubes and machines that are keeping her father alive.

'I just don't understand it. Why is this happening to him? He's so fit and well, he eats properly, he doesn't smoke. OK, he likes a drink, but God, it's just so unfair!' Steve squeezes her shoulder. She smiles at him gratefully.

'Some people have weak hearts I guess,' offers Emma in a small, weepy voice.

'Oh for goodness sake, Emma. That's not a very helpful thing to say!' cries Rachel.

'Sorry, I'm just saying,' says Emma sulkily.

'Girls, can you just be quiet please,' says Diana. The girls look at their mother and mumble ashamed apologies.

'I think we should all try to get some rest,' says Steve.

'We can't go anywhere,' says Rachel.

'No, of course not. Your mum can have the chair and I'll ask at the nurse's station for some mattresses and blankets.'

'What about the kids?' says Rachel.

'Sue says she can stay and take them to school in the morning. She said not to give it a second thought,' says Steve.

Rachel wishes she knew what to say to Steve. They haven't spoken properly since she stormed out the previous night. She had returned early in the morning, in time to take Will to school, and there had been a cursory exchange in the hall as he left for work. It was as if they couldn't bring themselves to start on a conversation for fear of where it might lead. All she knows is that she's so glad he's here at the moment.

Moments later, Steve returns with the bedding and soon, they are all tucked up around the room, like tourists on some bizarre camping holiday.

If it wasn't so terrifying, thinks Rachel, *this would be quite funny*. She looks at her mother, who is propped up in a hospital armchair with a blanket draped loosely around her shoulders. She is staring at Edward with a look of such love and concern, Rachel feels as if her heart will break.

'Mum?' Diana looks over at her daughter, slightly bemused. 'You should get some rest,' urges Rachel.

'I will, darling. You go to sleep.'

Emma wakes up and at first can't remember where she is. The room is dark and as her eyes adjust she can see her mother's shoes a few feet from her face and wonders if she's having another bizarre dream. She sits up and rubs her eyes, banging her head hard on the bottom of her father's bed.

'Ow!'

'Emma?'

'Mum?' Emma rubs her head and peers through the darkness at her mother propped up in the padded green hospital chair. She is alarmed to see her staring past her as if she is asleep with her eyes open. 'Mum, are you OK?' she asks, following her eyes to where Edward lies, his breathing steady through a jumble of tubes.

Diana's eyes don't leave Edward for a second. 'I'm fine.'

Emma isn't sure what to do next. She feels as if she's intruding on her parents and suddenly sees them as a couple in love and wants to cry. 'I think I'll go and get a drink. Will you be OK?'

'Of course,' says Diana not looking at her. 'We'll be fine.'

Emma tiptoes out of the room and down the corridor. It's deathly silent, which strikes Emma as strange for a building full of sick people. Suddenly she hears a moan from one of the other rooms. Its volume and frequency intensify and Emma looks round in panic. She walks towards the nurse's station.

'Excuse me? Excuse me? I think there's someone here who needs help,' she calls. A stout looking nurse with a weary face appears and heads towards the room without acknowledging Emma's pleas or presence. Emma stands alone feeling frightened and then turns on her heels and heads towards the exit. Once outside she breathes in cold night air, holding the wall for support. She looks up at the sky and for once in her life, she prays: 'Please, please don't let him die.'

The tears course down her face and the enormity of the situation hits her like a slap. She reaches into her pocket for her phone willing herself to be wrong about Richard. There are no messages, no consoling texts, and Emma Darcy is forced to confront a truth she would rather ignore. She hears the automatic doors open and feels her sister by her side.

'Hey, Em.'

'Hey,' says Emma her voice hoarse from crying.

'I thought I might find you here,' adds Rachel linking arms with her sister. 'Come on. Let's walk.'

They make their way across the car park. A heavily pregnant woman is lumbering towards the hospital, her husband beside her, looking helpless. She pauses every now and then as a ripple of pain surges through her body. Her husband takes her hands, his face ashen and concerned. Rachel shivers once they are passed.

'Poor buggers. I know how that feels and I certainly wouldn't want to go through it again.' Emma, already on an emotional knife-edge, bursts into a fresh round of tears. Rachel hugs her sister. 'Come on, Em, it's OK.'

'No, it's bloody not!' cries Emma. 'I've ballsed up everything with Martin. I've made such a fool of myself and him. I'll probably never get married or have children and now Dad's lying in hospital and he might die!' she says through a veil of snot and tears.

'Well, I have to say, little sis, you're unlikely to ever find another boyfriend with that amount of mucus streaming down your face.'

Emma snorts with weak laughter, grateful to her sister for trying to stop the onslaught of emotion but it's short-lived as she starts to cry again. Rachel holds her by the shoulders.

'Listen to me, Em. Since when did Edward Darcy ever give up on anything?'

'Never?' says Emma sounding unconvinced.

'Precisely,' says Rachel. 'Like he's going to leave us now with all our problems.' Emma gives her sister a quizzical look but Rachel doesn't want to dwell on her problems at this moment. 'Anyway, you will get married. I'm not having you left on the shelf. You'll only come and live with us and that would be bloody awful. I'd kill you within a week!' Emma laughs. Rachel pulls her sister to her. 'Everything will be fine,' she says, hoping and praying that this is true.

CHAPTER TWENTY THREE

'Good morning!' sings the cheerful Asian nurse as she picks her way through the assorted sleeping bodies on the floor. 'Ooh, quite crowded in here!' She picks up Edward's chart and casts her eye over the monitors and tubes. Then she scribbles on the notes and says, 'Doctor be here soon.'

Steve, Rachel and Emma all start to unfold themselves, stretching out their aching limbs. Diana is still motionless in the chair watching Edward, and Emma wonders if she has been like this all night.

'Right, why don't I fetch us some breakfast?' says Steve. Rachel smiles at him but notices that he doesn't catch her eye.

'I'll come with you,' says Emma. 'What does everyone want?' They are all waiting for Diana to answer but she doesn't move or seem to have heard.

Rachel kneels in front of her mother. 'Mum?' Diana blinks and looks down her daughter as if seeing her for the first time. 'Do you want some breakfast? Maybe a cup of tea and a croissant?' says Rachel gently.

Diana sighs. 'I'm not eating anything from that cafeteria. Pat Burley came in here for a knee operation and her husband caught food poisoning from their toad-in-the-hole.' Rachel exchanges an amused glance with her sister. 'It's not funny, Rachel,' says her mother. She looks at Steve. 'I'll just have a cup of tea, thank you, Steve.'

When they are gone, Rachel goes to the window and looks out at the car park below. The day is grey and unpromising. There are lots of spaces but cars are darting in by the dozen, laying claim to the precious parking spots. Rachel turns to look at her mother unsure of how to start the conversation. She tries for an easy option.

'So, did you manage to get any sleep last night?'

Diana's eyes are back on Edward's. 'Rachel, look!'

Rachel looks over at her father and can see his head moving ever so slightly, his eyelids flickering into life. They rush to his side.

'Edward! Edward, can you hear me?' implores Diana, reaching out for him. Edward's eyes open slightly and he catches sight of his wife.

'Is there any tea?' he whispers in a parched voice.

Rachel and Diana laugh and Diana touches his cheek. 'You horrible man. How dare you scare us all like that?' she says. The door swings open and the doctor from last night walks in.

'Goodness, you've had a long night,' says Rachel by way of greeting. The doctor smiles and doesn't disagree.

'Good morning,' she says, 'and good morning' Mr Darcy. How are you feeling today?'

'Thirsty,' says Edward. The doctor nods and starts to examine him. Rachel feels a little self-conscious but is compelled to stay and distracts herself by looking at the hand-washing instructions on the wall. When the doctor has finished she gives a little cough. Rachel and Diana turn to face her.

'As I told you last night, this was a sizeable heart attack.'

'What did I miss?' says Emma bustling into the room, cups in hand. 'Dad! You're awake!' she cries thrusting the cups into her sister's hand and flinging herself at him.

'Careful, Emma!' cries Diana.

'Sorry,' says Emma, and then to the doctor, 'sorry.'

'That's quite all right. As I was saying, it was a sizeable heart attack and there will be some resultant tissue damage. However, it is a good sign that you are already regaining consciousness, Mr Darcy. The next twenty-four hours will be crucial but I'm very pleased to see you're awake. I'll tell the nurses and then hand you over to my colleague, Dr Assan.'

Diana smiles proudly at her husband. 'Thank you, Doctor, thank you so much,' she says.

Rachel follows the doctor out of the room. 'Thank you again, Doctor.'

The doctor looks at Rachel, her face serious. 'It's good that your father is making such speedy progress but we're not out of the woods yet. He's obviously a fit and healthy man.'

'Yes and he knows how angry my mother would be if he left us now,' jokes Rachel and then wishes she hadn't.

The doctor smiles again. 'I'm sure. If you have any questions or concerns, just ask one of the nurses to page Dr Assan.'

Rachel nods and darts back into the room, which has now taken on something of a party atmosphere with Emma and Diana perched on the bed and Steve standing by Edward's head board telling him the football results from the previous night. Rachel goes to her dad and kisses him on the cheek.

'How are you feeling?' she asks.

'As if your children have been jumping on me all night,' says Edward hoarsely.

Rachel smiles. 'You gave us quite a shock, Dad. We expect this level of drama from Emma, but not you.'

'Shut up, cow-bag,' says Emma but she is smiling.

'And how my favourite patient?' says the nurse from earlier, who has appeared through the door. 'Very nice to see you awake, Mr Darcy. I get you some water and then we take it from there, OK? You need anything, you just call, OK?'

'Thank you, Connie,' says Edward, and Connie smiles at him.

After she has gone, Diana chuckles. 'Edward Darcy, you're such a flirt. I'll let you off, but only today.'

Edward tries to look innocent. 'You have to be nice to the nurses, my darling. They are modern-day angels and anyway, you do know I only have eyes for you, don't you?'

'Oh stop it,' says Diana with a giggle.

Rachel and Emma roll their eyes at one another and laugh. They eat their breakfast and sip their tea perched around Edward's bed. It reminds Rachel in a strange way of Christmas morning when they would all pile into their parents' room. After opening their presents, their mother would make toast and let them eat it in their bed for a treat, 'but only if you put the crumbs on Daddy's side'. If today's situation weren't so terrifying, thinks Rachel, it would actually be lovely and one of the rare occasions she gets to spend time on her own with Emma and her parents.

'Right,' says Steve, brushing toast crumbs from his chin. 'I better call work and let them know what's going on. Shall I give Sue a buzz?'

Rachel nods. 'Yes please and ask her if she's OK to have the twins today and thank her and tell her I owe her.'

Steve goes off to make his phone calls and Emma turns to her mother. 'Mum, why don't you go and freshen up. We'll stay here with Dad, won't we, Rach?'

''Course,' says her sister.

Diana looks over at Edward, unsure and a little frightened. 'You go, my darling. I'm not going anywhere,' he says.

'All right, but I won't be long,' says Diana plucking her handbag from the floor. 'I'm just going to powder my nose,' she adds which causes Emma to nudge her sister in amusement. When Diana has gone the girls sit either side of their father. He looks enquiringly at them.

'So, how are my girls? Did you sort out your problems with Martin and Steve?'

Rachel and Emma exchange glances and using quick-thinking sibling telepathy, decide to lie.

'Everything's fine, Dad. Isn't it, Em?'

'Absolutely,' says Emma. 'Very fine.' Rachel frowns at her unconvincing reply.

'You never were very good liars, were you, girls?' says Edward with a smile.

'Oh, Dad, I've made such a mess of everything!' cries Emma flinging herself at his chest.

Rachel shakes her head in annoyance. 'Emma, this is hardly the time!'

Emma sits back, wiping her face with the back of her hand. 'No, probably not. Sorry, Dad.'

'Don't be silly. What have I told you a hundred times? I just want you to be happy.' The girls nod. 'And I can see that you're patently not, but do you know what I also see?' Emma and Rachel look at him expectantly. 'I see the solution to your worries right in front of you. Do you? You just have to take the courage to admit what they are. The secret to a happy life isn't actually that complicated. Do you know one of my favourite things in life?'

'Fiona Bruce?' quips Rachel.

Edward chuckles. 'Well, she is rather special, isn't she? No, I tell you what it is. It's when you watch those wonderful children of yours, Rachel, when they don't know you're watching them.' Rachel nods. 'They get so absorbed in their little worlds and nothing else matters. They are just content in the moment, rather than looking for the next thing. Do you see? I know that life gets taken over by life sometimes, we all have to pay our bills and battle along, but strip it all away and what are you left with?'

Diana has come back into the room now closely followed by Steve. Rachel and Emma wish they could talk more but the moment has passed.

'How was Sue?' she asks Steve.

'Fine, she says you don't owe her a thing and she is happy to have the kids but that Alfie has been a bit upset this morning.'

'Oh, right.' Rachel looks round at her father.

'You should go and sort out the little man,' says Edward. 'Tell him that Grandpa sends him a big squeeze.'

Rachel feels a bit shaky and teary. 'OK, but you have to give it to me to pass on to him,' she says, putting her arms around her father and holding him close.

'Don't be so hard on yourself, wonderful girl,' he whispers. Rachel stands up and wipes her eyes.

Steve pats Edward's shoulder. 'I'll tape the game for you tonight,' he says.

Edwards nods and smiles. 'Thanks, Steve.'

As they open the door to leave, Martin appears.

'Hi, Mart,' says Steve shaking his hand. 'I gave Martin a call,' he adds to Emma by way of an explanation. 'Right, I'll take Rach home and we'll be back later, OK?'

Martin watches them go and stands in the doorway looking awkward.

'It's good to see you, Mart,' says Edward breaking the silence.

'I had to come when Steve called me. I wanted to check you were OK and see if there was anything I could do to help.'

Emma is watching him, unsure of what to say.

'Well, you could take Emma home to get a change of clothes,' says Diana.

'Oh. Right. Yes of course,' says Martin.

'There's no need. Really,' says Emma feeling cornered.

'Look, I am perfectly capable of looking after your father. I have been doing it for forty years. You go and come back later.'

'And you'll call me if anything happens?'

'Of course but everything will be fine now, won't it, Edward?'

'The grim reaper wouldn't dare call with your mother standing guard,' says Edward. 'You go and remember what I said, Em?'

'OK,' she says finally. 'But I'll be back in a couple of hours.' She hugs her father tightly and she and Martin say their goodbyes. They walk down the long corridor towards the exit in silence. This doesn't really seem like the time for small talk, which is a shame as it would have made them both feel less awkward.

'My car is over there,' says Martin. They drive in renewed silence until Martin says, 'I'm really sorry about your dad. I was so shocked to hear he'd had a heart attack. He's so fit and healthy.'

'Yes, it's all a big shock,' says Emma feeling as if she's delivering a line in a play and not doing it particularly well. She doesn't know what topic of conversation to follow with Martin. Anything from 'How are you?' to 'What have you been up to?' seems inadequate and very likely to lead to more uncomfortable topics. She opts for the uncomfortable silence studying the grey, drizzly view, mulling over what her father has said. She knows she's been a fool but she can't quite face the truth today. Once they reach the house, she is ready to leap from the car. She gathers her belongings and ventures a glance at Martin.

'Thank you for bringing me home. It was above and beyond the call of duty in the circumstances.'

'I'm very fond of your dad,' says Martin by way of an explanation.

Ouch, thinks Emma, *but I probably deserved that.* She gets out of the car and leans back to say, 'I'll see you.'

Martin nods but doesn't smile, turning back to face the road and driving away. Emma lets herself into a cold house. She dumps her bags and goes into the kitchen; flicking the switch on the kettle, firing up the boiler and turning on the radio, wanting to blot out the silence. She goes to the fridge to retrieve some milk and as she closes the door she picks off a photo of them all together at her parents' the previous Christmas complete with the obligatory paper hats. Steve is caught in mid-run having set the timer but not made it back to his place in time. Everyone else is looking at him and laughing, except for Edward, who sits at the centre with Alfie on his lap and Lily standing on his other side, her arms wrapped protectively around his neck. Edward is staring out of the picture: smiling, warm and utterly content. Emma hugs the photo to her and cries and cries with noisy, longing sobs.

'And did I tell you about Doreen?' says Diana, not waiting for her husband to answer. 'She's had a terrible time. Her daughter-in-law has run off – ' Diana pauses for dramatic effect and then leans in and whispers ' – with another woman!' Edward smirks at his wife, his eyebrows raised. 'What?' says Diana. 'It's no laughing matter, Edward.'

'Of course not, my darling,' says Edward, still grinning. 'But it does make for rather splendid gossip, doesn't it?'

Diana looks horrified. 'I do not gossip!' she declares, but her face breaks into a smile as she realises she's being teased. 'Much.' Diana never minds when her husband teases her and particularly not today. He is the man who stopped her taking herself too seriously and she loves him for it. She looks at him now, looking so poorly and pale, but Diana Darcy is a woman with determination. She also sees the twinkle in his eye and clings onto this as proof that all will be well. She perches on the side of the bed and reaches out a hand to stroke his forehead. 'Darling Edward,' she murmurs.

'Dearest Dis. Why don't you lie down with me, darling? You look exhausted,' he says.

Diana feels a little unsure, as if this would be vaguely inappropriate despite their forty years of marriage, two daughters and advanced years. She remembers a time when her mother had caught them cuddling on the sofa when they were newly engaged. She sees her mother's angry, unforgiving face in her mind and it gives her courage. She slides herself next to Edward, careful not to disturb the wires and tubes that are helping him to live. Edward puts his arms around her.

'That's better,' he declares.

'I'm never going to forgive you for this,' says Diana gently kissing his cheek.

He leans down to kiss her. 'Of course not, my darling. I know I'm on washing-up duty for the rest of my days,' he says.

Despite the beeping and whirring of the machines surrounding them, Diana feels a happy calm descend over her. Edward is warm by her side, his breathing steady. She feels sleep wash over her and as she falls, she hears herself say 'I love you' and she has never meant anything more in her life.

When she wakes she is confused by the thin, piercing sound, more urgent than an alarm clock. She sits up, suddenly aware of the situation and of people rushing into the room.

'Mrs Darcy, we must ask you to step aside,' says a nurse, taking her by the shoulders.

'No,' says Diana vehemently. 'I can't leave him.'

'Mum? Mum! What's going on?' cries Rachel, bursting into the room closely followed by Emma and Steve. Both girls stop and clutch their hands to the mouths.

'No!' cries Emma. 'No! This can't happen. He's OK, he's going to be OK! Rachel?!' She implores her sister to make it all right.

'I'm very sorry, but you must leave now,' repeats the nurse.

Diana still refuses to come. 'I must stay with him. He needs me,' she cries. Rachel helps Steve pull her mother out of the room.

'Come on, Mum, you have to let them do their job.'

They watch helplessly as various medical staff rush in and out of Edward's room. Rachel and Emma stand, their arms around each other. Diana looks through the window, her eyes never leaving Edward for a second. No one speaks. All they can hear is the sound of panic with that constant beeping screaming in their ears.

Please let him live, thinks Rachel, *I'll be a better person, I won't shout at the kids and I'll sort everything with Steve. I'm so sorry.*

At the same time, Emma is seeing herself properly for the first time. She doesn't like what she sees and wants to make everything better.

Suddenly the panic is over, the beeping has stopped and the family rush towards the room. The doctor meets them at the door, his face impossible to read.

'I'm sorry,' he says. 'We did everything we could.'

Just seven words and three worlds collapse.

CHAPTER TWENTY FOUR

Emma pads down the stairs as quietly as she can so as not to wake her mother. She walks into the kitchen and, unfamiliar with the switches, turns on the hall light as well.

'Emma? Is that you?' says a voice from the living room.

'Mum?' says Emma peering around the doorway, squinting through the darkness. 'What are you doing sitting in the dark?' she adds, flicking on the light. Her mother is sitting in Edward's favourite chair and Emma notices that she has wrapped his coat around her. 'Oh, Mum.' She goes to her mother's side and puts her arms awkwardly around her, leaning over Diana in a strange, standing embrace.

Tears come easily to Emma but Diana does not cry. She does realise that some kind of maternal reaction is required and pats her daughter's head with a hesitant hand. She has never dealt well with crying. Edward was always the one who comforted the girls when they banged their knees or fell over. When Diana was alone with them, she would try to rouse them out of their wailing with a 'There, there, don't cry. Be a brave girl for Mummy now.' Diana knew this wouldn't be appropriate now but she still wished Emma would stop. 'Shall I make us some tea?' she says at last.

Emma looks up surprised at her mother's composure, her face red and streaming. 'OK.'

Diana stands up and carries Edward's coat to the hall, placing it on a coat-peg and running her hand down the material as if reaching for the man who had once worn it. Emma follows her into the kitchen and they busy themselves with the menial tasks of filling the kettle and retrieving cups and milk. When it is ready, they sit at the kitchen table in silence. Diana looks ahead of her and Emma stares out of the window at the breaking dawn. The sky is glowing with the promise of a sunny autumn day. It would have been a day to lift one's spirits had circumstances been different. Emma looks at her mother, unsure of what to say. Diana clears her throat and Emma feels nervous at the prospect of a heart to heart.

'I'll give Pat a call in the morning. She lost her husband last year and they had a marvellous funeral director. He was very sensitive and very – ' Her voice breaks off. 'Your father liked him.'

Emma hears her mother's voice waver with emotion and is surprised by the novelty. She takes Diana's hand. 'Oh, Mum,' is all she can think to say.

'What am I going to do without him?' cries Diana, uttering a universal sentiment. Emma wonders if she is finally going to cry but Diana looks at her and it is as if something has clicked off in her mind. 'Anyway, we'd better try and get some sleep. There is a lot to do tomorrow,' she says finishing her tea.

'Yes, OK,' says Emma feeling a strange mix of disappointment and relief.

'I'll see you for breakfast,' says Diana in a matter of fact way. As she walks past her daughter, she reaches out a hand and squeezes her shoulder. Emma smiles at her mother, appreciating the gesture.

'Night, Mum.'

Diana makes her way up the stairs feeling suddenly exhausted. She walks into her bedroom and shuts the door behind her. Carefully she tiptoes round to Edward's side of the bed and climbs in. She lies down, inhaling deeply into his pillow, noting his cufflinks and alarm clock on the bedside table. She closes her eyes and weeps.

Rachel opens her eyes to silence. She finds this strange as she knows her family is still in the house. Downstairs she can hear Steve's deep, soft tones talking to the children and she picks out the odd word: ' . . . kind to Mummy . . . very sad. We all loved Grandpa very much.'

Rachel feels guilt and gratitude in equal measure and closes her eyes again. Her mind races back to the last time she saw her dad. *This time yesterday*, she thinks, *this time yesterday, he was still with us, still breathing. How can he be gone? What will we do?* Hot tears roll down her cheeks. She clutches her pillow to her body and rolls over onto one side, facing the window. The sky is glowing with sunshine and Rachel thinks how today would have been a day for her father to do some work in the garden and this brings on a fresh round of tears. She hears the door open behind her and assumes it will be Alfie, creeping in to snuggle up with his mum. She doesn't look round and is surprised to see Will appear by the bed, his face fixed in a frown of concern.

'I brought you this, Mum,' he says, holding up a slightly nibbled and melted chocolate biscuit. 'It was the last one.' Rachel can see that he is shocked by her appearance and does her best not to start crying again.

'Thank you, darling,' she croaks, taking the biscuit and wiping her eyes. 'I must look pretty scary today. Like something out of *Scooby Doo*,' she adds attempting a smile.

'Yeah, but it's OK, Mum,' says Will. 'I know you're very sad about Grandpa. I am too.'

'Come and give your old mum a hug,' she says offering her arms to him. Unusually for Will, he accepts and folds himself into her like a baby. They sit for a while, Rachel enjoying the warmth of the boy who was once her first and only baby. She feels his shoulders shaking a little and looks down to see that he's crying. Rachel cries too, unable to bear the pain her child feels.

'I know, my darling, I know,' she whispers.

After a while, they sit up and smile at each other through their tears.

'The thing you need to do,' says Rachel finally, 'is to remember all the happy times you had with Grandpa. That's what he would want. He's probably looking down at us now saying, "What are you lot moping about?"' Rachel laughs at the thought and wonders at herself – a middle-class atheist who still employs the heaven imagery as the only way she knows of making it all seem better.

'The day I went to the football with Grandpa and Dad, and Deon Burton scored a hat trick. It was the best day of my life ever,' says Will plainly.

Rachel looks at her son and feels untold admiration for him. Her father's words to her and Emma from yesterday echo in her head.

'I'm sad about Grandpa,' says Alfie from the doorway. Rachel looks over at his small, forlorn face. 'Can I have that biscuit?' he asks, forgetting his grief in a way that makes Rachel smile.

'Come in with Will and me, darling.' Alfie scrambles onto the bed and snuggles under his mother's other arm, munching happily on the biscuit. Rachel kisses the top of his head and pulls him in close. 'Oh my lovely boys,' she sighs.

'Where is Grandpa now?' asks Alfie.

'Well,' starts Rachel, feeling her voice wobble.

'He's up in heaven,' says Will with certainty.

'Oh, where's that?' asks Alfie, keen to know more.

'Up there,' says Will pointing towards the ceiling.

'Oh, up there,' says Alfie, eyes wide with wonder, looking upwards.

'Everyone all right in here?' says Steve, climbing the stairs. 'How are you feeling, Rach?' he added. Rachel shrugs, her face a picture of despair. Steve has been kind and supportive over the last few days but his hugs and comfort have been more like that of a friend than a husband. Rachel can't really blame him and she doesn't have the emotional energy to face it at the moment.

'Daddy, daddy! Guess what?' shouts Alfie, full of excitement.

'What is it, little man?' asks Steve.

'Grandpa is in the loft!' he cries, pointing up at the ceiling.

'No he's not you dum-dum,' declares Lily wandering in. 'He's in heaven, which is way, way up in the sky, even further than the moon.'

'Oh,' says Alfie sounding disappointed. 'When can I see him again?'

Rachel looks at Steve.

'Come on,' says Steve. 'Let's leave Mummy in peace. We can go downstairs and talk about it.'

'No, it's OK,' says Rachel. 'Stay. Please. Let's talk about it now.'

'OK, if you're sure,' says Steve.

Minutes later, all five of them are tucked up in bed, talking, laughing and crying about Edward. Rachel feels warm and loved and sad. *You were right, Dad. You were so right*, she thinks. She pulls her family to her and doesn't want to let go.

Diana wheels the trolley down the biscuit aisle and prays that she doesn't bump into anyone else she knows. She's already seen Brian from the golf club and Beryl who used to work in the school office. She held herself together when she told them that Edward had died but actually ended up feeling guilty at the distress it caused them. Their smiling faces dissolved into shock and despair, their brains desperately casting round for something to say. They couldn't believe that he'd only died yesterday and yet here she was, doing her shopping as if nothing had happened. *How many of the people you pass in the street*, thinks Diana, *are carrying round the tragic events of their lives, like little, hidden boxes of pain.* She knows it's absurd to be doing this today, but she had to get out of the house. Everything in it reminds her of Edward and Emma is doing her best, but it's like having her own Greek tragedy chorus wailing in the corner. Diana scans the shelves looking for the Crinkle Creams. She notes that they are on offer.

'Oh look, that's good. We'll have a couple of those, shall we?' she says, turning expecting to see Edward and then realising how it will be from now on. She breathes in sharply, feeling her hand go to her mouth. She wills herself to go on breathing and her chest heaves with short breaths that become deep sobs. She holds the trolley to steady herself.

'Mrs Darcy? Are you all right?'

Diana blinks at the concerned voice, seeing the face of a woman around Rachel's age staring back at her.

'I'm sorry – ' she begins.

'It's all right,' says the woman. 'I'm Sue. Rachel's friend. We met at the twins' birthday party. I'm so sorry to hear about Edward.'

'Oh Sue, yes of course,' says Diana, immediately warming to this sunny woman. 'I was just having a little moment.'

'Of course,' says Sue. 'When my dad lost my mum, it used to hit him at the strangest times. He once got invited to join a group of mothers for coffee when he got upset in his local library. He meets them every week now. Listen,

I've nearly finished my shopping and my son's at pre-school. Would you like to go for a coffee?'

Diana looks at Sue and is experiencing that life-enhancing feeling you get from the kindness of strangers. 'That would be lovely,' she says with gratitude.

Emma hears her mobile ring from the bathroom and dashes downstairs. Her first thought is that it might be Richard and her second thought is that she's a fool who has learnt nothing. She checks the caller ID and answers.

'Ella? Hello. How are you?'

'I'm fine. Miranda told me about your dad. I'm so sorry, Em.'

'Thank you. It's all such a shock,' sniffs Emma.

'Of course it is. I can't imagine how you must be feeling. Listen, if there's anything I can do, you know just to call, don't you?'

'Yes, thanks, Ella,' says Emma feeling suddenly weary.

'And don't worry about work, OK?'

'No, OK.'

'All right, I'll let you go because I expect you're really busy but take care and call me if you need me. Anytime. OK?'

'OK. Thank you,' says Emma, ending the call and sinking into a chair. She hears the front door open and Rachel's voice.

'Hello?'

Emma drags herself from the chair and wanders into the hallway.

'Hey, Em. Are you OK?'

'No, not really,' says Emma, starting to cry again.

'No, sorry. Stupid question,' says Rachel hugging her. 'Did Sue bring Mum back?'

'Yes, she's upstairs resting. She didn't say much. Do you know what happened?'

'She had a bit of moment in the biscuit aisle apparently.'

'Well, I told her not to go, but she wouldn't listen. You know how she can be.'

'Yes, well, I can understand why she wanted to get out of the house,' says Rachel, glancing at Edward's coats hanging in the hallway.

'Do you think we should move them?' asks Emma.

'No, I think we should let Mum decide when the time's right.'

'Mmm OK. Do you want a cup of tea?' asks Emma.

'I'm a bit tea-ed out to be honest. That seems to be what you do when tragedy hits. Drink tea.'

''Tis the British way,' says Emma half-smiling.

'I could do with something stronger to be honest,' says Rachel walking into the dining room and opening up the drinks cabinet.

'Cherry brandy?' giggles Emma, feeling like a disobedient child raiding their parents' booze supplies.

'No. This,' says Rachel pulling out a very acceptable thirty-year-old single malt.

'That was Dad's favourite,' says Emma, feeling unsure.

'And that is why I am going to toast him with it. Want one?'

'All right then. With ice please.'

Rachel looks at her sister as if she's just asked for a dog turd. 'You always were a bit weird.'

They make their way to the living room with their drinks. The sun is shining brightly through the window, illuminating the pictures on the mantelpiece. Emma picks up the photograph of her parents on their wedding day.

'They were a handsome couple,' she says, her voice breaking slightly.

Rachel smiles and takes the picture. She raises her glass. 'To Edward Darcy,' she declares.

'To Edward Darcy,' says Emma, clinking her glass against her sister's. She flops down into a chair.

'So,' says Rachel. 'Tell me the truth about Martin. What's going on?'

'Only if you tell me about Steve.'

'All right. You first.'

'Well – ' says Emma, unsure of where to begin. 'You know my new author? Richard Bennett?'

'The dishy one you mentioned in the pub?'

Emma thinks back to that night and feels as if that was a different life, as if she were a completely different person. 'Yes, him.'

'Well? What happened? Did you sleep with him?'

'Rachel!'

'What? You didn't sleep with him?'

Emma rubs her temples. 'No, but I wanted to.'

'Well, that's hardly a crime,' says Rachel, pondering her own misdemeanour.

Emma looks at her sister. 'I fell for him in a big way. He flattered me, paid me attention. We liked the same books, films. That kind of thing. We just clicked somehow.'

'More than with Martin?' says Rachel nodding, understanding.

'Different.'

'So how come you and Martin have split then?'

'Richard came round and declared his feelings for me.'

'So?'

'Martin was there.'

'Oh. Sounds like something from one of your poncey novels. Did he challenge him to a duel?'

Emma looks at her sister in surprise. It's as if she's found the final piece of the million-piece jigsaw that is Richard Bennett. Emma shakes her head at the revelation.

'You're right. It was like the plot of a bloody novel and I'm the flawed heroine falling for it like an idiot.'

'Oh, don't be too hard on yourself. Happens to the best of us,' declares Rachel.

'Oh yes. So what happened to you then? Who turned your head?'

Rachel looks ashamed. 'My next door neighbour.'

'Tasty Tom?'

Rachel smiles. 'The very same.'

'Well, I don't blame you but at least nothing happened, right?'

'Of course not,' says Rachel a little too quickly.

'Rachel?'

'We had a moment. Nothing happened. We kissed,' says Rachel. 'I sort of thought Steve was having an affair.'

'Steve? Are you sure? I can't think of anyone less likely to be unfaithful than Steve,' says Emma.

It's Rachel's turn for an epiphany. 'Yeah, I know. I guess Dad was right. Sometimes you can't see what you've got.'

'Until it's gone? Well, it looks as if we've both fucked things up, doesn't it?'

'Certainly does, little sis, but I fully intend to sort out my mess. What about you?'

'Dunno. I can't think about it now. Mum needs us and we've got stuff to do. I've made a list. Let's crack on shall we?'

Rachel puts her arm round her sister. 'OK, but you can phone Rosie.'

'Deal. You can phone Granny Liz.'

Rachel screws up her face. 'You drive a hard bargain but all right.'

When Diana comes downstairs half an hour later, the girls are surrounded by papers and busy with lists and phone calls. She watches them unnoticed, a feeling of pride creeping over her. Rachel looks up.

'Hi, Mum. How are you feeling?'

Diana sighs. 'All right. How are you getting on?'

'OK. We've phoned nearly everyone on your list.'

'Did you speak to Rosie?'

'Emma did.'

Emma pulls a face. 'It was all I could do to stop her coming over.'

'Well, I'm glad you managed it,' says Diana with a wry smile. 'Will you stay for dinner?'

The girls make positive noises and Diana is pleased and thinks how much Edward would have enjoyed this. She goes to the kitchen and starts on dinner in order to stop herself thinking about how much she misses him.

CHAPTER TWENTY FIVE

Rosie looks at the dining table loaded with assorted finger foods and tuts.

'*Vol-au-vents*? How ghastly. No one serves *vol-au-vents* these days,' says a voice next to her. Rosie glances over to see a frowning elderly woman, dressed in a fitted midnight-blue suit. The woman looks at her and Rosie holds out her hand.

'Rosie Temperley,' she says, and then in a confidential whisper, 'and I was just thinking the same thing.' The woman smiles, satisfied that she has found an ally.

'It's my daughter, you see, she never did have much taste, apart from her husband. Dear, dear Edward, so tragic. How she ever managed to win him and keep him, I'll never know.'

Rosie is delighted. 'Oh, you're Diana's mother. It's so lovely to meet you, and yes, it is an absolute tragedy about darling Teddy. I feel completely devastated by his loss,' she says. 'He and I were very close, old friends. I've known him a lot longer than Diana,' she adds.

'Really?' says Diana's mother. 'I'm Elizabeth by the way. It's good to meet you too.'

Rosie smiles warmly at her new friend. 'And do I detect that your divine suit is Chanel?'

'Of course,' says Elizabeth plainly. 'I rarely wear anything else during the day.'

'Are you OK, Grandma?' asks Emma joining them. 'Hello, Rosie.'

'Please, darling, don't call me Grandma. It's so ageing. Call me Granny if you absolutely must or Lizzy.'

'Darling girl!' cries Rosie, pressing Emma to her bosom. 'How are you keeping? You must be in pieces!'

Emma sniffs and nods. 'I just can't believe he's gone.'

'I know, dear heart, I know.'

'Great Grandmama?' says Lily, sidling up to Elizabeth and tugging at her skirt. The old lady winces and looks down at Lily as if she has just discovered the source of a particularly unpleasant smell.

'Ah, it's Lileth, isn't it?'

Lily stares back at her as if she is the stupidest person on the planet. 'No, duh! My name is Lily. Now, do you want to come and play a game or not?'

Elizabeth looks scandalised at the suggestion and Emma realises she needs to help. 'Come on, Lils, I'll play with you,' she says taking her niece by the hand.

'What an impertinent child,' remarks Elizabeth.

'Yes, I think Rachel's three are quite a handful,' observes Rosie.

'Well, it's young women these days, isn't it? They want it all, don't they? It just isn't possible. I have told Diana time and again how much she's spoilt those girls but does she listen?' says Elizabeth popping one of the much-maligned *vol-au-vents* into her mouth.

'Would you care for a seat?' asks Rosie, preparing to sit down and indulge in her favourite sport: criticising Diana.

'But why did Grandpa have to die?' asks Lily again.

'Well, his heart wouldn't work properly,' says Emma, wishing they could talk about something else.

'And where did you say he was?' asks Lily.

'Well, I think he's up in heaven watching down on us.'

'But we'll never see him again?'

'No.'

'But why?'

'Well, it's like this, Miss Lily,' says Martin joining them. 'Grandpa's body died, so that's like his clothes, and what was inside him, like a spirit, has gone up to heaven so he can keep an eye on you and Will and Alfie and make sure you're OK.'

Emma catches his eye, mouthing a heartfelt 'thank you'.

'Well, I think it's bloody unfair,' says Lily.

Martin kisses her on the forehead. 'Do you know what, Lils? So do I,' he says.

Lily clings onto him. 'I really like you, Martin. When are you going to be our uncle again?' she asks.

Emma holds her breath. 'I already am your uncle and I always will be,' he says.

'Yay!' shouts Lily and runs off to find her brothers.

Emma smiles nervously at him. 'Thank you for that. And for coming. I didn't realise you were here.'

'I nipped in to the back of the church. I had to come and pay my respects. I was very fond of your dad.' Emma can feel the tears welling in her eyes. Martin looks at her. 'Hey, come on, Em, come here.' He pulls her to him and they stay like this for a while. Martin is the first to pull away. 'I should go.'

'Please, don't. Oh, Martin, I'm so sorry. I've messed up everything.'

He sighs. 'You won't find me disagreeing with you, Em.'

'Can we at least talk about this?' she pleads.

Martin looks around the room. 'I don't think this is the right time, do you?'

Emma sniffs. 'I guess not. I am sorry I hurt you though.'

He nods. 'I'm going to go and say goodbye to your mum and Rachel now. Take care, Em,' he says, turning on his heel.

Emma watches him go and wishes that her father were here to tell her what to do.

Rachel observes her mother move around the kitchen, her face set in concentration, her lips mouthing words like 'sausage rolls' and 'need more crisps'. She looks over at Sue who shrugs helplessly.

'Mum, are you OK?' says Rachel, trying to sound matter of fact. Her mother looks at her with that blank glaze that characterises her appearance since Edward died.

'What? Oh yes, I'm fine, darling. I'm just trying to remember where I put the olives,' she says. Rachel stands alongside her and peers into the cupboard.

'Here they are, Mrs Darcy,' says Sue, reaching behind her.

'Ah, thank you, Susan, and please, call me Diana.'

'Listen, Mum. Do you want to come and stay at ours tonight? The kids would love to have you over,' says Rachel.

'Oh, well that's very kind of you, but I'm sure I'll be – '

'Diana!' calls a voice from the living room. Diana doesn't seem to hear until her mother appears at the kitchen door. 'Diana! What are you doing hiding in here?'

'Oh, sorry, Mother. I was just fetching some more food,' says Diana.

'Oh for goodness sake, Diana, you can't hide out here all the time. People want to see you and honestly, what are you wearing? You know I can't abide off the peg. I really think you need to come and see my hairdresser too and for heaven's sake touch up that make-up!'

'Sorry,' says Diana without a hint of fight. Rachel feels a surge of sympathy for her mother and utter indignation at her grandmother's insensitivity.

Just at that moment, Alfie bursts through the door. 'Granny, Granny, Granny! Can we have some more of these crisps, please!'

Elizabeth tuts loudly but Diana smiles and Rachel is proud of her. 'Of course, my darling,' she says taking the bowl from him.

'They were Grandpa's favourite,' says Alfie, his face a big round moon with two vast blue, wondering eyes staring up at her. He frowns and screws up his face. 'I miss Grandpa,' he says plainly. Diana stares at him for a moment. Rachel and Sue hold their breath. Then she sinks to her knees and pulls his tiny, perfect frame to her.

'So do I, Alfie. So do I,' she says through a veil of desperate tears.

Elizabeth shakes her head and is about to open her mouth when Sue takes her firmly by the arm. 'It's Elizabeth, isn't it? I'm Sue. You must come and meet Christa,' she says, ushering her away. She glances back to see Rachel mouthing the words 'I love you!' and grins.

'Caught you!' says Emma rounding the corner of their parents' summer house.

'Shit, Emma! Do you have to creep up on people like that?' says Rachel, taking a nerve-calming drag on her cigarette.

'Sorry, but it wasn't difficult to work out where you were.'

'How so?'

'Well, you're not in the house and as we're not electing a new Pope, I assumed the cloud of smoke rising above the summer house was probably you having a crafty fag.'

'Fair point. Want one?' says Rachel offering the packet.

'No thanks and you shouldn't be either.'

'Oh spare me. I've just buried my dad today, seen my mother humiliated by Granny and had to endure Rosie doing her "other widow" act.'

'OK, whatever. How are you feeling, anyway?'

Rachel throws one cigarette to the floor, stamps on it and takes another from the packet. 'Pretty numb. I keep expecting him to appear at any moment and offer to make us all ridiculously strong gins and tonic.' Emma nods. 'How about you?' asks Rachel.

'I can't believe he's gone. He won't be there to walk me down the aisle or see my children born. It's just not fair,' she says, brushing away the tears. Rachel puts her arm round her sister and they stand in sorrowful silence, staring out at the bare autumn garden.

'How do you think Mum is?' asks Rachel after a while.

'I dunno. OK I guess.'

'I just saw Granny give her a complete dressing-down. Poor Mum. I think I'm a bit harsh on her sometimes.'

'Yeah, maybe. Maybe we both are. She can just be so controlling,' says Emma.

'Yes, but we all are, aren't we? And I can see where she gets it from. At least she's not as bad as Granny.'

'True,' says Emma.

'What about you and Martin then? Is it all off? I saw him leaving.'

'I don't know, Rach. Everything seems to be imploding. I don't know what's going to happen to be honest. What about you and Steve?'

'I'm going to sort it this evening,' says Rachel with confidence. She is determined. One thing she has discovered about grief, is that it has a startling way of putting your life into perspective. She's going to square everything with Steve – apologise, beg, plead – anything it takes to make him see how sorry she is.

They hear someone walking down the path and Rachel kicks her discarded cigarette under a bush.

'Oh there you are,' says Steve. 'What are you doing out here?' Rachel and Emma exchange glances like two schoolgirls who've just been rumbled.

'Oh I was just having a fag and Rachel was standing with me,' says Emma with unconvincing loyalty. 'I'm going to go back to the house.'

When she has gone Steve says, 'I thought you'd given up.'

'Oh yeah sorry. It was just the one, you know. It's been a horrible day.'

'I know,' he says, turning back towards the house.

'Actually, Steve?' she says, reaching out to touch his arm. He flinches but doesn't pull away. 'Can we have a talk this evening?'

'Are you sure today's the right day?' he asks.

'I think we need to,' she says with a weak smile.

He nods. 'OK then. I do have something I need to say.'

'Rachel!' shouts Emma from the back door.

'What is it?' calls Rachel, walking up to meet her sister on the patio.

'It's Mum.'

'Is she OK?'

'She's fine, but she's just punched Rosie.'

Rachel follows her sister into the dining room, where Rosie is sitting clutching a bag of frozen peas wrapped in a tea towel to her injured cheek. There is a crowd of people comforting her as she wails a chorus of self-pity. Rachel ignores her and pushes through to the kitchen. Diana is standing by the sink while Elizabeth is letting fly with a torrent of chastisements.

'The trouble with you is that you have absolutely no self-control, never have done. I cannot believe that you're my daughter. I am so ashamed and embarrassed. Poor Rosie. It is completely unacceptable to behave in such a way, Diana. Diana? Diana? Are you listening to me?'

Diana is standing motionless, staring straight ahead, unmoved by her mother's speech. It is as if the words are washing over her and she cannot hear them. Emma and

Rachel move towards them, ready to defend their mother, but it is Diana who speaks as if a button has been pressed in her head. She looks at her mother, unsmiling, speaking in a low, soft tone. 'And your trouble, Mother, is that you are utterly devoid of human emotion and feeling and always have been. You gave me the most miserable childhood possible and never supported or loved me. I cannot believe that you are my mother and I am glad that I have finally given Rosie exactly what she deserves. Now if you will excuse me, I have just buried my husband today and would like to be alone. I am going upstairs to lie down. I'm sure Rachel or Emma will phone for a taxi to take you home. Goodbye, Mother.'

Diana sweeps from the room leaving Elizabeth opening and closing her mouth like a stuck pig. Rachel and Emma exchange looks of admiration as Christa comes into the kitchen.

'Wow! Your mum has good punch, *nicht wahr*. I was *sehr* impressed. Ah, hallo again Lisbeth. Are you OK?'

Elizabeth tries to answer but it still too shocked to speak. Much to Rachel and Emma's amusement, Christa puts her arm around her. Elizabeth looks horrified as Christa pats her arm. '*Ja* I know *Schatz*, it's been a *scheisse* day but at least that bitch Rosie got her comeuppance. *Und* now, I have to go. I will give you a lift, Elizabeth. Come.'

Emma and Rachel watch them go. 'She is amazing,' says Emma at last.

'Isn't she?' says Rachel smirking. Suddenly, the two sisters are laughing hysterically, tears rolling down their cheeks.

'This is certainly the happiest funeral I've ever been to,' says Sue, joining them in the kitchen.

'I know,' says Rachel through her laughter. 'Dad would have loved it!'

Emma sees Richard's car before he sees her and sighs. She hasn't spoken to him since he dropped her off at the hospital and has felt some relief at this, unable to find the emotional strength to deal with both her grief and her ailing relationships. She taps on the window causing him to jump. He smiles at the sight of her.

'Emma, darling, how are you?' he asks following her down the garden path, reaching out an arm to stroke her shoulder.

'Not too bad,' she lies.

'I'm so sorry about your dad,' he says.

'Thank you.'

He follows her into the house and down to the kitchen. 'No Martin then?' he asks looking around.

'No, he's gone.'

'Oh, I'm so sorry,' says Richard, sounding anything but.

'Richard, why are you here?' asks Emma suddenly angry.

'Darling, I've been desperate to see you,' he says trying to take her in his arms. She pushes him away. 'Emma, what's wrong?'

'I'm not sure. You tell me.'

'Why are you so angry?' he ask, his tone edged with irritation.

'Hmm, I don't know, maybe I'm a little pissed off because, my dad has just died and the only emotional support I've had this week is from my ex!'

'Well, like I told you, I'm not very good at the family stuff,' he shrugs.

'"The family stuff"?' says Emma, her anger rising. 'Sorry, but I thought you were in love with me and I hate to tell you this but I come with a family in tow!'

'I know, I know, Emma, and I'm sorry about your dad, truly I am. It's just that I never really had a proper family per se, so I struggle a little with it, you know?' He looks off into the distance. 'I guess you losing your dad brought back the pain of family life for me. I should have called.' He holds out his hands, palms upwards in a conciliatory gesture.

Emma looks at him and recalls a time when this kind of talk would have made her feel compassion. Now, all she feels is anger.

'How dare you?'

'Sorry?'

'I mean it! How dare you come round here and pretend you're sorry. It's all an act with you, isn't it? You weren't falling in love with me. You liked the idea of me, like a character in a novel. In fact, you're a character in a novel. You don't have a genuine feeling in your body.'

Richard looks hurt. 'Emma, that's a terrible thing to say.'

But Emma is in her stride now. 'And you do this hurt act so well, don't you? God, I have been such an idiot, such a fool. I let some lame attempt at a Byronic hero turn my head with his flattery. But I can see through you now. It's all an act. Go on, admit it.'

Richard is watching Emma carefully. 'All right, there were times when it was a bit like a game but then life's a game isn't it?'

'Not for me,' says Emma.

'But as time went on, I did start to fall for you. You're so different.'

'Yeah, yeah, I know, I'm so different. So different, you saw fit to turn my world upside down and destroy my life with Martin. Thanks a bunch. You must really love me.'

'I'm sorry, Emma. I'm sorry you feel like this. I thought we had a connection. I thought you felt the same,' says Richard quietly.

'I did for a while, until I realised what a fool I'd been.'

'I do love you, you know. That's the truth,' says Richard.

Emma throws up her hands. 'And so the lies continue. What am I? A Cathy to your Heathcliff? How romantic. No, Richard, it's over. You no more love me than you love Stella!'

Richard looks at her sharply. 'Who told you about that?' he says.

'About what?'

'About Stella and me.'

Emma stares blankly at him and then the penny drops. Richard similarly realises the mistake he has made.

'Oh you mean Stella from *The Red Orchid*,' he says, his voice small like a little boy whose misdemeanours have just been uncovered.

'Well I did,' says Emma, 'but I think we both know what we're talking about now, don't we? Why don't you run back to the real Stella? You deserve one another.'

Richard gives her a pained look but Emma has had enough. 'Get out!'

Even Richard sees when he's defeated. 'I'm sorry,' he says.

'So am I,' says Emma ushering him to the door and closing it firmly behind him.

'All quiet on the western front?' asks Steve, as Rachel plods into the kitchen.

'Yep. Were Alfie and Lily OK?'

'A bit tired and teary but fine. It's been a long and emotional day for all of us.'

Rachel nods and goes to the fridge to retrieve a beer. 'Want one?'

'Please.'

She hands it to him, sitting at the kitchen table and gesturing for him to do the same. He looks a little reluctant but plonks himself down opposite his wife.

Rachel takes a large gulp of beer. 'So,' she begins.

'So.'

'Steve, I want us to start again.'

'Rachel, I'm leaving.'

'What?' Rachel looks as if she's been shot.

Steve fiddles with the label on his beer, avoiding her gaze. 'I didn't want to talk about this on the day we buried Edward but as you're insisting, I think it best you know.'

'What are you saying?' says Rachel panicked.

'I'm going to go and stay with Mum for a while, give us both some space so we can work out what we want.'

'But I know what I want!' cries Rachel, the tears springing readily into her eyes.

Steve looks at her, his blue eyes full of sorrow. 'But I don't, Rach. I don't know what I want any more,' he says. 'You and I were such a great team, us against the world but now – ' His words trail off as if he doesn't want to finish the sentence.

'And now?'

Steve shakes his head. 'I just keep thinking what would have happened if Tom hadn't called a halt to things.'

Rachel looks at the floor ashamed at the memory. 'It was just a moment, Steve. I thought you were having an affair!' she cries in desperation.

'How could you think that, Rach? How could you think that of me.'

'I know, I'm sorry but you weren't being upfront about that thing with Sam. I just jumped to the wrong conclusion.'

'Yes. but I can't live like that with you not trusting me and then practically jumping into bed with someone else at the slightest doubt. That's not a marriage.'

'Don't say that.'

'I'm just telling you how I feel. Look, we're not going to resolve this tonight. I'm going to go to Mum's tomorrow and then we'll see.'

'But you're not giving up on me?' says Rachel half-joking, half-panicking.

'No more talking tonight,' says Steve. He picks up his beer bottle and goes into the living room. Rachel wants to follow him but she can't seem to haul herself into a standing position. She feels so tired. Her head is swimming and her body is heavy as if she's being dragged down by life. She hears fat drops of rain beating against the window behind her and stares out into the darkness feeling utterly alone.

CHAPTER TWENTY SIX

Emma stares at the manuscript next to her. It is decorated with only a scattering of red-pen strikes. She sighs and looks back to her laptop, allowing the internet to claim her once again. She has been grateful to Miranda for allowing her this time away from the office, but is starting to wonder if it's such a good thing. The trouble with the internet is that there is always something more exciting happening somewhere else and it is your job as the browser to find it. She checks her e-mails. There are several from Ella and Miranda, a couple from Rosie and one from Joel. She clicks on it: '*I am sorry for your loss. Joel.*'

Irritated by his cursory attempt at compassion, she turns back to the manuscript. Emma rereads the lines, casting her pen over every word. Somehow the characters no longer exude the life and passion of before. They all feel slightly one-dimensional and the only emotion she can conjure up for Stella is abject loathing.

'Consider killing off Stella?' she writes on a note pad next to her. *That would show the bitch*, she thinks, and then laughs at how ridiculous it is to want to punish a character in a novel. She hears a noise downstairs and freezes. She listens, willing her brain to be wrong, and is alarmed to hear someone climbing the stairs. She rummages in the cupboard for a suitable weapon, approaches the door and leaps out when she hears the intruder reach the landing.

'Haaaaaaaaaaaa!' she cries, and is mortified to notice that she is holding a broom, but relieved to see that the intruder is Martin.

'What's this then?' he asks with a wry smile. 'Death by sweeping?'

'Shit, Martin! What are you doing creeping around like that?'

'Sorry, I just came back to get a few things. I didn't think you'd be here,' he says.

'Oh, right, of course,' says Emma feeling chastened. 'Well, don't mind me. Help yourself.'

'Thanks,' he says disappearing into the bedroom. Emma loiters on the landing, unsure of what to do next. 'Do you want a coffee, Mart?' she says in a matter of fact way.

'What was that?' he asks, poking his head round the door.

'Coffee? I'm just going to make one,' she says.

It might be the look of desperation on her face that causes him to answer. 'Oh all right, just a quick one though.'

'Yeah. And a coffee, eh?' says Emma in a lame attempt at humour. Martin looks at her with mild amusement, shaking his head. 'Sorry,' she says, disappearing downstairs.

When he appears in the kitchen ten minutes later, he is carrying a large bin-bag and Emma notices he's holding a framed photo of their first Valentine's trip to Brighton.

'Are you taking that?' she asks, trying to sound disinterested.

'I thought I would, if it's OK with you?'

'Sure. Let's have a look.' They stand side-by-side, smiling at the memory; a snapshot in time. They both look so young and hopeful. Emma feels a pang of sadness.

'Of course, we may have to go to court.'

'What do you mean?'

'Over who gets custody of Robert,' says Martin pointing at the gigantic boggle-eyed frog nestling between them in the picture. 'I did win him after all.'

Emma smacks him on the arm. 'You so did not! It was me who knocked down those cans, love, and you know it.'

'Whatever.' They laugh and Emma is momentarily transported back to how things used to be. She moves to the table with their coffee mugs.

'Biscuit?'

'Thanks,' he says standing in the middle of the kitchen looking awkward.

'Don't make the place look untidy – sit!' cries Emma. She knows she's trying too hard but somehow she wants to keep Martin here for as long as possible.

He perches on the edge of the chair and sips his coffee. 'How's your mum?' he asks after a pause.

'She's struggling a bit, I think. She doesn't say much.'

'I'm not surprised. She and your dad were made for each other.'

Emma takes a sip of her coffee unsure if this is a dig. 'And how are you?' she asks.

He nods. 'I'm OK. Work's busy. Charlie's sofa's getting a bit uncomfortable. I need to find a flat soon.' He says this in such a matter of fact way that Emma feels irrationally hurt. 'Actually, sorry to bring this up but we probably need to talk about what to do with this place at some stage.'

'Oh right. Well, if that's what you want?'

'There's no point in prolonging things, is there?'

The question hangs there like a judgement on their relationship. *Yes there is!* Emma wants to cry. *We could try again – things would be different this time! I would be different this time!* But she sees Martin's face and can tell that he's shut himself off to her. She knows she's hurt him and she doesn't know if he will ever forgive her. 'I guess not,' is all she can say.

'Well look, I should go. Thanks for the coffee,' he says, rising to his feet and picking up the bin-bag. Emma looks up at him and feels utterly crushed. She longs to put her arms around him and tell him how sorry she is but it's as if she can't get near him any more. She follows him down the hall. He doesn't kiss her goodbye. He just gets into his car and starts the engine, but before he drives off, he glances at her and gives her a small, resigned wave goodbye. She watches him until he has driven off and his car is a tiny speck in the distance.

'Explain it to me again,' demands Lily.

Rachel takes a deep breath.

'Mum and Dad don't like each other and they are going to live apart so that when they see each other again, they can decide if they do like each other any more. It's called a trial separation. If they don't like each other any more, they will get a divorce,' says Will plainly.

Alfie looks alarmed and grabs his mother's sleeve. 'Noooo, Mummy,' he says, eyes wide and brimming with tears.

'Alfie, it's OK. Will, it's not like that. Where do you get these things from?' asks Rachel.

'School mostly. Ethan's parents are divorced and Dee's and Jessie's and Mason's. Lauren's are separated and Ella's dad has run off with the au pair,' says Will with grave authority. 'It's OK, Mum. It happens all the time.'

'Well, it's not happening to us,' says Rachel, hoping that this isn't a lie. 'Life is complicated when you're a grown-up and Daddy and I just need a little time apart to think about everything and sort stuff out.'

'Well, I think it's crap!' says Lily suddenly.

'OK, well, you shouldn't use that word but you are right, of course,' says Rachel.

'And it's your fault,' continues Lily, pointing a finger at her mother.

'That's rude, Lily,' says Will.

'No, it's OK, Will. Let her speak. Go on, Lily, what have I done wrong?'

'Well, you're always nagging us and Daddy. It's like you don't even really want to be here. I mean why don't you go and get a job in Tesco like Shamil's mum? She's always really smiley and happy and Shamil says she hardly ever shouts, whereas you shout all the time.'

'Is that what you really think?' asks Rachel quietly.

'Yes!' says Lily firmly. 'And the boys agree with me, don't you, boys?' Will and Alfie look at the floor and murmur something approaching the affirmative.

'Right, well, OK then. Thank you for telling me,' says Rachel feeling as if she's been punched. 'The important thing is that I don't want you to worry. You'll still see Daddy as much as possible and we are not getting divorced.' *Yet*, says her brain.

The boys nod sadly but Lily is still in fighting mood. 'Yeah, whatever. Why do grown-ups always say things are complicated when what they really mean is "we're not going to tell you what's really going on"?'

'OK, detective Lily, you are very clever but there are some things that just grown-ups have to know about, OK?' says Rachel.

'Well, I still think it's crap,' says Lily defiantly.

Rachel looks at her daughter and cannot disagree. She decides to change tack. 'I think we all deserve a treat. Who's for ice cream?'

'Me!' chorus Will and Alfie.

'Lily?'

Lily looks at her mother as if she were a piece of raw sewage. 'I don't want anything from you!' she says, rushing up the stairs and slamming her bedroom door.

Rachel feels miserable as she goes into the kitchen, filling the boys' bowls with too much ice cream and a multitude of toppings as if she can soothe away the pain with sugar. A heavy mood has descended upon the house. The boys are happy with their ice cream and then slope off to watch cartoons, but Rachel is disturbed by the eerie quiet. Feeling exhausted by life, she considers a nap on the sofa with her TV-watching sons but this plan is interrupted by the sound of someone knocking at the door. Expecting an unwanted visitor, she is relieved to find the smiling forms of Sue and Christa bearing two large slab bars of Dairy Milk, a jumbo bag of Doritos and carrier bags making happy, clinking sounds.

'We thought you could do with some company,' says Sue, stepping over the threshold and wrapping her friend in the tightest hug.

Christa kisses her on both cheeks and pulls two bottles of champagne out of her bag. 'Right, *mein Schatz*, Susan und I will put the *kinder* to *bett*, *Ja*? You go and pour a large glass of this and we'll see you in half an hour, OK?'

'OK,' says Rachel, feeling her eyes brim with tears again.

'*Nein, nein*. We are not doing the *weinen* and the weeping this evening. This is very good Kristal. We are going to drink to your papa and to your future, with or without Steve, yes?' Sue is standing behind Christa grinning all the while.

'OK,' says Rachel, 'but if you're not quick, I will eat all the Dairy Milk.'

'Ahh, you're welcome. Just don't drink all the booze!' says Christa.

An hour later, Rachel is laughing hard, but can't remember why. Christa has just told them a story involving Paris Hilton and a pig, which made Sue snort Kristal through her nose. Christa had become quite serious and chided her for wasting it. Rachel is enjoying the easy banter and can't remember the last time she laughed so much.

'So, Rachel, what are you going to do?' says Christa suddenly.

Rachel is still giggling but tries to answer her. 'Oh I don't know. I've really fucked things up, haven't I? I mean fancy trying to cop off with your neighbour?'

'What is this "cop"?' asks Christa looking confused. 'Is it *etwas* to do with policemen?'

Rachel and Sue dissolve into hysterical fits of giggles before Rachel calms down enough to say. 'No, I mean I tried to seduce him.'

'*Ach ja.* You mean Dom or Tom or whatever?'

'Tom.'

'*Ja. Sehr gut.* Well, I don't blame you, but your Steve is a very handsome man too. Are you just a bored *hausfrau* perhaps?'

'I dunno. Maybe. All I know is that I need to do something before I fall into some sort of life of depravity.'

'*Ja*, this happened to my *schwester*-in-law,' says Christa slowly. Rachel and Sue exchange glances.

'Oh really,' says Sue, her voice tight with laughter. 'What happened?'

'Well, she was living with my brother, Bruno, in a beautiful house in suburbs of Berne. Had everything, you know; the house, the husband, the kids, the money.'

'And?' says Sue waiting for the punchline.

'*Ach*, she got bored. The kids were at *schule*, she did not need to work and so she became a, how-you-say, madam?'

'You mean a prostitute?' says Rachel.

Christa throws back her head and shrieks with laughter. '*Nein, mein Schatz*, she wouldn't sell her pussy for money, she is very in love with my brother. *Nein*, she runs an escort agency, you know, very high class, for businessmen. It is a very successful business. She is one of the richest women in Switzerland,' says Christa proudly.

'Well,' says Sue, her face serious for a moment. 'There's a career path you hadn't previously considered, Rach.' She looks at her friend, poker-faced and they erupt into another fit of laughter.

Christa looks at them smiling and uncertain but happy to go along with the joke. 'More Kristal, girls?' she says.

'Don't mind if I do,' says Sue topping up their glasses. 'And I would like to propose a toast.' The three friends sit up in readiness. Sue lifts her glass. 'To Rachel and her future, wherever it may lead her. She is a better mum than she realises and a truly beautiful friend.'

'And she has great tits,' adds Christa with a wink.

'Christa!' says Rachel. 'I never knew you cared.'

'Sweetie,' says Christa. 'I am a very flexible and open lady. So if you ever get lonely, you just give me a call. Now, where is the loo?'

Rachel points her towards the stairs and then collapses with helpless laughter again.

'Well,' says Sue laughing. 'I'll give her one thing, she certainly knows how to take a girl's mind off things. Now top up my glass, will you? We're not nearly drunk enough yet!'

CHAPTER TWENTY SEVEN

Emma drums her fingers on the coffee shop bar, impatient at having to wait for her morning latte. *Calm down*, she tells herself. *You have to calm down.* Today is her first day back at work and she is nervous.

'Just a black coffee please, Gio, no mess, no froth and none of those filthy syrups,' booms a familiarly assertive voice.

'Morning, Miranda,' calls Emma from the other end of the counter.

'Darling girl! You're back! How are you?' says Miranda sweeping over, her voluminous turquoise silk outfit wafting behind her like a sail.

'I'm OK thank you.'

'Good, I'm very glad to hear it. We've missed you. Ella will be so glad you're back.'

'Is she all right?'

'She's blooming – the absolute picture of fecundity. And how are you faring with *The Red Orchid*?'

'It's finished,' says Emma, realising the true significance of this statement. They both have their coffees now and are making their way down the street to the offices.

'Well, you have been working hard. Is Richard happy?' she asks as they step into the lift.

'I think so. I haven't seen him for a while but we've exchanged e-mails.' Emma is trying to sound casual and hoping that Miranda won't notice. She is out of luck.

Miranda peers at Emma over her half-moon glasses and narrows her eyes, as if toying with a tricky cryptic crossword clue. 'Emma,' she says finally as they reach her office. 'You did heed my warnings, didn't you?' Emma bites her lip and looks guilty. 'I think you better come in,' says Miranda, ushering her inside.

Emma faces her, defeated. 'I've been an idiot, Miranda. I should have listened to you. I let my feelings for Richard get the better of me but I promise it hasn't affected the book. I would understand if you asked me to resign though. I'm just sorry I've let you down.'

Miranda folds her arms and looks at her. 'Emma, I can hardly chastise you for your actions given my past history but I did hope that you were a bit smarter than me.'

'I'm sorry,' says Emma again.

'I think it is you who needs my sympathy. Am I right?' Emma nods, blinking back her tears. Miranda walks around the desk and puts her arms around her. This small gesture of affection is so welcome to Emma, and the tears fall easily as she thinks about her grief and her loss. She has let everyone down: her father, Miranda and Martin, yes most of all, Martin.

'Do you think you came back to work a little too early, my dear?' asks Miranda softly, handing her a tissue. 'Grief is a very unpredictable thing and you clearly have a lot on your plate at the moment.'

Emma wipes her eyes. 'I can't stay at home any more. I need to get on with my life,' she says with more determination than she feels.

'All right, dear heart, but remember, my door is always open.'

'Thank you,' says Emma with a weak smile. 'And sorry for the outburst.'

'Don't be so hard on yourself. We're all human and it does us good to remember that sometimes.'

Emma nods and walks slowly out of Miranda's office and back to her desk. There is a bunch of bright pink and purple peonies smiling up at her with a card from Ella: 'Welcome back! We missed you. x' Emma strokes their soft petals.

'Oh, you're back! Damn, I wanted to be here to welcome you,' says Ella, lumbering into their work area.

Emma stares at her pregnant friend. 'Look at you!' she says, wrapping her in a tight hug. 'It's so good to see you.'

'And you, Em. Yes, I'm turning into quite a little fatty now,' says Ella with a grin.

Emma laughs. 'Thanks for the flowers. It's very sweet of you.'

'You're welcome. I'm sorry I couldn't make the funeral. I had my twenty-one week scan.'

'Oh wow! Do you know what you're having?'

'Yep, it's a boy and we're going to call him Stanley.'

Emma smiles with approval. 'Fantastic news and who's this "we"?'

Ella looks a little shy. 'Jamie and I have decided to make a go of things.'

'That's lovely, darling. I'm so pleased for you,' says Emma, sinking into her chair.

'And now, do you want the good news or the bad news?'

'Hmm, good first please.'

'OK, I have bought doughnuts to welcome you back.'

'You spoil me! And the bad?'

'We have a marketing meeting in five minutes.'

'Oh crap.'

'I know. Sorry,' says Ella wincing. 'I can cover it if you like?'

'No, it's OK. Straight back to it, eh?'
'Attagirl.'

Diana looks at the photos on the mantelpiece. She picks up each in turn and wipes them with a duster. She replaces them carefully. The grandchildren take the central position, Rachel's wedding photo on the right, Emma's engagement photo on the left. She considers removing this one, but decides against it. She knows how fickle girls can be. Finally, she replaces her wedding photo and then the portraits of Edward and herself when they were twenty-one.

'You bloody man,' she tells Edward. 'I wish you were still here so I didn't have to do this infernal dusting every day.' She feels emotion catch her throat, grabs the mantelpiece to steady herself and then sinks back into Edward's favourite armchair. She likes to sit here for her morning coffee. It still smells of him and she can do the *Telegraph* crossword a lot quicker. She smoothes the arms of the chair and picks up her coffee. People are always telling her to 'keep busy' but she doesn't know how. Her life has always been structured by the whims of her dependants. Her friend, Jean has tried to persuade her to go for coffee at the local community hall but Diana feels as if that would be giving in and she never gives in.

She looks at the remote control and considers turning on the television and then feels horrified. She never watches daytime TV and never allowed the girls to either. She is pretty sure that petty crime and vandalism could be eradicated if someone put a stop to Jeremy Kyle. Suddenly she remembers *Woman's Hour* and thanks the Good Lord for Radio 4. She moves to switch it on, but is interrupted by the telephone ringing. She contemplates leaving it for the answering machine; something she never used to do but something she has learnt to do since Edward died. Most people have been kind and thoughtful, but she can always hear their voices straining with the effort and she feels herself wanting to release them from the thrall of sympathetic chitchat. She almost prefers speaking to her mother, who is rude and direct, but Diana is used to this. She lifts the receiver and has barely had a moment to utter a greeting when the caller launches into a monologue of cooing interrogation.

'Darling Diana! How are you? I've been thinking of you and wondering how you were but I wasn't sure whether to call after Edward's funeral. I could tell you were very emotional on the day and I just want to tell you that I forgive you. I'm finding it so hard to cope without him, aren't you? I mean I just can't believe he's gone. It's so tragic.'

'Hello, Rosie,' says Diana, trying to break her flow.

'How are the girls? They must be struggling. They were so close to their father. I hear that Rachel and Steve are having problems and that Emma and Marvin are no longer together. Oh poor, dear Diana, your whole life falling apart around your ears, it must be ghastly. I feel for you, my dear, I really do.'

Diana wonders how long Rosie can talk without interruption and is now letting her do just that. Suddenly she feels a bubble of emotion well up inside her and wonders if she is about to cry. She is amazed when the sound that emerges from her mouth is a small giggle. Rosie is stopped in her tracks.

'Diana, dear, are you all right?'

'I'm fine, Rosie, it's just that – ' begins Diana and then she laughs again and finds that she can't stop laughing.

'Diana? Diana? What are you laughing about? Oh I see, it's hysteria. You poor thing. Do you want me to come round or call Rachel or Emma?' But Diana doesn't stop laughing and when she eventually recovers she realises that Rosie has stopped talking and hung up.

'Well,' she says to Edward's picture as she replaces the phone in its cradle. 'That's one way to stop the old cow talking. Scare her witless!'

The meeting room is almost full by the time Ella and Emma arrive. They find two seats next to Philippa, who smiles and squeezes Emma's hand under the table. Joel makes no acknowledgement of Emma's return.

'OK, guys, as you know Philippa is still learning the ropes and ultimately when she's up to speed and completely on message, we will be alternating the chairing of this meeting. So for today, I will chair, OK? Good,' he barks without waiting for a response.

Emma looks at the agenda. The first half is taken up with other editors' titles. Then she notices point number five, '*The Red Orchid* – update from Emma,' and feels her stomach lurch. She tries to concentrate on what people are saying but feels as if she's drifting somewhere in the corner of the room, as if none of this is entirely real.

Saskia, the designer, is trying to convince them to develop a book cover made entirely of PVC, but Eve, the production manager keeps shaking her head and trying to point out that this is commercially unviable. Saskia is becoming more and more excited, flapping her skinny little arms like an agitated bird, her voice reaching a pitch and crescendo that would only be audible to dolphins. She is now accusing Eve of having 'no creative backbone', to which Eve simply raises her eyebrows and looks over at Joel, willing him to take control of the meeting. Joel is whispering to Jacqui and it is Philippa who says, 'OK, Saskia, it's a very interesting idea and if you want to try to source it yourself, at a reasonable cost, I'm sure Eve would be happy to discuss it with you?'

Eve smiles gratefully at Philippa. Saskia looks a little sulky but nods anyway. Joel is visibly perturbed by

Philippa's presumption. 'OK, thank you, Philippa. I think I can handle this. All right, Saskia, you see what you can find and Eve will be there as a sounding board, yes?'

Saskia nods enthusiastically and bounces up and down in her chair like an excited puppy. Eve shakes her head and looks wearily at Philippa, who shrugs her shoulders.

'And so, let's turn now to our newest and probably most challenging title.' Joel looks sideways at Jacqui and gives a little chuckle. 'Emma, can you give us an update?'

Emma almost jumps at the sound of her name. She looks at Joel and is suddenly struck by the pointlessness of all this. Why does she spend her life battling with this man? She feels strangely calm. 'It's finished,' she says quietly.

'Well, that's lovely,' says Joel with a mocking grin. 'I'm glad we've got all the words in the right order. The question is, how do we pitch it to the market? I mean what's the genre? Where does it fit?'

Emma takes a deep breath. 'Well, I'm sure you'll have no problem marketing it. I mean we all agree it's a brilliant book, don't we?' Everyone in the room nods enthusiastically. 'So, as long as you've read it and you understand it, Joel, which I expect someone who loves *Don Quixote* will have no trouble doing, there shouldn't be a problem, should there?' Joel looks at Emma, a flicker of confusion crossing his face. *Is she flattering him?*

'Although if you're struggling, I'm sure Philippa can give you a few pointers. She's completely on message with the book,' says Emma, parroting Joel's marketing speak.

Emma can see a shadow of panic in Joel's face. 'I don't think that will be necessary. I'm sure I can manage. Thank you for the update, Emma,' he says, keen to end the conversation.

'You're more than welcome, Joel,' says Emma with a saintly smile.

Philippa gives her a thumbs-up under the table and Joel leaves Emma alone for the rest of the meeting.

'Daaaaa-deeeeeeeee,' cries Lily from the top of the stairs, hurtling down to greet her father. Alfie runs straight into his leg and clings on, looking up at him with a grinning moon-face, and Will stands casually at the living room door, half-watching *Ben 10*. 'Hi, Dad,' he says without emotion.

'Wow, what a welcoming committee,' says Steve. 'I should go away more often.'

'Are you staying here tonight?' asks Alfie.

'I am.'

'Yessss!' chorus the kids.

Rachel comes in from the kitchen, tea towel in hand, feeling a little shy, like a stranger at a party.

'Hi there,' she says smiling.

'Hi,' says Steve still with a child attached to each leg. 'I would say hello properly, but I am a little bit tied down at the moment.'

'So I see. Cup of tea?'

'Please.'

Rachel returns to the safe territory of the kitchen and listens to the excited squeaks and giggles coming from the living room. Eventually, Steve extracts himself and makes it to the kitchen. He reaches for the mug on the table.

'Lovely. Thanks, Rach,' he says.

'You're welcome and thanks for coming over tonight. It will be good to see Mum. We haven't really caught up properly since the funeral.' Rachel pauses and then reverts to safer, practical matters. 'So, there's a lasagne in the oven and there's garlic bread if you want to do that. Help yourself to whatever you want and – '

'Rach?'

Rachel is piling plates, knives and forks on the table, but looks up to see Steve staring at her, his face a picture of worry.

'What?'

'Is this how it's going to be from now on?'

'How do you mean?'

'You handing the kids over for visits and me being a stranger in my own home?'

'No, of course not. I just don't really know what else to say. I'm sort of waiting for you to give the word, seeing as – '

'Seeing as I'm the one who left?'

Rachel shrugs. 'Well yes.'

Steve sighs. He looks weary and worn down somehow. 'I miss the children,' he says after a pause.

And me, Rachel wants to cry, *do you miss me?* She is standing by the sink, a tea towel in her hand. She realises that she's squeezing the life out of it.

'And there's something else I need to tell you,' he adds, picking up a piece of cucumber from the chopping board and taking a bite.

You forgive me. You want me back. You're ready to trust me again, prays Rachel. 'Kate Winslet heard you'd moved out and asked you out on a date?' she jokes, trying to keep the conversation light.

'Well obviously but sadly I was out with Julia Roberts that night,' he retorts, a glimpse of the old Steve returning. 'But seriously, I've been offered another job.'

'Wow, that's great! It is great isn't it?'

'It is actually. I was headhunted and it's the same sort of job with more money and some international travel.'

'That's fantastic! Congratulations.'

'I haven't said yes yet. I wanted to speak to you first.'

Rachel feels a surge of hope at these words. At least she still figures in his plans. 'I think if it's what you want to do then you should go for it,' she says trying to sound reasonable.

Lily runs into the kitchen and leaps into her father's arms. 'Ah my little Pica-lily, I've missed you.'

'I've missed you too,' says Lily, resting her head on his shoulder and eyeing her mother with suspicion. 'I thought YOU were going to Granny's,' she says accusingly.

'Right, fine, I'm going,' says Rachel, realising she's not off the hook yet. 'Daddy's in charge,' she adds as she heads for the door. 'I'll see you tomorrow and congratulations on the job again,' she says to Steve.

He nods. 'Give my love to Emma and your mum.'

Emma peers through the living room window, looking for signs of life. She contemplates phoning Rachel, who is predictably running late, but tells herself that she can deal with this. Suddenly, she has a nightmarish thought that her mother has killed herself, or had an accident and she contemplates phoning Martin. 'This is ridiculous,' she tells herself and takes out her mobile, scrolling to find her parents' home number. She can hear the phone ringing inside the house and then it's picked up.

'Hello?'

'Mother?'

'Yes, is that you, Rachel?'

'No, it's me, Emma and I'm outside the house. What are you doing?'

'Having a bath, dear. I must have dozed off. What do you want?'

Feeling slightly squeamish about talking to her mother in her 'nature intended' form, Emma is keen to finish the conversation. 'Just let me in, will you, Mum? It's freezing out here.' She can hear noises from within the house, sees lights being turned on and eventually the robed form of her mother coming down the stairs. She opens the door, looking quite irritated and Emma wonders if she is going to block her entry. She moves aside for her youngest daughter and Emma suddenly recalls something she read in a bereavement leaflet about forgetfulness.

'Oh, you forgot we were coming,' says Emma, making her way to the kitchen and plonking a bottle of wine on the table.

'I did not forget,' says Diana, pulling her dressing-gown up around her neck like a defence mechanism. 'I told you, I fell asleep. I'm allowed to be tired at my age, you know.' Emma looks at her mother, reaches forward and gives her a gentle hug. Diana bears it for as long as she can before pulling away. 'What was that for?' she asks.

'I'm allowed to hug my mum, aren't I?' says Emma with a smile. There's a knock at the door. 'That will be Rachel. I better get this open. I know what she's like if she doesn't have a drink in her hand fourteen seconds after she's walked through the door.'

Diana leaves the kitchen and returns with a shivering Rachel.

'All right, tart-face?' says Rachel in greeting.

'Yes thanks, slag-bag,' says Emma in reply.

Diana pulls a disapproving face. 'I haven't got any food in. So we'll have to have one of those takeaway things,' says Diana. Rachel and Emma look at each other and giggle.

'OK, Ma, do you have any menus?' says Rachel. Diana looks blank. 'You know, they drop through the door? Pizza, curry, that sort of thing?' she continues.

'Rachel, do I look like the sort of person who encourages hawkers and purveyors of junk mail?'

'All right, Mum, calm yourself. I've got all the numbers in my phone. Do we fancy a curry then?'

'Ooh yeah, curry would be good. Is that OK for you, Mum?'

'Of course, order me a prawn jalfrezi, tarka dhal and a keema naan please.' Rachel and Emma look at her in surprise. Diana shrugs her shoulders. 'You young people don't have the monopoly on these things, you know. Daddy and I used to have a curry once a month, but he was the one who ordered for me. He knew what I liked.' Diana's voice drifts off and she looks lost. Rachel and Emma exchange worried glances and then Rachel leaps in.

'Christ, Em, haven't you got that bloody bottle open yet. Mum, we'll sort it all. You go and get dressed.'

Diana suddenly clicks back into gear. 'All right, but don't blaspheme, Rachel,' she says disappearing upstairs.

By the time Diana reappears, the girls have laid the table and found some candles to light. Rachel puts on an old Stevie Wonder CD and pours the wine. Her mother walks in and Rachel is struck by how grief has aged her. Her eyes still sparkle and dart around the room ready to find and fix their attention on anything which displeases her, but her demeanour has a weary, resigned look to it. When she sees the candles and hears the music, she can find no fault.

'This is lovely. Your father would have loved this,' she says, and Rachel wonders if she is going to cry. She picks up a wine glass and hands it to her mother and clinks it with her own.

'To Dad,' she says. Diana smiles but doesn't speak.

'Here we are,' says Emma returning with three bags of sweet-smelling curry. She plonks them on the table.

'Not there!' cries Diana. 'I don't want turmeric stains on my best table linen, thank you!'

'Sorreeee!' says Emma like a petulant teenager and Rachel laughs. She takes the bags from her sister. 'I'll dish up in the kitchen.'

'Have you warmed the plates?' demands Diana.

'Of course,' says Rachel still smiling.

As with all good takeaway curries they have ordered far too much so that by the time they have eaten their fill, the table is littered with half-eaten naans and several quarter-full containers.

Diana sits back and dabs at her mouth with a napkin. 'That was delicious.'

'Mmm, very good,' says Rachel, stabbing her fork into the leftover mushroom bhaji. 'I should take some of this home for Steve.'

'No wonder he left you,' says Emma with a grin.

'You cow. That is out of order!' cries Rachel.

'That is a little unkind, Emma,' says Diana. 'And may I ask, Rachel, if this arrangement with Steve is a permanent one?'

Rachel mouths 'Thanks a bunch' at her grinning sister. 'We're working things out,' says Rachel trying to sound as ambiguous as possible.

'That's a little vague if I may say so,' says Diana. 'What about Scotland and more importantly, what about the children?'

'Oh, we're definitely keeping them,' says Rachel with a lame attempt at levity.

'Rachel, I don't think this is the time for humour. Your life is falling apart around your ears. You need to take action.'

'Yeah thanks for that, Mum, but we're sorting it. Actually Steve's got a new job so Scotland is officially off the agenda.'

'Well, that is a blessing,' declares Diana.

'You need to get a job,' says Emma.

'And you need to get a life,' says Rachel.

Emma sticks out her tongue. 'My life is fine thank you.'

'Spinster!' coughs Rachel with a grin.

'Shut up, Rachel.'

'Girls please!' cries Diana looking heavenwards. 'What would your father say?'

Rachel and Emma look ashamed. 'Anyway,' says Emma after a pause. 'I really think you should get a job, Rachel. It would do you the world of good.'

'Aren't you forgetting something rather vital?' says Rachel as if addressing a very slow child. 'The three small people I work for? I can't exactly hand in my notice.'

'Mum could look after them.'

'What?' chorus Rachel and Diana with equal measures of horror.

'Well, you could at least think about it. I mean Mum needs something to do and she is brilliant with the kids and you really need to go back to work. You're starting to become such a whinger.'

'I beg your pardon?' says Rachel staring at her sister. She notices that Emma and her mother are nodding at each other. 'I am not a whinger.'

'Well, you don't always seem to be enjoying it, Rachel dear, and it would be good for you to have a break. Goodness only knows if I'd had your choices in my day, I might have gone back to work.'

Rachel looks at them both. 'Well, thanks for that, family.'

'Just think about it, sis, and now, who's for pudding? I brought brownies!' says Emma.

Later in the evening, Diana gets out some old photo albums and they look at the pictures together, laughing at the fashions of the seventies. Rachel stops at a picture of Diana at her wedding with her mother and father.

'Were you close to Grampy?' asks Rachel.

'Not really. I think he and Mother felt they should have children out of a sense of post-war duty. I was something of a disappointment.'

Rachel wonders if it's the wine making her mother this unguarded, but is pleased that she is opening up to them.

'For the record, Mum, I think Granny was out of order at the funeral and you were right to say what you did.'

Diana smiles weakly. 'Well, it's given Mother a lot of material to complain about, so I suppose some good came out of it.'

They turn the page to find photos of Diana and Edward when they were first married.

'You look like film stars,' says Emma, keen to carry on talking about the past and share memories of Edward. Diana looks lost in her grief and suddenly gets up from the table.

'I'll make us some tea,' she says sweeping out of the room. Emma goes to follow her.

'Leave her, Em,' says Rachel.

Emma comes back to the table and picks up her wine glass. 'I wasn't being mean, Rach. I just get the feeling that you could do with a bit of a break from the kids sometimes. I mean Lily and Alfie will soon be at school.'

Rachel nods. 'I know. It's just that everything's a bit up in the air at the moment.'

'Tell me about it,' says Emma.

Diana returns with the tea. 'Here we are. No, Rachel, don't pour yet. Didn't I teach you to let it steep properly?' scolds Diana. Rachel smiles and sees Emma smiling too. Eventually, Diana carefully turns the pot and pours out three cups. Stevie Wonder's 'I Believe' reaches a crescendo and they sit, nursing their tea, letting its joyous tones wash over them, each lost in a memory of Edward Darcy and wishing he were there to put everything right again.

CHAPTER TWENTY EIGHT

Emma loves airports. Despite the endless queues and mile-long walks to the departure gate, she always feels a bubble of excitement when she enters one. There's an air of expectancy and the phrase 'all human life is here' always echoes in her mind as she passes through. Really she would have liked to start this adventure on her own, but Rachel was determined to ensure her little sister safe passage to Heathrow. Will was devastated as he was unable to attend due to school commitments. He tried to persuade his mother that the trip would be educational but she was having none of it. Alfie opted to stay at home with his granny as he 'doesn't be liking the noisy planes', so it is just Emma, Rachel and Lily who now struggle with Emma's laden trolley, trying to avoid people's ankles on their way to the check-in.

'All girls together!' chimes Rachel.

Lily looks at her mother with distaste. 'I've only come because I want to see Auntie Emma off. I still think it's your fault that Daddy left!' says Lily with a determined pout on her face.

'Very well,' says Rachel, who has developed a rhino-thick skin over the last few months in an attempt to deflect Lily's persistent jibes. 'Well, you won't want to go for a milkshake afterwards so I can tell you my big surprise!' Lily looks at her as if to say, I don't think you know what you're dealing with. I won't be won over with measly milkshakes. 'Also, I saw that Hello Kitty rucksack in a shop over there and I thought we could go and spend some of your birthday money on it,' adds Rachel with a grin.

Even Lily has a limit. 'OK,' she says with pursed lips.

'Nice one, Rach. I thought the ice queen would never melt,' says Emma. 'Right, I need check-in numbers 42–45. Why don't you go and grab us some coffees and I'll take Lily for a spin on the trolley. OK, Lils?' Lily nods her head and climbs aboard. Grateful for a break from her tormentor, Rachel heads for the nearest coffee shop.

'So, Auntie Emma, why do they call New York, The Big Apple?'

'I don't know, Lils, but when I get there I'll find out and send you a postcard, OK?'

'Cool!' says Lily, bouncing up and down on the trolley. 'How long are you going for?'

'Well, six months to start with, but maybe longer.'

'I'm going to miss you.'

Emma kisses the top of Lily's head. 'I'm going to miss you too, sweet pea.'

'Can I come and visit you?'

'Of course you can.'

'Auntie Emma?'

'Yes, Sweetness?'

'Do you miss Grandpa?'

'More than I can tell you, Lils.'

'I miss him. And I miss my dad.'

'Ah, but you can still see your dad.'

'I know. I hate my mum.'

Emma takes her niece's face in her hands. 'Lily, you mustn't blame your mum. None of this is her fault.'

'Of course it is. She kissed Tom.'

'How do you know that?'

'I heard her and Daddy talking. I'm not stupid.'

'You're certainly not that, Lils. Now listen, you have to understand that grown-ups aren't perfect, so don't be too hard on your mum. She loves you and she and your dad will always look after you and do their best, OK?'

Lily sighs. 'OK, but when I'm a grown-up, I'm not going to lie to my children. I will always tell the truth and I won't let things get complicated.'

Emma smiles. 'Well, good for you, Lils. I hope you manage it.'

Rachel comes rushing back in a high state of excitement. 'Guess what?'

'You forgot to buy coffees?' says Emma, staring with disappointment at her empty hands.

'No, well yes, but this is much more important. I just had a call from Daniel!' Emma looks blank. 'Daniel? My old boss? You know how you told me to e-mail my old contacts to see if anything was going. Well, he's got a project for me! He wants me to start next month and the best bit is, I can do it all at home. I just have to go into the office for briefing meetings. How fantastic is that?'

Emma folds her sister in a hug. 'Rach, that is brilliant news. Good for you!'

'Does that mean you'll stop shouting at us?' says Lily unimpressed.

'Hopefully, Lils!' cries Rachel hugging her daughter.

'Excuse me?' says a slightly irritated voice behind them. 'There's a check-in desk free.'

'Sorry!' trills Rachel smiling manically.

Emma watches Lily and Rachel disappear towards the Arrivals Hall and wonders if she'll ever have children of her own. She glances at her phone, half-expecting a text or a call from Martin but knows she's probably being foolish. They have been exchanging e-mails over the past few months, ever since Miranda offered the sabbatical to the New York offices. She had been hesitant at first but Miranda had been encouraging. 'I think you could do with some time away, dear heart. It is a great opportunity as well and much as I will miss you, I think you will adore it over there. But if you come back speaking like an American, I will have to sack you!' When she told Martin of her plans in an e-mail, he had given her no reason to turn it down. 'OK, let me know what you want to do about the house,' he had replied without any hint of emotion. They had agreed to let it for the time being and Martin had cleared out the rest of his things one evening when Emma was out with Rachel. When she returned home, she found a photograph on the table. It was taken the day she, Martin, Steve, Rachel and her father had taken Will to a football match. Her father has his arm around his girls with Steve and Martin on the outside and a grinning Will standing in front of them all. Martin had left a note with it: 'I found this and thought you might like to take it to New York with you.' Emma had wept at the sight of them all and felt wretched with longing for the happy days she had taken for granted. She showed Rachel a few nights later and after a couple of glasses of wine, Rachel had made her e-mail Martin. Emma wasn't sure if it was the right thing to do but after she had written down how she was feeling and pressed send she'd felt better somehow. That was a week ago and she hadn't heard from him since.

Suddenly, her niece emerges like a bullet from a gun, dragging someone by the hand.

'Look who we've found. It's Daddy! It's my daddy!'

'Like a scene from *The Railway Children*,' says Rachel, emerging alongside them smiling.

'Hey, stranger,' says Emma pecking Steve on the cheek. 'And bye, stranger.'

He smiles. 'Bye, Em. Good luck.'

Emma kneels down to kiss Lily. 'Now remember, Lils, I'm relying on you to look after everyone while I'm away. You're the only one for the job.'

Lily nods gravely. 'I love you, Auntie Em,' she says, wrapping her aunt in a tight little hug.

'I love you too, Lils,' says Emma, blinking back tears.

'Hey, tart-face,' says Rachel. 'No weeping.' She clings on to her sister for a long moment and whispers in her ear. 'I'll miss you, Em.'

'Me too,' says Emma. After a moment she pulls away and cries, 'Later, slag-bag, and don't forget, you're coming for a debauched weekend of Cosmopolitans, *Sex and the City*-style!'

Rachel smiles and nods, brushing away a stray tear. Emma gives them a final wave before turning and disappearing into the jostling crowd.

'So,' says Rachel. 'Who wants to go home then?'

'Only if Daddy is coming.'

'Of course Daddy is coming. It's still his home too,' says Rachel, looking up at Steve for backup. The last few months have been the hardest of Rachel's life with Steve staying at his mum's, although he came round to see the children and help put them to bed as many nights as possible. Some evenings he stayed for a beer or a cup of tea and a chat but he always left at around nine o'clock. She hated it when he left and loathed going up to a cold empty bed. Some nights Alfie climbed in next to her and she let him stay, grateful for a human form in the bed beside her. She told herself that she had to give Steve time and space and let him sort things out for himself. It went against her usual analysing and problem-solving nature but she had this feeling that if she pressured him, she would lose him for ever. When he started his new job, his working patterns changed and he wasn't always free in the evenings, plus he had to go on a few overseas trips. Rachel had always offered to pick him up from the airport but he had declined the first few times. Last week he had phoned from Singapore to speak to the children but they were all immersed in the television so Rachel had got the lion's share of the conversation.

'How's Singapore?' she had asked.

'Sweaty. And busy,' he said.

'Sounds heavenly. Have you been to Raffles?'

'Of course. Our client took us there on the first night. You would have loved it, especially the Singapore Slings.'

Rachel laughed. 'So when are you back?' she asked trying to sound casual.

'Next Thursday. Actually – '

'Yes?' she blurted hopefully.

'I wondered if you wanted to come and meet me maybe with Lils and Alf if you're free?'

Yes I'm free, I'm free, I'll be there! Rachel wanted to cry. 'We'll be there,' she said, trying to keep her voice calm.

'I want to come home, Rach.'

Rachel couldn't hold back the tears. 'Oh Steve,' was all she could say, her voice cracked with emotion.

'I'll see you on Thursday then,' he said. She could hear the relief in his voice.

Steve picks up Lily and kisses her. 'Yes, I'm coming home, Lils.'

'For ever?' says Lily with a furrowed brow.

'Well, apart from when I have to go to work.'

'Yay!' she cries, squeezing him tightly round the neck.

He grins at his wife. 'Let's go home, shall we?' he says.

'Yes please,' says Rachel, wrapping an arm round his middle and leading them towards the exit.

Emma finds her seat and is thankful to be by the window. She stows her hand luggage in the overhead locker and stashes everything she needs for the journey in the pocket in front of her. She retrieves her phone and checks for messages – still nothing from Martin. She feels a little hurt, although she knows she has no right. She flicks to her e-mails and notices that Miranda has sent out a note about her move to New York. She has received a raft of well-wishing responses. She scans them and is amused to find one from Digby addressed to Ella.

She clicks on a message from Joel:

All the best to you, Emma. Thought you might like to see the synopsis for the MBS title I am currently working on. Could be of interest to your new American colleagues. Regards, Joel.

Emma clicks on the attachment and is taken aback to find a grinning picture of Joel under the title *Get A Grip On Your Life, Loser!* She immediately forwards it to the editorial team at Allen Chandler under the heading 'Takes one to know one'.

She notices an e-mail from her mother, who is taking lessons on the internet from Rachel. She snorts with laughter as she reads:

Be careful and try to avoid as many Americans as possible unless they look like James Stewart. Come home soon, Mum x.

Emma smiles at her mother's attempt at affection and then switches off her phone and closes her eyes. She is just drifting off when she hears a voice next to her.

'Excuse me, is this seat taken?'

She opens her eyes and is surprised and delighted to be looking up into Martin's handsome face. 'Martin! What are you doing here?'

He sits down next to her and gives a little cough. 'Oh, you know, I was just passing,' he says with a wry grin.

'Martin, we are sitting on an aeroplane bound for New York.'

He nods sagely. 'Well, I haven't had a holiday in ages.'

She grins at him. 'What does this mean?' she asks.

'You tell me.'

'Did you get my e-mail?'

'I did. Did you mean it?' He turns to look at her, studying her face. She suddenly feels as if she's looking at him for the first time in her life and she likes what she sees.

She leans forwards and kisses him and the feeling that surges through her body is warm and wonderful. She breaks away to look at him again and realises for the first time in her life that she is exactly where she wants to be.

'I meant every word,' she says.

ACKNOWLEDGEMENT

Big thanks to my early readers for their insightful comments and huge encouragement: Gill Mclay, Viv Peters, Heather Williams, Fiona Veacock, Sarah Livingston, Jenice Collins, Jane Clements, Mary Vacher and Lisa Stevens.

Thanks to Sally Williamson, Nicky Lovick and all at the Carina™ UK imprint for their support and enthusiasm, and to Jenny Hutton for putting me in touch with them. Thanks also to Charlotte Robertson.

Many thanks to Chris Cleave for allowing me to use the phrase 'angels and tigers' from his brilliant novel, *Incendiary*.

Heartfelt thanks to my mum and dad for instilling in me a great love of books.

Finally, special thanks to Lily and Alfie for being a daily source of inspiration and to Rich for never allowing me to give up.

Look out for Annie Lyons' next book,
DEAR LIZZIE.

We've laughed, we've cried and we've absolutely fallen in love with it—and we hope you will too!

CHAPTER ONE

July

The church was chilly. This came as a surprise to Lizzie Harris, walking in out of the summer sunshine, and she pulled her jacket more tightly around her for comfort. She almost hadn't come today. As she got ready that morning, she had thought about what would happen if she simply didn't turn up. No one would come to find her. Nothing would change. She would simply be living up to expectations. But she had come. She had come because of one person, the person she cared most about in the world and one of the few who cared about her.

So Lizzie had pulled herself together, pulling on the purple dress she'd bought especially for the occasion, dug out her only pair of smart shoes, dragged herself

into her car and arrived uncharacteristically early. She
had watched as other people arrived, keeping a safe
distance, not wanting to attract anyone's attention. Not
yet. She wasn't quite ready to face it yet. Every time
she spotted a recognisable face, she closed her eyes and
told herself that she was doing the right thing. She had
to see this through, had to be strong. She waited until
five minutes before the service was due to start. Only a
few stragglers were entering the church now. It wasn't
seemly to be late on such an occasion. Lizzie had to tell
her feet to keep walking as she made her way up the
path and into the church. *Breathe and walk*. Her stomach was churning with nerves as she looked around the
packed church. She spotted Joe sitting at the front, his
arm wrapped around Sam, who looked impossibly small
for a boy of ten. They were both staring out towards the
front of the church, where the coffin sat draped in a purple silk pashmina. One mourner, a man of around fifty,
approached them, resting a hand on Joe's shoulder. Joe
looked round and smiled weakly at him. Lizzie wondered if he might recognise her and lifted her hand in
greeting, but he turned to the front again, his face glassy
with grief, pulling his son closer to him. The congregation was a riot of colour, the women all dressed in vary-
ing shades of purple, the men wearing purple ties or but-
tonholes as requested. The church was heavy with the
scent of lavender and 'Hopelessly Devoted to You' was
piping through the speakers to the accompanying sound
of subdued whispers and the occasional loud sniff.

Lizzie was wondering where to sit when she became
aware of someone standing next to her. She turned and

looked into the face of a woman worn down by grief.

'Hello, Mum,' said Lizzie in a hoarse whisper.

Her mother surveyed her as someone might look at a persistent stain and Lizzie noticed something else behind this, something which she had always seen in her mother's eyes: disappointment.

'Well, at least you've made it to your sister's funeral,' she said. 'But I hope you're not thinking of embarrassing me by skulking at the back. At least do Bea the final courtesy of sitting at the front with her family.' And with that she turned, her skirt a flash of purple as she made her way down the nave and took her place to Joe's right.

Lizzie remained frozen to the spot. She had a sudden urge to rush out of the church, drive home and lock the door on the world. After all, who would really care if she did? It would confirm all her mother's worst opinions of her and Joe would understand if she put it down to grief. He was hardly a man to challenge anyone; he'd certainly never challenged his wife.

Olivia Newton-John's plaintive tones were fading and the congregation quietened in readiness for the service to begin. One of the vergers approached Lizzie and touched her gently on the elbow.

'Lizzie?'

She turned to face a woman she recognised from her childhood; Evelyn Chambers, the vicar's wife. 'Do you want to go and take your place at the front?' she said, ushering her forwards with practised efficiency. 'The service is about to start.'

Lizzie wasn't sure what she was doing as she made

her way down the nave. She felt numb, almost as if she was watching herself from above, unable to control her own body. She had no choice but to keep going. She noticed the odd nudged elbow and whispered comment as she passed. She reached the front and looked to her mother, who ignored her with stiff-lipped coldness. Joe glanced up and gave her a grateful smile of recognition, gesturing for her to sit to Sam's left. Lizzie took a deep breath and settled next to her nephew. He looked up at her in surprise and then, frowning at this father, said in a loud whisper, 'Who is that?' Lizzie could feel people around her shift at his words, but kept her face fixed to the front as the service began.

******

Everyone agreed that it had been a wonderful send-off; a fitting tribute to a much loved daughter, wife, mother and sister. The vicar had spoken warmly of the woman he'd known through childhood and into her adult life and the choir had sung with reverent fondness. Once Joe had delivered his trembling eulogy and the funeral cortège had carried Bea's coffin down the central aisle, with Sam leading them towards the door, the sobbing had reached a crescendo. Only Lizzie and her mother remained dry-eyed. Lizzie knew that her mother was not one to show her grief in public and Bea had given her sister strict instructions.

'No wailing like a banshee during my big finale, Lizzie Lou. We've done our crying. I don't want my last exit to be ruined by your mucus-stained face,' she had grinned. Lizzie had worried whether she would be able to obey these wishes. It was all very well agreeing to these things when Bea was alive. It was the easiest thing in the world to make promises when the person you loved most in the world was still there. It was a different matter when they were no longer there to guide you. Lizzie hadn't thought she would break down in a fit of hysterical sobbing, but she was surprised at how surreal she found the experience of sitting in the church, staring at her sister's coffin. She felt like a spectator, almost cocooned from the reality of the situation. She had no place here among these people. She was merely watching from the sidelines and she couldn't connect the sister she had known with the body in the coffin. Lizzie felt numb as if she were momentarily anaesthetised against the grief of her loss; it was still there, but buried deep inside.

The mourners in the pews behind them waited patiently for Lizzie and her mother to walk out together following the coffin. Ignoring her daughter completely, Stella Harris made her way out into the aisle behind the procession. Lizzie felt panicked as all eyes were drawn to her. She could almost hear their thoughts. *Surely she should be supporting her mother on today of all days. Mind you, she's hardly been the supportive one. Not like Bea.* Lizzie avoided their critical glances, concentrating instead on her sister's coffin, taking courage from her presence in death as she had in life. She fell in step behind her mother and followed her out of the church.

Once outside, Lizzie felt the sunshine warm her face and shielded her eyes as she watched Joe and the other attendants slide her sister's coffin into the waiting hearse. There was to be a cremation, but Bea hadn't wanted anyone to be there. 'Too bloody sad. When they shut that curtain like the door finally closing on your life? No thanks, I want it to be a celebration. I want it to be like the kind of party I would enjoy. Why does everyone get so hung up and sad about death when it's actually as natural as life?' Most people didn't share Bea's sentiment. They honoured her wishes; they wore purple, played the music she'd requested, even ordered the tombstone cake, but they were the ones left behind. They were the ones who had to deal with life without her and, particularly when they saw Sam, a ten-year-old robbed of his mother, it couldn't be a celebration. It was a tragedy playing out in front of them.

It was different for Lizzie. She didn't know their version of Bea's world. She only knew the world of Lizzie and Bea as sisters. She wasn't part of Bea's life in this community, as a successful lawyer, devoted wife and mother, beloved daughter. To Lizzie, she was just Bea. Just Bea. The one who had picked her up so many times, who had always been there for her. She was the only reason Lizzie was here now and, as she watched the hearse pull away, she could see no other reason to linger.

As the mourners began to disperse, Lizzie decided to escape. She planned to go back home, put on her pyjamas and watch Bea's and her favourite film, *Grease*, whilst drinking as much red wine as she could handle or possibly a little more. She wanted to slip away from the helpless feeling that her life was like a sailing ship, cut loose by her sister's death, with no hope of getting back on course. How would she cope without Bea to guide and protect her? She had known this moment was coming for the past six months. She and Bea had talked about it but, still, nothing quite prepared you. In a fight-or-flight world, Lizzie's instinct had always been to flee, but you couldn't flee death. You could ignore it, pretend it wouldn't happen, dismiss it from your mind, but you couldn't escape its inevitability.

When Joe had phoned Lizzie to tell her that Bea had died, she had greeted his call with quiet resignation. It had felt odd to be receiving news about her sister from a man she hardly knew. She had wanted to end the call as quickly as possible. Joe's voice had been heavy with grief and Lizzie had no idea what to say to him.

'Thank you for letting me know,' she had said, embarrassed by the inadequacy of her response.

'I'll call you with the funeral arrangements,' he had said before ringing off.

Lizzie had stared at the phone after he'd gone, wondering how she was supposed to feel. Bea was gone. It was over. Lizzie was alone now. And yet, there she stood, two feet on the ground, the sun shining outside, life continuing without her sister. Part of her was stunned. She had half expected the walls to start closing in or the ground beneath her feet to shift at the moment of Bea's death. She had also expected tears—racking sobs of loss and grief, but none came. Minutes became hours became days. Lizzie thought about Bea during every waking second at her job in the bookshop, on trips to the shops, whilst making dinner, but still no tears came.

Every night she would fall into bed exhausted from thoughts of her sister, but did not cry; she couldn't and the worst thing was, Lizzie didn't know why. She had thought that the funeral might be a catalyst for tears, but remained dry-eyed. The grief was still there, though. It felt like something heavy and solid at the very centre of her being.

She could see Joe and her mother surrounded by people, all wanting to offer their condolences, as if their words could soothe away the pain of loss. They were all glad it wasn't one of their loved ones and who could blame them? No one approached her and she felt this gave her the permission she needed to escape. She put on her sunglasses and started to walk to her car without a backward glance. Once inside she exhaled with relief and placed the keys in the ignition. It was at this moment that she heard a light tapping on her window. She glanced over to see Joe's worried face peering in at her, with a frowning Sam at his side. She felt her insides sink with shame as she pressed the button to open the window. How could she let this poor bereaved man and his son follow her as she tried to escape? His opening words made her feel even worse.

''llo Lizzie. I'm sorry I didn't get a chance to speak to you in the church. I just wanted to say thank you for coming.'

Lizzie mumbled a response along the lines of, 'Of course.' There was an awkward pause and she wondered if it would be OK to start the car, whilst inwardly praying that she didn't run over her brother-in-law's foot as she sped off.

'We're having a party for Mum,' said Sam, his face fierce and suspicious. He was clearly offering her a dare.

'Oh right, well, I'm not sure if—' stammered Lizzie.

'You should come,' said Sam, as if it was the simplest thing in the world.

'Sam, I'm not sure if Lizzie is able to come,' said Joe, trying to placate the situation and making Lizzie feel both grateful and wretched at the same time.

'Why not? Mum would want her to be there. She's her sister,' declared Sam.

'Well, of course, if you would like to come, we would love you to,' said Joe.

Lizzie looked at Sam and knew that there was no getting out of this. He had an air of Bea in his frowning face; it was a look that said, 'Come on, sis, do it for me.' And like everything else her sister had ever asked her to do, Lizzie agreed without question.

'I'd love to come,' she said, with a small smile.

'Excellent,' said Joe. 'We'll see you back at the house.'

******

The Goode family lived just outside Smallchurch, very close to where Lizzie and Bea had grown up. When Bea and Joe married, she had made it clear that she wanted to stay near to her parents and give their children the countryside upbringing that she had enjoyed. Joe had been so in love with Bea that he would have lived in a sewer if she told him to and so they settled in a rambling old farmhouse surrounded by large fields and impressive views over rural Kent. Bea loved it because its boundary was flanked by cobnut bushes and fruit trees. The house itself needed a great deal of work and they had spent a lot of money and time making it into a comfortable family home.

Lizzie had never been to the house but she wasn't surprised by its size or decor. Her sister had always had great taste and an eye for style. She felt sick as she parked her car at one corner of the gravel drive and made her way through the open front door. An impressively large staircase sat in the middle of the hall, sweeping up towards a wide landing. Lizzie imagined an exquisitely decorated Christmas tree sitting at the top of the stairs. When Bea and Joe bought the house, she remembered her sister telling her that, 'It has room for two Christmas trees. I've always wanted a house big enough for two Christmas trees!' Along with a lifelong passion for the musical achievements of John Travolta and Olivia Newton-John, Bea was also hopelessly devoted to all things festive. Lizzie smiled at the memory, but the moment was interrupted as she heard voices approaching the door of the room to the right of the staircase. She made a beeline for the left-hand room. She needed to give herself a little more time before speaking to anyone. The food was laid out on a long rectangular table and in the middle was the tombstone cake. She smiled at her sister's dark humour. As she walked over to get a better look, she became aware of someone else in the room. Sam was standing in front of the fireplace, staring up at a large canvas photograph of him with his mother and father. It was an informal shot of the three of them, wide-eyed and laughing. Lizzie noticed Bea's arms locked protectively around Sam's body. If it hadn't been for her sister staring down at her, Lizzie could have been looking at a photograph of any family. She felt as if she were intruding. This place had nothing to do with her. As she hesitated, Sam turned around to face her. It was like an electric shock jolting through her body. His resemblance to Bea was astonishing.

He didn't smile, but he wasn't frowning any more either. His face was more a picture of curiosity. 'Do you want a cake?' he asked, wandering over to the food table and helping himself to a large chocolate muffin. 'Mum and I made these before she died. We put them in the freezer so that they didn't go off before the funeral,' he added.

Lizzie's stomach groaned with a mixture of nerves and hunger, but there was something about Sam's casual acceptance of her that made her take one. She nibbled the top. 'They're delicious,' she said.

Sam seemed satisfied. 'Come on,' he said. 'I'll show you my rope swing.'

She watched him walk towards the door, unsure whether she should follow. She had been on the verge of leaving and yet she was torn. He paused in the doorway and looked her straight in the eye. There it was again. That look. That determination.

'Come on,' he repeated.

Lizzie couldn't refuse him any more than she could refuse his mother. She followed him out into the garden, across the sweeping lawn which led down to a stream. The rope swing hung from the bough of a sturdy-looking apple tree.

'Can you hold my cake?' asked Sam. Lizzie obliged and watched as he took hold of the fat stick which served as a seat and swung across without a sound. He stared at her triumphantly. Lizzie realised that some sort of reaction was required, so she said, 'That's very clever,' although it sounded flat to her ears. Sam probably felt this too and swung back to stand next to her and reclaim his cake. 'You can have a go if you want,' he said, offering her the stick. Lizzie didn't think her mother would appreciate her estranged daughter making an exhibition of herself at Bea's wake, although she suspected that Bea would have loved it. 'It's all right. I'm enjoying watching you,' she said, realising that this was true. Sam nodded solemnly and embarked on another swing, cake in hand this time.

'Why haven't you ever come here before?' he asked once he was back at her side. Lizzie admired his candour. For Sam, this was merely a question that needed an answer, whereas for Lizzie it was a can of worms she'd stuffed in the back of the cupboard a long time ago. Why hadn't she returned to the place of her childhood for fifteen years? Why had she stayed away so long?

'Well, I live a little way from here.'

'Where?'

'Just outside London,' said Lizzie, hoping Sam's geography wasn't up to much.

'That's not far,' he declared. *Damn*, thought Lizzie, *why are kids so clued up these days?*

'Well, I work a lot,' she said.

'Oh,' said Sam, seeming to understand this. 'Mum used to work a lot too before she got sick.' Lizzie nodded, hoping the subject was closed. It wasn't. 'I suppose we could have come to visit you, though.'

'I suppose you could have.'

'Why didn't we then?'

Lizzie didn't know what to say. This was the first time she'd properly met Sam and it was clear that he and Bea shared more than just facial resemblance. There was something in his honest and direct questioning that reminded her so much of her sister. 'You're so like your mum,' she said fondly, hoping to buy a little time.

'Everyone says that,' observed Sam, sounding bored. 'So why didn't we see you then?'

Lizzie sighed. 'It's complicated.'

Sam kicked at a stone. 'Adults always say that.'

Lizzie didn't feel qualified to deal with this. Sam needed answers. She just wasn't sure that she was the one to give them. 'I used to see your Mum.' She knew how inadequate a response this was even before the words were out of her mouth.

Sam narrowed his eyes. 'Don't you like kids?' It was black and white to Sam. Y*ou chose not to see me. You don't like me.*

'It's not that.'

'What then?' Lizzie was silent. 'Is it something to do with Granny?'

'Yes,' said Lizzie uncertainly.

'Because she never mentions you. Or rather we're not supposed to mention you when she's around.'

'Oh. Right.' *At least I know where I stand,* thought

Lizzie. 'Did your mum ever talk about me?'

Sam shrugged. 'Sometimes. She said you'd fallen out with Granny and so didn't want to come home.'

Lizzie nodded. 'That's about the size of it.'

'Do you miss my mum?' he asked, eyeing her closely.

'Very much,' said Lizzie without hesitation.

Sam nodded, satisfied that he was getting an honest answer. 'I'm going to get another cake,' he said, heading back up the lawn without a backward glance.

Part of Lizzie longed for him to stay. It might be odd to confide your innermost feelings to a ten-year-old, but Lizzie got the sense that he understood, that he knew Bea like she knew Bea, an uncomplicated relationship based on love and trust. They had both lost the source of their comfort and protection. The difference was that whereas Sam had his father and grandmother and no doubt plenty of friends to envelop and help him through his grief, Lizzie had no one. She was alone. She had deliberately built her life in this way because she had always had Bea. Now that Bea was gone, she literally had no one to turn to. She felt her stomach twist with panic at the realisation of this truth. She stared at the house, trying to imagine her sister appearing at the back door, waving and wandering down the garden to join her.

'I miss you, Bea,' she whispered. She considered going back inside to find Sam, but then she ran the risk of bumping into Joe or, even worse, her mother. It was at that moment that she noticed a male figure make his way out on to the lawn and walk towards her. At first she thought it might be Joe, but, as she shielded her eyes against the sun, she recognised him. She felt an overwhelming urge to run away, but he was striding purpose-fully towards her, waving and smiling, so she stayed rooted to the spot. It was fifteen years since she had seen him and, as she watched him stroll down towards her, she was immediately transported back in time. She re-membered how her heart had surged whenever he had walked into the room, her teenage self filled with long-ing for his attention. He had made her feel protected and special until it had all turned sour. He must have noticed her guarded expression, because at first he looked unsure, studying her face for a clue as to wheth-er he was welcome. She told herself to stay calm. She didn't need to deal with this now; in fact she was unsure if she ever wanted to deal with the hurt this man had caused her. She wanted to be on her way. She looked into his clear blue eyes and did her best to keep her face neutral. He smiled confidently. He had always been con-fident. It had been one of the things she had liked most about him. As a teenager he had been boyishly good-looking, with the charm of youth to carry him. Age had allowed him to grow into his looks, his once dark hair flecked with a little grey.

'Hello Lizzie,' he said. 'It's good to see you.' His voice was warm and genuine, but Lizzie wasn't about to be drawn in by his easy charm. Too much had hap-pened since the time she had been his girlfriend. He had been one of the reasons she'd left Smallchurch and one of the reasons why she hadn't come back until now.

'Hello Alex,' she said coldly. He either didn't pick up on her tone or chose to ignore it. 'How are you holding up?' he asked, reaching out to touch her on the arm.

She took a step back. 'Yes, OK thanks,' she said. It was a complete lie, but she wasn't about to share confidences with this man. 'I was just leaving, actually.'

He looked surprised, but gave a small nod of his head. 'Of course, I had to tell you how sorry I am about Bea. I know how close you were.' His eyes misted with grief and Lizzie felt enraged. *How dare he try to hijack her loss? How dare he try to act as if he understood anything?* 'If there's anything I can do,' he said.

Such kind words, thought Lizzie, if they were uttered by another person, but from Alex they were like a cheap unwanted gift. She could have reacted in a hundred different ways, said everything she'd practised in her head over the years, but today wasn't about Alex Chambers. Today was about Bea, her darling lost sister. 'I'll be fine, thank you,' she said, turning away and walking back towards the house. It was another neat lie. Five reassuring words that meant nothing.

She hurried through the patio door, past a small gathering of people, chatting in hushed tones over the strawberry pavlova. They turned as she entered, but she ignored them all. She was giving herself permission to flee. Bea wouldn't want her to stay, not after her encounter with Alex. She had almost made it to the front door when she heard a voice behind her.

'Oh, Lizzie. I didn't realise you were here.' From another person, this might have been a declaration of pure joy, but from Stella Harris it managed to sound both cold and critical.

Lizzie turned to face her mother. In the gloom of the church, she hadn't looked at her mother's features properly. Now, in Bea's brightly lit hall with the sun streaming into Stella's face, Lizzie was shocked by how much she had aged in fifteen years. Her mother had been forty-five when she had last seen her. If someone had described Stella as being in her late sixties, Lizzie would have believed it. Her face was a mass of wrinkles, like a map of her life's experiences. She observed her daughter, unsmiling, unimpressed. Lizzie couldn't bear that look. 'I'm going now. Would you say goodbye to Joe for me?'

'I most certainly shall not,' snapped Stella.

Her mother wanted a fight. Lizzie saw this now. 'Goodbye,' said Lizzie, turning away. She couldn't handle this. Not today. She knew it had been a mistake coming to the house. It was like being smacked in the face by the past over and over again. She might have been able to deal with this if Bea had been here, but not on her own.

'Well, I don't suppose I'll see you again then,' said her mother. There was something about the way she said this that was less critical and more regretful.

Lizzie turned back and looked at her, seeing sadness in her face that masked her own. She couldn't bear it. 'Goodbye, Mum,' she repeated.

She hurried to her car and flung open the door, flopping down into the driver's seat and telling herself that it was nearly done. She had almost made it through the day. All she had to do was drive home and she would be safe. Someone tapped on her window and she jumped. It was Joe. He was holding his hands up in apology, a parcel tucked under his arm. She sighed as she wound down the window.

'Hi Joe. Sorry, I was going to say goodbye, but I couldn't find you,' she lied.

'No worries,' said Joe, ever reasonable. 'I just have something I need to give you. From Bea.' He held out the parcel and Lizzie stared at it. As soon as she saw Bea's writing and the name, 'Lizzie Lou', she felt her pulse quicken.

'Do you know what's inside?' asked Lizzie, her voice almost a whisper, as he handed the parcel through the open window.

Joe shook his head. 'No, but Bea was very precise in her instructions. I was to give it to you on the day of her funeral. You know what she was like,' he said, with a fond smile.

Lizzie nodded. She looked down at the writing and ran her hand across it. Joe took a step back as if he were intruding on a private moment. 'Well, I should let you go,' he said. 'Thank you for coming. It meant a lot to Sam and me.'

Lizzie knew that she should have a better response for Joe, something heartfelt and consoling, but she was too caught up with thoughts of Bea's parcel and the need to be on her way. She laid the parcel carefully on the seat next to her, like a mother placing her newborn in its cot.

'Thank you, Joe. Goodbye,' was all she could manage before she drove off. She didn't make it very far before she pulled over at the side of the road and sat with her hands on the steering wheel, staring out at the bright summer sky, her mind racing with thoughts of her sister. She picked up the parcel and hugged it to her chest as the tears fell easily and the sobs overcame her so that she thought they would never stop.

Printed in the USA
CPSIA information can be obtained
at www.ICGtesting.com
LVHW040156080823
754624LV00010B/284

9 780263 250350